RL AKERS

ESCAPE FROM
OVERTWIXT ™

ILLUSTRATED
BY JesseLewis

table of contents

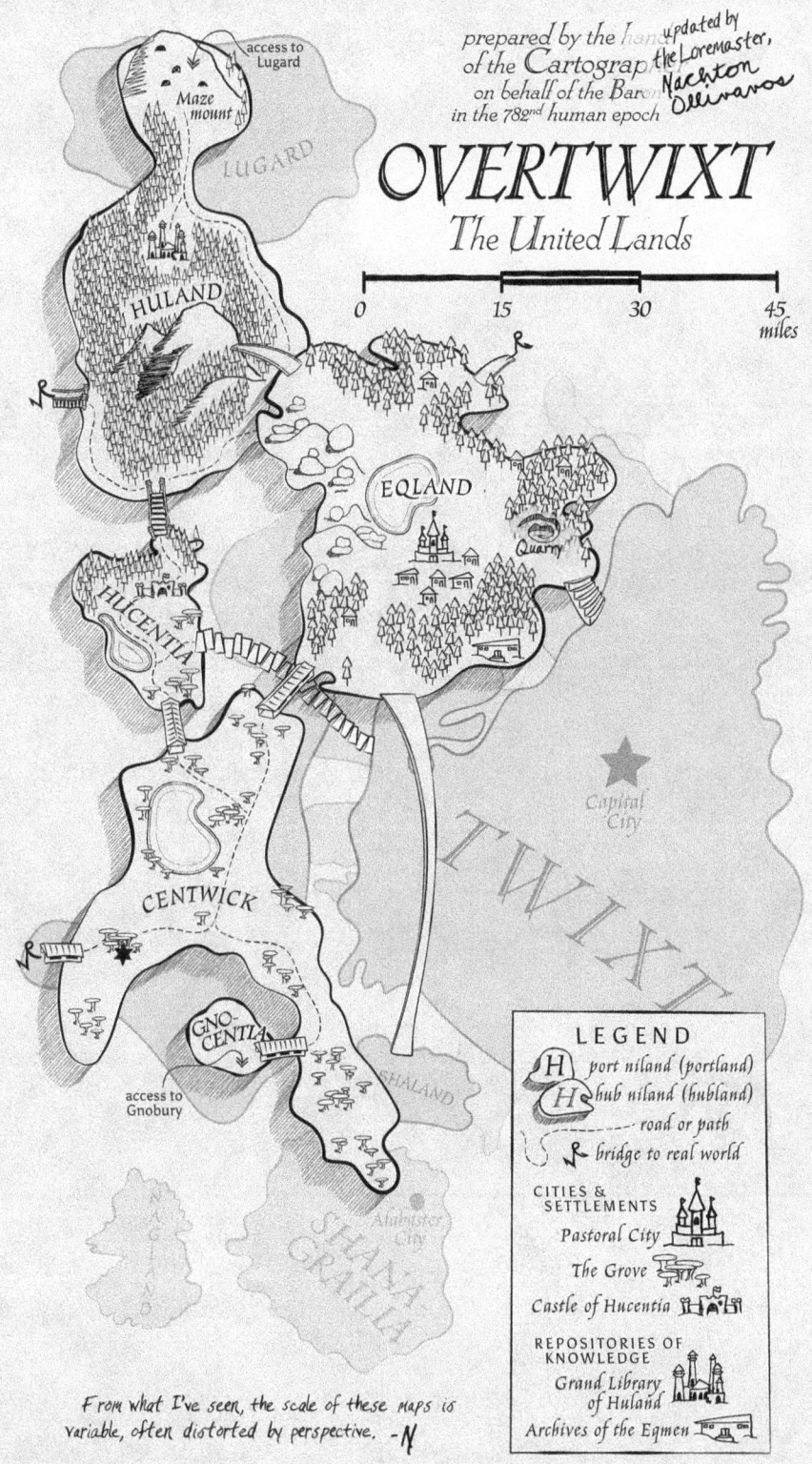

access to Lugard

Maze mount

LUGARD

HULAND

prepared by the hand ~~updated by~~
of the Cartograp~~the~~ Loremaster,
on behalf of the Baron Nachton
in the 782nd human epoch Ollivaros

OVERTWIXT
The United Lands

0   15   30   45
miles

EQLAND

Quarry

HUCENTIA

Capital City

CENTWICK

T W I X T

GNO-CENTLA

access to Gnobury

SHALAND

Alubister City

SHANA-GRAILA

LEGEND

H port niland (portland)

H⁄S hub niland (hubland)

- - - road or path

bridge to real world

CITIES & SETTLEMENTS

Pastoral City

The Grove

Castle of Hucentia

REPOSITORIES OF KNOWLEDGE

Grand Library of Huland

Archives of the Eqmen

From what I've seen, the scale of these maps is
variable, often distorted by perspective. — N

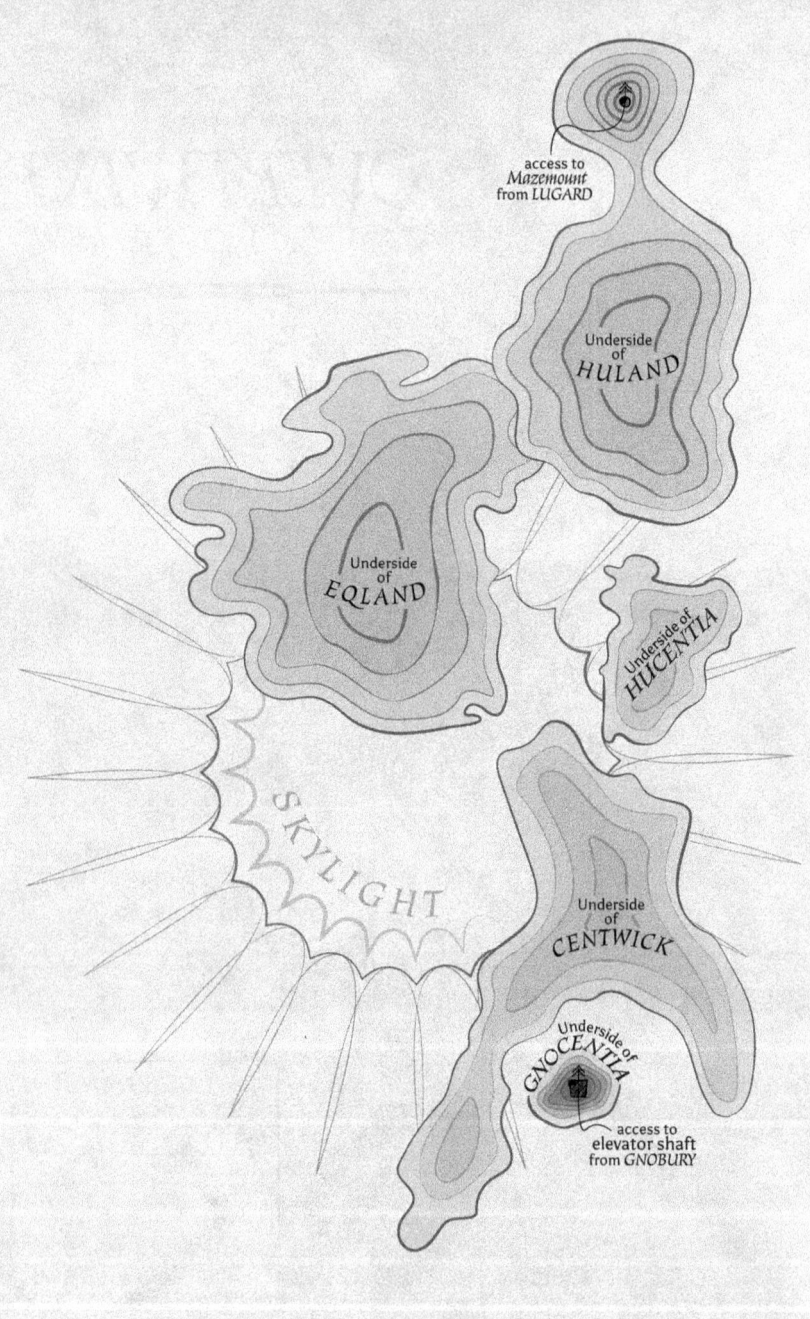

access to
Mazemount
from LUGARD

Underside
of
HULAND

Underside
of
EQLAND

Underside
of
HUCENTIA

Underside
of
CENTWICK

SKYLIGHT

Underside of
GNOCENTIA

access to
elevator shaft
from *GNOBURY*

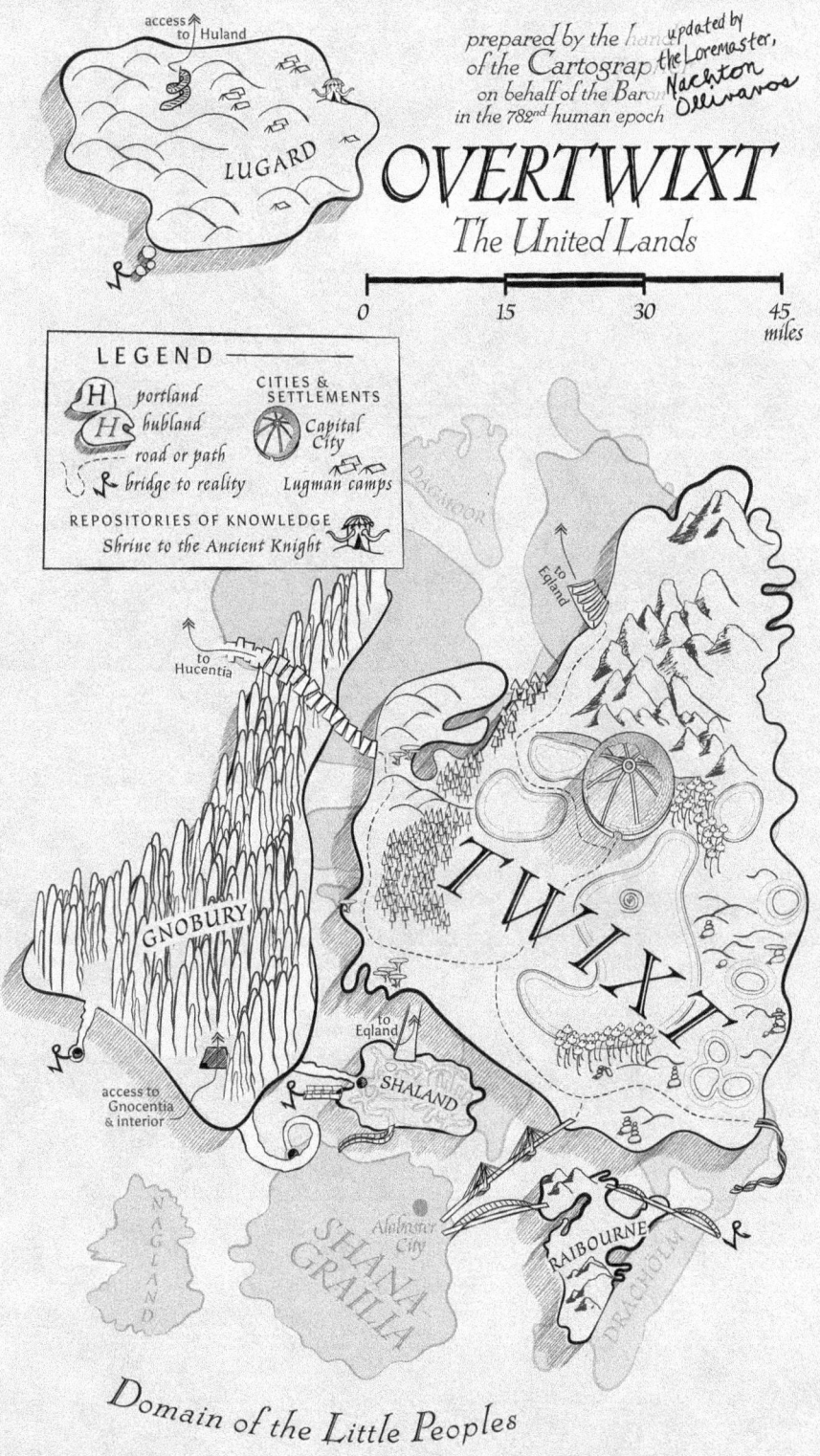

access to Huland

LUGARD

prepared by the hand updated by
of the Cartograp the Loremaster,
on behalf of the Baron Nachton
in the 782nd human epoch Ollivaros

OVERTWIXT
The United Lands

0   15   30   45 miles

LEGEND

H portland
H hubland
- - - road or path
bridge to reality

CITIES & SETTLEMENTS
Capital City
Lugman camps

REPOSITORIES OF KNOWLEDGE
Shrine to the Ancient Knight

DAGGADOR

to Eqland

to Hucentia

GNOBURY

TWIXT

to Eqland

SHALAND

access to
Gnocentia
& interior

Alabaster
City

NAGLAND

SHANA
GRALLA

RAIBOURNE

DRACHOLM

Domain of the Little Peoples

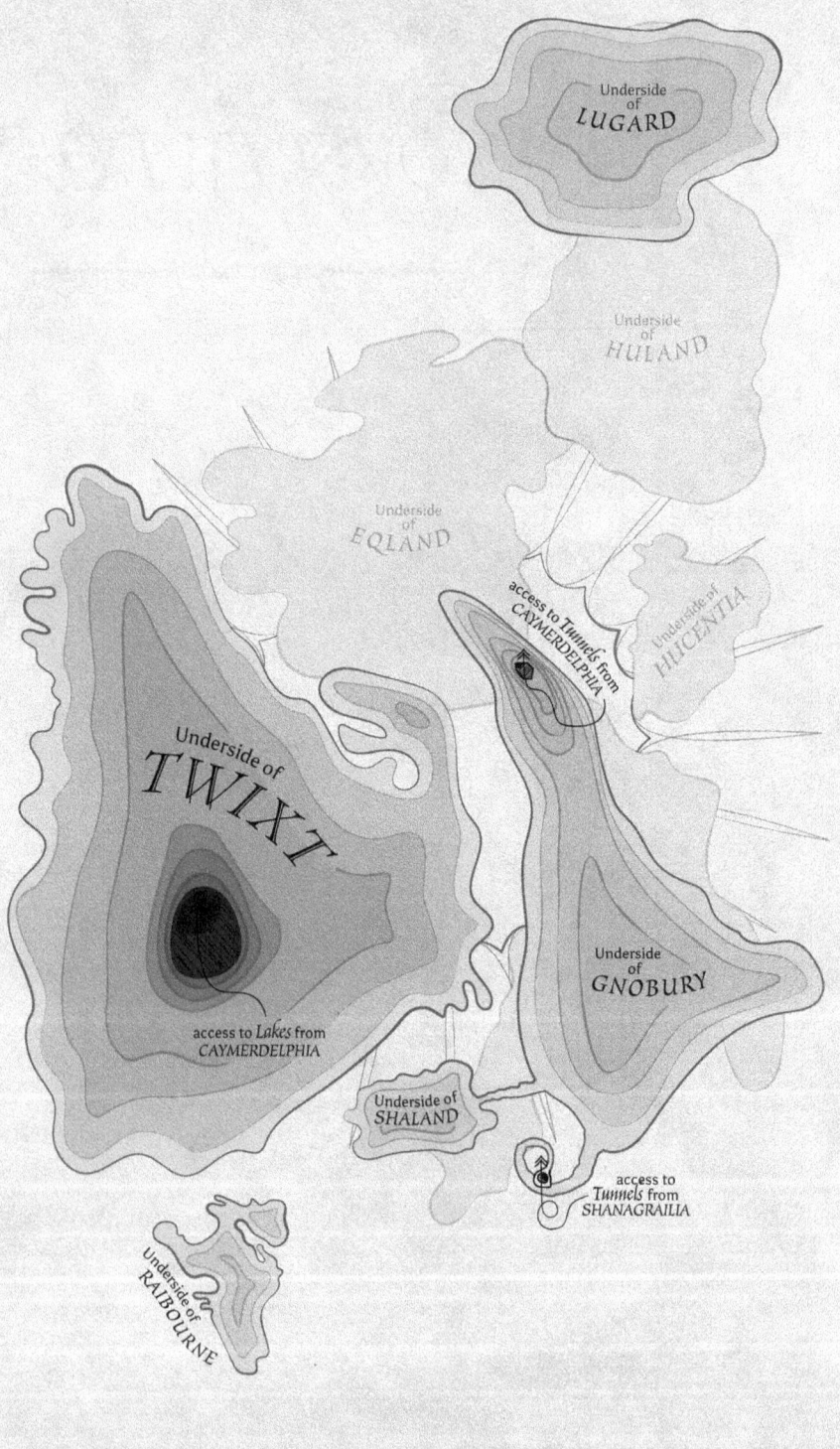

prepared by the hand *updated by*
of the Cartograp *the Loremaster,*
on behalf of the Baro *Nachton*
in the 782nd human epoch *Ollivaros*

OVERTWIXT
The United Lands

0   15   30   45
miles

Worlds of Water

DAGMOOR

beaches

MERPOOL

IMPSTEAD

CAYMERDELPHIA

access to
Gnobury

LEGEND

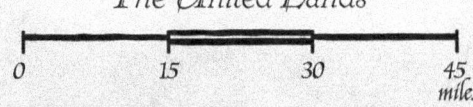

H portland
H hubland
--- road or path
bridge to reality

CITIES &
SETTLEMENTS

Crystal City

Nagman Cliff
Dwellings

Alabaster City

REPOSITORIES OF
KNOWLEDGE

Mystic's Tower

CAYPOOL

access to
Twixt

DELPHYRD

PHOLAND

to ↑
Shaland

to
Gnobury ↑

to Twixt ↑

to Raibourne ↑

NAGLAND

SHANA
GRAILIA

Docks

DRACHÖLM

Domain of the Little Peoples

Underside
of
LUGARD

Underside
of
MERPOOL

Underside of
CAYMERDELPHIA

Underside of
CAYPOOL

Underside
of
GNOBURY

Underside of
DELPHYRD

Underside of
TWIXT

Underside of
SHALAND

Underside of
RALBOURNE

Underside of
SHANA-
GRAILIA

Underside of
NAGLAND

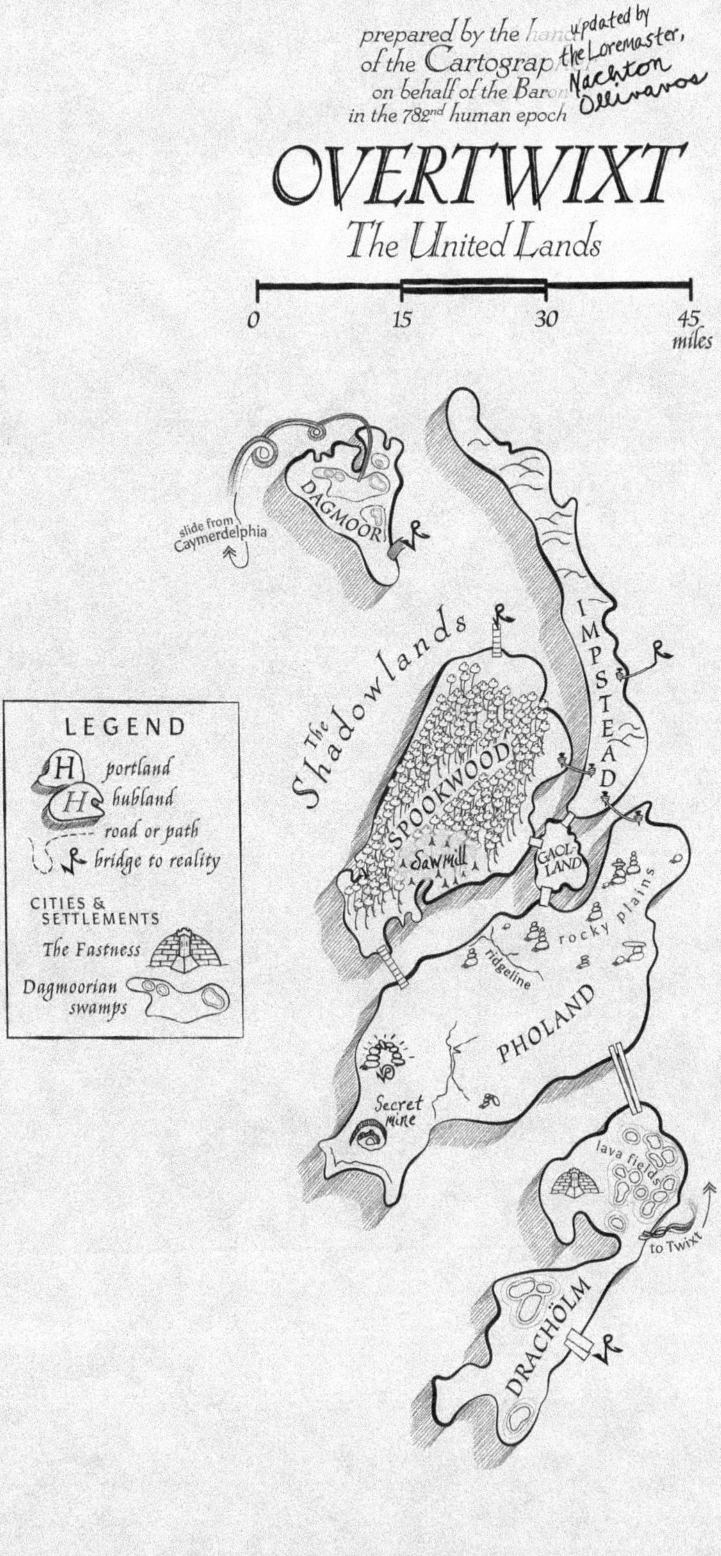

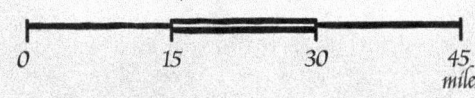

prepared by the hand
of the Cartograp~ updated by
on behalf of the Baron the Loremaster,
in the 782nd human epoch Nachton Ollivaros

OVERTWIXT
The United Lands

0   15   30   45
miles

slide from
Caymerdelphia

DAGMOOR

The Shadowlands

IMPSTEAD

SPOOKWOOD

Sawmill

GAOL-LAND

rocky plains

ridgeline

PHOLAND

Secret mine

lava fields

to Twixt

DRACHÖLM

LEGEND

H — portland
H — hubland
--- — road or path
— bridge to reality

CITIES & SETTLEMENTS

The Fastness

Dagmoorian swamps

The Five Fundamental Laws
of Overtwixt

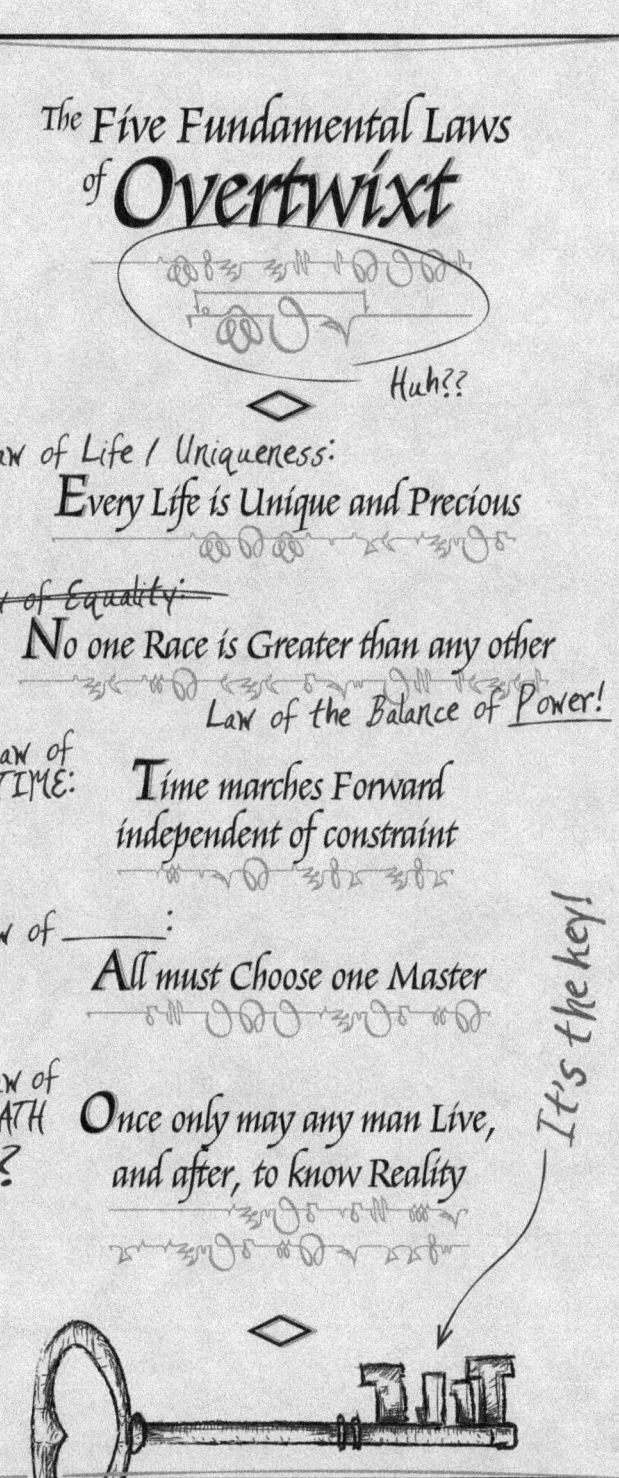

Huh??

Law of Life / Uniqueness:
Every Life is Unique and Precious

~~Law of Equality:~~
No one Race is Greater than any other

Law of the Balance of Power!

Law of TIME:
Time marches Forward independent of constraint

Law of _____:
All must Choose one Master

Law of DEATH ?
Once only may any man Live, and after, to know Reality

It's the key!

Still for Ian, Sadie, Emme, and Nate...

my own personal Knight, Princess, Empress,
and Loremaster

· prologue ·

(Nachton)

Nachton's little brother Ewan, the 5-year-old Knight of Overtwixt, had been smoked. Despite their Guide-given mission to overthrow the evil Vizier, it had been the Vizier who defeated Nachton and Ewan's entire strike force—turning them to yellow smoke and expelling them from Overtwixt forever. *

Nachton alone had survived.

The images of that disastrous confrontation kept replaying in his mind:

The lugman Berserker, blown away by one of Nachton's own green fireballs, contemptuously redirected by the Vizier.

The eqman Squire, tripped up by another of Nachton's ineffectual attacks, screeching as the Vizier snuffed him out without even looking.

The shaman Weaponsmaster, frozen in midair by the green mist Nachton himself had

---

* All major concepts and characters from the first *Overtwixt* are described (along with pronunciation clues) in the complete Glossary of Persons, Places, and Things on page 271.

flung at their enemy, nunchucks barely spinning. Crushed into nothing by one squeeze of the Vizier's fist.

And Ewan—poor, sweet, innocent Ewan—cut down effortlessly by the Vizier's elegant saber… even though the little boy wore one of Sovereign's Relics, the ancient Diamond Armor that supposedly made its wearer impervious to evil attacks.

After that, Nachton had run away. He, Nachton Ollivaros—the powerful Conjurer of Overtwixt—had hitched up his robes and *fled* the Archives in a desperate bid for survival. But the Vizier had caught him anyway, flinging a green cloud of his own to freeze him in place. Sobbing, Nachton had screamed for help, naming everyone he knew… and of all people, it was the *Guide* who rode to his rescue.

Another series of images then, burned into his memory: the Vizier unleashing a massive fireball at Nachton… the Guide placing himself between Nachton and danger… the fireball splashing harmlessly against the Guide's centman flanks. Obviously, Nachton's eyes had been playing tricks on him in the midst of his terror, for that was impossible. He'd been more focused on the centman's outstretched arm anyway. "Take my hand," the Guide had said, and Nachton didn't argue. The moment he gripped those fingers in his, the freezing magic had dissolved, and the Guide pulled Nachton onto his back.

Now they were galloping, fleeing still, and Nachton hadn't even stopped to consider *where* they might be going. Instead, he wept openly, despite being fifteen years old. "He's gone," Nachton moaned when the Guide slowed at last. "Ewan's *gone*… The Vizier killed him, and… and…"

The Guide turned at the waist to look Nachton in the eye. Taking a deep breath, he said, "You should know—"

"Oh, I know, I know!" Nachton interrupted. "Ewan wasn't actually *killed*." He took an unsteady breath but forced himself to keep talking. "The Fifth Fundamental Law: after being ejected, you return to the real world."

Nachton and Ewan and their two sisters, Amélie and Cécilie, had arrived in Overtwixt by accident (though the Guide said otherwise), passing through the wrong gate at the Atlanta airport in their human real world. While the two brothers had embraced the adventure of this magical world between worlds, Amélie had always been more interested in escaping Overtwixt as soon as possible.

Well, her wish had come true, partly. "Ewan's probably back with Mom and Dad already, telling them all about how I let him fight with a real sword. They're gonna ground me for sure." At least Nachton *hoped* the little boy was soon reunited with their parents in the real world. The four kids had been in Overtwixt for weeks—or even *months*, depending which one of them you asked. (Time passed irregularly in this place.) After so long, their parents had surely left the airport, expanding the search for their lost children.

Regardless, this was a disaster, even if Ewan *was* now safe at home with Mom and Dad. "It's just... he's not *here* anymore, and he can never come back! The greatest adventure of our lives, and he'll miss out on the rest of it. I don't even know when I'll see him again!" And Nachton's tears resumed their flood down his cheeks. He knew he was making a fool of himself, but he just couldn't stop it. Ewan...

The Guide looked like he might say something more—some stupid platitude, probably, about how sorry he was—but Nachton barreled on before the centman could speak.

"It wasn't my fault!" he growled, though no one had said it was. "It was that lying spook! He was a Spy after all!" He meant Ewan's bat-like friend, the one Ewan called "Shark" (though no one knew the little monster's actual name or role in Overtwixt). So far as Nachton was aware, *all* of the flying creatures—including the bat-like spookmen—

were bad guys. "That filthy creature warned the Vizier we were coming. Or— or— he told the Vizier about us, and the Vizier had him lure us to the Archives! The Vizier *knew* we were coming, otherwise he never could've stood against me!"

The Guide scratched his bearded chin for a long, thoughtful moment. Then he asked gently, "Are you so sure of that?"

Nachton had said the words by reflex, but inside, he *wasn't* so sure anymore. Still, what other explanation could there be? "I've studied. All I've done since coming here is study, starting with the Five Fundamental Laws, just like you told me to. I'm pretty sure I understand the workings of power in Overtwixt!" he concluded with a sarcastic confidence he didn't really feel.

"Then you know all, now? Is it not possible you... misunderstood something? Or that magic works differently from how you think? From how you want to believe?"

This made Nachton doubt all the more, but he waved a hand impatiently. Who was this centman to question *him*, anyway? The Guide was a glorified doorman, tasked with greeting each new visitor to Overtwixt and offering a selection of three roles to choose from. The tall centaur-creature wasn't even that good at his job. Instead of guiding Nachton to his obvious calling as Conjurer, he'd tried to shove him into a minor support role—that of Loremaster.

But Nachton took another deep breath, forcing himself to choose his words carefully. "Look," he said finally. "Thank you for... for your assistance back there." Assistance, that's all it was, not a *rescue*. Nachton's eyes had *definitely* played tricks on him. "But," he continued firmly, "let *me* worry about questions of magic and power."

The Guide nodded humbly. "Very well."

Nachton took another steadying breath, on the verge of losing control yet again. Ewan... oh, Ewan. *I will get revenge on the person responsible for this,* he promised his brother. *When I get my hands on the Vizier* and *that spook...* He looked around then, suddenly aware of his surroundings. "Where are we?" he asked the Guide. "Where have you brought me?"

"We're nearly to Pastoral City, and your sister's new Palace," the centman responded. He meant the younger of Nachton's two sisters, the 8-year-old Cécilie, who had been named Princess of Eqland. Right before the disaster at the Archives, Nachton and Ewan's strike team had led an uprising on Eqland, soundly defeating the Vizier's flying minions. The horse-like eqmen (and their new allies the gnomen) had been quick to accept Cécilie as their ruler after that. "I assumed you and the Princess would want to be together during this difficult time," the Guide concluded.

Nachton gritted his teeth but forced out another polite response. "Thank you."

"What will you do next?"

"I... I don't know." The loss of Ewan left him feeling adrift. Both Ewan and Cécilie had fulfilled the quests given them by the Guide. And their 12-year-old sister Amélie was off building a coalition, stepping into her Guide-given role of Empress to make herself a rival of the Vizier (who claimed that *he* was Emperor). But what had Nachton accomplished? Taking on the role of the Conjurer, he'd been sure he could defeat the Vizier. But whatever the reason, no matter whose fault it was, Nachton had failed to do that. Spectacularly.

"If I may suggest," the Guide began hesitantly, "stay at the Palace for a time, with the Princess. If I understand correctly, the Empress will return here soon. Her efforts have not been as fruitful as she hoped. She and the Princess will both need your support in the days to come, and... minus one of the four of you, it'll be more important than ever that the rest of you are united."

Nachton wasn't so sure—he wasn't ever sure of anything the Guide said—but he nodded anyway. Better to just agree than give the annoying centman the impression that Nachton needed convincing. "Fine," he said.

The Guide stopped moving. "Then this is where we part ways."

"What?" Nachton said in surprise. He stared into the darkness, and realized he could see lights. They were nearly to the outskirts. "You're not taking me all the way?"

"I am not welcome there," the Guide said simply.

"The eqmen?"

The Guide nodded. "Among others."

Nachton was suddenly fearful again. "What if the Vizier attacks?"

"He will not. Not tonight, at least." The Guide turned, staring off into the distance. "The Vizier is already making haste to the Shadowlands, thoughts consumed by his many schemes—and the amulet your brother returned to him. He will not pass this way."

"Amulet... you mean that necklace?" After Ewan had disappeared in an explosion of yellow smoke—and after his worthless Diamond Armor had winked out of sight too—a strange ruby necklace had clattered to the floor. Nachton hadn't realized the little boy was wearing one, though he *had* seen a similar necklace on a ribbon around their sister's neck. "Cécilie has one too. What *are* they, exactly?"

"Magical artifacts of the same sort as Sovereign's Relics. The Vizier thinks them his own creation, but their magic is far older—and far more evil—than even he knows."

"The Vizier can make relics too?" Nachton said in surprise. "And they're more powerful than Sovereign's?"

"No," the Guide answered with a sharp, confident shake of his head. "For that to be so, the Vizier himself would have to be more powerful than the Sovereign. And none is more powerful than the Sovereign, not even the Adversary."

"Then how could the Vizier defeat the Diamond Armor so completely?" Nachton demanded. "He cut through Ewan's Armor like it wasn't even there!"

The Guide gave Nachton a penetrating look. "The Diamond Armor could not protect your brother... for the same reason the Diamond Lens could not grant you wisdom."

Nachton stiffened. *His* quest from the Guide had been to obtain knowledge and wisdom. Lame as that was (next to his siblings' quests to obtain weapons and armor and thrones), he had invested months of study at the Grand Library of Huland anyway. And in the end, despite cutting some corners along the way, he'd uncovered another of Sovereign's Relics that had been lost to history: the Diamond Lens of Discernment, a pair of spectacles that bestowed unusual insight. Nachton had felt even greater confidence in his strategies against the Vizier, knowing that he wore the Diamond spectacles... and now the Guide had the audacity to suggest their magic had never worked in the first place?

"*Why?*" Nachton demanded. Why had Ewan's invincible Armor—and Nachton's insightful Lens—failed to have the promised magical effect?

The centman gazed at the human for a long moment. "If you've studied magic as much as you say you have, then you already know the answer to that question. But you can't acknowledge the truth because you've deceived yourself—*about* yourself." He shook his head. "Until you recognize just how wrong you are, you'll be incapable of seeing the truth about Ewan or the Vizier either."

Nachton stared back at the Guide, a dozen new questions flitting through his mind. But he refused to give the infuriating centman the satisfaction of asking. He slipped off the Guide's back and stepped away. "Fine then," he said in a level tone.

The Guide looked sad. "Be well, Master of Lore. And bear your responsibility wisely." He said nothing more, whirling instead and galloping back into the woods.

Then Nachton was truly alone, for the first time since losing Ewan. Suddenly, this didn't feel like such an adventure after all. Had Amélie been right all along, trying so desperately to return home with all possible haste? They'd been in danger since the day they arrived, and now one of the four siblings had finally succumbed to that danger. Unless Nachton's little brother really was the lucky one.

At least Ewan had already escaped from Overtwixt.

Nachton walked the rest of the way into Pastoral City. Before long, he was surrounded by eqmen dancing and singing in the streets—celebrating the liberation of their niland from the Vizier's creatures of darkness. Some of the revelers noticed Nachton and stared at him with awe, remembering that *he* had been the architect of their freedom.

Could Nachton return to Cécilie? Could he bear to look her in the eye and tell her Ewan was gone? Hardly—and he certainly wasn't ready to endure the high and mighty *Amélie's* scathing disapproval. Before he submitted himself for judgment, he wanted to have a new plan to offer, a way for the three remaining siblings to recover from this mess. And even before that, he needed to figure out how the Vizier defeated Nachton's team so quickly. Obviously, that filthy spook's warning gave the Vizier time to prepare, but that still didn't explain how. Nachton needed to understand *how* the Vizier had bested him, then determine what to do next.

Still, he couldn't just leave his sisters hanging. They deserved to know the truth about Ewan.

Nachton tore a sheet of paper out of a notebook from his satchel, then beckoned one of the eqmen in the street. "I need you to get a message to the Princess. Can you do that?"

"Oh yes, wise one!"

Nachton nodded. And feeling like slime for doing this in a letter, he scribbled his note with ink and quill. When he was done, he rolled the paper and sealed it with wax, then winced when the eqman took it gently in his teeth.

"Um, try not to drool on that too much."

"Uh cose, why one," the eqman tried to say.

But Nachton had already walked away, turning his back to Cécilie and the Palace—directing his steps toward the Archives once more, now that he knew the Vizier was gone.

He *would* reunite with his sisters soon enough, as the Guide suggested. But first, he needed answers, and the Archives seemed a good enough place to start looking. Nachton would figure out how the Vizier had defeated him, and he would figure out how to defeat the evil tyrant in turn.

Then Nachton, Amélie, and Cécilie would take their revenge on the Vizier.

Even as Nachton fantasized about that vengeance, however, the light from a nearby torch caught his Diamond spectacles and made them glitter—and a quiet voice deep inside reminded him that revenge was never the answer.

Part I
Reunion

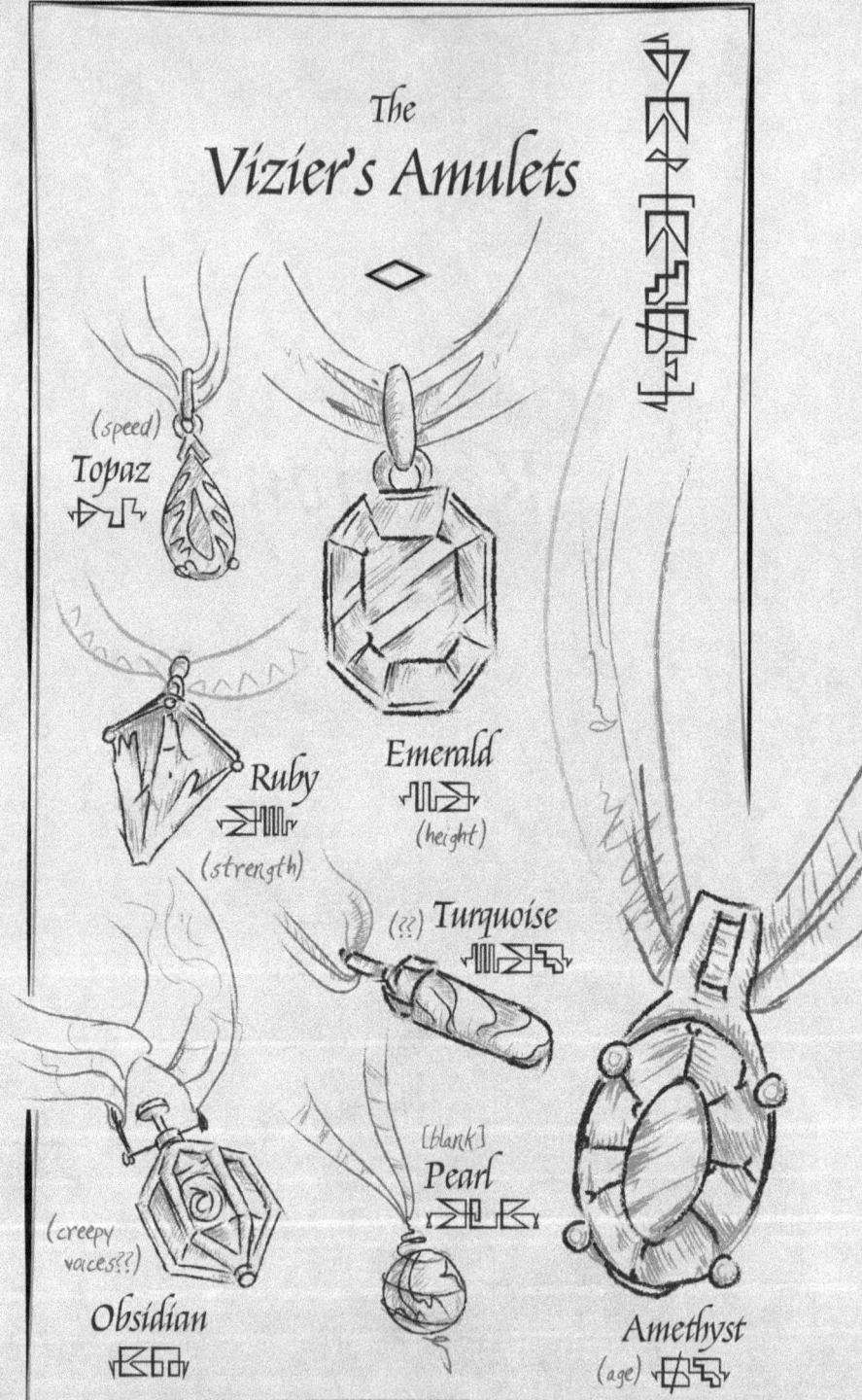

The Vizier's Amulets

(speed)
Topaz

Ruby
(strength)

Emerald
(height)

(??) Turquoise

[blank]
Pearl

Obsidian
(creepy voices??)

Amethyst
(age)

· one ·

(Cécilie)

"Long live the Princess!" the horses and unicorns and gnomes shouted. "Long live the Princess!" Even hours after winning their battle, Cécilie's new followers continued to break into spontaneous cheers.

She could still hardly believe it. *Her*— 8-year-old Cécilie Ollivaros—an actual *princess*, ruler of the floating island princedom of Eqland. She touched her head just to make sure the silver tiara was still there. Cécilie had been crowned by the horses (and the unicorns, who were really just girl horses in Overtwixt) right after she swore her oaths as Princess. She also still wore the flower garland that the gnomes had woven for her earlier in the day.

Wearing those two crowns *and* her pink princess dress *and* the magical amethyst amulet (which made her look more mature, without any freckles), Cécilie felt beautiful.

If only she was *actually* beautiful.

Cécilie banished the thought as her subjects cheered yet again. "All hail the Princess! Long live the Princess!"

One of the unicorns—a dapple-gray called Matron—noticed Cécilie grinning stupidly, and she arched an eyebrow. The new Princess stood straighter immediately, adopting a facial expression that was more regal. She raised one hand in a small, proper wave to acknowledge the cheers, and the Matron nodded approval. After all, it was her job to make Cécilie more lady-like.

Then another unicorn nuzzled Cécilie's hand. "Relax, your highness. This is a party, after all!" It was the Handmaiden, a much younger unicorn with a pure-white body and long pink hair. She was one of Cécilie's ladies-in-waiting — and more importantly, Cécilie's new best friend.

Cécilie giggled, throwing her arms around Handmaiden's neck as the Matron pretended not to notice. "You're right!"

The girls went back to dancing, moving into the center of the ballroom of Cécilie's new Palace. The celebration had already been going on for hours, ever since the new Princess entered Pastoral City at the head of a victory parade. Everywhere the human girl looked, faces were joyful. And why shouldn't they be? With the help of Cécilie and her brothers, the people of

Eqland had defeated the Vizier's army of flying bad guys, freeing their floating island* from slavery.

Now, her new subjects danced with all their might, accompanied by their exotic music—enchanting vocals sung by the horses in seven-part harmony, punctuated by rhythmic beats tapped out on stone or wood by the little gnomes. The dancers moved in ways Cécilie never would have thought possible... and as soon as Matron slipped away to sample refreshments in the next room, Cécilie let her own dancing get a little crazy too. When she couldn't reproduce the horses' four-legged steps, she settled for some of the elaborate dance moves she'd learned from videos on the Internet back home. Before she knew it, the youngest horses and unicorns were mimicking *her*.

Of course, they weren't really horses or unicorns. Cécilie needed to stop thinking of them that way, for there was no such thing as animals in Overtwixt. The graceful four-legged creatures surrounding her were eqmen and eqwomen, intelligent *people* with their own culture and customs. The same was true of the skillful little gnomen, who used to be bitter rivals of the eqmen— until the Vizier's slavery made them unlikely allies.

When Cécilie was finally too exhausted to dance any longer, she and

---

* Known in Overtwixt as a "niland." See complete Glossary of Persons, Places, and Things on page 271.

Handmaiden moved into the feast hall. The long, elaborately carved table was heaped high with fruits and candied carrots, finger sandwiches and oatmeal cookies. And that was just the eqman food! Even as Cécilie collapsed into a magnificent chair at the head of the table, gnoman chefs began bringing out trays of delicacies native to *their* real world, such as fragrant sweetbreads and intricate hard candy twists.

Eyes wide as saucers, Cécilie began pointing. "I want one of *those*, and a handful of *those*, and at least three peppermint rolls," she gushed.

"Me too!" Handmaiden squealed.

As the servers began filling plates with food for their Princess and her lady-in-waiting, Cécilie's closest supporters gathered around the table and selected food for themselves. The eqmen remained standing while the gnomen pulled up chairs of their own.

Soon, they were all recounting the events of the battle, and even Matron was smiling broadly. "I simply cannot believe the imps were so foolish," she said, shaking her maned head. "To abandon their post like that..."

The battle for Eqland had begun with a ruse at the Vizier's quarry, east of Pastoral City. That was where most of the eqmen and gnomen were being kept as slaves, chained up and forced to cut huge slabs of stone out of the ground, for use in the Vizier's secret building projects. They were guarded by countless impmen—gray-furred gargoyles who flew in circles above the quarry, cackling gleefully and cracking their whips at any worker who slacked off. Fortunately, imps weren't the most intelligent people. When Cécilie's army of free eqmen charged the quarry, then seemed to panic and flee back into the woods, every single imp had followed eagerly.

Which was when Cécilie and Handmaiden rode to the rescue of the slaves.

"*I* can't believe we galloped past those imps all by ourselves," Handmaiden said with a shiver, grinning at the same time. "I think that's the bravest, scariest thing I've ever done. If they had seen us..."

"It *was* very dashing and heroic, wasn't it?" Cécilie agreed grandly. Then she sighed dramatically. "It's almost a shame they *didn't* see us." Thanks to the magic of another amulet, Cécilie's topaz necklace, she and the little unicorn were moving so fast that they probably looked like a blur to everyone else. It had shocked the slaves in the quarry when Cécilie took off that amulet, returning to normal speed.

"It was like you done appeared outta thin air, Princess," said the Wrangler. He was a muscular eqman who spoke in a humble, aw-shucks sort of way. "I reckon my heart 'bout stopped, or near enough," he drawled.

"How *did* you manage to appear and disappear like that?" asked the gnowoman Seamstress, another former slave. "Do you have special powers too, like the Vizier?"

Cécilie froze in the middle of reenacting her heroic gallop to rescue the slaves, arms held comically in front of her like when she rode her unicorn. "Ummm," she said slowly, and suddenly she didn't feel quite so dramatic. After all, she really *wasn't* much of a hero, no matter what it looked like. It was only her enchanted necklaces that made Cécilie special, which was why they had to stay a secret.

She had found her collection of amulets in the Grand Library of Huland on her first day in Overtwixt, but that was just luck. *Anyone* could have found those amulets and used their magic to rescue the horses and gnomes. If her new followers ever learned the truth—if they found out how young and completely un-special Cécilie herself really was— would they still respect and adore their new Princess then?

Handmaiden was the only one who knew about all of Cécilie's amulets. And seeing Cécilie's hesitation, the little unicorn came to her rescue. "It was magic!" she blurted, not explaining any further than that.

To Cécilie's surprise, everyone seemed to think that was a perfectly sensible and sufficient explanation. Seamstress went back to sewing the new outfit she had promised to Cécilie, a formal ankle-length gown. (Cécilie still loved the knee-length pink skirt she'd worn since arriving in Overtwixt, but having a change of clothes *would* be nice.) Next to her, the gnoman Engineer just nodded. He didn't say much, but his eyes glowed with gratitude for Cécilie's rescue.

The Mayor of Pastoral City spoke up. "For my part, I am still astounded by the ingenuity of those net traps you designed, Master Crafter."

The third gnoman in their group—the Crafter—sniffed and stroked his chin, though he clearly loved hearing the praise. He was one of the few gnomen to escape the quarry on his own (weeks prior to the battle), and he'd used his talents to prepare the forest battlefield with traps before the imps arrived.

Mayor turned to the Seamstress and Engineer. "You should have seen it! The imps chased us into the forest, zipping between the trees on those ratty leather wings of theirs. Then Crafter threw a switch, and just like that"—he stomped one hoof sharply on the tile floor—"there were big nets strung between the trees. The imps were flying too fast to stop, and they plowed right into them."

"Poof!" Handmaiden cried. "Yellow smoke!"

"That's right," the eqman Steward agreed. "More than a few of the foul creatures were smoked right then and there. And the ones still alive couldn't escape, because of *more* nets trapping them from above."

"I reckon that's about the time we caught up to y'all," Wrangler put in. As soon as Cécilie unchained him and the others, the freed slaves had galloped to join the battle. Bursting into the forest, the newcomers had trampled the impmen who were forced to land because of the nets. Some of the gnomes had even been *riding* their eqman allies, which made Cécilie smile, considering how much they used to hate each other.

"And *we* took out a bunch of bad guys too!" Handmaiden said excitedly, reminding everyone how she and the Princess had ridden through the battle, spearing imps on her unicorn horn, turning still more of them to yellow smoke.

Even Matron couldn't help but smile. "That you did, young one." Her eyes shifted to Cécilie. "And your little brother the Knight defeated more than his fair share of enemies also." She lifted an eyebrow. "More magic, I suppose?"

Cécilie nodded, stuffing a cinnamon twist into her mouth so she wouldn't have to answer. Ewan had been wearing *another* of her amulets (she had a whole bunch of them), a priceless ruby that granted him immense strength. The little boy had even managed to pick up a fallen *tree* and smoke a bunch of imps with it! That memory should have made Cécilie smile, but she suddenly felt glum. She wished Ewan was here celebrating with them. She even would have liked for Nachton to stay. Instead, both of her brothers had run off to the Archives (the local eqman library) right after the battle. Cécilie still didn't understand why, and she hadn't heard from them since. That was hours ago.

Sensing Cécilie's change in mood, everyone else grew more serious as well. "It was your big brother who really saved the day," Mayor said, and Cécilie nodded again, looking away. "When the Warlord showed up and started tearing down the nets, I thought we were done-for."

The Warlord was the Vizier's chief henchman, commander of his flying army of darkness—and almost as evil as the Vizier himself. He was essentially a dragon, huge and scary, with a long barbed tail and vicious fangs. Unlike Cécilie, Nachton had learned to use magic on his own, without having to wear an amulet. He had woven some amazing magic spells out of bright green light, using them to fight the monstrous dragon, but their duel had eventually ended in a stalemate. Even so, the Warlord lost the keys to the Palace in the process, and he was forced to abandon Eqland and lead his army back to Capital City on Twixt.

In other words, the villainous dragon was still out there somewhere. And that meant Cécilie and her family would have to face him again someday. She only hoped Nachton would be there to fight the dragon that day too, because there was no way *Cécilie* could.

"It sounds like your entire family is blessed with great magic," the Seamstress said conversationally. "What about your sister the Empress?"

"I don't know," Cécilie said. "Maybe." She'd never *seen* Amélie use magic, but they'd been separated for more than a month, ever since Amélie left on her quest to unite the peoples of Overtwixt. Who knew how much had changed? Cécilie had even begun to miss her big sister, something she'd never dreamed would ever happen!

"How *is* your family blessed with so much magic?" the Steward asked with a thoughtful frown. "So like the Vizier himself. Perhaps it's a human thing?"

Cécilie could only shrug. How she missed Mom and Daddy and her brothers and sister. She wouldn't even mind if they accused her of being a drama queen (like they always did), if it meant she could just see them again.

It was very late when the celebration in Pastoral City finally ended. Cécilie's good mood eventually returned, and she sat around the table talking with her friends until she couldn't keep her eyes open any longer. Then Steward and Handmaiden gently roused her, and began leading the Princess to her royal sleeping chambers at the top of the Palace's tallest tower.

"Mr. Steward," Cécilie asked, stifling a yawn. "Why is this place called Pastoral City?"

"Because it's a simple city, quiet and charming, situated amidst Eqland's grassy pastures. That's where the word *pastoral* comes from, you know—pasture. Ah, here we are." The Steward stopped suddenly at a doorway, then stepped back and waited to see Cécilie's reaction.

She had been yawning again, but she forgot sleep when she saw her new room. "This... this is all mine?"

"Only the best for our Princess," the Steward said, and the Handmaiden giggled with delight.

Cécilie had never gotten a room to herself before—she always had to share with Amélie—and definitely not a room this *big*. This must be what Mom called luxury. The bed was shaped like a giant circle, with the softest mattress she'd ever felt. Beautiful wooden furniture lined the walls (including dressers, wardrobes, and chests), and there was even a full-length swivel mirror. On the far side of the room, steam was rising from a great big bath tub, and beyond that were doors leading onto a balcony (though they were closed at the moment).

"How?" Cécilie whispered. "These are human things, not eqman." Horses didn't use beds or furniture, did they?

"The Palace staff has been preparing this room ever since we arrived," the Handmaiden explained. "And some of the gnomen carved and built this furniture, just for you."

"That fast!?" Cécilie exclaimed.

"It's amazing what eqmen and gnomen can accomplish, working together," the Steward said. "I never would have guessed."

"But they missed out on the party!" Cécilie objected.

"This was how those individuals chose to celebrate," the Steward assured her. "And they will not regret it when I tell them how pleased you are. You *are* pleased, aren't you?"

"Yes!" Cécilie blurted. "This is the best princess bedroom ever!" she declared, and it really, truly was.

He smiled. "In that case, your highness, I will take my leave of you. Please call if you need anything."

"Same for me, highness," the little unicorn added. "My room is just down the hall."

Cécilie nodded, still stunned. Seeing this place, she wasn't even tired anymore. First she was going to jump into the hot tub, and so what if she splashed water everywhere? After a nice long soak, she would comb her hair with the beautiful ivory-handle brush she saw sitting out on that dresser; then she would try on some of the dresses that must be hanging in that wardrobe. After that, she'd probably call Handmaiden back in, and they could stay up even later sharing secrets.

"Oh!" the Steward added. "I almost forgot. A letter came for you a short time ago." He had a small satchel hanging around his neck, next to the big brass Palace gate key that Nachton had returned to him after the battle. The Steward shoved his muzzle into the satchel and pulled out a roll of paper, which Cécilie took. "Good night, your highness."

Cécilie inspected the paper as the two eqmen bowed and left. There was a bit of dry wax holding the roll together, but that broke when she opened the paper. It was a letter, with Nachton's signature at the bottom:

Cécilie —

We were betrayed. Ewan fell in battle, fighting the Vizier. He's okay, but he got kicked out of Overtwixt. If we ever want to see him again, defeating the Vizier is more important than ever. I must return to my studies. I will be at the Archives if you need me.

I love you, Nachton

Cécilie stared at the letter until big wet spots started blurring the ink, and she realized she was crying. Ewan was *gone?* No, that wasn't possible.

For the longest time, her mind simply couldn't believe it, even while her emotions began running out of control. Her heart was aching like Ewan had *died*, though she knew he was safe in the real world—Nachton's letter said so. But even if that was true, when would she see him again? Cécilie's new subjects were all wonderful, and she loved the Handmaiden, but Ewan was her *bestest* best friend.

What was the point of this whole adventure if Ewan wasn't right here next to her, doing it with her?

Looking up from the letter, Cécilie caught her reflection in the swivel mirror. She appeared mature and sophisticated, despite the wet streaks running down her face. She looked *regal*, like a Princess should be. Suddenly angry, Cécilie ripped off the amethyst necklace—and just that fast, she was her normal self again. An awkward little girl.

Until now, she'd been so worried what people would think of her without the amethyst. If her subjects knew the real Cécilie, they might stop following her entirely. Or maybe they'd start treating her like the kid she was, instead of taking her seriously. But now she just didn't care. The necklace was a *lie*—and when she wore it, she was a liar, pretending to be someone she wasn't. Ewan knew the real Cécilie, and he loved her just the way she was. Why should she want to lie about herself, just to impress people she barely knew?

Crying angrily, Cécilie flipped open the lid on a nearby chest, then threw the amethyst necklace inside. She threw it so hard, she felt like the gemstone should have shattered. When it didn't, she picked it up and threw it again, harder this time. Sobbing now, she pulled all the other necklaces out of her pockets and threw them into the chest too, slamming the lid closed.

Then Cécilie crawled into her big new bed and pulled the covers over her head, fully intending to cry herself to sleep.

That was when she heard a sharp knock at the door— but not the door leading into the hallway.

The knock came from the *balcony*.

· two ·

(Amélie)

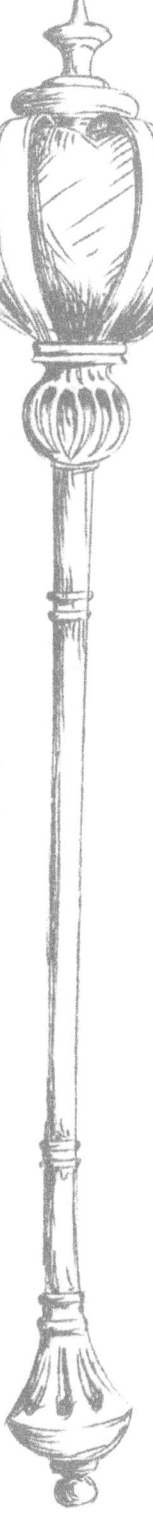

A mélie Ollivaros stared off into the nighttime sky, overcome with the wonder of this place called Overtwixt. When she'd first arrived, she'd been so afraid: afraid of the strange creatures here; afraid that one of these impossible floating nilands would suddenly fall away beneath her; afraid that she and her family would never find their way home. Those fears still existed, but she had begun to grow in confidence as well—both in herself, and in the magic that made Overtwixt possible.

The 12-year-old girl clutched her new scepter to her chest, and she felt her fears quiet once more. All would be well in the end, whatever may come.

Amélie was the new Empress of Overtwixt, having selected that role from the Guide on her first day here. The Guide had then tasked her with an impossible quest: building trust and loyalty among the peoples of Overtwixt, overcoming their many prejudices, and uniting them beneath her banner—all in the name of overthrowing the Vizier. Presumably she, as Empress, would then rule in his place for a time. The Vizier had committed many atrocities, including the destruction of all the bridges back to the various real worlds. Amélie would need to have those rebuilt, if her own family ever hoped to return home safely.

Almost immediately after choosing her role, circumstances had separated Amélie from her three siblings, leading her on a whirlwind tour of other nilands as she attempted to recruit the peoples of Overtwixt to her cause. Escorted by her new centman protectors, she had spoken before the Council of Centwick as well as the Assembly of Caymerdelphia, making an impassioned plea for unity in the face of tyranny.

And she had failed, completely.

At Centwick, the Councilmembers simply hadn't trusted her, nor did they trust the Guide (despite the fact that he was a centman like them). From the Council's perspective, Amélie was just another power-hungry human, not so different from the Vizier. One Councilman went so far as to suggest that Amélie didn't understand her own mission.

At Caymerdelphia, things had gone even worse. At the very moment when Amélie thought she'd convinced the aquatic peoples to join the fight, news had arrived about the battle for Eqland—how Nachton, Cécilie, and Ewan had fought to free the eqmen and gnomen from slavery. Despite their victory, Amélie had been *furious* to learn that her siblings disobeyed her orders, launching the attack without her... and the Caymerdelphian Committee members had seen her anger. They too had withheld their support, pointing out that Amélie could hardly unite the peoples of Overtwixt if she couldn't even unite the members of her own family.

And so here she was, more than a month after arriving in Overtwixt, with only four followers: the Captain, Ranger, Operative, and Scout, her personal centman protectors. Meanwhile, her spunky little sister Cécilie—the new Princess of Eqland—had done more to advance Amélie's cause than

Amélie herself. Cécilie had won the support of two entire races when she liberated the eqmen and gnomen.

Everything about the situation continued to infuriate Amélie, threatening her mood whenever she let herself think about it. But then she forced herself to take a deep breath as she clutched her scepter. Peace washed over her again.

Amélie's return from Caymerdelphia to Eqland had been an adventure all by itself.* She'd been separated from her four guardsmen along the way, and chased from one niland to another by agents of the Vizier. But her pursuers had turned back once Amélie reached Eqland, unwilling to step foot on this niland again after their defeat by Cécilie's forces. And finally, just minutes ago, Amélie had been deposited safely here.

On the balcony of the tallest tower of Cécilie's new Palace.

As Amélie gazed out at the distant, twinkling Sky Lights, she felt peace and confidence that the Captain and his men would make their way safely here over the next few days; there was nothing more she could do to help them in any event. It was time to do something about the things she *could* control. First she needed to confront her siblings with their disobedience, and then she needed to unite her own family as an example to the rest of Overtwixt.

She took a deep breath, trying to ignore her ratty, travelworn appearance. Instead she needed to act, even *be* regal. She was the Empress, after all. She knocked on the balcony doors like she owned them.

"Cécilie?" she called. "It's me, Amélie. Can I come in and see your new Palace?" Without waiting for a response, she pulled open the double doors and swept inside.

---

* The tale of Amélie's journey back from Caymerdelphia, and how she acquired the scepter, is told in the novella *Perilous Flight*.

Then she stopped, almost immediately, at the sight of Cécilie curled up in the fetal position in the middle of a big round bed. Yet she was obviously awake. For a long moment, the little girl only stared back at Amélie in shock. Then she threw off the bedcovers and bolted across the room, colliding with Amélie in a violent hug. Amélie squeezed her sister back, surprised by just how much she'd missed the little girl—and by just how much Cécilie had obviously missed *her*. It felt like things were going back to the way they should be, their family coming together again.

Then Amélie felt the Princess shuddering against her chest, and she realized her sister was sobbing. "Cécilie?" The little girl craned her neck to look up, and Amélie saw that her eyes were swollen and red from tears. She'd already been crying, even before Amélie arrived. "Cécilie, what is it?" she asked in alarm. "What's happened?"

Cécilie bit her lip and took an unsteady breath. "It's Ewan," she managed to say. "He's... he's..."

· three ·

(Nachton)

Nachton spent at least a week cleaning up from the fight in the Archives. The eqman library was like a big warehouse, all one floor, with row after row of shelves. But instead of books, the shelves were filled with *seashells*—each one an audio recording, a much more effective way of storing information for the horse-like eqmen, who didn't have hands or fingers for writing. The diverse collection of shells had once been elaborate and beautiful, but after the fight, they littered the floor in a shattered mess. The Berserker had knocked over so many bookcases trying to flee the Vizier, and each one home to so many recordings... it took a full day just to straighten the shelves, and the rest of the week to sort intact shells from the broken ones, returning them to their proper places and sweeping the shards into a pile near the door.

The pile of broken pieces was far too big.

Nachton did a lot of thinking while he cleaned. At first, he was consumed by thoughts of revenge, dreaming up elaborate fantasies of how he would punish the Vizier as well as Ewan's traitorous friend Shark. But that was hardly practical, and it got old fast. What Nachton still didn't understand was *how* the Vizier had bested him—and he was gonna need to figure that out if he hoped to get his revenge the next time they faced off. So as the week went on, Nachton began trying to formulate specific questions to research. He wasn't going to find an archive recording titled "How the Vizier Defeated You in Three Easy Steps," after all. But where *would* he find his answers?

The Guide had implied that Nachton didn't understand power and magic in Overtwixt as well as he thought he did. It made Nachton's skin crawl to even consider the possibility that the centman was right, but... well, it was just Nachton here. It couldn't hurt to revisit his most basic assumptions, right? So the Five Fundamental Laws of Overtwixt* would be a good place to start. After that, he decided he would research Sovereign's Relics some more. They must have a weakness, no matter what people said about them. Sure, the Guide claimed nothing was more powerful than Sovereign or his Relics, but in the next breath, he'd *admitted* their failure to work for Ewan or Nachton. Surely some wise eqman from ages past had examined the question of how such failure was possible; Nachton just needed to find the proper recordings.

He spent weeks researching, as he had before. How many weeks, he couldn't say, for he lost track of time entirely. It didn't really matter, considering that time was passing more slowly in the outside world anyway.

And all alone, with no one else to accuse him, Nachton finally let himself consider the possibility—the *possibility*—that he really had misunderstood some things... that he

---

* The Five Fundamental Laws are basic rules governing the innerworkings of Overtwixt, as established by the Sovereign when Overtwixt came into being. They are listed at the start of this book.

might've even made a mistake confronting the Vizier so soon. And as a result, he began to find the answers he sought.

Terrible answers.

"Ho there!" a distant voice called, accompanied by the clatter of hooves. "Master of Lore, are you here?"

With a sense of déjà vu (the feeling that he'd been in this situation before), Nachton rose from his studies and began closing the various notebooks he had spread out before him. This was just like that day, surely months ago now, when a delegation of eqmen arrived on Huland to tell him about the Vizier's conquest of Eqland. "I'm back here," he called in answer, returning the last seashell recording to its place on a shelf.

A minute later, the Captain, the Operative, and the Ranger all joined him. These three were centmen like the Guide, except they were all cleanshaven and much less infuriating. Along with another centman called the Scout, these men had sworn to serve Amélie as guardsmen and protectors. They all nodded their heads in acknowledgment of Nachton, but it wasn't much of a bow.

"I see you found your friends," Nachton said to the Ranger, who had traveled along with Nachton for a time, temporarily acting as a protector for Cécilie and Ewan. The last Nachton had seen of the guy, he was off to report to Amélie about the liberation of the eqmen and gnomen. "I guess that means my sister the exalted Empress has returned here to Eqland?"

"Actually, we got separated on the way back, but yes," the Ranger said. He was the biggest of Amélie's guardsmen, with thick red hair covering most of his muscular body. He was usually the friendliest of the bunch too, but he didn't seem that way now. "Although *we* only just arrived, the Empress has been back for a week now. And she has been very eager to speak with you." His face gave nothing away.

The oldest of the centmen spoke up. "Your sister is disappointed that you haven't already returned to the Palace of your own accord." Known as the Captain, he was the leader of the Empress's guard (and before that, the old Baron's guard), and he had silver running through his chestnut hair. "Therefore, you have been formally summoned. At the Empress's command, we are to collect you and return with you to the Palace at once."

Despite his recent soul-searching, despite admitting to himself that he'd messed up, Nachton still felt his anger flare at being treated this way. "What, Amélie's arresting me? One messenger wasn't enough; she had to send all *three* of you?"

The Captain blinked, and the others looked even more surprised. "Arresting you?" the leader of the guardsmen said. "No, of course not. But her majesty was definitely concerned for your safety, being out here alone."

"My safety," Nachton repeated bitterly. But it was a valid concern. It turned out Nachton really *wasn't* capable of defending himself, not against the Vizier. Not by a long shot.

"And considering what happened to the Knight..." the dark-skinned Operative trailed off uncomfortably.

"You know about that, huh?"

"Young master, everyone knows about that. The entire princedom of Eqland is in mourning. Your sister the Princess is heartbroken."

Nachton winced, turning away so the three centmen wouldn't see the tears forming.

"And the Empress is eager to see you," the Ranger added gently, "despite everything that's happened."

"Besides, the time has come," the Captain intoned. "We must hold another council of war."

Nachton steeled himself, then nodded. "Okay," he whispered. "Let's go."

· four ·

(Amélie)

Amélie couldn't help herself. No matter how relieved she was at seeing Nachton again, she started yelling the moment he walked into Cécilie's new throne room in the Palace. "How could you!?" she demanded from where she stood on the dais. "How could you be so *stupid?* Attacking the Vizier, and taking Ewan with you!?"

Shame-faced, Nachton stopped where he stood, eyes dropping to the floor.

"He's *five*, Nachton. He's no warrior, no matter how cool his new Diamond Armor is!"

"I'm sorry," Nachton whispered. "I..." He swallowed hard. "I was wrong."

"I can't *believe* you. How could you do something so idiotic and pig-headed and—"

"I said I was sorry," Nachton repeated, obviously getting frustrated.

"And *I* said you were supposed to wait for me at the Grand Library on Huland," Amélie shot back. "I specifically told you not to do anything until I came back from my quest. We were supposed to go to Eqland *together*, to claim Cécilie's throne *together*. Was I unclear about any of that?"

"Oh, you were clear all right," Nachton said, his temper flaring. "You *commanded* me to stay at the Grand Library. That was the word you used: *command.*"

"Exactly!"

"You're not the boss of me, Amélie!"

Amélie felt like she might explode; she was so mad right then. "That's *exactly* what I am, Nachton."

They stared at each other furiously. Then Amélie remembered that they weren't the only people in the throne room. Cécilie was beside her, of course, staring back and forth between her older siblings, and much of Cécilie's retinue too—including Mayor, Steward, and members of the Palace staff. Scout was still guarding the door, and Amélie's other three centmen had returned with Nachton.

"Perhaps we should withdraw," the Steward said awkwardly. "Give your family some privacy—"

Amélie gestured angrily, forbidding anyone from leaving, and all eyes were drawn to the scepter she now carried in that hand. She knew people had questions about it, but this was hardly the right time to tell the story of her perilous flight from Caymerdelphia. Amélie also wore a formal evening dress now—lavender satin, with a regal high collar—just fashioned by the gnowoman Seamstress. Between the gown and the scepter, she finally looked every inch like the Empress she was supposed to be.

"Well?" Amélie demanded, focusing on Nachton again. "Are you going to explain yourself?"

"The liberation of Eqland speaks for itself," Nachton said coldly. "I will not apologize for that. By freeing the slaves at the quarry, we ended a great evil and won the trust of both the eqmen and the gnomen."

Amélie sucked in a breath to retort.

"But confronting the Vizier..." Nachton went on, now both angry *and* remorseful. "That—" He heaved a frustrated sigh. "That was a mistake."

"What were you *thinking?*" Amélie demanded again.

Nachton scowled. "I don't know. I thought I understood how the battle would go down. I was wrong, but... But we were betrayed, too. There was this spookman, a friend of Ewan's, and—"

"You trusted a *spook?*" the Captain demanded, obviously appalled at the notion.

"We *didn't* trust him! Not at first. But Ewan swore he was a good guy. Then the spook told us where we could find the Vizier after the battle, all alone, and—"

At that moment, Cécilie's little unicorn Handmaiden came galloping into the throne room from a side entrance. "Your highness! Your highness!" she called excitedly.

Amélie silenced her with a glare.

The Captain had whirled on the Ranger. "Did you know of this?" he demanded. "A *spook?*"

"Yes, sir," the guardsman mumbled.

"What were *you* thinking? *You* actually know better!"

"We didn't trust him very far," the Ranger said quickly. "Besides, he claimed to be the old Baron's informant, the one that was helping us at the end."

Captain frowned. "What did this spook call himself?"

The Ranger shrugged. Nachton said, "He's a *spook.* What does it matter? He was one of the Spies, I guess."

Cécilie chewed her lip. "Ewan called him Shark."

The Captain looked up sharply. "Say again?"

"Ewan called the spookman *Shark.*"

Nachton waved a hand. "Obviously not his real name. Ewan's only five. He doesn't always—"

"The Charlatan," Captain said quietly. "That spook... it must've been the Charlatan. Of *course,*" he growled. "One of the most accomplished liars and swindlers to ever make a name in Overtwixt." The centman rubbed his face with both hands. "No wonder you all were deceived."

"Who cares!" Amélie interrupted angrily, afraid she might burst into tears at any moment. "Ewan's *gone.*"

To Amélie's surprise, Nachton agreed with her. "You're right. It really doesn't matter." He took a deep breath and seemed to let go of his own anger. "Betrayed or not, what happened to Ewan was my fault. All of it."

Amélie stared at him.

Nachton's throat worked as he tried to process his emotion. "For the longest time, I wanted to blame the Vizier. But of course he was going to cut down our team, given the opportunity. He's the bad guy. But *I'm* to blame for giving him that opportunity... for taking my innocent little brother into a battle none of us was prepared for yet." Tears filling his eyes, Nachton came the rest of the way onto the dais and knelt before both of his sisters, taking their hands in his.

"I'm *sorry*," he said genuinely. "I was wrong... and stupid... and... will you forgive me? Can you ever forgive me?"

Amélie still just stared at him. Who *was* this?

"Are you sure he's still alive?" Cécilie asked, so quietly Amélie almost couldn't hear the words.

"Yes, I'm sure," Nachton said.

"But *how*? You said he fell in battle, that the Vizier defeated him!"

Nachton sighed. "It's just the way it works. If you're hurt badly enough, you get expelled from Overtwixt."

Amélie opened her mouth to disagree. That might be what all the books in the Library said, but she wasn't so sure after some of the discussions she'd had with her guardsmen during their travels. What if the Scout was right, and everything was different now that the Vizier had destroyed the bridges?

But before Amélie could say all this out loud, she noticed Cécilie's pale face... and the glimmer of hope that had appeared there. "So Ewan's with Mom and Daddy now?"

"I hope so," Nachton said. But he still looked unsure, and Amélie knew what he was thinking. Even if the little boy *was* back in the real world, it had been well over a month since the kids entered Overtwixt. By now, their parents must have returned home, thinking the children kidnapped or worse. Ewan would need help from the police or someone at the airport just to phone Mom and Dad... except he didn't even know their phone number, much less the spelling of his own last name.

"Can he just come back?" Cécilie said, even more hope shining in her eyes. "Can he *bring* Mom and Daddy?"

That was one question Amélie could answer for sure. "Not with the bridges down," she said sadly. "I'm sorry."

"Not even if the bridges still existed," Nachton said even more sadly. "It's the Fifth Fundamental Law. Only *one* life can a person live here in Overtwixt. If that life is ended..." He swallowed. "I'm sorry, Cécilie. There are no do-overs."

Cécilie finally lost control of her emotions. Amélie pulled her hand free from Nachton's and wrapped both arms around the little girl, still holding her new scepter too, of course. She beckoned to Nachton, and he scrambled to his feet, making it a family hug. Amélie was *so angry* with him, but she also felt her anger fading as waves of peace washed over them. She didn't want to be angry with him. She wanted everything to be okay between them. She needed the love of her family just as much right now as Cécilie did.

"I just can't believe it," Amélie whispered. "I mean, Ewan, *gone...*"

"Please forgive me," Nachton begged.

"Of course I forgive you."

"Me too," Cécilie squeaked.

Someone cleared a throat nearby, shattering the moment, and Amélie looked up irritably. "What!?"

It was the Handmaiden, and she was standing *right there*, well within the personal bubble Amélie usually reserved for family alone. The little white unicorn was hopping from foot to foot, her long pink hair swaying as she tossed her head impatiently.

"What is it?" Cécilie asked more sweetly.

"I'm sorry to interrupt, it's just really, *really* important, and it kinda changes everything. I raced back here as soon—"

"Just get to the point," Nachton said.

"It's about my friend Debby—I mean Debutante, we just call her Debby for short—" Amélie gestured impatiently, and the little unicorn went on. "She lived here in Pastoral

City until the day the Vizier and the Warlord attacked, but then..." Handmaiden became emotional.

The Mayor spoke up, his tone gentle. "Debutante was one of the ones we lost, when the Vizier's army first invaded Eqland." He gave Amélie and her siblings a knowing look. "Yellow smoke."

Amélie sighed. "I'm so sorry," she apologized, realizing that the Handmaiden was grieving for her friend the same way she and her siblings were grieving for Ewan. Cécilie hugged the little unicorn around the neck.

"But what's that got to do with anything?" Nachton demanded. "I mean, I'm sorry too, but..."

Oddly, the Handmaiden started bouncing up and down again—not at all like someone grieving. "That's just it! Debby's *not* gone. I just ran into her in the street, here in Pastoral City!"

For a long moment, everyone stared at the little unicorn. "But," Cécilie said loudly, "if Debby's not gone, maybe *no one*'s gone."

"Exactly!" the unicorn said gleefully. "What if your brother Ewan is still in Overtwixt too?"

· five ·

(EWAN)

E wan *hurt*. He couldn't say where. He just... hurt. Like the time his family went to the fair and walked around in the bright sun *all day*, making him tired, and thirsty, and his head all fuzzy. He just felt *ugh*.

And he was scared.

He tried not to cry, though. That was really hard—he could *feel* his bottom lip shaking—but he didn't cry. Some tears squeezed out, but that didn't count. He didn't *need* to be scared, 'cause Nock promised to protect him.

"Nock?"

"He's not here, sir Knight," said a tired voice with a fancy accent. "Not yet, anyway."

Ewan sat up and looked around. "Skire Horsey?"

"Indeed. A little the worse for wear, but... it is I." The horsey smiled a horsey smile at him, then groaned.

"But you dead!"

"No more than you, it seems."

"But I saw you! Viziguy, he use fireballs, and..." Ewan trailed off. Skire Horsey—the big black eqman

· 43 ·

everyone else called 'Squire'—really was alive. Ewan could see him standing there with his own two eyeballs. And that was good, 'cause the black horsey was the first new friend Ewan ever made in Overchix, *and* Ewan's personal horsey whenever he rode into battle. Ewan was the Knight, after all, and everyone knew knights rode horseys. "I'm so glad you still alive!" he yelled at his friend.

Someone else groaned nearby. "Could ya keep it down with that racket?" The voice reminded Ewan of his Aunt Judy from New Jersey.

"Fight Guy?" Ewan guessed excitedly.

"Unfortunately," the little dude muttered. Fight Guy was the fast-talking little half-dolphin dude that everyone else called 'Weaponsmaster,' but Ewan couldn't pronounce that. Really, he had tried.

But if Skire Horsey and Fight Guy were both still alive, even after the Vizier smoked them...

"Bazooka!?" Ewan demanded, looking everywhere.

"Is here too," the big guy boomed. He stood up in the corner of the room, and his rhino head touched the ceiling. He was a lugman named 'Berserker.'

"Bazooka!" Ewan squealed happily, proving he could pronounce *that* friend's name just fine. Suddenly the little boy didn't hurt so bad, knowing his friends were okay—even though he still felt *ugh*, and even though he realized he wasn't wearing his special shiny Armor anymore either. He tried to rush over and hug his friends, but there were rows of metal bars going from floor to ceiling in the middle of the room, keeping everyone separated. "What *is* dis place?" Ewan said in wonder, really looking at the room for the first time. It was all gray, with metal bars on the windows too. There was only one door going in or out of the room, and Ewan couldn't get to it.

"Is jail," Bazooka rumbled. "I try escape, but... no escape." And just to prove it, he grabbed a bar in each hand and pulled them away from each other as hard as he could. They didn't even budge.

"Let me try!" Ewan said. "I'm *awesome*, you know." But nothing happened when he pulled the bars either. Huh? He was supposed to be *strong* in Overchix! He had lifted a whole tree trunk in the battle for Eqland, using it as a weapon against the wimpy dudes. One time, before he and Bazooka were friends, he even lifted *Bazooka*, slamming the giant barbarian back and forth into the ground until the big guy begged for mercy.

"I have a better question," Fight Guy said, and he didn't sound happy. "How in the hungry hag's hopscotch did we get here?!"

Skire Horsey just shook his mane, and Ewan shrugged. Then *another* voice spoke. "The Vizier slew you in battle... but instead of being ousted from Overtwixt, you rebounded here to this place."

"Shark!" Ewan cried happily. The little spooky bat was hanging from the ceiling in the jail cell next to Skire Horsey's.

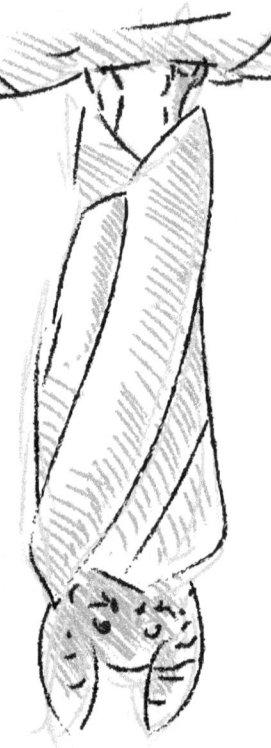

"We *rebounded?*" the horsey repeated with a neigh. "That's not possible! It breaks the Fifth Fundamental—"

"The Five Fundamental Laws of Overtwixt remain intact," Shark said. "But the Vizier found a way to... *bend* that one. Destroying the real world bridges wasn't just about preventing new visitors. He wanted to stay in Overtwixt forever, to give himself eternal life. Which means he kinda did the same thing for everyone else, too." The little spook shook his head in awe. "Now when someone gets smoked, they bounce *here* instead of going back to their real world—into one of these cells, which the Vizier controls."

"That's ridiculous!" Fight Guy said.

"Is crazy talk!" Bazooka agreed.

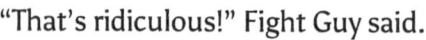

"Wait a moment," Skire Horsey said, looking at Shark with suspicion. "How did *you* get here? You weren't with us at the Archives on Eqland."

Shark sighed. "No, I was not."

The door slammed open, and a *huuuuge* dwagon thing slid into the room. Ewan jumped up, terrified, and ran to the back wall of his cell, as far away from the creature as he could get. "It's him!" he gasped. The *Warlord*.

"Oh goodie!" the dwagon thing said, in a really nice-sounding voice. "You're all awake! How do you feel?"

"Um..." Fight Guy said.

"Any nausea or discomfort? Lingering dizziness?"

"I... uh... no," Skire said.

"I bet you're all hungry though, right?" The dwagon actually winked at Ewan. "*You're* hungry, aren't you, little fella?" And he handed a bowl of hot soup to Ewan through the bars. It smelled wonderful. He handed bowls to everyone else too, except Shark. It was amazing the dwagon was able to carry them all at once.

"I don't get it," Fight Guy muttered. "The Warlord, serving *soup?*"

"Oh, I'm not the Warlord," the dwagon laughed. "That's my cousin. I'm the Jailer. Though I'll tell you a secret..." He lowered his voice. "I used to be the Proprietor. All I really care about is keeping people warm, fed, and happy, ya know? But... well, the Vizier wanted to change my name, just like he did for my cousins. So who was I to argue?" He shrugged his big shoulders. "Anyone need anything? A blanket? A softer pillow, perhaps?"

Everyone relaxed a little. "You... said we were asleep?" Skire Horsey asked. "How long?"

"Oh, I don't know. A few days, maybe a week. Except for that one." He pointed at Bazooka, then made a fist and rapped on his own skull. "You know lugmen. Hard-headed. He's been up and about at least a day. *Anyway.* You folks sure I can't get you anything? No? Very well, I'll send in your visitor, then be back to check on you in a few hours." And with that, he slid back out through the door, pulling himself along with his two muscular arms. He caught the door with his barbed tail and pulled it closed after him.

"Whoa," Ewan said softly.

Skire Horsey turned to face Shark. "Well?" he demanded in his fancy accent. "How did you get here?"

Shark sighed again. "I'm afraid you're not going to like the answer, friend eqman."

The door slammed open again... and this time, something far scarier than a dwagon entered the room.

The Vizier.

Ewan's eyes got as big as dinner plates, and his heart started thumping. The Vizier's clothes were all black. He was even wearing a cloak that blew behind him like a cape, with a collar that hid half his face. He was so tall that *his* head almost touched the ceiling too.

"I very nearly captured the lot of you, didn't I?" the bad guy said in his recognizable deep voice, which seemed to echo off the walls and come from everywhere at once. "I believe I shall add *all* of you to my collection. Alas, I only have room for one at the moment." He opened his hand to show Ewan two glittery gems—a white pearl hanging from a gold ribbon... and a red ruby hanging from a silver ribbon.

"My lucky neckace!" Ewan said, recognizing the ruby. "Give dat back!"

The Vizier threw back his head and laughed. "Yours, is it? I think not. This amulet belonged to *me*, along with dozens more like it. And when I find out who stole them, I will make the traitor suffer for all eternity." His wide eyes got all shiny and scary when he said this.

"I don't get it," Fight Guy said. "Amulets?"

"Magical relics of my own invention—the Vizier's Relics, I call them, and more powerful than anything Sovereign ever created. For one thing, I can make as many as I wish, though it's a taxing process."

"But what do they do?"

"They preserve and enhance a single talent or ability harvested from a... donor."

Fight Guy and Skire Horsey looked confused.

"Allow me to demonstrate," the Vizier said, and Ewan could tell the bad guy really liked showing off. The tall human touched the necklace he was already wearing, a glittering green emerald on a black ribbon. "This was the only one I had left when that traitor stole my old collection and burned all my notes—and only because I was wearing it at the time. I'll let you guess what it does."

He took it off, and suddenly he was short. Like, *really* short for an adult—barely taller than Amélie, and not scary at all! "How you do dat!?" Ewan demanded.

The short Vizier just smirked. He put on Ewan's ruby necklace, but nothing changed. Then he grabbed the bars to Fight Guy's cell and bent them out of the way, easily.

Everyone gasped. "Sir Knight..." Skire said. "All your feats of strength... Is that necklace how you did all those things you did?"

Ewan stared. "I thought I awesome," he whispered.

The Vizier just laughed. He removed the ruby and put the emerald necklace back on, and suddenly he was tall again. "I am most grateful to you, *sir Knight*, for returning my property to me. Decades of research lost, or so I thought. I tried studying this one, of course"—he tapped the green emerald—"but it was the first I ever made, and it took many years to manufacture. Reverse engineering *that* would have been pointless. I learned better techniques in the years that followed, but lost them when my notes burned."

"That's why you were in the Archives!" Skire blurted.

"Trying to reproduce all of my old research, yes," the Vizier agreed with a scowl. "It's all I've done since the day I became Emperor, moving from library to library across the United Lands, poring over old tomes... and making very little progress." Then he smiled an evil smile. "But all that changed when you returned this ruby to me! Studying *it* helped me reconstruct my newest techniques... and I was able to create a brand new blank amulet in only a week."

The Vizier held up the other necklace he'd shown Ewan earlier: the pearl dangling from its gold ribbon. Then he stepped between the bent bars and into Fight Guy's cell.

The little shaman backed away. "Sir Knight? Sir Knight! Help me, please." Fight Guy was the best fighter Ewan ever met, but the little guy didn't have any weapons. "Please," he begged the Vizier, "not like this."

The Vizier smiled and started weaving his hands in the air. "Any last words?"

"*Please*," Fight Guy blubbered, "put a blade in my hands—or something, *anything*. Give me a *chance*. Don't send me out like this, defenseless and—"

The Vizier finished weaving, and Fight Guy disappeared with a pop. There was no smoke. He was just gone.

But the pearl started glowing green.

The Vizier's smile got even bigger as he took off the emerald necklace, got short, then hung the pearl around his neck. He drew his elegant saber.

Taking a deep breath, the Vizier launched into a flurry of motion, swinging his saber in every direction, faster than Ewan's eye could see. It was like the bad guy was *dancing* with his sword. When he finished, he slammed the blade back in its sheath in a single motion. "Yes!" he cried joyfully. "The Weaponsmaster was skilled indeed!" Then he swapped necklaces again, got tall, and left the cell.

He stopped at the door and looked at Ewan. "Don't worry, I'll be back for the rest of you as soon as I create more blanks." He cocked his head. "Charlatan?"

There was a flutter of wings, and to Ewan's surprise, Shark darted between the bars of his cell and landed on the Vizier's shoulder.

"Shark? You not a pwiz-o-ner too?"

"A prisoner?" the Vizier said with a laugh. "The *Charlatan?* Of course not! The Charlatan is my most trusted servant, the only one of all my minions whose original name I left intact. This fine creature is a spy and a thief like so many of the other spooks, but more talented than any of the fools I renamed Spy or Thief. The Charlatan is... well, exactly what the Guide first declared all those years ago: Charlatan. A pretender, a deceiver, dare I say a conman." The Vizier smiled slyly. "Definitely not a prisoner."

Ewan swallowed hard, and his lip began to tremble. "But... Shark my fwend too."

Shark didn't say anything.

"He my *fwend*," Ewan repeated. "And I'm *his* fwend. He *pommise*. Right, Shark?"

Shark still didn't answer, and the Vizier started laughing again. The sound of his laughter continued even after the Vizier and Shark exited the room, leaving Ewan alone with Bazooka and Skire Horsey.

Ewan finally stopped fighting his tears.

· six ·

(Cécilie)

Cécilie couldn't believe it—Ewan was still here in Overtwixt?! It was like Christmas and Easter and birthday all rolled into one. She and the Handmaiden looked at each other with huge smiles and started giggling together.

"I don't get it," Nachton said, voice full of emotion. "All the books agreed, and everyone I talked to said the same thing. Yellow smoke means you're *gone*. How can Ewan or this Debutante still be here?"

Everyone was standing around Cécilie's throne dais now. "I don't know," the Captain said, also sounding stunned and looking very unsure of himself—which was unusual for him. "I don't understand it myself."

"Obviously, I was right," the Scout said with a snort. "Everything is different now that the Vizier is in charge."

"Yes, but how is this *possible?*" the Captain asked.

"And where is Ewan now?" Amélie added.

No one answered until Cécilie spoke up. "I bet the Guide knows," she said confidently.

Lots of people snorted at this, but the Handmaiden nodded eagerly. "Maybe you're right," Nachton said, surprising Cécilie. "The Guide *does* seem to know a lot, but... he's not always forthcoming with information."

"You can say that again," the Scout muttered.

Amélie frowned hard. "But Nachton, the Guide was with you after Ewan got smoked. Surely he would've told you if he knew, if he even had an idea."

"Maybe," Nachton said again, thoughtfully. "Honestly, I wasn't being the best listener that night," he admitted. "I, um, may have interrupted a few times, assuming I already knew what he was trying to tell me. Besides," Nachton added hurriedly, blushing, "I think the Guide really *does* like us to figure stuff out for ourselves sometimes."

"What if we just asked him?" Cécilie suggested. This was something she had learned from the Matron during their journey across Eqland, that the Guide was always ready to help people with their quests.

The Scout snorted again. "That might work if the Guide was actually *here*. But I don't see him lurking around, do you? I can't remember the last time I saw him, much less being helpful—"

"That's enough," the Captain interrupted quietly.

Cécilie took a deep breath and spoke loudly. "Um, Mr. Guide?" She thought for a moment, then yelled at the top of her lungs. "Mr. Guide, can you hear me?"

The Scout started laughing bitterly.

Cécilie felt her cheeks getting hot, but she yelled, "Why aren't people getting kicked out of Overtwixt anymore?"

"Because of the Vizier's great evil," a strong voice said from the door. Everyone jumped in surprise, then *stared* as the Guide walked into the throne room. The Scout's eyes looked ready to pop out of his head.

Nachton actually gave the newcomer a respectful nod before saying, "The Vizier's great evil? You mean he's worked some terrible magic?"

"Not magic," the Guide said. "I refer to the destruction of the bridges. The Scout *was* right."

At this, the Scout's jaw actually dropped open.

The Guide cocked his head. "Children, do you not remember what I told you the first time we met? By destroying the bridges, the Vizier stranded everyone. *All* passage between here and the real worlds is interrupted."

The Ranger groaned. "All those Spies we shot on our way to the battle at the quarry... We thought we were keeping the army's approach a secret!"

"Instead, you were actually sending those spooks straight back to their masters, to report your position." The Guide nodded gravely. "Fortunately for you, there is a period of... disorientation... following such a traumatic event. And your campaign to retake Eqland was rapid enough that you still surprised the Warlord."

"So you know where people go now?" Amélie asked eagerly. "You know where *Ewan* went?"

The Guide simply nodded.

"This changes everything!" the Captain interrupted, shaking his head. "And not in a good way. The enemy soldiers we defeat in battle will just be back to fight us again later. And the Vizier... you're telling us he can't be defeated!"

"That *was* one of the things the Vizier hoped to accomplish by destroying the bridges," the Guide agreed.

Cécilie didn't fully understand all this, but it seemed to depress everyone else. People were staring at the floor now, like the situation was suddenly hopeless. Everyone except Amélie. "But what about *Ewan?*" Amélie demanded.

"Yes, if people aren't expelled from Overtwixt anymore," the Captain asked. "Where do they *go?*"

"To a destination of the Vizier's choosing," the Guide said. "And this redirection *did* require a tricky bit of magic."

The Handmaiden spoke up. "My friend Debby, she woke up in some sort of jail cell, but she wasn't there long. They chained her to a bunch of others and started using them like *workhorses.*" She made that sound like a dirty word. "Eventually they ended up back here, one of the slaves at the quarry." Cécilie and Handmaiden had only unchained some of the slaves personally, leaving those people to free others. And there were so many eqmen in Pastoral City now; it was no wonder a week had passed before Handmaiden and Debutante ran into each other.

"Which niland was this jail on?" Captain persisted.

The little unicorn shrugged. "Debby thinks the whole niland was the jail. She says they crossed a drawbridge over nothingness on their way out of the building."

"That's absurd," Scout said, finding his voice again. "There are no such nilands in Overtwixt. Not in this realm, anyway."

The Guide raised an eyebrow at this but said nothing.

"Well, Debby *was* disoriented, and scared," Handmaiden said with a sniff. "But she's sure the jail was somewhere in the Shadowlands."

"Wait a sec," Nachton said, flipping open his satchel and digging out a notebook. "I transcribed all the current maps from the Grand Library on Huland," he said as he started flipping pages.

"I'm as familiar with those maps as anyone in Overtwixt," the Captain said, "but I don't know of any jails, not in the Shadowlands or anywhere else." He glanced at the Handmaiden. "And an entire *niland* jail? Scout is right. New nilands may come into being from time to time, but they don't grow that large overnight. I would have heard of it."

"There!" Nachton said victoriously, stabbing a finger down on a page. "Right *there.*"

Everyone leaned in to look at Nachton's map. He was pointing at a small niland labeled *Gaoland*.

"Um... Gay-ole-land?" Amélie said uncertainly.

Nachton smirked. "You're mispronouncing it. I did too when I first saw that name on the map, which is why it didn't catch my attention. But that's an Old English spelling."

Everyone stared at him blankly.

"It's pronounced Jail-land," Nachton said, rolling his eyes. "The name of that niland is literally *Jail-land.*"

The Captain smacked a hand to his forehead. "Of course, I'd forgotten all about that little niland. The Vizier took over its cultivation from the moment it appeared, way back during the early days of the United Lands. I imagine no one except the Vizier and the Shadowlanders themselves have ventured that deeply into the Shadowlands since then. I had no idea the Vizier was turning it into a *jail.*"

"Is he right, Mr. Guide?" Cécilie asked, pointing to the map. "Is that where Ewan is?"

The Guide simply nodded, smiling like he was proud of Nachton for figuring it out.

"So how do we get Ewan out?" Amélie demanded.

"I don't know," the Captain answered. "That's *deep* in the Vizier's territory. This isn't like dodging spooks up here, where the locals are friendly." He shook his head. "To get to that jail—to get to *Gaoland*—we have to go through Impstead, Pholand, or Spookwood."

"But we could fight our way through," Nachton said. "We have allies now, right?"

Amélie sighed. "Fewer than you think."

"We have the eqmen, at least. And the gnomen."

The Captain shook his head again. "You can't fight through that much enemy territory without losing people." He hesitated, uncomfortable, then asked, "Exactly how many eqman lives is the single life of your brother worth?"

The Mayor and the other eqmen seemed uncomfortable. Handmaiden looked away.

"Your brother is important to the fight against the Vizier, I know," the Captain continued, "but he's still just one person. And the First Fundamental Law tells us that *every* life is unique and precious. The Knight's not any more special than the people who would be risking their lives to save him."

"Except that they're *not* risking their lives," Nachton replied, gesturing impatiently. "The destruction of the bridges changes everything, remember? If our people fall in battle, they'll just end up on Gaoland with Ewan!"

The Captain hesitated. "It's still a traumatic experience. The, um, Guide just said so."

"I get that. But anyone we lose going after Ewan, we would immediately rescue *with* Ewan when we got there!"

"That raises another point, though," the Ranger said. "We can't possibly surprise that prison. Any bad guys we smoke on the way to Gaoland will *also* wake on Gaoland. They'll know we're coming days before we get there."

Everyone got quiet again.

Finally, Amélie said, "We can't take an army, then. It has to be a small enough group to sneak all the way there."

No one seemed to like this idea, but one by one, everyone nodded. All except the Guide. "What do *you* think?" Cécilie asked him. "Is this the right thing to do? Should we even be trying to rescue Ewan?"

"Cécilie!" Amélie exclaimed. "How can you even ask that question?"

The Guide now smiled proudly at Cécilie. "The Princess is wise to ask such a thing. Wiser than you give her credit for, Empress." He nodded slowly, thoughtfully. "But yes, I believe an attack on Gaoland would be in your best interests—assuming you indeed keep it a surprise."

"Won't the Vizier expect an attack, though?" the Operative asked the Guide, speaking up for the first time. "Even if we avoid spooks and imps entirely, he has to know we'll come for the Knight."

"Actually, no," the Guide said. "Because he would do the opposite in your position. He would never mount a rescue, because he doesn't value individuals. *He* would entrench himself at his Citadel, surrounding himself with armies and the trappings of power." The Guide smiled. "If you can convince him that the Empress has done the same, he'll never expect an assault on the prison."

"But I don't have a Citadel," Amélie said.

"Don't you?" the Guide asked, eyes twinkling.

"The Castle at Hucentia!" the Operative exclaimed, referring to the old Baron's abandoned Castle, where Amélie and her guardsmen had once camped for the night.

The Captain nodded thoughtfully. "I think we can make it look like the Empress and her siblings are going to Hucentia. Enough to trick any lingering Spies."

Nachton nodded firmly, taking control like always. "Good. You oversee the planning of that operation, Captain. But keep the circle small. Obviously we don't want the secret getting out." He looked at the Guide. "Meanwhile, *we* will plan the assault on the prison." He hesitated suddenly. "Um, I mean, if that's okay, Empress?" He blushed as he said this, but he sounded sincere.

Amélie smiled brilliantly. "That sounds good to me."

Nachton nodded again, looking relieved. "I can't participate in the attack personally—not as a combatant. But I've got ideas. And besides, the Guide has said all along that I'm supposed to be a counselor, primarily."

"I don't understand," the Ranger said. "You can do incredible things with magic! The green fireballs, the green whips, the freezing green clouds of mist… Why wouldn't you participate in the attack?"

Nachton took a deep breath. "Because I just can't."

The silence lasted a long time and got really awkward. Finally, Nachton took a shaky breath and explained.

"Me chasing after magic, that's the reason Ewan and his friends got hurt in the first place." He glanced at the Guide, who nodded. "I deceived myself *about* myself, about my role here. The Guide told me not to study magic, but I ignored him. I knew my cause was noble—defeating the Vizier's evil—so I thought that anything I did in pursuit of that cause was justified. But…" He swallowed hard. "I was wrong. The ends never justify the means, and my motives were never pure anyway."

He looked ashamed of himself, and Cécilie put her hand on his arm, to remind him how much she loved him.

"I wanted to be powerful, respected," Nachton went on. "But that was selfish. That's why Sovereign's Relic, the Diamond Lens, failed to grant me wisdom. The selfishness in my own heart, which is also a kind of evil, nullified the Relic's power in my life." He laughed, but it sounded bitter. "I thought I was so wise, but I was just a fool wearing a pair of fancy spectacles."

Everyone was watching Nachton with compassion, but no one knew what to say. No one except the Guide. "Friends," the centman said softly, "would you clear the room please? Captain, you might begin planning that diversion, as the Loremaster has suggested."

The Captain straightened and saluted sharply, pounding his fist on his chest.

"Good," the Guide concluded. "I wish to talk privately with the three humen. I think they are ready to speak certain truths to one another."

· seven ·

(Nachton)

The Guide gave Nachton all the time he needed to work through his emotion. It took almost that long for the Captain to herd the others out of Cécilie's throne room anyway.

When everyone was gone except the Ranger and Scout—who took up guard position at the two entrances—the Guide put a hand on Nachton's shoulder. "You fell to the very same temptation as the Vizier," he said gently.

This comparison made Nachton feel even worse.

"But *you* have forced yourself to face the truth, something the Vizier has never been capable of doing. Not only have you now acknowledged your wrong, it sounds like you're willing to change your ways."

Nachton nodded fervently. "I'm done with magic!"

"But this still doesn't explain Ewan," Amélie interjected. "*He* was pure of heart. How come the Relic *he* was wearing didn't work?"

The Guide nodded toward Cécilie. "The Princess might have some idea why."

Cécilie looked up in surprise. "Me?"

"Yes, you. Tell me, can you wield—or wear—more than one magical relic at the same time?"

"No," Cécilie answered without thinking. "If you put on more than one, only one of them does what it's supposed to do."

"That's true enough in this case," the Guide confirmed with a small smile. "When a person wields a relic of deception, that magic undermines all else. And if you wield—or wear—more than one deceptive relic, it's always the *most* deceptive that holds sway. The one that tells the biggest lie."

"Wait," Amélie gasped. "How does *Cécilie* know that?"

Cécilie blushed furiously, and Nachton spoke up. "Because she found some of the Vizier's magical amulets at the Grand Library. She's been wearing one to make herself look older; but obviously she found at least one more than that, since Ewan had one too when we fought the Vizier."

The little girl nodded jerkily. "It gave Ewan super strength," she said. Near the door, the Ranger cursed under his breath, like something suddenly made sense to him; the Scout was also staring at Cécilie. Clearly, they could both hear every word of this "private" conversation.

"But Ewan's heart was *pure*," Amélie objected again.

"A person cannot simply dabble in evil," the Guide said sadly. "No matter the nobility of your intentions, or your ignorance of the truth. Evil will always corrupt—*always*."

Amélie spun on Cécilie. "I can't believe you would mess with these things! And you gave one to Ewan too?!"

"I was just trying to help!" Cécilie said, words coming out in a rush. "I wanted to protect him. He never woulda beat Bazooka without the ruby, and if I hadn't used the topaz, we never coulda gotten past all the *other* lugmen. And the horses never woulda followed *me*. I'm just a little kid! I *had* to use the amethyst."

"Wait-wait-wait!" Amélie cried, waving her new scepter at Cécilie, making Nachton wonder again where she'd gotten it. "Exactly how many of these amulet things *are* there?"

"I dunno," Cécilie mumbled, looking away. "Like... twenty?"

"Are you wearing one now?"

"No!" Cécilie almost shouted. "Not since Ewan—" She shook her head, swiping at her eyes. "I stopped wearing *any* of them! I hid them in a chest in my room, and..." She was so emotional, she struggled to find the right words. "They... they *lie*, all of them. They make things seem like they aren't, and... and I don't *want* to lie anymore. I just wanna be *me*, the me I'm supposed to be! I want Ewan back, and everything the way *it's* supposed to be!"

Nachton pulled his littlest sister into a fierce hug. A stillness fell on the throne room, and he realized that the Guide was smiling.

"Congratulations, Princess of Eqland," the bearded centman said.

"Huh?" Cécilie asked, pulling back from Nachton and wiping her cheeks.

"You have completed the quests I set before you," the Guide explained. "Not only have you claimed your throne— and kept it, though you wear no amulet now—you also discovered a truth that no one else could teach you."

Cécilie nodded slowly, understanding. "Trying to be someone I'm not... it's miserable, always wondering if people actually like me, or just the person I'm pretending to be." She thought for a second. "Doesn't mean I can't try to improve, to *become* a better me. But I should never be fake."

Nachton blinked. "Wow. You actually sound like an adult now, even though you don't look like one anymore."

Cécilie slugged him, but not very hard.

"Which brings us to you," the Guide said, facing Nachton. "Acquiring knowledge was never the greater of the challenges I placed before you. Acquiring the wisdom to properly *wield* that knowledge, on the other hand..."

Nachton nodded soberly. It was now his turn to share what he'd learned from his experiences—the realizations he'd come to over the last week in the Archives. "Not all knowledge is equally valuable," he said. "Not all knowledge is equally *true*, either. And not all knowledge is beneficial." He looked down at his hands. "I wish I didn't know a lot of what I know now. I wish I hadn't been so quick to rush into things I wasn't ready for."

"You have endured *and* caused terrible pain," the Guide said. "But you've also learned from your mistakes. And these truths you have spoken aloud today—they are not knowledge only, but the beginnings of wisdom."

Nachton nodded his acceptance of this compliment, assuming that's what it was. But he couldn't feel good about it. Acquiring that wisdom had cost too much.

"Now, oh Master of Lore, I will tell you something you might find difficult to hear."

Nachton steeled himself.

"You are *not* done with magic. You must wield magic again if you're to rescue your brother from Gaoland, much less defeat the Vizier."

"What?!" Amélie said.

"But you tried to steer me *away* from magic!" Nachton repeated.

"I tried to steer you away from *focusing* on magic, obsessing about it, which is exactly what you did. Tell me, did you truly earn the right to unlock the dangerous knowledge at the top of the tower of Magic?"

"No," Nachton admitted, thinking immediately of his scavenger hunt in the Grand Library of Huland, which had required him to solve a series of puzzles to recover the pieces of an ancient skeleton key. Only with that entire key reconstructed should he have been able to access the locked room at the top of the tower of Magic. But Nachton hadn't possessed the patience to complete the challenge as intended, so he partially forged the key and forced the lock instead. "The scavenger hunt..." he said, "It was designed to help me acquire knowledge on a broad scale. If I'd actually read all those books, I still would've found all the pieces of the key eventually... except that way, I would have been *ready* to wield magic by the time I finished."

The Guide nodded.

"But that would have taken too long! I never would have learned magic in time to defeat the Vizier."

"Perhaps, perhaps not. But the way you did it was unnatural. You forced the matter, seizing hold of knowledge you were not yet ready for. And then you named yourself Conjurer and began wielding that knowledge as a weapon. You redefined yourself according to your ability to hurt people with magic."

Nachton buried his face in his hands as tears threatened to come once more. "I know! I'm sorry!"

"You've already sought—and received—forgiveness. Now it is time to put your hard-earned wisdom to good use." The Guide lifted Nachton's chin to meet his eyes, and Nachton saw great affection there. "I never wished you to earn your wisdom through such great suffering. But now that you have, do not squander it! I tell you again: you are not done with magic."

"But magic is *evil*," Amélie said with a shiver, and Cécilie nodded emphatic agreement.

"If that were so," the Guide asked gently, "how could the Sovereign have created his Relics? Or Overtwixt itself?"

That made everyone pause and think.

"Sovereign created Overtwixt for the express purpose of offering people the experience of magic. Your 'real world' is a place constrained by natural laws, is it not? *This* place *defies* your laws of physics, very much on purpose."

Nachton stared at the centman.

"All people have a degree of magical potential," the Guide told Nachton, "and you especially, considering your interest in it. I would not rob you of that joy. I only wished you to experience that joy in the proper context, at the proper time."

"Why didn't you tell me this in the first place?!" Nachton asked, frustrated. "Why not tell me I *would* be allowed to use it someday?"

"Would that have made any difference?"

Nachton hesitated. "I... I don't know."

The Guide smiled sadly. "Much of what I say is ignored. I'm afraid it's the fate of most young men and women to ignore wisdom, then acquire it only through the experience of personal suffering. I wish it were not so. But I have learned to speak only when my wisdom is desired, and to speak not at all when it serves no purpose."

Nachton's brow furrowed, but he couldn't stay upset. The Guide was telling him it was okay to use magic now! "Where do I start? What *is* the proper context?"

"Your heart must be pure, of course—you know that much already—*and* your intentions noble. Both your means and your ends must be just."

"Yes?" Nachton said, urging the Guide to continue. He felt like he should start taking notes.

"It is a question of whose good you seek to serve when you take magic into hand. No person can serve two masters. Wielding magic, you can either hurt and destroy... or you can protect and preserve."

Nachton didn't want to forget a word of this, so he decided he *would* take notes. Sitting down on the floor, he opened his notebook across his knees and unstoppered an ink bottle. Quill scratching at the paper, he began scribbling excitedly.

"The power of preservation lent by Sovereign's magic is more powerful by far," the Guide went on, "but the power of destruction lent by the magic of his enemy, the Adversary, is a corrupting influence. As you've learned—as the Princess has confirmed—no person can wield both simultaneously, for the latter will always undermine the former."

"It's green vs. blue!" Cécilie blurted suddenly. "Green is the evil magic—what Nachton was using before, the same color my amulets were glowing. But *blue* is the *good* magic. That's the same color Ewan's Diamond Armor glowed when he first found it. He told me so! Except..." She looked confused. "It *stopped* glowing when he put it on."

"Because he was already wearing a relic of the Vizier's magic," the Guide said softly. "The *Adversary*'s magic."

"Nachton!" Amélie exclaimed. "Your *glasses* are glowing!"

Indeed they were, Nachton realized. The spectacles he had continued to wear after the fight in the Archives, despite their uselessness, had begun emitting a soft light.

A soft *blue* light.

The Guide smiled at Amélie. "The Diamond Lens of Discernment has been glowing for some time, in fact, ever since the Loremaster began to admit the truth to himself. That glow may have been feeble at first, but the more he exercises wisdom— free from the taint of selfishness— the more brightly it will shine." He turned his smile on Nachton. "Well done, Loremaster."

Nachton beamed, stoppering his ink and getting to his feet. Even Amélie started smiling. "I'm so proud of you guys," she said to both Nachton and Cécilie. Her tone was a bit patronizing, as if *she'd* never made any mistakes, but Nachton forced himself to ignore it. "Now that this is all settled," the Empress went on, "can we figure out the assault on Gaoland? Ewan is still in prison, after all."

The Guide watched Amélie for a long moment, until she began to squirm. "What?" she asked finally.

"*Is* everything settled between you and your siblings? Or are there other truths yet to be spoken?" He paused. "Perhaps the truth of what transpired in Caymerdelphia?"

Amélie flushed deeply. "What happened in Caymerdelphia doesn't matter right now. Besides, we're already doing exactly what the Committee said, aren't we? The three of us are working together now, and we're going to go rescue Ewan so that we truly *are* united."

The Guide raised an eyebrow but let the matter drop.

"So let's talk about the assault on the prison," Amélie repeated.

And with their relationships to one another restored, the three Ollivaros children got down to details. Nachton did a very good job acting in his new role as advisor, if he said so himself, and even Cécilie offered some good suggestions. They called the Captain back into the room, along with the others, and everyone contributed to the planning. Soon enough, they had a workable strategy.

But even over the days that followed, as Nachton surrounded himself with a team of designers and began building the siege equipment they would need to assault Gaoland—even as he got lost in all those details, while continuing to struggle with thoughts of vengeance against the ones who had wronged Ewan—he couldn't help but wonder...

What exactly had happened to Amélie in Caymerdelphia? And what impact would it have on their plans to rescue Ewan?

The End of
Part I

Part II
Rescue

Alabaster City
of Shanagrailia

· eight ·
(Amélie)

One week after Amélie's arrival at the Palace on Eqland, her new carriage rode forth with great fanfare. The carriage was gorgeous, painted dark red and trimmed in gold filigree, designed and built just for her by the gnomen. It was drawn by a team of six eqmen and escorted on either side by the centmen Ranger and Operative, and it even had curtains over the windows so no one could look inside. All the rest of the eqmen and gnomen trailed behind, leaving Eqland to take up residence at the Castle on Hucentia, which was much better fortified than the Palace. Considering the amount of celebration, there was no chance any spookman Spies lurking in the trees failed to notice the carriage's departure.

Amélie herself stayed behind, of course, hiding in the Palace with her siblings and a few others. They waited a full day, then left under cover of darkness.

Traveling in the other direction.

They took the route the Captain originally suggested when they had left Centwick weeks earlier, crossing the great white arch to Shaland, from which they could access Shanagrailia. Amélie rode the Captain and Nachton rode the Scout, while Cécilie looked super cute perched atop her unicorn Handmaiden. Three more people accompanied them, all recruited by Nachton to help plan the assault on Gaoland: the Crafter and the Engineer, both gnomen, and a muscular eqman named Wrangler who was pulling the cart with all their siege equipment. Both Engineer and Wrangler had been among the slaves Cécilie rescued from the quarry.

The view of Overtwixt from the great white arch was breathtaking, or so the Captain told Amélie. Traveling at night, she saw nothing—which was good, considering her terrible fear of heights. Then again, seeing nothing was the point anyway. If *they* couldn't see for miles, then no one for miles around would see *them* passing from Eqland to Shaland. It was such a dark night, they could barely see ten feet in front of them, and only that far because of the soft blue glow of Sovereign's Relics.

The spectacles Nachton wore were glowing more than ever, but so was Ewan's Diamond Armor. Recovering the Armor (again) had been one of Cécilie's tasks during their week of preparation; she had ridden Ranger back to the cave on Eqland, finding the Armor just where Ewan found it in the first place. Now it was stacked in the cart next to Amélie's scepter, covered with a cloak so it didn't glow *too* much. There were also some other weapons, along with Squire's caparison-cape and saddle gear, which had remained in the Archives when everyone got smoked that terrible night.

The great white arch *was* "great," so big that it took many hours to ride across it. The Sky Light was just turning toward day when they reached the other side, and they quickened their pace to reach cover before full light.

Like Huland, Shaland was mostly uninhabited. There were dozens of shamen in Overtwixt, of course, but they tended to mingle with the other races, serving as advisors or mentors to prominent people (like the Weaponsmaster "Fight Guy" had done, joining Ewan as his trainer). That left only a few people on Shaland itself, and they were easy to avoid, since Shaland was covered by a network of gullies that Amélie's party used to travel quickly and secretively across the niland. The Scout argued constantly that there was still a danger, that the group should move more slowly while he scouted ahead, but his boss wouldn't allow it. The Captain insisted that everyone should stick together, and Amélie was perfectly happy to follow that advice.

Two days after leaving the Palace, they reached the bridge from Shaland to Shanagrailia... and finally encountered their first problem.

Imps. Two on each side of the gap between nilands, guarding the bridge, plus *another* two in the air to keep close watch over the ones on the ground.

"They learned from my trick," Nachton hissed. "Either that, or they're just being more careful now."

"What are you talking about?" Amélie whispered. They were still hiding in a gully, and so far, the bad guys hadn't seen them.

"When we snuck onto Eqland. We knew we couldn't just shoot the bridge guards, because the next patrol would've known someone came through. So I used the green magic to time-freeze them while we passed. I assumed they woke later and never knew." He gestured at the imps in the sky. "But those two are too high to reach with magic."

"And that kind of magic is evil anyway," Amélie said.

"I'm just saying. I wasn't going to try that trick again," Nachton assured her.

"So how *are* we gonna sneak across?" she asked.

"I'm not sure we can, your majesty," the Captain spoke up. "But I don't see any other options for getting across into Shanagrailia, unless we turn back and go around."

"There will be guards on all the bridges into Shanagrailia," the gnoman Engineer said quietly. "It's an occupied niland."

"Same for any bridge to the Shadowlands," the Crafter added. "We'll face this problem anywhere we go."

The Captain nodded and grimaced.

"Surely your magic is still good for *something*," the Scout said, scowling at Nachton.

Nachton licked his lips uncertainly. "Even if I knew a blue spell that would help, I don't think I should be using magic on our enemies. It's... well, it seems wrong."

"What if you cast a spell on *us* instead?" Amélie asked suddenly, thinking back to her escape from Caymerdelphia.

"On... us?" Nachton repeated stupidly.

"Yes," Captain said musingly. "Maybe to disguise us? It wouldn't have to be much. The Wrangler is already drawing a cart. Make that cart look like a load of quarried stone. Then make the rest of us look like prisoners in shackles."

"But what about us humen?" Nachton asked.

"Turn us into imps!" Amélie suggested. "Wings and everything."

Nachton chewed his lip for a moment, obviously thinking through how he might do something like that.

"Wait a sec," Cécilie said. "How is this not *bad* magic? It's the same kinda thing I was doing with the amulets! Lying about who we are!"

"Yes," the Captain said patiently. "But for what purpose? Because we want to be something we're not? Or because we want to preserve and protect ourselves, against people who wish to hurt us?"

"It does seem different," Nachton admitted. "Wearing a disguise for protection is different from lying to our friends, or trying to impress people."

"There's an easy-enough way to find out," Amélie prompted him impatiently.

Nachton took a deep breath. "Okay. But if I can't do it with blue magic, I'm not doing it at all. I refuse to dabble in evil. Not again."

The Captain smiled and nodded.

Nachton closed his eyes and began to weave. "I'm focusing my thoughts on my sisters... my friends... how I want you all to look," he said quietly, distractedly. "I'm letting my desire to *protect* you fuel my spellcasting. I—" He straightened suddenly, like a jolt had run up his spine. Then Amélie felt it too, and she gasped. Looking around at her siblings and friends, she gasped again.

The cart was now laden with stone, or at least looked that way. Iron collars fastened around the necks of the gnomen, eqmen, and centmen, with chains connecting them all together. As for Nachton and Cécilie, and Amélie herself...

"You did it," she said in wonder, raising an arm to look at one web-like wing. "We're imps!" Even her clothes were different: ratty pants, and long strips of colorful cloth wrapped around her upper body. "Ugh, my *nails!*"

"Gross!" Cécilie exclaimed, touching the fine gray fur on her arms. Her nails were long and sharp too. "Am I as ugly as you guys?"

"Uglier," Nachton replied automatically. Unlike the girls, he was bare-chested—and *very* muscular. He smiled when he noticed that detail.

Heart pounding excitedly, Amélie tensed her legs and started flapping her arms—

Everyone stared. "What are you doing?" Cécilie asked.

"Um...
trying to fly?"

Captain shook
his head, waving a
hand through the chain
connecting him to Scout. "This is
an illusion only."

Amélie's heart sank. "You can't make it
real?" she asked Nachton. "Real wings, at least,
so we can fly?"

"You mean an actual shapeshift? I wouldn't
have the first clue how to do something that advanced," he
admitted. "As it is, we'll have to be careful. I'm not sure how
long I can keep this up."

"Then we'd best get moving," Captain said.

Everyone took a few calming breaths. Then they left
their hiding place, walking up to the two *actual* imps guarding
this side of the bridge.

"Halt!" one of them cried. "Halt in the name of the
Emperor!"

Amélie's heart almost stopped in her chest.

The other imp scowled at his friend. "Why are you
telling them to halt, you fool? They're on *our* side!"

"I'm just practicing," the first one said sheepishly. "I
finally got it right, didn't I? I said *Emperor* this time."

"What are you fools babbling about?" Nachton
demanded with a sneer. On his fake bat-like face, the
expression was so disgusting Amélie actually shivered.

"It's a long story," the second gargoyle replied. "Short
version: ole Stooge here let a coupla centmen and their new
huwoman Empress get the drop on us on Centwick. We
spent a few weeks in Gaoland on account o' that mistake."

Amélie's eyes widened. These were *those* impmen?!

"That was your mistake too, Flunky," the Stooge muttered. "'Sides, I heard the little Empress ain't a huwoman at all. She's a *fairy*—she can *fly*."

"And *I* heard she's nothin' but a scaredy-brat child ready to faint away at the sight of her own shadow," Flunky said, rolling his eyes. "That don't make it true. There's a hundred rumors goin' 'round about the little Empress." He turned back to Nachton. "I see you caught a coupla centmen of your own," he added with a nasty smile. "Hideous, ain't they?" He raised a hand to slap the Captain across the face.

Nachton caught his arm. "These two are for the boss himself," he said hurriedly. "Doesn't want 'em damaged."

"Ooh-ee!" the real imps chortled.

"Know where we can find him?" Amélie asked. "The Viz—um, the Emperor, I mean." Knowing the Vizier's location would make him easier to avoid, after all.

"Still on Gaoland," Stooge answered. "Makin' hisself some new jewelry from all the prisoners we been takin'."

"Bet he'd make a mighty fine amulet outta *that* one," the Flunky added, winking at the Captain.

Amélie forced herself to laugh with them, just like Nachton was doing. "That's where we're headed, then."

"Gaoland it is!" Nachton agreed.

"Hey, if you's in a hurry," the Stooge said, "ask for the Dockmaster when you get into town."

"The... Dockmaster?"

"Yeah. He's organized a ferry service for the boss. Hits all the important nilands. You know, for prisoner transport— so you don't have to rely on bridges for these *groundwalkers*." He said the word like it was an insult.

Nachton slowly nodded, then smiled. "A ferry service, huh?" He glanced at Amélie. "Yeah, I think we'll check that out. We *are* in a hurry, after all. A very big hurry indeed."

· nine ·

(EWAN)

"**G**o Troll!" Jail Guy roared victoriously, spittle spraying out between his fangs. Even though the huge dwagon dude was smiling, Ewan almost peed his pants.

"You suppose to say *Go Fish*," Ewan said, pretending he wasn't still a little scared of the guy.

The Jailer shook his big bat-like head. "No, I recognize this game now. Where I'm from, it's called Go *Troll*."

"Troll?" Skire Horsey muttered. "That's even more confirmation I do *not* want to visit where *you're* from."

"Ah, yes!" Bazooka exclaimed. "I know this thing. Is right, sir Knight. In my home, is called Go *Trawl*." He scrunched his eyebrows. "I still no like this game."

Ewan licked his lips and looked at the playing cards he held in his hands. They weren't like the paper cards he was used to. These were really big and made of thin *wood*.

"Go Troll," Jail Guy reminded him.

Ewan picked up a card from the deck, but it wasn't the card he'd asked for. "You turn," he told Jail Guy.

The dwagon grinned really big and rearranged the three cards he held. "Hmm... Friend Berserker... do you have any *nines?*"

Bazooka squinted at his cards, then handed one to Jail Guy. The dwagon roared, "I win! I win!" and Bazooka bellowed, "I hate this game!" before throwing the rest of his cards on the floor.

Ewan started giggling at the Jailer. Seeing the ferocious dwagon get excited about a card game was *funny*.

Jail Guy reached through the bars into Ewan and Bazooka's cells and collected all the cards. "Anyone need anything? Top off your beverage?"

Ewan and Skire shook their heads. Bazooka was still muttering under his breath.

Jail Guy cocked one of his big bat ears at Ewan and winked. "I could bring up some hors d'oeuvres, perhaps?"

"What *orr durves?*" Ewan repeated.

Skire Horsey chuckled. "Snacks, sir Knight. Appetizers."

Jail Guy wiggled his talons. "Finger foods, if you will."

"Oh!" Ewan said. "You gots any candy?"

"I... well, no," the big dwagon said with disappointment. "But I made some lovely little prosciutto

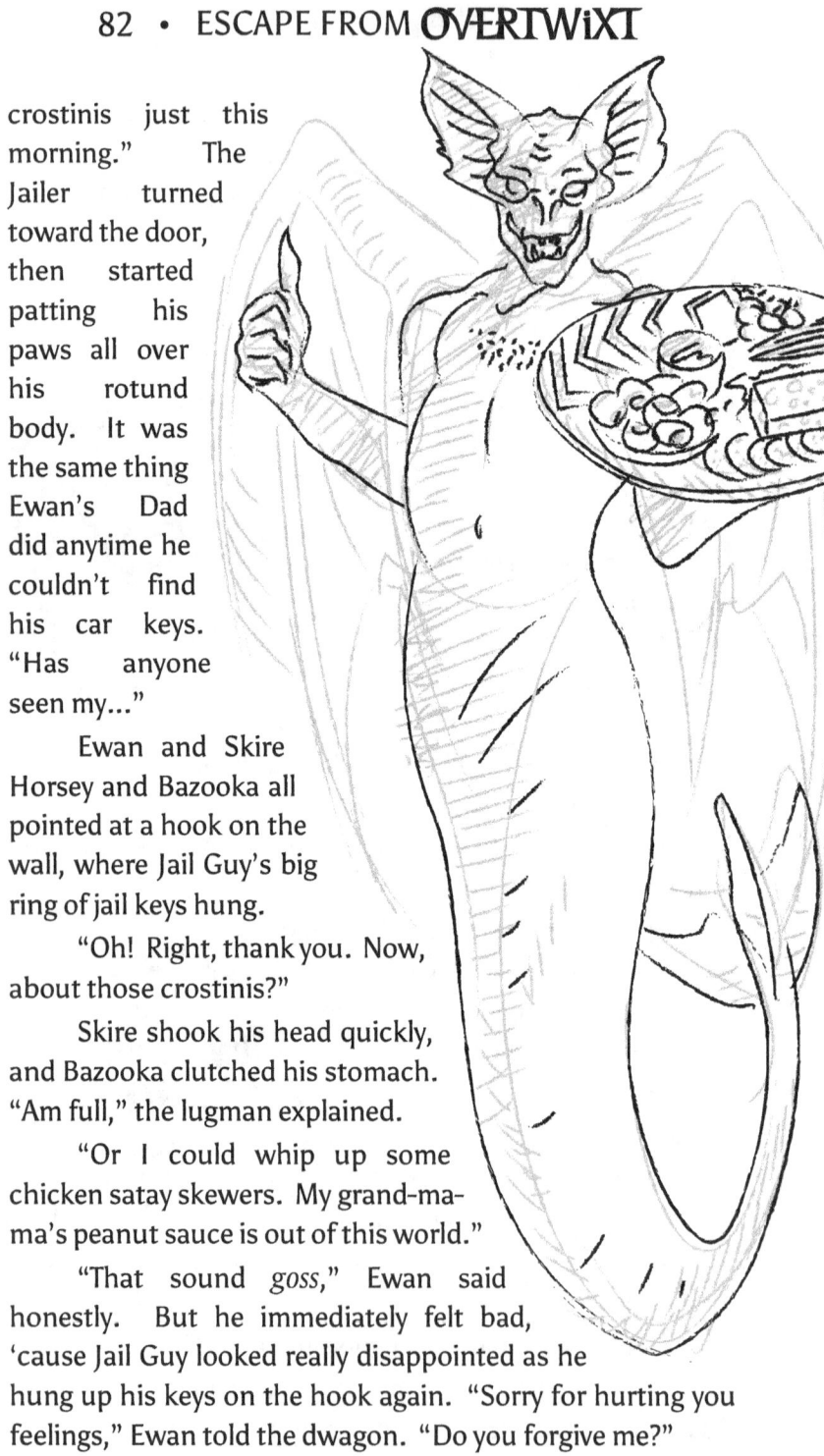

crostinis just this morning." The Jailer turned toward the door, then started patting his paws all over his rotund body. It was the same thing Ewan's Dad did anytime he couldn't find his car keys. "Has anyone seen my..."

Ewan and Skire Horsey and Bazooka all pointed at a hook on the wall, where Jail Guy's big ring of jail keys hung.

"Oh! Right, thank you. Now, about those crostinis?"

Skire shook his head quickly, and Bazooka clutched his stomach. "Am full," the lugman explained.

"Or I could whip up some chicken satay skewers. My grand-ma-ma's peanut sauce is out of this world."

"That sound *goss*," Ewan said honestly. But he immediately felt bad, 'cause Jail Guy looked really disappointed as he hung up his keys on the hook again. "Sorry for hurting you feelings," Ewan told the dwagon. "Do you forgive me?"

"Of course, young human."

"Can we be fwends, Jail Guy? I mean, you really nice, and... um..."

Jail Guy smiled a big smile. "I would like that. But please call me Proprietor. All my friends do."

"Puh— Puh-ruh— um... I can't say dat."

The dwagon roared a laugh. "Jail Guy it is, then." He paused. "Just so long as you understand that I can't let you out of your cell, friends or not. The Vizier's orders—I mean, the *Emperor's* orders—are very clear."

Ewan shrugged. "Wanna play another game?"

"Oh goodie!" Jail Guy said.

"No more Fish Trawl!" Bazooka whined. "We play War next, yes?"

"Okey dokey!" Ewan agreed, but Jail Guy and Skire Horsey both groaned.

"Not *that* game again," Skire said. "I beg of you."

"War is so pointless," Jail Guy agreed. "It never ends, and no one ever wins."

"What 'bout Old Maid?" Ewan suggested.

"You mean Decrepit Damsel?" Jailer asked.

"Personally, I'm partial to Raibournian Rummy—" Skire Horsey began, but then the door opened...

And the Vizier walked in again.

It was the first time Ewan saw him since that day he made Fight Guy disappear. Ewan glared at the Vizier like he was ready to fight, but inside, his heart was thumping.

Jail Guy straightened and his eyes got really wide, even though he himself was a lot bigger and scarier-looking than the Vizier. "Your majesty, what an honor—"

"What is the meaning of this?" the Vizier boomed.

"I was just seeing to the prisoners' needs..."

The Vizier noticed the playing cards clutched in the dwagon's paws and sneered. He flicked his wrist, and the cards burst into green flames! Jail Guy yelped and dropped the deck, then started sucking his fingers. The Vizier leaned in very close to the big guy's fangs and said, very quietly, "Do not forget your purpose. You're not here to make friends."

"Of course! Of course, master."

"Disappoint me again, and I may decide to use this on *you*." The Vizier raised his fist, and Ewan saw he was holding another necklace. This one had a gem Ewan never saw before, all blue-green with black wrinkles in it.

"You've created another blank amulet, master?"

"Yes," The Vizier said absently, turning slowly to face the jail cells. He glanced at Bazooka and Skire Horsey, then focused on Ewan. "What talents do you possess, little boy?"

"I dink you a big meanie!"

The Vizier frowned. "Courage, maybe? I can't decide if you're actually that gutsy, or just faking it."

Ewan kept staring at the tall bad guy. They stared at each other so long, Ewan almost gave up and started crying again. Any second, the Vizier was gonna wave his hands, then Ewan would *pop* and be gone, just like Fight Guy.

The Vizier sighed and turned away. "Best not to risk it. I think I'll hold onto this blank for now, in case I run into someone *truly* special on Hucentia."

"Hucentia?" Jail Guy asked. "You're leaving us?"

"Yes, and I'm taking most of your guards with me. It seems the kid's sister is already making her move, setting herself up at the old Baron's Castle." He snorted a laugh. "Empress? What a joke. I spent half a lifetime planning my ascension, and she thinks she can steal my empire in a matter of weeks?"

"Ridiculous," Jail Guy agreed in a mumble.

"She has no idea the size of the army I'm about to bring crashing down on her," the Vizier went on. "By this time next week, the Castle at Hucentia will be reduced to rubble, and *all* the eqmen, gnomen, and centmen will be in chains."

He looked at Ewan and smiled. "But don't worry, little boy. Your days of being surrounded by all this non-human scum are nearing their end. You will be reunited with your family soon—very, *very* soon."

· ten ·

(Cécilie)

Shanagrailia was the most beautiful place Cécilie had ever seen (aside from Eqland, of course!). After crossing the bridge onto the niland, they followed a narrow pass through the mountains, and they found the Alabaster City nestled beside a great waterfall in a valley inside.

"I've never seen buildings so white!" Cécilie blurted. They practically glowed under the rays of the Sky Light.

The Captain smiled. "That's why they call it the *Alabaster* City."

"Alabaster is a type of stone," Nachton explained. "White, almost clear sometimes."

Cécilie was barely listening. She was staring at the needle-like white spires stretching into the sky. They seemed to grow right out of the gray stone valley floor. And at different places in the sides of the spires, *trees* grew through holes to climb up the sides of the buildings!

"That's the Mystic's tower," the Captain said, pointing to the tallest spire. Unlike the others, this one had so many trees growing at the top that its tip wasn't even visible. "The old Mystic has lived there in seclusion since abdicating as leader of the little peoples."

Nachton glanced at Cécilie. "Abdicating means giving up the throne, quitting the job of being ruler."

Captain nodded and gave Cécilie even more of an explanation. "Like your predecessor, the Prince of Eqland, the Mystic peacefully stepped down to let the old Baron rule his nilands. Back when the Baron united what we now call the United Lands."

Scout snorted. "Not that they're very united."

"Not since the Vizier overthrew the Baron," Captain agreed quietly.

"Should we go see this Mystic?" Amélie asked, her bat-like impwoman face wrinkling uncertainly. Cécilie was still a little weirded out, seeing her siblings like that, even though she realized she was just as hideous at the moment. "I mean, that was the original plan, and we're finally here."

"That might be risking too much, even with these disguises," the Captain said. "As you can see, the Vizier now has full control of the Alabaster City, and I would imagine the Mystic is watched most closely of all."

Sure enough, Cécilie noticed dark shapes flitting all around in the skies over the city—imps and spooks. She saw Handmaiden shudder.

"I suggest we remain focused on our purpose," the Captain went on. "Get through Shanagrailia cautiously but as quickly as possible. The bridge to Drachölm is on the cliffs on the far side of the niland; I'd imagine this Dockmaster and his ferry service are near there too."

"You think we should take the ferry?" Nachton asked.

"It's a risk," the Captain said, sighing. "It would mean mingling with more impmen, and flying straight into danger if the ferry goes to the prison directly. If that's the case, we wouldn't have a chance to surveil the prison ahead of time either." He took a deep breath. "On the other hoof, taking the bridges through Drachölm and Pholand—like we planned—is a circuitous route. The ferry would shave days off our journey, and if it deposits us *inside* the prison walls..."

"Seems a waste, building that catapult for nothing," Crafter complained, bristling with wounded professional pride. The other gnoman, Engineer, stayed quiet as usual, but he nodded in agreement.

"Still," Amélie said. "It sounds like it's worth the risk." The Captain nodded. "The ferry it is, then," Amélie concluded. "How're you holding up, Nachton? Any danger of our disguises slipping?"

For the first time, Cécilie noticed the sweat on Nachton's fake imp face. Apparently, it was a strain keeping their disguises in place, but he shook his head. "We should be okay. Still, let's not waste any time."

They went the rest of the way down the path into the city: the Captain and the Scout, the gnomen Crafter and Engineer, the unicorn Handmaiden, and finally Wrangler pulling the cart with the disguised catapult; the three Ollivaros kids stuck to the outside of the group, pretending to be nasty imp taskmasters.

The buildings of the Alabaster City were even more beautiful up close, and Cécilie decided it must be a wondrous place to live in normal times. But right now, up close, she realized how terrible life must be for the little peoples. Thanks to the Vizier's reign of terror, the impmen were in charge here, and they were *not* acting very nice.

Gnomen were being mistreated everywhere, and nagmen too—little creatures that looked like shaggy ponies. Lots of these nagmen stood on street corners playing musical instruments (they had *fingers* on their front hooves!) and the imps were laughing and throwing vegetables at them, telling them to play songs the poor ponies obviously didn't know.

"That way," the Captain said quietly, and Amélie pretended to pull him by his chain down a side street. There, they saw a trio of impmen making scary faces at a small gnomaid. The little girl was shrieking in terror, tears streaming down her cheeks as the gargoyles laughed.

Enraged, the Crafter started forward to rescue the little girl, but Nachton yelled, "Get back, slave!" Then he added in a whisper, "Let me handle this."

Walking up to the three impmen, Nachton grabbed one by the shoulder and spun him around. "What are you fools doing?"

"Havin' us some fun, that's all," the guy spat back. "What's it to ya?"

"You're supposed to be on guard duty, at the bridge to Shaland."

"First I heard of it," the imp sneered.

"Yeah," one of the others said. "That's the Stooge's job. Gonna be his job from now 'til forever, they's sayin'."

"Punishment," the third added. "Didn't you hear? He was *this close* to those human meddlers and didn't realize 'til it was too late. Him and Flunky is the fools!"

Nachton gave them a mischievous grin. "Yeah, well, Stooge says you got a face like a prune, and... and... your *mama* has a face like a *shriveled* prune!"

"How dare he!" the imp demanded furiously. "And what the heck is a *prune?!*"

"I don't know," Nachton added, "but he said it about all *three* of you!"

"I'm gonna knock his lights out," one of the others snarled, flapping his arms and leaping into the sky. "C'mon, boys. That fool needs a lesson in manners."

Grinning, Nachton offered a hand to the little gnomaid, but she squeaked and ran away.

"That was well handled," the Captain said quietly. "But we can't help everyone, Loremaster."

They made it to the docks without further incident, though Cécilie saw the members of her group clenching their fists angrily at all the injustice they saw around them.

The docks were a bunch of shabby platforms built onto the side of the cliffs, hanging out over the empty white space that stretched between nilands. They weren't beautiful like the rest of Shanagrailia, so Cécilie guessed the impmen just built them recently. Most of the docks had flat *boats* sitting on them, surrounded by gnoman slaves loading or unloading stone and logs. One boat was full of potbellied dolphin-horse creatures, all chained up.

"Raimen," Handmaiden told her in a whisper.

The Dockmaster was the ugliest imp yet, with a patch over one eye and a scar running down that side of his face, under the patch. He just grunted when he saw them walk up. "Where to?"

"Passage to Gaoland," Nachton grunted back.

The Dockmaster barked a laugh. "This your first rodeo? You know we don't fly straight there."

"Why not?" Amélie blurted. Her voice was *way* too high-pitched. She made her voice gruff and quickly added, "Why not, you ugly fool?"

The Dockmaster bared his fangs at her. "Emperor's orders. Believe me, I'd rather we *did* fly straight there. It would simplify logistics. But the boss seems to think there's a risk of enemy magickers putting on disguises and using the ferry to sneak into the prison. He said direct ferry service would introduce a *security vulnerability*."

Nachton swallowed so hard, even Cécilie heard it. "Uh, right. So what's the closest you can get us?"

"Spookwood," the Dockmaster growled. "We've got a logging operation there." He narrowed his eyes. "Seems to me that's where this lot should be going anyway, not Gaoland. Most prisoners these days is being shipped *outta* the jail, to the worksites. Prison's bursting at the seams."

Nachton shrugged. "Emperor's orders. Uh, Spookwood is fine, I guess."

The Captain stomped a hoof.

"I mean," Nachton added hastily, "what about Pholand? Do you offer service to Pholand?"

The Dockmaster glared at Nachton suspiciously. "*Pholand?*"

"Yeah. There's, um, something we need to pick up along the way."

The Captain cringed, and Cécilie remembered suddenly. They had planned to assault Gaoland from Pholand because of all the rock formations on the phomen's niland. If they had to use the catapult to attack Gaoland after all, they would need the rocks for ammo.

The Dockmaster got up real close in Nachton's face. "I offer service to Spookwood, Impstead, and Twixt, with connecting flights to Raibourne and Eqland. You don't like those options, you can take a bridge."

"Uh, Spookwood will do nicely."

"Fantastic," the Dockmaster growled back.

Twenty minutes later, the gnoman slaves finished unloading logs from one of the boats, and Cécilie's group climbed aboard. A bunch of impmen flew over and grabbed hold of ropes attached to the sides. They got into an argument with Nachton, insisting that he and Amélie and Cécilie should help carry the boat, but Nachton refused; after all, they only looked like imps (they couldn't actually fly), but he could hardly tell *them* that! Instead, Nachton argued that someone needed to guard the fearsome centman prisoners, and the Dockmaster eventually sided with him, calling over more impmen to help carry.

The flight to Spookwood was even scarier than Cécilie expected. She spent the entire trip gripping the railing, trying not to look at the white emptiness all around, even though Amélie stared at the sky wistfully. (When had *that* changed? Amélie had always been afraid of heights before now!) And Cécilie barely noticed when the rest of the group started whispering excitedly; apparently, they had seen a huge army of imps and spooks flying the opposite direction, with a human riding a drachman at the front. The Vizier? Cécilie didn't care; she was just trying not to be sick.

Finally they landed, and Cécilie's group of friends slipped away into the murky forest of Spookwood. As soon as they were safely out of sight among the trees, Nachton collapsed to his knees and the disguises disappeared.

"What now?" Amélie asked, helping him up. "We still need to get to Pholand, don't we?"

"I'll scout ahead," the Scout said, already moving.

"No," the Captain said sharply. "We stick together."

"But Captain!" Scout argued. "There could be *Spies* between here and the bridge. These humen sound like a whole herd of woolen mammadons tromping through the forest; any enemies would hear us coming a mile away. But *I* can sneak ahead to look for any Spies, then come back and lead us around them. *Please*, sir. Let me do my job!"

That was different. Usually Scout was sarcastic and blunt. Cécilie had never seen him so passionate about anything.

"No," the Captain repeated. "We stick together."

The Scout stomped his hooves in annoyance—and suddenly, Cécilie noticed something *else* different about the centman.

"Quickly now," the Captain said. "We're close. Let us make haste for Pholand, that we may rescue our allies."

Everyone except Cécilie and the Scout gave a quiet cheer at this, and Cécilie decided to start watching the surly centman more carefully.

· eleven ·

(Nachton)

Nachton's group made camp on Pholand, in the shadow of a ridge. According to his maps, there was a vast plain just over that rise, filled with strange rock formations... and beyond that, the niland ended, only a narrow gap separating it from Gaoland.

Everything down here was draped in shadow. Nachton had always assumed Spookwood, Impstead, Pholand, and Drachölm were called "the Shadowlands" because they were home to the creatures of darkness. But these nilands were literally in the shadow of the nilands above, which prevented direct illumination from this realm's Sky Light.

With the Captain's blessing, the Scout finally rode ahead to reconnoiter the rocky plain and surveil the prison. He would return in one hour—about the time the Sky Light set for the night—with recommendations for the assault, based on the number of guards he observed. Then everyone would go to bed early, so they could *wake* early, cross the plain in darkness, and begin their assault with morning's first light.

Nachton helped with the various responsibilities of setting up camp, surprised to find he enjoyed it. After spending so much of his time in Overtwixt convincing other people he was important, it was refreshing to just be helpful, not caring what people thought of him. When the chores were done, he checked over the siege equipment with the Crafter and Engineer, reviewed the assault plan with the Wrangler, then settled down next to the fire to chat with the Captain.

"Amélie tells me there are only two phomen in all of Overtwixt," Nachton said.

The Captain nodded. "And only three drachmen. It's one of the reasons I supported your plan of assaulting from Pholand, and why I planned to get here by way of Drachölm. I knew these nilands were deserted."

"What are they like?" Nachton asked slowly. "Phomen, I mean. I saw them from a distance, but..."

"Unnatural, freakish creatures," the Captain said at once. "More so than any other I've met in Overtwixt."

"Evil," Nachton said, nodding his understanding.

The Captain barked a laugh. "No, just different. True, the two phomen left in Overtwixt, the Inquisitor and the Enforcer, *are* very bad people. But there used to be many other phomen, and it was the Vizier who expelled them all. That won him a lot of popularity, back when he was new here, in the service of the Baron." The centman chuckled again. "Nobody likes phomen, not really. They look like walking skeletons, and they have this bizarre ability to hear each other speak, no matter how much distance separates them. But... that doesn't make them evil." He shook his head. "The Vizier's campaign to oust them from Overtwixt—all but two of them—is proof of that."

Nachton frowned thoughtfully. "Any idea where they are now? The Inquisitor and the Enforcer?"

"I wish I knew. They chased the Empress and me across Centwick, but we lost them in Gnobury. You sure they weren't at the battle for Eqland?"

"Pretty sure."

"Then no one has seen them since, that I know of." The Captain thought for a moment. "I imagine they're flying toward Hucentia now. It's rumored the Vizier could talk to them across vast distances too, as if *he* was phoman. Yet another bit of magic on his part, I suppose. No doubt he's called them to join his army."

Nachton grimaced. The eqmen and gnomen would be well defended at the Castle on Hucentia. Still, he hated using them as bait, knowing what the Vizier and his cronies would do to them if they got past the Castle's defenses.

The teenage boy felt a familiar flash of anger every time he thought of the Vizier. Even after accepting that he himself was responsible for what had happened to Ewan, Nachton continued to struggle with thoughts of vengeance. He didn't need the Guide or anyone else to tell him that was wrong. Heck, he'd seen enough movies to know that people never felt better after getting revenge, only worse; and besides, wise books like the Bible and others made it pretty clear revenge was unhealthy.

Finding out Ewan was still here in Overtwixt had changed things. It gave Nachton something more important to focus on: rescue instead of revenge. Still, his fury at Shark—the Charlatan!—and the Vizier continued to simmer in the back of his mind.

They would get what was coming to them. But first, Ewan. *Just hold on, buddy. I'm on my way.*

The Scout returned to camp right on schedule, just as full night settled upon them. Unfortunately, he had nothing but bad news to report. "Gaoland is crawling with guards," he said. "Hundreds of them, and that's just the ones I saw on the walls. There are surely more inside."

"So many?" the Captain asked in dismay. "But the army we saw flying away with the Vizier was so large, and considering what the Guide told us…"

The Scout snorted. "Since when do you care what the *Guide* has to say?"

Amélie rushed into the circle around the fire, pushing past Handmaiden and Wrangler. "Has anyone seen Cécilie?" she demanded. "I've searched the whole camp, and I can't find her anywhere!"

"I'm right here," Cécilie announced, appearing suddenly out of the darkness. She certainly knew how to make a dramatic entrance.

Amélie gave her a big hug. "Where were you?" she demanded. "I was worried sick!"

"Your majesty," the Captain said, "we have a bigger problem. Scout says the prison is crawling with guards."

"Hundreds," Scout repeated.

Cécilie moved to stand between Handmaiden and Wrangler. Touching them both on the snout, she drew their heads down low so she could whisper to them.

"I really think we should reconsider attacking tomorrow," Scout said. "Wait a couple days, think through our options. Maybe call for backup."

"Backup?" the Captain said. "From where?"

"But what about Ewan?" Amélie objected.

"What are you doing?" Nachton asked Cécilie suspiciously. He'd been watching her and the eqmen, so he was the first to notice when Handmaiden moved around to Scout's other side. Suddenly, Handmaiden and Wrangler sidled up next to Scout, squeezing him tightly between them.

"What is the meaning of this?" the Captain demanded, hand dropping instinctively to grip the big curved sword that hung from the scabbard at his side.

The Scout was trying to get to his own sword, but he couldn't; it was pinned to his side by the Wrangler's body. "Get off of me!" he said angrily.

"How many bad guys did you say?" Cécilie asked the centman loudly, her eyes wide with pretend surprise. "I'm not sure I heard you right the first time."

"What?" Scout growled. He glanced at the Captain. "What is this silly child talking about?"

"How many *impmen*," Cécilie clarified, still loudly, "did you say you counted on the walls of that horrid prison?"

"Hundreds! I don't know. Too many to count!"

"And yet," the little girl declared, turning even more dramatically to face the rest of them, "*I* only counted *ten!*"

"What *are* you talking about?" Nachton demanded. "And stop being such a drama queen. Just tell it to us straight."

Cécilie's shoulders slumped a little, but she did as Nachton asked, explaining in a more normal tone. "Amélie asked where I was. Well, I followed *him*." She pointed accusingly at the Scout. "I scouted for myself, up on the ridge and down to the plain." Her eyes lit up again, and she smirked a little. "Some 'Scout' he is... he didn't even know I was following him! Anyway, I watched for a long time. And there were definitely only *ten* imps on the walls."

"I don't understand," Captain said. "You're accusing the Scout of *lying*? Why would he do such a thing?"

Amélie spoke up. "Cécilie, you must be confused."

But Nachton had been watching the Scout through all of this, and he realized Cécilie was right. "Maybe, maybe not. Look at him, how nervous he is. I think he *is* lying."

"This is absurd," the Scout spat, but there was no question. The sour-faced guardsman was definitely hiding something.

The Captain had his sword half out of its sheath now, but he was looking everywhere at once, clearly unsure what to do or who to believe. "Would someone please explain what's going on?" he demanded.

Cécilie flung her arms wide. "This centman is a vile traitor!" she declared victoriously. "*That* is what's going on!"

"But Cécilie," Amélie objected. "Scout's been with me since the beginning! He's served me faithfully!"

The Captain's face hardened. "All due respect, Princess, this is a very serious accusation. I dearly hope you have some proof to back it up."

As if Cécilie needed any more encouragement. Eyes blazing excitedly, chest swelling, the little girl walked right up to the Scout and raised her hand suddenly. He actually flinched away, like he thought she might hit him. Instead, Cécilie rested her hand lightly on his wrist—or rather, on something that was wrapped *around* that wrist.

"Exhibit A," the little girl stated. "Nothing but a simple bracelet. Or *is it?*" With one last flair of showmanship, she ripped it free of Scout's wrist. "A-ha!" she squealed. "It's just as I suspected! This is no mere bracelet... it's an *amulet*. One of the Vizier's evil relics!"

Now that Cécilie was displaying it for all the world to see, Nachton could tell that the ribbon was longer than it first appeared. Scout must have wrapped it around his wrist several times, for this was more like a necklace than a bracelet... and there was, indeed, a glittering black gemstone hanging at the end of it.

Surrounded by a green glow.

Amélie swallowed hard. "Is that—"

Cécilie held up a hand for quiet. Abruptly, she was all business, retying the ribbon and hanging it around her own neck. For a long moment, she just stood there, looking into the distance... and then her eyes widened. "Just like in the maze," she whispered, then clapped a hand over her mouth. She removed the necklace and handed it to the Captain before saying anything further. "Put this on and listen," she told him. "Don't say anything. Just listen."

The Captain did so, and *his* eyes soon widened too. He finished drawing his sword and placed the point at the Scout's neck, then passed the necklace to Nachton.

The moment Nachton touched it, he knew. "It's evil," he whispered. "The Vizier's magic—I would recognize the feel of it, the *smell* of it anywhere." Squeezing his eyes shut, Nachton placed the amulet around his own neck.

Immediately, he heard raspy voices in his head:

"—*there tommmorrow if we hhurry.*"

"*Masster will reward us greatly if we prevent thissss.*"

"*If only we could contact hhim—*"

Nachton ripped off the amulet and threw it to the ground before himself, breathing heavily.

"It's one of the amulets I found in the Library," Cécilie said excitedly. "I thought I recognized it yesterday, but I wasn't sure. So I started watching the Scout more closely."

Nachton understood something suddenly. "The Vizier created this amulet from a phoman! He harvested a phoman's telepathy, and stored it in this gemstone!"

"Telepathy?" Amélie asked, confused.

"Yeah! That or something like it. The ability to talk across vast distances, using only your mind." Nachton turned to the Captain. "Don't you see? That's how the Vizier communicated with his phomen in the past!"

"Those are the same voices I heard in the maze," Cécilie was saying. "Remember me telling you? On the way to Lugard, way back when Ewan and I left on our very first quest, I was talking to Ranger about Amélie going to Shanagrailia. I think I mentioned Gnobury too. Then suddenly I heard those creepy voices, asking who Amélie was—and I was wearing that amulet at the time!"

"So that's how the phomen knew the Empress's name," the Captain said, squeezing his eyes shut briefly. "It also explains how they knew where to find us."

"But how does that make Scout a traitor?" Amélie wanted to know.

"It doesn't," Nachton admitted. "I don't think he betrayed us until today, though he's been looking for a chance. All those times he asked to scout ahead..."

The Captain leaned in close to the Scout, looking furious. "Where did you get the amulet?"

The Scout's face twisted with anger and shame. "From the chest in the Princess's quarters. Where she said she hid them." His nostrils flared. "I took *all* of them."

"How dare you dishonor our people this way," the Captain said. "How could you do such a thing?!"

"Save me the speech," the Scout shot back. "Why is it that humen always rule over centmen—can you tell me that? As far back as anyone remembers, every Baron has always been human! Then we allow the Vizier to take over?" Scout shook his shaggy blond head angrily. "Now these *children* show up, and everyone just stumbles over themselves to worship at their feet? Even the eqmen serve one of them now, though they've never before named anyone Prince or Princess except one of their own! And next, you want to put a human Empress on the throne of this realm? How is that any better than a human Vizier?!"

"So you violate your oaths?" the Captain cried. "You sell your soul to the Vizier? You *hate* the Vizier!"

"I hate all humen!" Scout snarled. "But the Vizier is already in charge. At least this way, I get something out of it. The phomen assure me I'll be rewarded handsomely for warning them of this plot to assault the prison."

Nachton spoke up. "That's why he waited. He could've betrayed us on Shanagrailia, to the Dockmaster or any of the other imps. But he didn't, because there was nothing in it for him." He turned to the Scout. "So what's your reward? What did the phomen promise you in exchange for double-crossing us?"

The traitor looked back at him sullenly. "I'm to be the new Baron. A *centman* Baron, finally."

"You fool," the Captain spat. "You'll still be subject to the Vizier."

The Scout barked a bitter laugh. "Only until I overthrow him. Then *I'll* be Emperor, and I'll name another centman as the next Baron." His eyes grew earnest. "It could be you, Captain. *You* could rule after me, if only you'll—"

"No," the Captain said coldly. "I swore to serve the Empress and the greater good, never myself. I will not betray those oaths." He flicked his wrist, slicing neatly through the Scout's belts and sending his weapons clattering to the ground. "Crafter, Engineer," the Captain called gruffly to the two gnomen, who had been watching this whole confrontation with wide eyes. "Kindly bind the traitor's hands, then tie him to a tree. Make it tight. Use twice as much rope as you think you need."

Amélie cleared her throat. "We're still attacking then?"

"The phomen will be here tomorrow," Nachton said. "I heard them say it, through the amulet."

"You were trying to delay us until they got here!" the Captain accused the Scout. "But just how early tomorrow will they arrive?" The Scout refused to answer. "Bah!" The Captain said finally through clenched teeth. Then he heaved a sigh, forcing himself to relax. "It doesn't matter. We need rest after that journey, and we can't attack before first light anyway." He turned to Amélie. "I say we continue as planned, if it please your majesty?"

Amélie nodded.

"Then let us sleep. But not before setting a watch. I don't want those foul phomen surprising us in our beds." And with that, the poor betrayed centman stalked off.

Nachton turned to face Cécilie. The little girl was smiling up at him expectantly, clearly hoping for a bit of praise. Nachton could only smile back and shake his head wryly. "Cécilie, you are *such* a drama queen!"

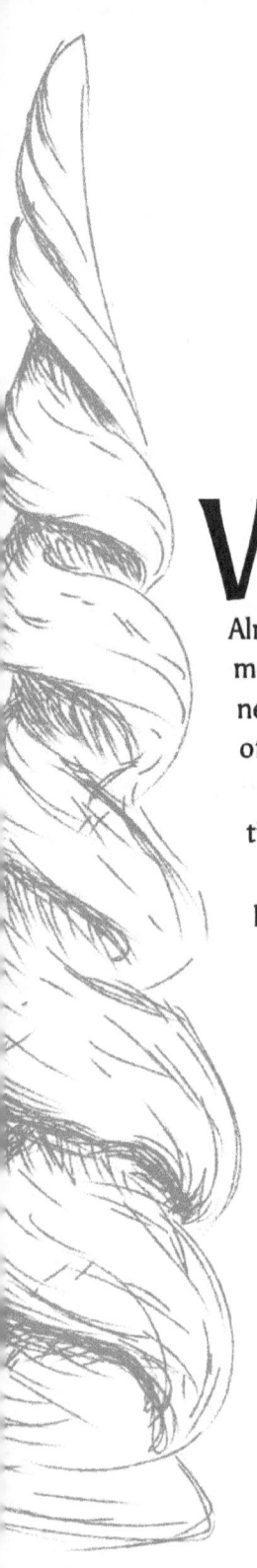

· twelve ·

(Cécilie)

When Amélie shook Cécilie awake a little later, the little girl sat bolt upright in her sleeping bag bedroll thing. "What? Already?" she complained. It didn't look like morning; it was still completely dark! Besides, "I never even fell asleep," she swore. She was sure of it!

"You definitely fell asleep," Nachton said tiredly.

"You slept quite soundingly, your highness," the Captain agreed.

"He means you were snoring loudly," Crafter felt the need to add.

Cécilie folded her arms and huffed. "I don't snore," she muttered.

They put a gag in Scout's mouth, then left him tied to his tree. Since Cécilie was the only other person who did any scouting yesterday, *she* led her friends and family over the ridge onto the plain beyond. It was kinda steep for the cart, but the Wrangler managed.

"Wow, you're really strong," Cécilie told the eqman.

If horses could blush, Cécilie woulda sworn that's exactly what the muscular eqman was doing right then. "Aww shucks, yer highness. It's nuthin'."

They set out across the plain, walking among the strange rock formations that loomed over them in the dark. And it was *very* dark. The only reason they could see at all was the dim light of the stars—distant Sky Lights. The silver nighttime glow of their own Sky Light was completely blocked by the nilands of Delphyrd and Caymerdelphia, floating directly above them.

When the walls of Gaoland were barely visible ahead, they stopped and looked around. "We should set up the catapult somewhere with a greater concentration of rocks," Nachton said.

"Over here!" one of the gnomen hissed.

"Perfect!" Nachton agreed, and they put the catapult in the middle of three tall rock formations. The towers were made up of stacked stones so big Cécilie couldn't wrap her arms around them.

"But how do we get them down?" she asked. "So we can use them with the catapult-thing?"

The Wrangler chewed the inside of his cheek. "I reckon you could just use one o' them amyalets, Princess."

Cécilie hadn't considered that. Even though *she* had left the necklaces behind, the Scout had stolen them and brought them along on their journey; Captain had found them in the traitor's supply bags. Could one of them help knock down a few rocks? Maybe it wouldn't hurt to use the bad magic a *little*, since her intentions were good.

No, that's not the way it worked. Cécilie remembered the Guide's words: "You can't just dabble in evil," she said, quoting to the best of her ability. "No matter your intentions, evil always corrupts, always."

Nachton grinned at her. "Bravo, sis. You're absolutely right again. I wish I hadn't even put on that one amulet yesterday, even though I had no intention of using it."

Cécilie grinned back, then got serious. "But what else can we do? To get these rocks down, I mean."

"I think I have a way," her big brother said. "Assuming everyone's ready to begin the assault? Once I start this, it's gonna be like a beacon to the imps on those walls."

The Captain studied the sky for a long moment. "First light will come any moment now. Yes. Do it."

"Everyone gather in tight around the catapult," Nachton said. He began waving his hands, weaving his magic. The glow of his glasses got a little brighter, and suddenly, a matching blue *dome* appeared above them, like an upside-down bowl covering them and the catapult.

"Whoa!" Cécilie breathed.

"The difference between magic used for good and magic used for evil is obvious to me now," Nachton said, a slight strain in his voice. "Weaving blue magic, I can't intentionally harm others, like I did before with green. But I *can* protect people—and the more I love them, the easier it is to do that kind of magic. This dome is something I've been working on in my head. It's a *shield*."

"But how does it help with the rocks?" Amélie asked.

"Watch." Nachton waved his hands toward one of the three rock towers, and the dome stretched in that direction. It pushed against the big stones at the base of the tower, then pushed them right out from under the ones on top! A *bunch* of big rocks tumbled down, causing Amélie to scream and cover her head. But the rocks just bounced off Nachton's shield, rolling down the sides to land safely on the ground.

"Sorry about that," Nachton told Amélie, though a small smile pulled at the corner of his mouth. "I guess I should've explained." He started waving his dome toward the next tower. "Oh hey, Cécilie. Speaking of protection, I think you should wear the Diamond Armor today."

"But that's Ewan's Armor."

"Maybe. But it's not doing him any good right now."

"The Loremaster is right," Captain agreed, and Amélie nodded emphatically. So Cécilie pulled the cloak off the Diamond Armor where it was piled in the back of the cart that held the catapult. She started putting on the Armor with Amélie's help, piece by piece; they finished just as the last rock formation collapsed. Nachton's dome disappeared.

And suddenly, Cécilie's glowing blue Armor was the brightest thing in sight. "I look silly."

"No, your highness," Handmaiden breathed. "You look amazing—like a *Warrior* Princess!"

"We've got incoming!" the Captain bellowed.

The first glimmer of daylight was peeking out from beyond Caymerdelphia above... and in that yellow light, Cécilie could see three impmen flying straight toward them.

"Protect the catapult!" Nachton yelled.

The bad guys had bows and arrows, and they started firing down at Cécilie and her friends. Nachton was already weaving, and he started flinging blue globs back at the bad guys. The globs flattened and hardened, creating little shields in midair to catch the arrows, then disappear.

"Make the big dome again!" Amélie said.

Nachton shook his head. "Too much effort, and the catapult can't shoot out of it. This will work for now."

The gnomen were already firing their slingshots back at the impmen, while the eqmen—Wrangler and Handmaiden—pulled in tight to protect Cécilie and Amélie. The Captain looked from one person to the other, then muttered, "Guess I'll load the catapult." He used the ratchet to get the contraption into launch position, then bent down and heaved a big stone into the basket.

All three imps were still dancing around in the sky, just far enough away that it was hard to hit them with a slingshot. When one of the gnomen's shots *did* connect, it didn't hurt the bad guy enough to matter.

The Captain kicked the catapult lever, and the basket whipped the first huge stone into the air, faster than Cécilie's eye could follow. The rock plowed straight through one of the impmen, releasing a puff of yellow smoke, then traveled across the gap to hit the prison wall. It missed the closed drawbridge by a *lot*.

Shrieking, the remaining imps flapped their wings hard to get farther away. That made them *impossible* to hit with slingshots, but also made it easier for Nachton to protect everyone from their arrows.

"Reload!" the Loremaster cried.

"I'm getting to it," the Captain muttered. "Why didn't we think to bring more people capable of lifting these stones?"

"We did," Nachton said with a snort. "He turned out to be a traitor, remember?"

The gnomen had put their slingshots away, and they were already ratcheting the catapult basket back down. "Friend eqman," one of them said, "kindly adjust our trajectory six degrees leeward."

"Say wha?" Wrangler replied.

"Just nudge the cart thataway."

The big eqman did so, just as the Captain dropped another large stone into the basket. The Engineer kicked the lever, and this stone rocketed across the gap to bounce off the wall on the *other* side of the drawbridge.

"And a hair back the other direction," Crafter said.

Wrangler obeyed, and they did the process of reloading again. The next big stone hit the drawbridge dead center!

And did absolutely nothing.

The two remaining impmen stared at the catapult for a moment, then at each other, before retreating to the protection of Gaoland's walls. There, they and the rest of their friends—about nine or ten total, just like Cécilie saw last night—started laughing and calling insults.

"Just as well," Nachton said with a grin. "This way, I can pitch in with the heavy lifting."

The next time the siege equipment fired, it sent *three* big rocks catapulting across the empty space. When they hit, a sharp wooden crack echoed back to them.

The impmen stopped laughing. They looked at each other again, and then *all* of them were attacking.

"We've got more incoming!" Nachton yelled, in case anyone had missed it.

"It's worse than that!" Amélie shrieked. "Behind us!"

Cécilie spun to look the other direction—and there, swooping down out of the sky, was a sight even scarier than a drachman: two horse-shaped skeletons flying with big black bat wings. Their evil eyes flashed red, and their white fangs glistened in the morning light.

The phomen had arrived.

"Here!" Amélie told Cécilie, shoving the handle of a short sword into her hands, then grabbing another sword out of the cart for herself. She left her scepter in the cart, afraid to let the phomen see that she had it. "Get ready to fight!"

"I don't know *how* to fight!" Cécilie shouted back.

"I'll protect ya, highness!" the Wrangler cried, diving between Cécilie and one of the flying black horses as it touched down nearby.

"Hhow dare you defile our hhome," it hissed—apparently referring to the fact that they were attacking Gaoland from Pholand, the phoman portland.

"Ha!" Wrangler laughed. "Aren't you just a big ole hypocrite." He reared up on his back legs to pummel the phoman with his front hooves, but the bad guy swept his wings backwards, jumping out of the way.

Cécilie turned to look toward Gaoland again. The impmen from the walls were all here now, fighting Nachton, Amélie, and Handmaiden, and more were flying toward them from inside the prison.

Meanwhile, the gnomen were operating the catapult as fast as possible, the Captain reloading it just as quickly. They fired another big stone, then Nachton dropped another blue dome over the good guys, trapping three impmen inside with them—but leaving Wrangler *outside*.

Cécilie turned around just in time to see the big eqman launch another attack at a phoman. That bad guy danced away, but the other one darted forward—*way* fast—and sank its sharp teeth into Wrangler's neck. Wrangler bellowed, then disappeared in a puff of yellow.

"No!" Cécilie shrieked.

"You're nnnexxt, little hhuwoman."

And then, to Cécilie's dismay, the magic blue shield— the only thing separating her from the phomen— disappeared again.

· thirteen ·

(Ewan)

Ewan didn't want to wake up. He dreamed he was home in his own bed, and Mommy was snuggling him, singing songs. But Skire Horsey kept nudging him with his nose. "Sir Knight! Sir Knight, awake!"

Finally, Ewan rolled over and opened his eyes. It was very dark, but he was still in his jail cell. Skire Horsey's head was sticking between two bars, leaning over Ewan. The horsey opened his mouth, and out came his tongue—

"I up! I up!" Ewan shrieked, scrambling away before the horsey could lick him. "That *goss*, Skire!"

The horsey pulled back into its own cell. "Sir Knight, something's happening! Listen."

Ewan listened hard. Just when he was about to complain that he didn't hear anything, there was a big *thump* from somewhere else in the jail.

"What was *dat?*" he asked, eyes wide.

"Is siege," Bazooka boomed quietly.

"Huh?"

"An attack," Skire Horsey explained. "Someone's attacking the prison!"

Ewan's eyes got even bigger. "Nock! And Ommie and Sessy!"

"That seems a safe assumption," Skire agreed.

There was another *thump*, and this time the walls seemed to shake, causing dust to float down from the ceiling. Then something jingled and clattered nearby.

"Jail Guy's keys!" Ewan cried.

"He must've left them here on accident, hanging from the wall!" Skire Horsey said. "I didn't even notice!"

Jail Guy *was* always doing that, but Ewan knew better. He could see a dark shape through the open doorway. Someone had *thrown* the keys in here!

"Is no matter," Bazooka interrupted. "Sir Knight, can you reach?"

Ewan stretched between the bars, straining as far as he could... "Yes!" He pulled the big key ring toward himself, then tried different keys until he found the one that unlocked his cell. After that, he unlocked Skire Horsey, then Bazooka.

"What now?" Skire asked.

Ewan squinted through the doorway into the rest of the jail, but the person who helped them was gone. He took a deep breath. "Now we free evveybodies."

They went from cell to cell, unlocking doors and letting pwiz-o-ners out. There were lots of little no-mans, and other small people too, like shaggy pony guys, and fat little dolphins with legs that Skire called "ray-men." Plus a bunch of other horseys and cent-guys and even a couple slimy dudes covered with spiny fins. The jail was *big*, with lots more cages than Ewan guessed, and most of them were full. Ewan and Skire Horsey kept saying "shhhh" to everyone as Ewan unlocked the doors. The more cells they unlocked, the closer they got to the booming *thumps*.

When Ewan and his friends went through a door into the fourth big room of the jail, they came face to face with Jail Guy and a wimp dude. "Alarm—" the wimpman started to scream, but then Bazooka's fist turned the guy's face into yellow smoke. An instant later, the wimpman reappeared in an empty cell nearby, looking really dizzy. He took two steps, then tripped and fell down.

Ewan and Skire and Bazooka and everyone else looked at the Jailer, whose eyes were wide. "Please don't hurt me!" Jail Guy squeaked.

"But—" Ewan began.

"Just lock me in a cell," the dwagon begged.

"Join us!" Ewan blurted. "You could be a *good* guy!"

Everyone froze, waiting on Jail Guy's response. The big dwagon looked down at his paws. "I cannot openly defy the Vizier," he whispered.

"But—"

"No," Jail Guy said more firmly. "If I go with you, then who will take care of the prisoners? There *will* be more. And... this is my mission, from the Guide."

"That's the most ludicrous thing I ever heard," Skire said. "The Guide wouldn't want you *here*, helping the Vizier."

"Is crazy," Bazooka agreed, backing Jail Guy into an empty cell.

Ewan felt his lip trembling, but he stepped forward with the keys, locking the cells that now contained Jail Guy and the wimpman. "Thank you," he whispered to the big dwagon. His newest fwend. "For evveything."

"It was my pleasure, young human," the dwagon whispered back sadly.

Ewan and his other friends finished unlocking pwiz-o-ners throughout the rest of the jail, and they didn't see any other bad guys in the whole place—except a few more dizzy ones that appeared suddenly in cells they passed. They locked those cells back again, and started locking *all* the cells after freeing the pwiz-o-ners.

"Follow me!" a ray-man called when they were done, waddling ahead of them on all fours. His round belly swung from side to side as he ran. "There's a drawbridge this way!"

The *thumps* got louder the closer they came to the drawbridge. They were almost there when Ewan heard a big *crack*. Suddenly there was dust all around, and sunlight coming in from up ahead.

Bazooka pushed past Ewan. "Is way out!" he cried. When Ewan caught up, he found the big lugman ripping pieces of the drawbridge off its hinges and throwing them over a gap, to create a way across. On the other side of the gap was a floaty desert island.

And on that island was his family, locked in battle.

Skire Horsey knelt beside him, making it easy for Ewan to get on. "Shall we, sir Knight?"

Ewan grinned and scrambled up. "You bet, Skire Horsey." He filled his lungs with air and raised one fist overhead. "For Overchix! For Empess Ommie and Overchix! Charge!"

And he went galloping out of the jail to help his family, closely followed by Bazooka—who was looking *very* scary— and an entire army of freed pwiz-o-ners.

· fourteen ·

(Nachton)

N achton was exhausted. He knew the siege of Gaoland had barely started, but it felt like the battle had been raging for hours. Sweat poured from his face, and his arms ached from the effort of weaving magic. He couldn't even maintain the dome shield any longer; it took too much out of him.

To his left, the gnomen Crafter and Engineer kept ratcheting and firing the catapult as fast as their deft little hands could move. The Captain was with them, still lifting stones to reload the catapult when needed, but doing it all one-handed—while fighting back attackers with his *other* hand, wielding a great curved sword.

Of Nachton's sisters or the eqmen, there was no sign.

A monumental *crack* split the air, and even the bad guys paused in their fighting to turn toward Gaoland.

The big doors had been shattered.

"Woohoo!" the gnomen cheered, then started giving each other high-fives. "How many stones was that?" one asked. "Twenty?"

"Who cares?" the other replied. "It worked!"

There was movement inside the prison, and shapes started appearing out of the dusty gloom, but Nachton didn't have time to stare longer—for in that moment of shocked silence, he heard one of the girls scream. "Help!"

His head whipped around to look in that direction. He noticed the Handmaiden first, fighting her way through a sea of imps; when one got too close, she speared him with her horn, turning him to yellow smoke. Beyond the little unicorn—in the direction she was trying to go—Nachton finally saw Amélie and Cécilie.

Trapped between the two phomen.

And the phomen were *playing* with them! Even as Nachton started fighting his way toward them too, he saw one of the skeletal winged horses dart in to nip at Cécilie's shoulder.

She screamed, pulling away just in time, and stumbled into her sister. Amélie, meanwhile, was facing the other direction, trying to keep away from the *other* phoman.

"Hhow do you tasste, little hhuman?" one cackled.

"Like chhicken, brothher," the other answered gleefully, finally sinking his fangs into Cécilie's shoulder. Fortunately, Cécilie was still wearing the Diamond Armor, all except for the helmet. The only person hurt by the phoman's bite was the phoman himself, who started howling, "My tooffff! Shhe bwoke my tooffff!"

"You'llll pay for thhat, filthhy hhumen!" the first phoman screamed, then charged the girls.

The girls had already lost their swords, so they had no way of defending themselves. Summoning the strength from somewhere, Nachton starting flinging globs of glowing blue magic, letting them harden as they flew to his sisters' defense. One of them hit an imp partway there, knocking him down and leaving him dizzy, but the other little shield sprung up between Amélie and the uninjured phoman just as he twisted his head to bite at her neck.

No teeth got broken this time, but the phoman was clearly surprised when his face bounced right off the hardened blue glob. "Whhat ssorccery iss thissss?"

And then Handmaiden was through the crowd, coming to Cécilie's defense. She started harrying the broken-toothed phoman, dashing in quick circles around him and jabbing at soft spots with her horn, but never staying in one place long. Between that and the Armor, Nachton decided Cécilie was safe and focused on keeping blue shields between Amélie and the other nasty creature.

He didn't expect the phoman to turn and charge *him*.

There were still a half dozen impmen separating them, and they had finally noticed Nachton pushing their direction.

Dropping the shield that protected Amélie, Nachton formed one in front of himself, just as two imps attacked with swords. Nachton's strength was failing rapidly, and the sword strikes were already half past his new shield before he finished weaving it. His shield formed *around* the blades, trapping them in place.

Surprised, Nachton jerked backwards with his magic, ripping the swords out of their owners' hands! Shrieking, the disarmed imps fled. Nachton let his shield disappear, then caught one of the swords before it could drop. He created a new shield—very small—with what strength remained, adding straps so he could wear it on his other arm. Then he turned to face the charging phoman.

The beast came in fast, teeth bared. When Nachton raised his shield, the phoman threw his shoulder against it, staggering Nachton back on his heels. Nachton jabbed with his sword, but it slid harmlessly off the phoman's hide, like the creature's skin was made of metal.

The skeletal horse hissed. "I would knnnow your nnname before I sslay you, chhild."

"I am the Loremaster. And you might be surp—"

"I am the Vizzier's Enfforccer," the phoman hissed back. "Let my nnname ring in your earss as I rend your flesshh from your bonessss."

"*Ew,*" Nachton said, making a face. "Do you talk to your mother with that same mouth?"

"Whhat?" the Enforcer replied, seeming perplexed.

Nachton attacked furiously. He charged the phoman with his shield, but the Enforcer just swept his wings forward, blowing sand in Nachton's face. Crying out, Nachton clenched his eyes shut, but the damage was done. He jabbed blindly with his sword, but it was no use.

Then skeletal hooves pounded on his shield, slamming it into Nachton's forehead. Stunned, Nachton tripped backwards and fell to the ground, losing the shield. Swiping at his eyes, he cleared them well enough to look up... and saw fangs descending toward his neck.

One of the girls screamed from nearby, and then Cécilie was throwing herself across Nachton's body. The Enforcer howled with pain as *his* teeth encountered the Diamond Armor. "Filthhy hhuman chhild!" he spat, then headbutted Cécilie, knocking her off Nachton.

The Loremaster seized the opportunity, jabbing upwards as hard as he could, but with even worse luck than before. This time, the sword shattered in his hand... and the annoyed phomen grabbed what was left of the blade between his teeth and tore it from Nachton's hand!

This definitely wasn't going well.

Then Nachton had a flash of inspiration. He stopped *fighting* and relied entirely on the blue magic to protect him, the way it was intended. Still barely able to see, he wove his hands, and manacles of brilliant blue light came into existence around each of the Enforcer's ankles—then snapped together, causing the creature to tumble onto his side. A much larger band of blue snaked around the phoman's skeletal chest, trapping his furled wings to his back. At last, a glowing blue muzzle clamped the foul creature's fanged mouth shut.

Nachton heaved a relieved sigh and swiped at his eyes to clear the last of the sand. Almost too late, he'd remembered just how strong the phomen were, with only two of them left in Overtwixt. Nothing short of the Sovereign's magic would be effective against them.

He smiled at Cécilie. "Thanks for the help, sis."

She grinned back at him. "Anytime, *bro*." At Cécilie's side, Handmaiden giggled.

"Help!" Amélie screamed.

Nachton turned to stare. The other phoman—the Inquisitor, he remembered—had stopped complaining about his tooth and started attacking again. He had backed Amélie to the very edge of the niland, and there was no way Nachton could get there in time to help, no time or strength to even create a shield.

"For Empess Ommie!" someone yelled in a boyish voice, and then a big black blur was colliding with the phoman. Both shapes went down in a rolling tumble, raising a cloud of dust. When the dust settled, Nachton recognized *two* people facing the Inquisitor—a big black eqman named Squire, and the little human Knight who had ridden the horse to the rescue.

Ewan.

The little boy screamed, "Stay away from my sister!" and then attacked with a vengeance. He'd picked up a sword from somewhere, and he began wielding it with surprising skill, thanks to all those lessons with the Weaponsmaster. In the next moment, Nachton realized his brother was also completely unprotected, since Cécilie was wearing the Diamond Armor. Ewan didn't even have the ruby amulet to grant him strength.

You wouldn't know it by the way the little boy fought, however. Whatever fear Ewan had shown in the face of the Warlord or Vizier, there was no sign of it now as he valiantly protected his big sister. He wielded his sword expertly, as much defending himself from the Inquisitor's lunging snaps as jabbing back at the phoman. With the help of Squire's own rearing attacks, Ewan steadily pushed the phoman toward the edge until it was forced into the air. Then a streak of blue light shot past and very nearly hit the phoman.

"What was that?" Nachton gasped, climbing to his feet. Was there someone *else* wielding magic here?

No... at least, not in the same way Nachton did. It was the *Captain*. Advancing on the phoman, the centman reloaded his crossbow with another glowing bolt and fired again, producing another blue streak. The Inquisitor sobbed in sudden fear as he twisted out of the way—barely. But that put him off-balance when Squire attacked again, the eqman's thundering hooves knocking into the phoman's head, making him dizzy, driving him to the ground. One last blue streak from the Captain's crossbow entered the phoman's chest just as Ewan's sword descended, and the phoman disappeared in yellow smoke.

Nachton stared at the Captain's crossbow. "What manner of magic is *that?*"

The centman smiled, just a little. "You didn't think you children were the only ones blessed to bear one of Sovereign's Relics, did you?"

Nachton could only laugh.

The Captain headed toward Ewan and Squire. "I must recover my Diamond Bolts, however. There are only seven, and I've already lost one of them..."

Ewan came running up and gave Nachton a big hug. "You rescue me!" he blurted joyously.

Nachton squeezed his little brother tightly in his arms. He realized he was crying. "I'm so sorry, Ewan. I should have protected you. You never should have *needed* rescuing. Can you ever forgive me?"

Ewan pulled back in Nachton's arms, looking into his eyes with a big smile. "It okay," he said with a shrug, and Nachton could tell the little boy meant it completely. If he had ever blamed Nachton for his terrible blunder that night at the Archives, it was obvious he had long since forgiven him and practically forgotten about it.

The girls rushed up, and then they were hugging Ewan together, too impatient to take turns. "You rescue me too!" Ewan told his sisters gleefully.

Amélie laughed through her tears. "And you immediately returned the favor."

Ewan pulled out of the hug and shrugged nonchalantly, like it was no big deal. "I'm da Knight."

"Empress," the Captain said, striding up. "Princess, Loremaster," he acknowledged the others, then grinned as he added, "Sir Knight, it's good to see you again."

"You too, Mr. Cap'n Guy!" Ewan bellowed.

"Your majesty," the centman continued, "there are some people here you should probably meet."

Nachton suddenly remembered the impmen, but when he looked around, he discovered there were only two still visible on the plain—one in each of the Berserker's immense hands. Even as Nachton watched, the huge lugman kept swinging the screaming villains against the dusty ground until they finally puffed into yellow smoke. Nachton grinned. It was good to see Ewan's big friend again too.

But there were a whole lot of other people on the plain now also: gnomen and eqmen and centmen, plus pot-bellied raimen and shaggy pony nagmen of the sort Nachton had seen in Shanagrailia. There were even a half dozen sleek creatures that could only be dagmen—dark-skinned and human-shaped, but with spiny fins sprouting from every joint on their bodies. All told, there had to be a hundred, maybe two hundred people, many of them holding rocks or pieces of broken wood—makeshift weapons that they must have used to defeat the rest of the imps.

"Who *are* all these people?" Amélie asked in wonder.

"Pwiz-o-ners!" Ewan replied gleefully.

"But... they all look so healthy," Amélie objected.

That struck Nachton as strange too, come to think of it. He had expected any prisoners they freed to be tired, sick, and hungry. But these weren't.

Ewan shrugged. "Jail Guy is a good guy… kinda."

The rescued prisoners were all whispering among themselves, and Nachton heard the word "human" on many lips. Apparently, Amélie heard it too. "It's true," she announced, loudly enough for all of them to hear. "We are human. But we're no allies of the Vizier. We're here to defeat him."

The whispering intensified.

"I won't lie to you," Amélie continued. "We came here to Gaoland to free my brother, the Knight." Ewan grinned really big and waved at the other former prisoners. "But I am overjoyed to see all of you freed too."

"If he's a Knight," a nagman called, "who are all of *you*?"

Amélie smiled down at the little pony, who had interesting patterns shaved into his shaggy hair. "People of Overtwixt," she announced, "allow me to introduce the Knight's sister—the Princess of Eqland." Cécilie offered a shy but regal wave, and Handmaiden darted forward to stand with her. "And this is the Knight's brother," Amélie continued, gesturing to Nachton. "The Loremaster."

The people were no longer whispering. They were talking aloud to one another, their voices awed. And while they were focused on Cécilie and Nachton, Amélie walked casually to the catapult and retrieved her new scepter from the back of the cart. Nachton could hardly blame her; holding that staff made her look very royal indeed.

"I am the Empress," she said now, drawing all eyes back to herself. "And as the Empress, the Guide has tasked me with uniting all the peoples of the realm against the Vizier, overthrowing him, and rebuilding the bridges he destroyed."

She took a deep breath. "Nothing would please me more than doing exactly that... and then returning home to my real world. I have no desire to rule once the Vizier is defeated."

The rescued prisoners met her solemn gaze, and Nachton could tell they believed her. Despite her failures convincing anyone else before now, every single one of *these* people believed... and were ready to follow her.

One by one, the gnomen, nagmen, raimen, eqmen, and centmen dropped to their knees before her. "Long live the Empress!" someone cried, then all of the others were repeating it, their voices combining to sound like thunder. Only the dagmen stood apart, but not for long. Glancing back and forth between that scepter and the other prisoners, still bowing, the dagmen began grinning. "I fink we best fall in too, mates!" one of them said. And then they were leading the others in another round of "Long live the Empr'ss!"

The Captain turned to Amélie, a zealous light in his eye. "This is it, your majesty. The opportunity you've been waiting for." He swept his arm across the crowd of people. "You have an army. You can take the fight to the Vizier!"

Amélie looked uncertain. "But I'm supposed to unite the peoples first."

The Captain's smile grew deeper. "You *have*, don't you see? Most of the peoples are represented here. We even have dagmen to represent Caymerdelphia. The only thing we don't have—other than creatures of darkness—is a shaman."

Nachton frowned, realizing the Captain was right. What had happened to Ewan's shaman companion, the Weaponsmaster? He should have been among the prisoners freed today.

"I don't know if this truly counts as uniting the peoples," Amélie replied to the Captain hesitantly.

The centman's face hardened. "Do not be cautious when you should be bold. As we speak, Ranger and Operative and our other allies are most likely under attack on Hucentia. They need the aid this army can render. It's time to attack the Vizier head-on."

"I would agree," Amélie answered calmly, "if we knew how our allies were doing or where the Vizier is. But we *don't* know... and I've had enough of acting rashly."

The Captain looked exasperated, but Amélie turned to Nachton and Cécilie. "What do you guys think?"

"Ask the Guide," they said together, then laughed.

"*Exactly* what I was thinking." Amélie took a deep breath, as if she realized just how foolish this was going to look, but going through with it anyway. "Guide?" she called loudly. "I need your help. What should I do?" She swallowed. "Can you hear me?"

"Of course," the Guide answered.

Nachton spun, surprised to see the Guide there in the crowd with the other prisoners. Had he been there the whole time? Nachton hadn't looked very closely at the rescued centmen before now, but... somehow he doubted he would have seen the Guide before this moment.

How did the strange centman *do* that?

"Your course of action is for you to decide," the Guide answered Amélie's question. "I can only offer guidance."

"Then tell me, please," Amélie said. "Do you know what's happening on Hucentia?"

The Guide nodded, then seemed to stare off into the distance. "The Vizier's forces attacked the Castle this morning, at much the same time your siege of Gaoland began. The Castle proved little defense against the imps and spooks, who simply flew over the walls and attacked your allies within. However, the Ranger and Operative followed the plan carefully. Traps were set throughout the Castle. As the impmen chased the eqmen and gnomen down hallways and into chambers, many were tripped or caught in netting. Most of your allies have escaped the Castle, fleeing in different directions so the Vizier doesn't know who to chase."

Nachton felt a weight lift from his chest. Amélie looked relieved too. "What about the Vizier?"

"Unfortunately, he *was* able to capture one of your allies and learn the truth about your plans. Realizing that you've attacked Gaoland and freed the prisoners by now, he has retreated to his Citadel in Capital City, on the niland of Twixt, recalling all his troops from across the realm."

There were expressions of joy from everyone at this. "*All* of them?" an eqman cried. "He's on the run!"

"And Shanagrailia is free!" a nagman exclaimed.

"Is it possible?" Amélie said wonderingly. "We've really freed Overtwixt from the Vizier, that easily?"

"Alas, no," the Guide said. "Retreating to Twixt was always part of his plan. You've forced him to move up his timetable—Capital City's defenses are not yet complete—but the Vizier is still very much a threat."

"But all the slaves have been freed!" Nachton said.

The Guide shook his head. "When the Vizier's troops left Shanagrailia, they took many of the gnoman and nagman workers back with them."

"And," the Captain added, "many of Capital City's citizens are still trapped there, from when the Vizier first seized power. He's no doubt been using them to help build the wall around the city... and now that he has *more* slaves, the wall will go up even faster." He took a deep breath. "Your majesty, if the Vizier has returned to Capital City, then that's where we need to attack. We must take this army and strike now, before he finishes that wall!"

Amélie turned to the Guide. "*Should* I lead this army to attack the Vizier on Twixt?"

The Guide only smiled and looked to Nachton.

Nachton considered the question carefully. He put aside any desire he had for personal glory. He considered the needs of all the peoples of the realm, then balanced them against the risk to each individual who might fight in the upcoming battle. He pondered the right and wrong of each course of action... and noticed his spectacles glowing brilliantly, the blue light visible even in day. Then he met Amélie's expectant gaze. "Your majesty the Empress," he said formally, "I counsel you to release these rescued prisoners. Give each one leave to return to his people."

"What?" Amélie blurted.

"You can't be serious!" the Captain scoffed.

The Guide only smiled.

Nachton went on. "Encourage them to tell their friends and family of all they've seen and heard this day, holding nothing back. And *if* their leaders wish to join us in our cause, to meet us on the niland of Twixt... where we will unite beneath your banner, Empress, and lay siege to Capital City and the Citadel of the Vizier."

Even though he intended his words for Amélie alone, Nachton realized he'd spoken loudly enough for all to hear. They began cheering wildly. And Amélie didn't look even the least bit upset. "I believe I will follow your counsel," she told him with a grin.

The Captain looked as frustrated as Nachton had ever seen him, but he finally took a deep breath, let it out, and nodded grudgingly. "Can we at least make a foray into the prison before we go? To release some of our friends who fell in the fighting just now?"

"Like the Wrangler!" Cécilie blurted.

"Easy-peasy!" Ewan announced, holding up a big ring of keys. "I gots da keys to all the cages!"

"They'll be pretty disoriented," Squire warned.

"We can dump the catapult and let the Wrangler and any others ride in the cart," Nachton said.

"We should also collect the Scout," the Captain added woodenly. "Lock him in one of the cells. I do not trust those ropes to hold him forever."

Amélie nodded. "Very well. And after all of that, we journey directly to Twixt... and hope to meet representatives of all the other peoples there." She glanced at the Guide hopefully. "Will you go with us?"

The Guide smiled. "I will not travel as a member of your party, no. But as you've no doubt come to realize, I'm never far, whether you see me or not. Know that I'm pleased with all of you, the things you've accomplished, and the lessons you've learned—and are still learning."

He eyed Amélie for an uncomfortably long moment.

"As you embark on this final phase of your mission," he concluded finally, "remember this: So long as you remain united in purpose, trust one another, and rely upon no magic except the Sovereign's, the Vizier cannot stand against you."

And with that, the Guide disappeared before their very eyes.

The End of
Part II

Part III
Rebellion

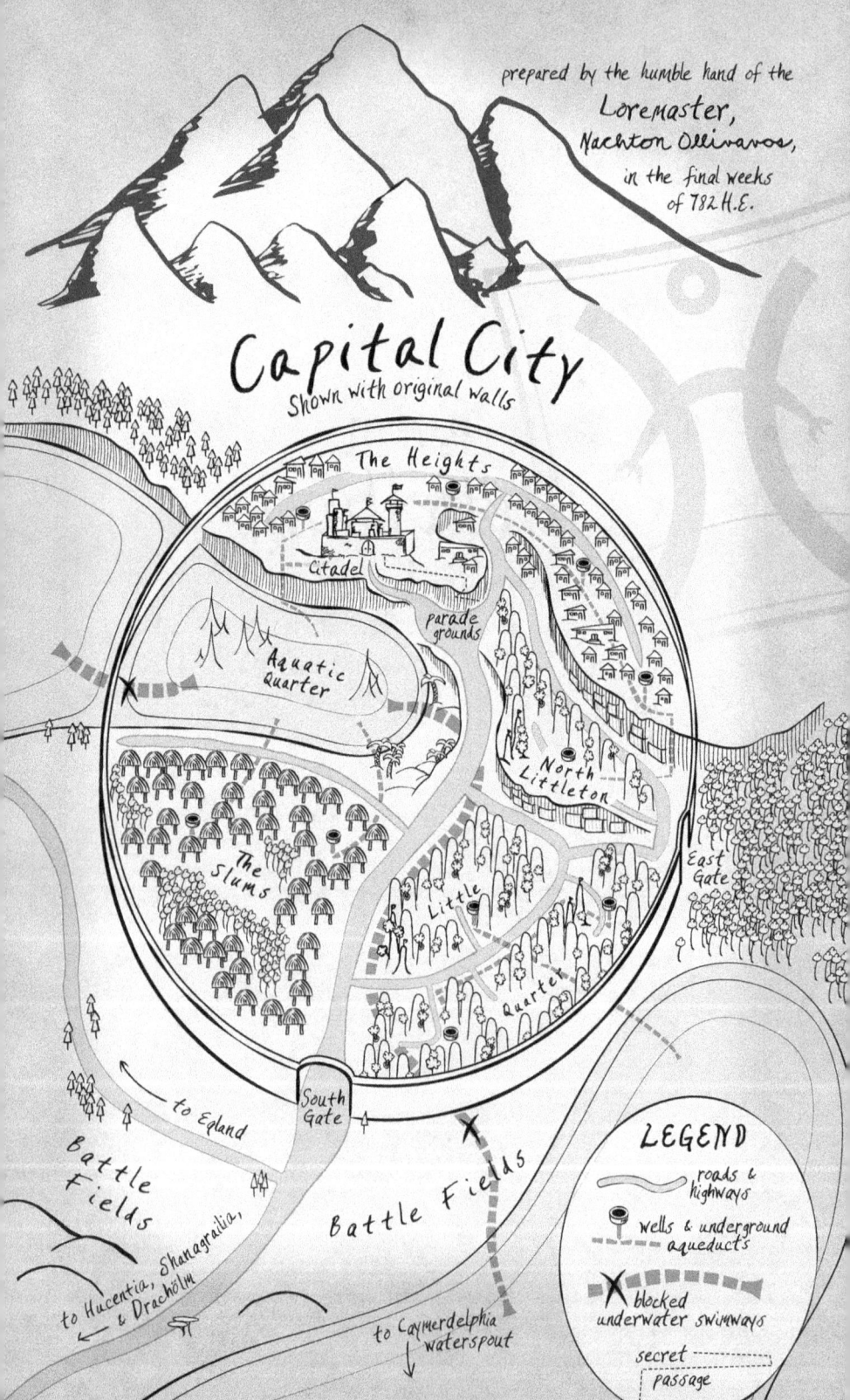

· fifteen ·

(Amélie)

Twixt was the grandest niland of all. As Amélie's eyes swept the horizon, she recognized features from many of the other places she and her siblings had visited: to the west, the rolling red hills of Lugard gave way to the grassy plains of Eqland and the forested slopes of Huland; to the east, the lava pools of Drachölm mixed with the rock formations of Pholand among the sandy dunes of Impstead; and straight ahead, the glittering lakes of Caymerdelphia fronted mountains worthy of Shanagrailia, which reached almost as high as the Sky Light itself. Twixt had obviously been created to represent all the nilands of this realm.

Originally cultivated as a hubland connecting the five United Lands, Twixt could be reached via bridges from Hucentia, Eqland, Shanagrailia, and the Shadowlands; Amélie saw no sign of any other bridges beyond that, but the Captain assured her that Caymerdelphia had access too.

When Amélie and her followers came in sight of Capital City, everyone stopped and stared.

"That's... that's impossible," the Captain breathed.

The Vizier's wall around Capital City was no longer just a wall. It was a *dome*. A massive structure built of stones quarried from Eqland and Pholand, arching up and over the entire city. As construction projects went, it was an incredible undertaking... and it was almost complete.

The Captain took a shuddering breath. "The last time I was here, the night the Baron was defeated, that wall surrounded half the city at most. When the Guide said it wasn't complete yet, I thought he meant there were still gaps at ground level. Not... *this*."

"But why a dome?" Amélie asked.

There can be only one reason," Captain replied. "To defend against enemies who can fly."

"But all the flying peoples serve the Vizier!"

"You know better than that. Or have you already forgotten your perilous flight from Caymerdelphia?" The Captain shook his head. "No, only the flying peoples of *this*

realm serve the Vizier. Among all the other infinite realms of Overtwixt, many other races are loyal to the Sovereign. The Vizier must fear that someday, eventually, the Sovereign will send flying armies to put down this rebellion."

Amélie nodded understanding. "Well, let's see if we can take care of the Vizier before that's necessary."

The Captain barked a laugh, pointing at the wall. "Don't you get it? He's already filled in all the gaps *we* could use to get inside!"

The centman was right, Amélie realized. Though portions of the dome remained incomplete, those holes were dozens of feet in the air. There was no way for her armies to get inside.

She took a deep breath and shook her head. "I refuse to accept that. The Guide wouldn't have sent us here unless there's a way inside. We just have to find it." She glanced at her followers, still standing in awe behind her. "Everyone start making camp. We'll wait here for our allies to join us."

Amélie's people obeyed quickly, unpacking supplies and pitching tents on the hill where they stood, beside a great lake. There weren't many of them yet, unfortunately: the Captain; Nachton, Cécilie, Ewan, and their friends; and the eqmen and gnomen they rescued from the prison. Some of *them* had actually fought in the battle at Hucentia, waking up on Gaoland after they were defeated—not counting the ones Amélie already sent back to Hucentia, with orders to round up the others who had managed to escape the Castle.

The young huwoman Empress returned her attention to the domed city that stood across the water from them. Atop this hill, she was able to look down into the city through one of the holes in the dome... and what she saw inside the city was just as amazing as the outside.

If Twixt was the grandest niland of the realm, Capital City was easily the grandest city, even more so than those on

Shanagrailia or Caymerdelphia—for like Twixt itself, Capital City incorporated elements from the rest of the realm. Beneath that huge dome, she could clearly see an area of town made up of brilliant white buildings with trees and shrubs growing out of their windows. Captain said that was the Little Quarter, designed to look like Alabaster City. There was also a lake inside the dome, with glass structures growing out of it, called the Aquatic Quarter. And the worn-down section of town beside that was the Slums, where Capital City's imp and spook populations lived.

That left the Heights: the last section of Capital City, according to the Captain, where eqmen and centmen and the occasional lugman lived. That was where the Baron had built his beautiful capitol building.

Which the Vizier had turned into a Citadel.

Amélie shivered, gazing at that distant, terrible place. Apparently, the dome over Capital City wasn't enough for the Vizier, for he had converted the capitol building into a fortified structure too. Even inside the dome, the Citadel's brown walls stood twice the height of the Castle of Hucentia and three times the Palace of Eqland—and that was only its outer walls. Within those walls, twenty different buildings stretched even higher into the sky, each one set with beautiful stained-glass windows. The Captain pointed out the tallest structure as the Vizier's tower, at the rightmost corner of the Citadel grounds; it was there, he explained, that the old Baron had made his final stand against the Vizier's evil. Colored pennants representing each of the sixteen races of this realm flew from the Citadel's many buildings, and a huge black flag flapped above the Vizier's tower.

And almost everywhere she looked, Amélie saw activity. Little people standing on scaffolds high in the air, turning cranks to lift stone blocks for adding to the dome. Impman taskmasters cracking whips at them, just like Amélie had seen in Shanagrailia. A huge drachman shape circled near the very top of the dome, wings grazing the ceiling—the Warlord, she guessed, keeping an eye on everything. By now, the creatures of darkness had surely seen Amélie's people on the hill across the lake, but they seemed content to ignore them, safe within their dome.

About the only place Amélie didn't see movement was the Aquatic Quarter. "The aquatics managed to get out, that night," the Captain explained. "They have their passage back to Caymerdelphia. When I told them of the Baron's order— a quiet evacuation—they were gone in minutes. The eqmen too, considering how fast they can gallop."

"But not the little people," Amélie said quietly.

The Captain turned away. "I should have helped them. I should have known the eqmen wouldn't."

Amélie nodded slowly. "But then you would have been captured too, and enslaved. You couldn't have helped *me*."

"It was still wrong of me. Selfish."

Amélie nodded again, not disagreeing. "Well, we will help them now. Are you sure there's no way inside? No secret passage?"

The Captain straightened, all business once more. "There is, in fact. A secret way in and out of the capitol building—the Citadel—that we constructed for the Baron's use. I bet the Vizier doesn't even know about it."

Amélie started to get excited. "So..."

"It won't help us get inside the *dome*, just the Citadel, *after* we're inside the dome."

"Oh. Right." And she went back to studying the dome, confident that there must be a way in.

When all the tents were pitched, Nachton led a group to the east to chop down trees and collect rocks for more catapults. Cécilie moved among her eqmen, offering smiles and encouragement, spending a few minutes with each one. And Ewan mounted Squire to practice swordplay with Berserker, even teaching his moves to a few gnomen when they asked.

Amélie's siblings had changed since arriving in Overtwixt, in a positive way. When Nachton spoke, his words contained true wisdom, and he showed as much concern now for the good of others as he did for himself. Cécilie was less worried about what others thought of her and more focused on doing the right thing, no matter what. As for Ewan... on the surface, he was much the same as always: loud and energetic, apparently ready to win the coming battle all by himself. But down deep, he had changed too. His greatest hero in all the world, Nachton, had failed him; and his friend Shark—the Charlatan—had betrayed him. Even so, Ewan chose to continue trusting his brother, and he spoke constantly of his new friend the Jailer, confident he would become "a good guy" before the end. Amélie knew from experience that forgiving people was hard enough. But choosing to trust again, even when you knew how badly you might get hurt? That was really mature. Ewan was growing up too.

And what about Amélie? Had *she* changed at all?

Yes, actually.

When Nachton returned to camp at nightfall, Amélie called all three of her siblings to her tent. Nachton arrived with a wrapped package tucked under his arm, and he eagerly tried to show it to her, but she made him wait. There was something she needed to say first. Something she knew the Guide had wanted her to learn all along.

"I've been thinking a lot about this," she began. "My quest was to build trust, overcome prejudice, and unite the races. The Guide said this would be the most difficult of our quests, and he was right. He said oaths would need to be sworn; but so far, *no one* has sworn any oaths to me, aside from the Captain and his guardsmen."

"That won't last," Nachton encouraged her. "The peoples of Overtwixt will answer your call. I'm sure of it."

Amélie smiled at his enthusiasm. "Thank you, Nachton. I hope you're right. But..." She took a deep breath. "Wow, this is *not* easy to say," she added, looking at her siblings awkwardly. "But I think I misunderstood what the Guide meant about oaths. I assumed he was talking about the peoples of Overtwixt swearing to follow me, but now I realize that's wrong. He meant someone else would have to swear the oaths first."

Nachton stared at her. "You think he meant *us?* As in... Cécilie and Ewan and I have to swear oaths to you, like you're our master or something?" The idea clearly made him sick to his stomach. Even so, he slowly lowered himself to his knees. "Okay," he said levelly. "What are the words?"

Amélie was staring at *him* now. "What? No! That's not— It's... I wasn't saying that at all!" She blushed furiously. "*I* need to swear an oath to *you*." She pulled Nachton to his feet, then she got down on her knees herself.

Taking all three siblings' hands in her own, Amélie said, "I understand something now that I didn't before. Being your leader doesn't mean I'm always right, or that I get whatever I want. If anything, being a leader means giving up *what* I want for the good of my people. So..." She realized there were tears in her eyes. "I hereby vow to put your needs ahead of mine, to work for *your* good, and to sacrifice for my people if necessary. I vow to lead in love. Since selfishness is evil, I vow to live self*less*ly, so I can do *good*."

Nachton was grinning so big it looked like his face would split in two. He pulled Amélie onto her feet and into his arms, and then Cécilie and Ewan joined them in a fierce hug. The little boy's arms were surprisingly strong for someone so tiny, who wasn't even wearing a strength amulet.

"Now," Nachton announced, "if we're finished with all these distractions, I've got a gift for you, Empress." He handed her the package he'd been holding, but then pulled the string to untie it himself. Folded bunches of deep purple fabric tumbled free.

"What's this?" Amélie asked in wonder.

"Something I've had the Seamstress working on," he explained. The little gnolady was one of the people who'd been smoked at Hucentia, then rescued from Gaoland along with Ewan. Nachton gestured to the purple fabric. "Something you'll need if you hope to complete your quest."

Amélie just looked at him, not understanding.

"It's your *banner*, sis. You're not just supposed to unite the races of Overtwixt, Amélie. You're supposed to unite them *beneath your banner*." Nachton grinned big. "Well, now you have a banner. You're welcome."

Hands trembling, Amélie slowly unfolded the long stretch of fabric, laying it out on the floor of her tent. "The color..." she whispered. "It's so rich."

"Purple is the color of royalty," Nachton said.

"And this..." She brushed her fingers across the simple white embroidery at the center of the banner, a very large flower. "A daisy?"

"Close. It's an aster—the *flower* of royalty. Symbolic of wisdom, purity, and innocence."

Amélie looked up at her brother with more tears in her eyes. "I love it," she said.

"Where's *my* banner?" Cécilie demanded, but she was obviously joking. Everyone laughed.

"Your majesty!" the Captain called, voice recognizable even from outside the tent. "Empress, an army approaches!"

They hurried outside to see a parade of little people approaching from the south: nagmen and raimen and shamen and even more gnomen marching in rows, with the roundest potbellied raiman Amélie had ever seen marching at their head. "That's the Mystic himself!" Captain said. "I'm surprised he got free when the impmen left Shanagrailia. He must have rallied every single little person left in Nagland and Raibourne!"

Amélie was still smiling at their appearance when the Captain pointed a different direction and announced, "Look there! More of the Princess's people, coming from Eqland!" Sure enough, many of the missing eqmen and gnomen who'd fought at Hucentia were coming over the crest of a hill from the direction of Eqland, accompanied by the Ranger and Operative.

Leaping onto the Captain's back, Amélie galloped forward to greet the new arrivals. But before they even arrived, the Captain slowed to a stop, an amazed look on his usually stern face. "What's that?" he demanded. "Who's that behind them?" Amélie strained to see in the distance, but then the Captain turned and smiled.

"What is it?" Amélie asked.

"The rest of *my* people!" he said excitedly, and he was right. Fifty or more centmen trailed behind the procession of horses and unicorns. "They must have emptied out the Grove completely!"

When everyone arrived, Amélie greeted the Mystic and the Council of Centwick warmly. The evening turned festive as old friends were reunited and new friendships forged, and everyone helped the newcomers make camp. And Amélie's heart was happy when she lay down to sleep that night, surrounded by more than *seven hundred* allies.

Suddenly, defeating the Vizier on his own turf was looking much more doable.

· sixteen ·

(Amélie)

I n the morning, the Captain introduced Amélie to the
Volunteer (a centman not much older than Amélie
herself), newly recruited to fill the Scout's place in
her guard. Then it was down to business as all the
leaders began discussing the Capital City assault. For
an hour or more, Amélie, Nachton, and their friends
argued excitedly with the Mayor, the Mystic, and the
Council about the best way to breach the Vizier's
fortifications.

"There's no way around it," Nachton concluded
after a time. "We have to go through one of the gates.
But trying to get the South Gate open would be too
costly." He pointed across the lake to the city's obvious
front entrance, the huge South Gate. It was protected
by a portcullis, a strong grid of iron bars that could be
raised or lowered. "The defenders can easily shoot
arrows through the portcullis at anyone who
approaches."

"Can't we just use the catapults to beat the gate
down?" one of the centman Councilmembers asked.

"No more easily than we can beat the *wall* down,"
the gnoman Engineer replied softly. "That wall is twenty
spans thick at its base, and reinforced around the gates."

"Could some of the slaves help us?" Squire asked. "Maybe they could unlock the gate from the inside?"

The Operative was shaking his head. "I spent half the night sneaking close, then watching through that gate. The slaves are shackled hand and foot, and chained all together like they were at Eqland. Plus they've been badly mistreated. Even if they got free, they're in no shape to fight their way to the gate. Especially without weapons!"

The Mystic cleared his throat. "He among us who is capable must utilize what ingress exists," the raiman said cryptically, slowly turning the glowing bracelet he wore on his right foreleg—one of Sovereign's Relics, obviously. "That he, in turn, might grant access to those *in*capable."

Everyone stared at the little creature, trying to figure out what he meant. The Captain had warned Amélie about the tendency of raimen to speak in riddles, but...

"You're saying we should find someone who can climb that wall," the Ranger asked, "so they can sneak inside through one of the unfinished holes in the dome? Then *that* person can unlock the front gate?"

The Mystic nodded seriously.

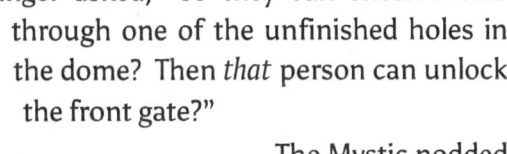

"Forgive me, your eminence," the Engineer said with great respect, "but that won't work either. Not at the South Gate. That portcullis is heavy; it'll require a dozen or more gnomen, working together, to raise the gate."

"Is me, then!" Berserker said with a smile. "I climb wall, I raise gate!"

The Engineer eyed him doubtfully. "Assuming you can climb, that might work... if we had three of you. Yes, the gate is that heavy. Either way, it's more people than we can probably sneak in through a hole in the wall."

"What about the East Gate?" Nachton asked, looking at the Operative.

"It's barely even a gate," the dark-skinned centman said. "More like a big doorway, hidden in that copse of trees over there." Everyone looked, but no one pointed, in case the bad guys were watching.

"So maybe we can use the catapult on this smaller gate?" the same Councilmember asked hopefully.

The Captain shook his head. "No room to maneuver the equipment through the trees."

"Could a single person open *that* gate from the inside?" Nachton asked, a gleam in his eye.

The Operative shrugged. "I guess so. But I couldn't see inside that gate. I don't know how heavy the barricades are."

"He among us who is capable must utilize what ingress exists," the Mystic repeated, as if he hadn't said the same exact thing just a minute ago. "That he, in turn, might grant access to some chosen elect. And *they*, in turn, to the entire assemblage."

The Ranger translated: "Someone goes through a gap in the dome and opens the *East* Gate, letting a small strike force within the walls? Then *they* fight their way to the front, raise the portcullis together, and defend the gatehouse long enough for the main army to get inside?"

Again the Mystic nodded.

"But again, who is capable of such a climb?" another of the centman Councilmembers asked.

"Is me! Is me!" Berserker repeated.

"And where on that wall," the centwoman went on, "could even a *gnoman* climb up without being seen? Much less a lugman?"

"Could we climb at night?" Ranger suggested.

"Too dangerous—"

And so the discussion continued. More than once, Amélie or Nachton called for silence, then asked the Guide aloud for assistance. But for the first time since meeting him, the Guide did not appear when called. Yet he had hinted he would be with them anyway, even if they couldn't see him. So the Ollivaros kids endeavored to do what he'd told them: remembering the lessons they'd learned, trusting in each other, and relying upon the magic of Sovereign's Relics to grant wisdom—not just Nachton's spectacles, but also the Mystic's bracelet and the pendant worn by the ancient centman Councilmember.

Eventually, Amélie ended the discussion with the other leaders. "These are all good suggestions," she said, though she had yet to hear an idea that wasn't terribly risky. "We must wait for the rest of our allies before finalizing our plans, however."

"The rest of our allies?" the Mayor asked, confused.

"Yes," she replied. "From Caymerdelphia."

No one said anything for a long moment. "Your majesty," the Captain finally said, gently. "If they're not here by now, they may not be coming."

"How would they even get to this niland?" the Mayor asked awkwardly. "And even if they could get here, how would they help? I mean... not to be rude, but... they're *aquatics*, and this will be a land-based assault."

Amélie met the eyes of all the other leaders, one after another. "They have a way. I don't understand the details, but the Captain assures me their passage even connects to the Aquatic Quarter inside the city—or at least it used to. Perhaps *they* can get us inside."

Everyone shifted uncomfortably. "Why would they help us?" the Crafter asked finally. "None of their people is at risk."

Amélie licked her lips. "I don't know," she answered honestly. "All I know is that I'm supposed to unite *all* the peoples under my banner. I can't do much about the creatures of darkness... yet... but what I *can* do is give the Caymerdelphians a chance to join us in ridding Overtwixt of this evil. I will wait as long as I possibly can. The aquatic peoples must be represented."

The wizened old centman from the Council of Centwick gave her a look that said he approved. No one else seemed to, but Amélie remained firm. Calling an end to their meeting for now, she suggested that everyone begin preparing weapons and armor for the assault. If and when an opportunity presented itself, Amélie wanted her coalition ready to fight. Besides, there was always a chance the enemy would attack if they thought Amélie's forces were unprepared.

Fortunately, Amélie didn't have to wait much longer. Just before midday, the water at the center of the lake began bubbling. A whirlpool formed, spinning faster and faster, and shapes began to appear—rising up and out of the vortex, rather than draining down into it. Those shapes were *people*: delphmen and dagmen and merpeople, and even a few caymen too.

"Your majesty!" someone cried, and Amélie hurried to the lakeshore to greet a familiar-looking delphwoman.

"Hostess," Amélie cried delightedly, recognizing the woman who had first welcomed her to Caymerdelphia. It seemed so very long ago. "Is that you?"

"Yes, your majesty!"

"You came! But... *how?*" Even knowing there was some sort of underwater passage to Caymerdelphia, Amélie couldn't understand how it connected—invisibly, apparently—to an entirely different niland.

It was a pair of dagmen who answered, and Amélie thought she recognized *them* from her arrival in Caymerdelphia too. "We gots our very own bridge 'tween Twixt and home, ain't we?"

"It's a waterspout," the Hostess explained, "spun up by a set of turbines the mermen built with the help of the gnomen, long ago. We can turn it on and off as needed."

Now Amélie recognized other figures swimming toward her at a more respectable pace, members of the Committee of Eleven. She took a deep breath, preparing to welcome them formally—but before she had a chance to speak, she was interrupted by the sound of a booming voice. A voice that seemed to come from all around, and from right next to her as well. A voice that could only belong to one person:

The Vizier.

· seventeen ·

(Nachton)

"**Y**ou think you've amassed quite the army, don't you, little Empress?" the Vizier boomed. He was nowhere in sight, but just like when Nachton faced him at the Archives, his voice seemed to come from everywhere at once.

Neat trick, that.

Nachton stared at Capital City, eyes searching. "There!" he told Amélie, pointing. In the middle of one of the gaps in the dome was a group of shapes—two hulking drachmen flapping their wings to stay in place, and in between, a slender human figure standing on a platform held up by a bunch of flying imps. The Vizier, obviously.

"*Oh, little Empress, little Empress,*" the Vizier's voice mocked her with an obvious sneer. "*How gravely mistaken you are.*"

"Is that the Warlord and the Jailer with him?" Amélie whispered. "I thought we left the Jailer in a cell on Gaoland."

"We did," the Captain replied. "That other drachman must be the Blackguard. She swore herself to the Vizier long ago as his personal bodyguard, but he usually doesn't let her serve in that capacity." He smiled just a little. "If she's at his side now, it means he's scared."

The Vizier was still talking. *"You think you can undo, in a matter of weeks, what I've spent decades planning and achieving?"* The villain laughed easily. *"You cannot take this triumph away from me!"*

"You're the one who's mistaken," Amélie responded loudly—but the Vizier just kept talking, giving no sign he heard her. Of course. *His* voice was booming across the entire niland, while she still spoke normally.

"Hold up," Nachton said as the Vizier continued ranting, obviously trying to discourage the army arrayed against him. "Let me try something." Squinting, Nachton studied the dome and the flows of magic barely visible in the air between here and there. Weaving a variation of that same spell, he turned to Amélie and smiled. "Try now."

"Fight me, and you will wish *for death before the week is out,"* the Vizier was saying, *"but I will not grant it. This is* my *empire, little Empress, not yours—"*

"And yet *I* was named Empress," Amélie interrupted, her own voice now amplified across the distance between them. She smiled gratefully at Nachton. "Whereas *you* were named Vizier, advisor. You rise above your station."

It took the Vizier a moment to respond; he was obviously surprised to hear her talking back. *"How dare you,"* he snarled. *"I am Emperor, ruler of—"*

"You obviously don't know what it means to be a ruler," Amélie shot back. "A good ruler wishes to serve his people, not be served *by* them. Maybe this *is* my empire, but I do not want it for myself. I want it for my people."

Before the Vizier could seize control of the conversation once more, Nachton wove a flow of blue magic to protect and preserve Amélie's voice, making interruption impossible.

"As soon as I win this empire back from you," Amélie went on, "I will lead the peoples of the realm in rebuilding all you destroyed, so that I can step down and return home to my real world. Then this place can go back to the way it was before you got here."

Nachton released his second spell, letting the Vizier break in finally. "—*nothing but a little girl. You think taking anything away from me will be that easy!?*"

"Look around," Amélie said. "You've already lost the nilands of the realm. This city is all you have left."

The Vizier burst into crazed laughter. "*I care nothing for those nilands, or the pathetic creatures left on them. They were only a means to an end.*" Nachton frowned in surprise. "*THIS was always going to be my crowning achievement,*" the Vizier crowed, and despite the distance, Nachton could see the villain gesturing at the domed city around him. "*When this dome is complete, even the Sovereign won't be able to get in! And none of my slaves will ever get out, either! I will make* this *the place where the dead respawn—not Gaoland—and then I will reign here forever, immortal and invincible.*"

Amélie's nose wrinkled in disgust, but Nachton finally understood. This *had* always been the Vizier's plan. To build this city and populate it with people to serve him... then enclose it entirely so no one could come or go. This was the ultimate goal behind everything he'd done, both before and after the Baron confronted him. Even the Vizier's study of magic had been about defeating the Fifth Fundamental Law so he could stay in Overtwixt forever.

"*So I offer you a choice,*" the Vizier concluded. "*Run away now, and escape my wrath. I'm on a tight schedule to complete this dome, so I haven't the manpower to chase you off. Yet.*"

"We will never run!" Amélie replied forcefully. "Not as long as you hold anyone inside that city against their will."

"So be it. When my allies arrive from Gaoland—including the phomen and everyone else you thought defeated before—we will meet you on the field of battle... and utterly overwhelm you."

Amélie hesitated, looking concerned. Her encounters with the phomen had been terrifying, Nachton knew. The Vizier's attempt to discourage her was beginning to work.

Weaving a spell for himself, Nachton spoke up quickly. "No one is coming from Gaoland to help you, Vizier. We left all the cells locked, and *we* still have the keys." He glanced at Ewan, who proudly held up the Jailer's big keyring, which he always carried with him these days. "I studied the magic you poured into building that place," Nachton went on. "Very impressive, and not easily defeated. I should think it would hold even *you*, given the chance. So unless you happen to have a spare set of keys, I don't think any of your allies will be getting out soon."

The Vizier chuckled genuinely. *"Do I look like a fool to you? Of course I had a spare set of keys."*

Nachton blanched. Oh.

"And I sent those keys back to Gaoland days ago with several of my most trusted Soldiers. By now, everyone has surely been released, and they're all flying back to me here—the Inquisitor, the Enforcer, the Jailer, and every single Soldier, Spy, and Messenger you thought defeated before. They will be here within the day," the Vizier cackled gleefully. *"So I repeat: If you wish to live, run now."*

Amélie gave Nachton a grim look, and he wished he hadn't opened his big mouth. "We shall see," she answered the villain finally. She made a cutting motion with her hand, and Nachton released the magic amplifying their voices. "Are we private?" she asked. "Good."

The Vizier continued ranting... but as Nachton looked around at all the faces of their allies, he realized they were not discouraged by the villain's tactics. Rather than listening to him, they had their eyes focused on Amélie, their leader.

Amélie turned to face a half circle of individuals treading water—the Committee of Eleven, if Nachton had to guess. "I see you've finally built a true coalition," a merman said. "You are united now, even within your own family."

The Empress nodded solemnly.

"What's more," an ancient centman spoke up from nearby, "she finally understands her mission from the Guide." The centman's eyes glittered almost as brilliantly as the Diamond hanging from a circlet around his forehead, obviously one of Sovereign's Relics. "You heard her yourself: she knows what it means to be a real leader."

This brought a smile to Amélie's lips.

One of the caymen spoke to Nachton. "*Does* she lead you now? Even you, her elder?"

Nachton glanced at his sister and smiled genuinely. "Yes, even me. She and I both understand our roles now. And I can honestly say I would follow this kind of leader anywhere... even if she *is* my kid sister."

Amélie's eyes grew misty, and several people chuckled.

"Good," the merman Committee member said. "I see you've even acquired the King's scepter, which must make for quite a tale all by itself." A tale Nachton was *still* waiting to hear; the right moment just hadn't come yet. "Now," the merman concluded, "there is only one thing you lack."

Amélie gave a little start. "What?"

"Compassion," the merman said gravely.

Amélie may have matured greatly these last few weeks, but she was still Amélie. She immediately started arguing. "But I *am* compassionate!"

"So compassionate as to put the needs of other people *completely* above your own? To sacrifice yourself *wholeheartedly*, for the good of your followers? To be utterly and entirely selfless?"

Amélie goggled at the merman, and Nachton did too. No one was that selfless. Nachton wasn't sure he *wanted* his sister being that selfless!

"Tsk, tsk," a delphwoman chided the merman. "Selflessness of that sort is impossible for mere mortals."

"And yet she must demonstrate it all the same," the merman argued back. "If she's to lead us, even for a short time, she must be selfless beyond her own capacity."

"And she will be," the delphwoman answered, "but only with Sovereign's assistance."

The merman heaved a sigh but nodded. Turning back to Amélie, he said, "Step forward, your majesty. And kneel, please, so I can reach you."

· eighteen ·
(Cécilie)

Cécilie watched in fascination as a bewildered Amélie complied with the merman's strange request. The Empress was soon kneeling in the shallow water, her elegant gown billowing around her.

The merman brought his hands above the surface, and in them was a glowing blue crown. "I bestow upon you the Diamond Crown of Compassion," he told Amélie simply. "May the selfless love of the Sovereign guide your leadership, this day and all days, so long as you serve this realm as Empress."

He placed the Crown on Amélie's head, and it pulsed once... then kept right on glowing.

"That Crown!" Nachton gasped quietly from beside Cécilie. "It's the last of the Relics gifted by Sovereign to the human race! I *knew* there must be four of them, but I never found any reference to this last one." Cécilie's older brother wasn't even looking at her as he spoke, and she realized he was mostly muttering to himself in wonder. "All the books talked about was the Plate-Armor of

Assurance, the Great-Sword of Justice, and the Lens of Discernment. But this makes sense! Two Combat Relics: the Armor for protection and the Sword for correction; and two Command Relics: the Lens for wisdom and the Crown for humility. The powers they bestow are balanced."

"Right," Cécilie agreed, though she didn't have a clue what he was talking about. "The powers they bestow are balanced. Exactly."

"But where did you get that?" Nachton demanded, addressing his question to the aquatic Committee members as if he didn't even hear Cécilie.

A cayman rolled on his side to eye Nachton. "Caymerdelphia has safeguarded the Crown for millennia, ever since the time of the ancient King of Caymerlot—who was a friend to your ancient Knight, if I recall."

"But it's a Relic for humen," Nachton argued. "You're not saying your ancient King was *human*, are you?"

The cayman laughed. "No, no, of course not. He was dagman... which I suppose is even harder to believe," he added in a mutter. "Be that as it may, this Crown was gifted to the King by his friend the Knight. All peoples of the realm chose to follow the King, and so they all gifted him their Relics of Rulership. The King was surely unable to wield their power, but the gesture was meaningful nonetheless. For someday, an heir of that ancient King of Caymerlot—a *new* King—will come to reunite these lands once more. Not with violence, as the Vizier has done, but with love. And ultimately it will be this future King—not the Vizier, and not even your majesty the Empress—who will be called Ruler over all Rulers."

Ironically, it was a nearby dagman who chose that moment to produce a rude sound with his fish-like lips. He gestured impatiently for the cayman to hurry up.

"Uh, forgive me," the Committee member said quickly. "I forgot where I was, and to whom I was speaking. You care not for such details. Regardless, that is why we have the Crown, and why we have the privilege—and responsibility— of presenting it to the Empress... if only for this short time of need."

Amélie nodded gravely. "Thank you, peoples of Caymerdelphia."

Everyone fell silent, and Cécilie realized the Vizier had finally stopped ranting in the background. The bad guy must have finally figured out no one was listening anymore.

She spoke up hesitantly. "What now? The phomen..." Cécilie couldn't help but shiver at the very thought of them. "The Vizier said they'll be here *today*."

"We need to attack before that happens," the Captain agreed grimly.

"But how?" Nachton asked.

Amélie eyed the Caymerdelphians. "Is it true your underwater passages connect to the Aquatic Quarter, inside the dome?"

Several of the Committee of Eleven looked toward a delphman floating nearby. "I checked," the young man said. "The old passages are all sealed. There's no way back into the Quarter." He hesitated. "I *did* feel water moving through a smaller duct beneath the city, however. I think it feeds one or more of the wells."

"Of course!" Nachton said excitedly. "Even if the Vizier closed off your passages, he would still want fresh water for drinking."

"This duct..." one of the centman Councilmembers said musingly. "Is it big enough to admit a person?"

The Mystic cleared his throat. "He who is capable—"

"We want to sneak someone inside," the Ranger explained hurriedly, with an apologetic look at the raiman. "In order to unlock the East Gate for us."

The delphman looked uncertain. "I don't know. It would have to be someone very small *and* very brave. A gnoman, perhaps, or..."

All eyes turned to Ewan, who was playing with two of the skeleton keys from the Jailer's keyring and speaking excitedly under his breath, narrating an epic swordfight between the keys. He was wearing his Armor again, which Cécilie had returned to him after the prison break. Better yet, it was glowing bright blue now too.

Amélie sucked in a breath to object, then caught herself and nodded. "Why not?" she said. "Now that we know why it wasn't working the last time, Ewan should be practically invincible in his Diamond Armor."

"Except..." A merman spoke up uncomfortably. "He, um, can't wear Armor underwater. He'd sink like a rock."

Ewan was paying attention now, the keys forgotten. "I go swimming?" he exclaimed gleefully, then immediately began tearing off pieces of glittering Armor.

"Now just hold on a second," Amélie objected.

"It okay, Ommie. Sessy can wear it!"

Nachton ignored Ewan. "What if we entrust the Armor to the strike team waiting at the East Gate? When Ewan lets them in, he can put it back on then."

"And go with them to open up the South Gate?" Amélie asked thoughtfully. "Maybe."

"What about me?" Cécilie asked. "Obviously you two are leading the battle from the front. But what will *I* do?"

Nachton and Amélie both looked stricken for a moment, and Cécilie realized neither of them had given any thought to how *she* would contribute in this battle. "You can, uh, help coordinate from the rear," Nachton said finally. "Where it's safe."

"I want to lead the strike team through the East Gate," Cécilie said with fierce determination.

"Out of the question," Amélie objected. "It's too dangerous."

Cécilie folded her arms and huffed.

"I want Sessy wear the Armor!" Ewan repeated. "For da whole battle! Then she be safe."

"And how will *you* stay safe?" Amélie demanded. Cécilie opened her mouth to argue—but to her surprise, Amélie held up a hand and disagreed with *herself*. "I'm being selfish again, aren't I?" she said quietly. "I promised to be a leader who sacrifices for my people, putting their needs ahead of mine. But I'm hardly doing that if I let everyone else take risks that I won't even let my own siblings take."

Cécilie blinked. She was used to Amélie being selfish, but she didn't understand how wanting Ewan safe was selfish. Still, Nachton was nodding.

"Besides, nowhere in this battle will truly be safe," Amélie continued slowly, "and I have no right to hold back my loved ones from danger. Not when the Guide has entrusted them with leadership too." She took a deep breath. "Very well, Cécilie, you can lead the strike team waiting at the East Gate." Cécilie grinned big. "Your strike team will consist of Squire, Wrangler, Crafter, and Engineer—and Handmaiden, obviously. Your eminence," Amélie added to the Mystic, "please pick out more of your people to join them, as many as the eqmen can carry. Along with a few who don't mind getting wet, to go with Ewan."

Several little people immediately raised their hands.

"When Ewan gets the door open, all of you will ride together to the South Gate, to get *it* open." Amélie eyed Engineer. "Will that be enough hands to raise the portcullis?"

The gnoman nodded excitedly.

"Then Nachton and I can lead the main army inside."

"And the Armor?" Nachton asked.

Amélie looked away, squeezing her eyes shut. "Let Ewan and Cécilie decide who wears it."

"Sessy wear it," Ewan said immediately, as he finished taking off the last piece.

Cécilie immediately began putting the Armor on herself again, piece by piece. "What will we do once our whole army's inside?" she asked her sister.

"We fight our way to the Vizier," Amélie said solemnly, "and we capture him."

"The Vizier will never surrender," the Captain said.

"We have to capture him anyway," Nachton said. "We *have* to. We can't just smoke him, or else he'll end up back in Gaoland. I know he said he called back all of his troops from there, but I bet he left at least *one* minion to let him out of his cell, just in case he falls in battle today. And if that happens, we're back where we started."

The Captain looked uncomfortable. "But how, exactly, does one capture the *Vizier?*"

"I honestly don't know," Nachton admitted. Everyone fell quiet as they pondered the question.

Cécilie finished with the Armor, then gave a little twirl to get a look at her reflection in the surface of the lake. When she'd donned the Armor last time—just before the assault on Gaoland—it had been dark, and the glow of the Diamond had been blinding. This time, she noticed that the Diamond Armor looked a little different on her than it did on Ewan, almost like it adapted to the wearer. That shouldn't have surprised her; she already knew it changed magically in order to fit the size of the wearer, considering that Cécilie was three years older and a few inches taller than Ewan. But even the *style* of the Armor had changed subtly to fit her, becoming more graceful and feminine on her body.

"I don't know how we'll capture the Vizier yet either," Amélie admitted finally. "But we *can* do it," she added firmly, "if we work together." She looked intently at Nachton, and Cécilie knew she was thinking about the night when he forced that first disastrous confrontation with the Vizier.

Nachton and Cécilie nodded. Ewan shrugged.

"Captain," Amélie said, looking around. "And the rest of you—our other allies—we would welcome anyone's assistance when we finally face the Vizier. But ultimately, my family has to remember and rely upon what the Guide told us all those weeks ago, when we first arrived in Overtwixt."

"Only the four of us humen," Nachton remembered, "working *together*, are capable of ending the Vizier's reign of terror."

"Exactly," Amélie agreed.

"Okay," Nachton said, clapping his hands together. Ewan and Cécilie looked at each other, smiling, and Amélie nodded with determination. "Let's do this thing."

· nineteen ·
(Ewan)

Ewan took a big breath, stuck his head underwater, and stared at the girl floating next to him. Her top half looked *normal*, like maybe one of Ommie's friends back home. But her bottom half looked like a *fish*.

The whole time Ewan stared at her, the girl stared right back at him, eyes big. Finally, Ewan went up to get some air.

"So *weird*," the mermay girl said.

"Yeah, so weed!" Ewan agreed loudly.

Standing on shore wearing her new Crown, Ommie asked, "You remember what you need to do?"

"Youbetchaaa!" Ewan bellowed loudly, and all the little no-man dudes and mermays in the water with him agreed too. Ewan turned to look at the big dome city, but he couldn't see it from here. That's 'cause Nock made them get in the water where the bad guys couldn't see *them*, so they wouldn't know they were coming.

"Very well," Ommie said. "May the Sovereign protect you all." Man, she really did sound like a queen-lady.

Ewan's new mermay friend giggled and grabbed his hands. "You ready?" she whispered.

Ewan sucked in a huuuge breath, then nodded.

The girl hugged him and pulled him underwater with her. Ewan kept his eyes open, but the water around him got dark *quick*. They were moving so fast! He couldn't see much except shapes all around, and the mermay's tail kept beating against his feet with powerful strokes.

Ewan knew he was gonna have to hold his breath a long time, but even so, it seemed like a *really* long time before his head finally came up again. He sucked in a *huuuuuuge* breath this time and started coughing. Ewan could hear the no-dudes doing the same thing around him, but he couldn't see them; it was completely black now.

"Sorry," the mermay girl told him, even though she giggled again. "Catch your breath. The second half is gonna be even longer."

"Where we be?" Ewan sputtered.

"In a trapped pocket of air beneath Capital City," she whispered. "Near the old entrance to the Aquatic Quarter. The wellwater ducts are nearby."

"Okey doke," Ewan said, even though he was starting to get scared. The rest of the trip would take *longer*?

"If you're ready, we'll go then," the girl said. "Keep your arms around me and your legs straight. It's gonna get tight. Big breath now!"

Ewan sucked in another big breath, and then they were underwater again. Almost immediately, Ewan felt walls close in around him. Even though the mermay said not to, he reached out a hand and scraped it on a wall. Wow! Now he understood why the mermay *kids* were swimming them inside; the adult mermays couldn't fit through here any better than Nock or Ommie!

Ewan's mermay was moving super-fast like before, but it started feeling like she was barely moving, even though it was fast enough to keep scraping his hands and back on the walls. It felt like they were inside the tunnel *forever.*

Just when Ewan thought his lungs would *splode*, he saw light again, and his head popped out of the water. He started coughing really loud, but the girl put a hand over his mouth. "Shhh. There could be bad guys."

Ewan tried to cough more quietly. It didn't work.

They were at the bottom of a long brick tube now, with a bucket hanging nearby from the end of a rope. There were also ladder rungs in the side of the brick tube, going all the way to the top—beyond which, Ewan could see the sky through a hole in the dome ceiling far above.

All three of the no-dudes came up in the water around him, coughing too. When they could breathe normally again, they said thanks to their new mermay friends, flashed grins at Ewan, and started up the ladder. Ewan gave the mermay girl a big hug, blushed furiously when she planted a kiss on his cheek, then followed.

Two of the no-dudes had reached the top and gone over the side when a harsh voice yelled. "*Halt! Stop in the name of the Emperor!*"

"*Escaped slaves!*" another cried. "*How'd you get out of your chains?*"

"*They ain't* slaves, *you fool!*" the first voice yelled back. "*They's part of the little Empress's army!*"

"*But how'd they get* here?"

"*Who cares? Attack!*"

The last no-man looked down at Ewan with big eyes. "Stay here," he hissed. "We'll draw them off. Wait 'til it gets quiet before you come up. Remember, the East Gate!" Then he pulled a slingshot out of his pocket and was gone.

And just like that, Ewan was all alone, his heart thumping. He listened to the whizzing of slingshots and the whistle of swords in the air, yells of anger and cries of pain, then finally footsteps running... until everything went quiet. And he never moved a muscle.

Finally, he forced himself the rest of the way up the ladder, peeking over the edge of the well. There were really-white buildings all around him, with green vine plants coming out of the windows, but there were no people. Moving quickly, he climbed out, then threw himself behind some vines to hide.

Why was he so scared all of a sudden? He was the Knight—he was a hero! He'd never been scared in Overchix before! Except that time with the Vizier. And the time before that, with War-Dwagon Dude. And the time before *that*, when they first got to Overchix. That was like barely never at all. Ewan Ollivaros didn't get scared!

Well, he was scared now. Terrified. Because he was alone, and he didn't have his Armor, and he didn't have his lucky necklace. And *now* he knew how bad hurting could really hurt.

But Nock and Ommie were counting on him. So he clenched his fists, took another huuuge breath, and forced himself out of his hiding place.

Then, heart still beating fast, he picked a direction and started sneaking along the wall, hoping desperately he was going toward the East Gate.

· twenty ·

(Amélie)

The banner of Amélie Ollivaros, Empress of Overtwixt, flapped gloriously in the wind. Sewn from the deepest purple fabric, with an immense white flower embroidered at its center, the banner was *long*—stretching back almost twenty feet from its pole, which the Ranger was holding.

United beneath that banner, the races of Overtwixt stood facing Capital City. More than seven hundred humen, centmen, eqmen, gnomen, shamen, nagmen, and raimen—along with a single hulking lugman—formed the bulk of Amélie's army, which spread across three hills. Beside them in the lake, several hundred more delphmen, mermen, caymen, and dagmen floated in eager readiness, prepared to participate in the coming attack however they were able.

It didn't really matter that the attack was just a diversion, a way of distracting the bad guys inside so that Ewan and his gnomen friends could sneak to the East Gate more easily. It was still absolutely critical to Amélie's battle plan.

"It's time, your majesty," the Captain said quietly at her side. "Give the order."

Across the entire landscape, nothing moved except that banner. This was the calm before the storm. Once Amélie gave the order to attack, nothing would *stop* moving until the Vizier was defeated... or Amélie and her siblings were defeated instead.

So she didn't give the order, not immediately. Instead, she took a moment to look around at the coalition she had created among *all twelve* of the oppressed races of this realm. This was what she'd been working toward since the day she entered Overtwixt, and here, finally, she was close to completing her mission. Her excitement at the prospect of finally going home, finally seeing Mom and Dad again, was almost more than she could contain. But beyond that, she was impressed with herself at what she'd managed to accomplish. Staring at the assembled armies—who had sworn to follow *her*—she felt a flash of pride.

And in the next moment, she felt an overwhelming sense of humility. These people were looking to *her* to lead them. To use their service for the greater good, making each and every decision with wisdom and humility. Looking at her followers through sudden tears, Amélie loved them, and she swore to herself—again—that she would safeguard their lives to the best of her ability, making *sure* their sacrifice mattered.

She gave the order.

· twenty-one ·
(Nachton)

As soon as the order came, Nachton's crews began loading their catapults with the massive stones they'd collected the day before. In the day and a half since their arrival, they had managed to build twelve of the big siege weapon contraptions. Now, as the centmen, gnomen, and nagmen finished ratcheting the baskets down, Nachton yelled, "Fire!"

The first round of huge stones crossed the short distance and struck the dome wall, sounding like thunderclaps when they hit. The hill they fired from was not the same one where they'd camped; Amélie had moved the armies closer as soon as Ewan and his friends swam away. The attacking force now stood at optimal catapult range, just far enough away that they didn't have to worry about return volleys of enemy arrows.

"Reload!" Nachton cried. "Reload and fire at will!"

This time, some of the stones struck the South Gate portcullis with a booming clang, but they caused no more damage than the stones that struck the dome. The wall around and over Capital City was just too thick.

Not that Nachton expected any different. The bombardment really was just a diversion, to draw the impmen here, allowing Ewan to move safely through the city. Except...

It wasn't working.

Sure, a handful of impman taskmasters had turned from their duties to watch, but they only laughed at Nachton's feeble efforts to beat down the wall. They weren't worried. This was just like Gaoland, when Nachton began his assault on the prison—except this time, his persistence would *not* pay off. It could take weeks of bombardment before he caused any real damage, and the bad guys knew that just as well as he did.

This was no good. Nachton needed the attention of every spook and imp focused on *him*, or else Ewan was going to be in big trouble.

Then he had an idea. If he couldn't *scare* them into attacking the catapults, why not enrage them?

"Hold!" he cried, and the rhythm of bombardment came to a ragged stop. The crews stared at him, surprised. "Aim for that gap in the wall there," Nachton yelled, pointing.

Now the crews *really* stared at him. "You want us to fire *into* the city?" someone asked, incredulous.

"I got family still lives there!" someone else yelled.

"I don't want you to fire just anywhere in the city," Nachton assured them. "I want you to fire through that gap specifically," he said, still pointing calmly at the big opening over the western side of the city, far from where Ewan or the slave workers were supposed to be.

Nachton could see some of his crewmembers running the numbers in their heads, calculating where the stones would fall, based on their knowledge of Capital City. And then they began to smile.

Working quickly, they adjusted their aim, ratcheted down the baskets, and reloaded.

"Fire at will!" Nachton yelled again.

And a dozen massive stones went soaring up toward the big gap in the dome. A few missed, hitting the wall, but most soared right through... and crashed with destructive force into the section of city known as the Slums.

Where the spooks and imps lived.

The taskmasters' laughter turned to screeches of rage, and without another moment's delay, they began flying from the city walls in droves. They zipped straight toward the siege equipment, pulling bows from their backs and preparing to fire arrows at Nachton's crews.

Their commanding officer, the drachman Warlord, appeared behind them—shouting for order, insisting they fall back. The impmen wouldn't listen. The catapult crews barely had time for one more volley before the Vizier's minions reached bow range, then started raining arrows down on Nachton's people.

It was way too many arrows for Nachton to think of blocking with individual blue globs of magic, like he'd done in the Gaoland assault. He only really had one option if he wanted to prevent a slaughter.

Summoning his strength, Nachton desperately wove a single magical shield to protect all twelve catapults, and more importantly, the people manning them. It sprang into existence just in time, a glowing blue dome of the sort he'd made before, but far larger—representing the single greatest outpouring of magic he'd ever attempted.

Hundreds of arrows struck and bounced off, even as Nachton's people flinched and gasped in relief. But Nachton

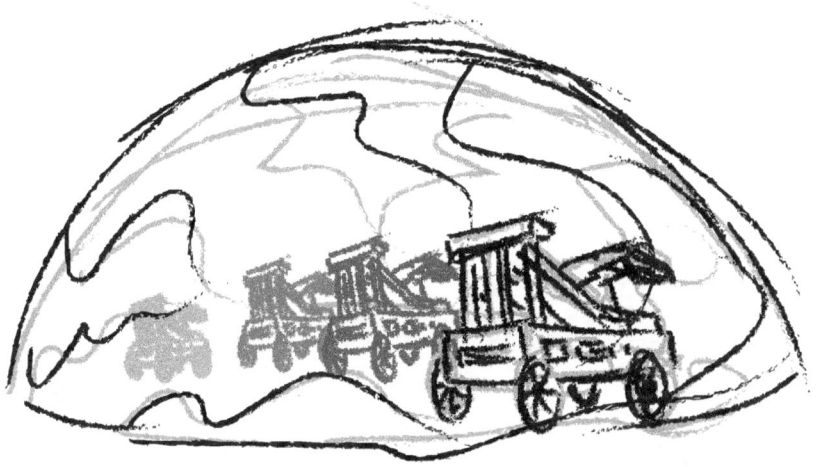

felt every one of those arrows chipping away at his flows of magic. He threw *more* effort into the weaving, exhausting himself... but also feeling strangely exhilarated. Somehow, he understood that his magic was being fueled now by his love for these comrades he barely knew, and also by the responsibility he felt for their safety. Sweat began pouring from his face, and his spectacles pulsed blue in time with the beating of his heart.

Furious at having their arrows blocked, the bad guys closed the rest of the distance between the city and the catapults. Putting away their bows, they landed and drew their swords, then began hacking at the outside of Nachton's blue shield.

"Form ranks!" Nachton called through clenched teeth. "Work together, and defend each other!" He gasped as he felt his shield starting to fail beneath the onslaught. "Focus more on protecting your allies than attacking your enemies. Let them come to us!"

And with that, he dropped the shield... then collapsed to the ground himself.

· twenty-two ·

(Ewan)

Ewan was lost. Nock and Ommie had showed him a map before he went swimming, but he didn't really pay attention. He thought the no-guys were gonna be with him!

Now he was wandering around part of the city with old wooden buildings. The buildings were stinky and *goss*, with peeling paint, and they looked ready to fall over. He knew he was in the wrong place, that the East Gate was close to the pretty white *stone* buildings, but... he wasn't really sure how he got here, or how to get back.

Then he heard whistling, getting louder fast, and he hid inside a hut. Ewan wished *he* could whistle like that. But who was making that sound? A bad guy? They must have the biggest lungs in the unee-verse, 'cause—

The hut across the street *sploded*, and then the hut *next* to that hut sploded too! Even the hut Ewan was inside started shaking, and he ducked down, covering his head. Slowly, he stood up again. The whistling had stopped. When he looked across the street, he saw something mixed in with the rubble: a big boulder-rock, bigger than he was!

Whoa. Did *Nock* do that?

Ewan was getting ready to leave the hut when he heard another noise, the sound of wings flapping, getting louder.

Suddenly, bunches and bunches of little spooky bats came flying around the corner. They looked lots like Shark, except most of them were bigger. And they were *mad*. Their fangs and claws and red eyes flashed as they screeched, "Our homes! They're destroying our homes!"

"Let's get 'em!"

"No!" a raspy voice called. He sounded really in-charge, like Dad when he got mad. "Pull it together. Fall in for inspection!"

The bat critters hissed and complained, but they obeyed. Eyes wide, Ewan stumbled back from the open window just before three of them landed on the edge of the roof—hanging upside down, of course.

"You think you're just gonna fly out of here and attack the Empress's army, is that it?" the in-charge bat went on.

"Yes!" they screamed. There had to be, um, *lots* of the little guys, and they were hanging on every roof edge Ewan could see. *Definitely* more bats than Ewan could count.

"Wrong!" the leader shouted. "Don't you see that's what the little Empress wants? Why do you think they attacked our homes?" That raspy voice... it sounded so familiar.

"Then what are we supposed to do?" one of the bats in Ewan's window asked. He was looking the other direction, but if he turned even just a little, he would see Ewan.

"We inspect the dome for damage," the leader said.

"*What!?*" the bats screeched back, the ones in Ewan's window especially.

The leader appeared in Ewan's window suddenly, swooping down to face the loudest complainer nose-to-nose, flapping to keep himself in air. It was Shark! *"Fool,"* Shark rasped. "What is most important to the Vizier?"

"The dome," the bat mumbled.

"The dome," Shark agreed. And then he looked straight past the other guy and saw Ewan—and his eyes got really big.

For a *looong* time, Ewan and Shark stared at each other, and Ewan knew he was in super-big trouble.

Then Shark started shrieking orders. "To the dome! I want every inch of it inspected for damage. Use your chalk and mark even the smallest crack. To the dome, I say! Fly, *fly*, double-time!"

Heart pounding, Ewan watched the bad guys leap into air again, then disappear from view. He waited, and waited, and—

"It's safe now, human." Shark reappeared, landing upside down on the roof edge and facing him.

The two of them studied each other for a long time, like they didn't know what to say. Last time Ewan saw Shark, it really seemed like he was friends with the Vizier too, like he was a *bad* guy. But if Shark was a bad guy, why didn't he tell the other spooks about Ewan just now?

"I'm sorry," Shark rasped finally. "About last time we spoke."

"So... you my fwend again?"

Shark scowled. "I have always been your friend. And you are mine. As I promised, when first we met."

Ewan couldn't help it. He started smiling. "You was never a bad guy at all!"

Shark's scowl disappeared, and he flashed his glistening fangs in a smile of his own. "I'm an actor—the preeminent performer in my world, before the Vizier trapped me here with everyone else." He shrugged. "It's my *job* to pretend to be someone I'm not."

"You really good! Everyone thought you a bad guy pretenning be a good guy. But you a *good* guy 'tenning to be a *bad* guy!"

"I think I deserve a little more credit than that," Shark said, puffing out his tiny chest. "At one point, I was a good guy pretending to be a bad guy who went undercover as a good guy to betray the other good guys *to* the bad guy..." He trailed off at Ewan's look of confusion. "Never mind. But..." He gazed at Ewan earnestly. "You believe me, right? I mean, it would be a wonder if anybody believed me ever again, so easily do I change roles."

"I believe you," Ewan said, just as earnestly.

The little bat heaved a sigh of relief. "So," he said, his voice even hoarser than usual. "Tell me the plan."

For just a second, Ewan wondered if that was a good idea. What if Shark really *was* a bad guy, just trying to trick Ewan? Then the little boy shrugged and decided to trust his friend. So he told Shark *everything*.

"The East Gate!" Shark exclaimed. "How'd you get way over here?"

"Um..."

"No matter. I know all the patrols between here and there. Follow me, and we'll get that gate open together. After that... there's something I really want to show you."

· twenty-three ·

(Cécilie)

Cécilie watched the battle from far away, trying really hard not to feel left out. This was what she asked for, wasn't it? To lead the strike team through the East Gate. But that was just it— she'd had to *ask* to participate. The Guide kept telling them they needed to be united, but no one except the eqmen had asked what Cécilie thought about *anything* since they rescued the prisoners from Gaoland.

Now, she was starting to wonder if Nachton and Amélie tricked her into leading the strike team. Her team had been hiding here in the trees for more than an hour now—Cécilie and Handmaiden and Squire and Wrangler, plus five more of the strongest eqmen in Overtwixt, each one carrying at least two gnomen. They were waiting for Ewan to open the East Gate and let them in, but it was taking way too long. What if Nachton and Amélie actually sent Ewan to the South Gate instead, and they were just trying to keep Cécilie safe in these woods?

She ground her teeth and stared across the lake at the armies under Amélie's banner. *Everyone* was fighting now. More impmen than she'd ever seen had swarmed out of the city, focused on Nachton's catapults especially, but attacking the rest of the armies also. Even so, the good guys were doing okay. Cécilie just wondered why the spooks weren't attacking too. If the spookmen ever joined the battle, things might get really bad for the good guys.

Was that why Nachton and Amélie were keeping her out of it? Even Ewan was trying to keep her safe, making her wear his Armor, though he was the one inside the city. This was so frustrating! Ever since she stopped wearing the amethyst necklace, everyone just treated her like a kid again!

For a very long moment, she seriously considered pulling out one of the Vizier's old amulets. She had them all in one of her saddle bags again, having taken them back from Scout on Pholand, after he stole them from her chambers on Eqland. Surely it wouldn't be *that* bad to use one for a little bit, today of all days. They needed all the help they could get! Just a few minutes wearing the strength amulet would let her kick open the East Gate all by herself! She wouldn't *need* to wait for Ewan. He might not be coming anyway!

Before she knew it, she was reaching for her saddle bag, her hand practically moving on its own—

And then Wrangler stepped up next to her. "I, uh, wanna let you know sumpin', yer highness." As always, he spoke awkwardly. If he were a human, Cécilie imagined he would be turning a big cowboy hat in his hands as he talked. "It's been an honor, a real honor, follerin' you into battle. Back on Gaoland, and here again today. Ain't no one I'd rather foller, that's all." Then he ducked his horse-like head and backed away again.

Cécilie felt a flush of pride and shame, all at the same time. Had she really been ready to do something she *knew* was wrong, just that quickly? And all because she let herself believe something that wasn't true? Nachton and Amélie *had* given her an important part to play. They wouldn't have sent Wrangler, Crafter, and Engineer with her otherwise—not to mention Squire! And the eqmen, her people, loved her even if she was just a kid.

"We will stay united," she whispered.

"Yes, your highness," Handmaiden agreed.

"And I will trust my family and friends," she decided. "I will trust Nachton's wisdom coming up with this plan, and I will trust Ewan to get that gate open for us, no matter how long it takes."

"Uh, about that, your highness..."

Cécilie looked up quickly. Sure enough, the tall and narrow doorway of the East Gate was now standing wide open—and little Ewan was standing there waving, a huge grin on his face.

"Yes! Let's go!" Cécilie called softly.

Ewan disappeared back inside the city. Handmaiden darted after him, followed by all seven of the other eqmen, moving single-file through the entrance as their gnoman riders held on tightly. Cécilie and Handmaiden were first through the doorway, but even so, Cécilie barely caught a glimpse of Ewan's blond head disappearing down a side street inside—going the wrong direction entirely!

"Ewan!" she hissed. "That's the wrong way! South Gate is *that* way." There was no answer.

Torn, Cécilie considered chasing after him. But if she didn't get the front gate open to let the rest of the army into the city too, everything would fall apart. Nachton and Amélie were trusting *her* to do that now.

"Squire!" she called. "Follow my brother! Everyone else, we gotta go to the South Gate. Be as quiet as you can!"

· twenty-four ·
(Amélie)

The battle was going surprisingly well, aside from the fact that it was meaningless. Amélie could hardly forget that, considering they were still locked out of the city. What was taking Ewan and Cécilie so long!?

At least it was only the imps her armies had to fight so far. Amélie was grateful she hadn't seen any of the spooks yet, and she was *really* grateful the phomen and others had yet to arrive from Gaoland. But that might change at any moment.

On the front lines, nagmen locked blades with impmen, defending themselves well despite the fact that impmen were so much taller. It helped that the gnomen behind them were firing slingshots over the nagmen's heads, stunning and sometimes blinding the bad guys so the nagmen could dart forward and create yellow smoke. The raimen weren't fighting much, but they dove willingly into danger to collect slingshot ammo for reuse—and while they were at it, demonstrated an uncanny ability to tangle themselves in the imps' legs.

Here and there, shamen fought with all manner of bizarre weapons—flinging daggers and throwing stars, spinning nunchucks or battle axes, even using lassos to grab hold of impmen just out of reach. From what Amélie had heard, none of them had the Weaponsmaster's skill, but they were all just as dexterous.

And a small army of dagmen had come out of the water to form an orderly square. Wielding tridents and nets, they pushed into the mass of impmen one step at a time—spearing the ones on the ground, and flinging nets over the ones who tried to fly away. They fought with surprising precision, considering what pranksters they were, though they *did* hurl insults at their enemies the whole time.

In the water, the battle raged just as viciously. At first, the imps had tried to ignore the aquatics stuck in the lake, knowing they offered no threat to the city. But then the delphmen had started spouting great jets of water from the blowholes on their heads, blinding and distracting the impmen with their spray—it was kinda like getting spit in your eye, after all! Then the merpeople were throwing grenades made of *glass*; when the volatile oil inside exploded, it created enough glassy shards to turn more than one bad guy to smoke. A contingent of impmen had finally turned to fight the aquatics over their own domain... which only brought them within reach of the caymen, who could heave themselves a surprising distance. Time and again, an imp would swoop low to attack a delphman or merman, and a cayman would explode out of the water, wrap his fins around the bad guy, then drag him below—never to be seen again.

And the lugman Berserker was glorious, standing all by himself in the midst of a horde of imps, halfway between Amélie and the portcullis. He was fighting the way he fought best: cudgel in one hand, half-unconscious imp acting as a shield in his other hand.

Meanwhile, centmen and eqmen led sorties past enemy lines in every direction, rearing up to pummel isolated imps with their forehooves. The centmen also fought with spears or longbows, the eqmen with their teeth.

Even Amélie's centman guards saw regular action. The Ranger, Operative, and Volunteer had long since put away their longbows, drawing curved swords instead, though the Captain kept his crossbow handy. Because of Amélie's banner, not to mention the way her new Crown glittered and glowed, she attracted attention easily. One reckless imp after another attacked from above, forcing Ranger (whose back she rode) to move around constantly. The centman had finally been forced to plant the banner pole in the ground, just so he could help his fellows cut down Amélie's attackers.

The good guys took losses too, of course. Not as many as the impmen, but then, there were far more impmen to start with. The wind atop these hills kept the yellow smoke from lingering long, but even so there was a *lot* of it.

Amélie had lost sight of Nachton, but his crews still fought tenaciously to defend each other and the siege equipment too, though the catapults themselves had fallen silent. She could only hope that Nachton was doing okay in the midst of all that violence, but—

Four imps dove at Amélie out of nowhere. "Down!" the Captain barked, shoving her off Ranger's back to hit the ground painfully. For a scary half-minute, hooves trampled the ground all around, but not one of them struck her; the centmen fought to create a perimeter, pushing the attackers away, creating an open space around the fallen Empress.

Then *another* foursome of imps dropped out of the sky, landing hard and standing over her with swords drawn. Amélie opened her mouth to scream—

—and a streak of blue shot straight through *three* of them, turning all three to yellow smoke in an instant. The last imp still could've attacked Amélie, but he turned instead and fled in horror. The Captain galloped up and stood over her while he reloaded his crossbow. "Only four Bolts left," he muttered. "Must use them wisely... Irreplaceable..."

Amélie stumbled to her feet. "Thank you," she told him genuinely. And then she saw Ranger. "Your back!" she cried, hurrying over to inspect the new claw marks on his flank, right where she'd been sitting. "Oh Ranger, I'm so sorry."

The wound was leaking a steady stream of yellow wisps, but it didn't appear serious. "I'll be okay," he said, though he winced when she touched him.

In the distance, Amélie caught the Warlord watching her again. He had given up on calling his troops back to the city. Now he just yelled orders, pointing out where Amélie's armies were weakest, and trying to get his impmen to exercise at least a little strategic thinking. But always, his eyes found Amélie again.

"Why doesn't *he* attack?" she asked. If the drachman attacked her personally, even all four of her centmen working together would have a hard time fighting him back.

"He's afraid," the Captain said simply.

Amélie snorted in disbelief. "Afraid of what? Drachman skin is indestructible; everyone says so. And Nachton says *that* guy's skin is probably even tougher since there are only three drachmen left in Overtwixt. It makes them more powerful. So what could he possibly be afraid of?"

The Captain simply hefted his crossbow. "This. Drachman skin might be *almost* indestructible, but if there's any weapon that can pierce it every time, it's one of Sovereign's Relics of Correction. So long as I stand by your side, he will hesitate to attack you." An imp screamed toward them suddenly, but the Captain sidestepped neatly, dispatching the bad guy with a smooth sword stroke. He gave her a small smile. "Fierce though the Warlord might seem, he does know fear. Sometimes, being *almost* invincible makes a person even more the coward."

Amélie opened her mouth to respond, but before she could, a warbling horn sounded from inside the city—then another, and another. All at once, the creatures of darkness whirled in surprise and horror.

And with a loud *creak*, the iron grid of the portcullis jerked one foot off the ground, stopping suddenly.

Amélie's armies started whooping excitedly, while the imps rose back into the air. The good guys fought all the harder, trying to keep the impmen here, buying Cécilie's people time to finish their task. Still, the sight of that gate opening accomplished what the Warlord could not. Hundreds of impmen started streaming back toward gaps in the city's dome.

"Archers!" Amélie bellowed. "Fire everything you've got!" There was a moment's delay, then volley after volley of arrows shot into the air from the centmen and many of the little people. The dagmen heaved their tridents after the fleeing bad guys, giving up any chance of recovering the weapons again, and one catapult crew even managed to fire a stone that took out half a dozen of the winged creatures. But the imps didn't turn back.

The portcullis jerked a little bit higher, stopping again, just as suddenly.

Of all Amélie's allies, Ewan's lugman friend was closest to the gate. Standing all alone now, he had his head cocked, and he was staring at the portcullis.

"Berserker!" Amélie cried. "*Bazooka!*" That got his attention. "Don't just stand there. Charge the gate! Don't let it come back down. Keep it open no matter what!"

He stared at her stupidly for a moment, then a slow smile crossed his face. He turned and ran toward the city.

"Everyone!" Amélie cried. "Charge the gate! *Charge the gate!*"

· twenty-five ·

(Nachton)

"**A**bandon the catapults!" Nachton took up his sister's call. "Charge the gate! *Charge the gate!*" And he joined everyone in running as hard as he could for the entrance to Capital City, despite the fact that he'd fallen over from exhaustion once already today.

By the time he got there, Berserker was on his knees, hands under the portcullis, muscles bulging. There was no way the lugman could raise the iron gate higher than it already was, but at the very least, he might keep it from closing again. On either side of the big guy, little people were shimmying underneath. Some attacked the imps standing just inside, who were trying to stick Berserker with arrows; others grabbed anything they could find to shove under the portcullis; still more disappeared up the stairs to the gatehouse, hoping to help Cécilie's gnomen with the gate controls.

And slowly but surely, the portcullis began to ratchet up higher. Soon Nachton could get through, and after that the eqmen and centmen too, and finally Berserker himself.

Dodging more arrows, or producing little blue shields to protect himself and others, Nachton found his way to where Cécilie, Handmaiden, and Squire were hunched beside a stack of big quarried stones. Others followed, diving inside buildings or finding cover wherever they could. *Everyone* was yelling. "Beware!" Squire yelled too, trying to be heard. "They're on the roofs all around us!"

"Where's Ewan?" Nachton yelled back.

Squire traded a look with Cécilie, and both of them turned toward Nachton with a guilty expression.

"You *lost* him?" Nachton demanded.

"We never *had* him," Squire insisted. "He took off right after letting us in."

"He went into the city!" Cécilie said, the two of them tripping over each other to explain.

"I followed his scent as far as the Heights," Squire said, "but then his trail got jumbled. I finally gave up and galloped back here."

Nachton buried his face in his hands. "He's going to the Citadel." That was, after all, where they expected to find the Vizier. "Ewan's going to attack the Vizier by himself."

For weeks now, Nachton had managed to repress his fury at the Vizier and his crony, that filthy spookman Shark. Now, the thought that Ewan might end up facing one of them again, being harmed by them *again*, was almost more than Nachton could bear.

"We need to get there too," he snarled, barely in control of himself. "Quick as we can!"

"Yes, but *how*?" Squire demanded. "The Princess may be invincible in that Armor, but the rest of us aren't. And with these impmen pinning us down..."

Nachton peeked around a stone block—and just missed getting stuck with an arrow. He saw enough, though.

There were countless imps standing on the roofs above, using the lip of the roof as cover while they fired arrows into the street. There were also gnomen crawling out of the insides of those buildings onto top floor balconies, using those same roof eaves to stay hidden from the bad guys they were clearly about to attack. "Get ready," Nachton said. "In about ten seconds, we're going to have an opportunity."

The others didn't question; they just did what he said. Cécilie jumped on Handmaiden's back, and Squire nuzzled Nachton, giving him permission to mount up. "Just this once," the big horse muttered.

And then impmen were shouting in surprise, some screaming in pain. "Now!" Nachton cried, and the four of them darted out into the street.

Nachton hauled back on Squire's mane, pulling him to a stop so he could look around for Amélie. His sister's armies were *still* streaming through the gate, but there was no sign of Amélie herself—and they couldn't afford to wait.

"For Overtwixt!" Nachton bellowed, raising one fist high in the air and almost falling off when Squire reared on his back legs to heighten the effect. "Whoa," Nachton gasped, grabbing hold with both hands again. "Um, for Empress Amélie—for Empress Amélie and Overtwixt!"

The answering cheer was deafening. At once, all the people who'd been hiding from impman arrows began filling the street again. Nachton wheeled Squire around, jabbing him in the ribs with his feet. "Charge!"

"Are you *kidding me?!*" Squire complained. "I'm a *person*, not some stupid animal from your world! Just *tell* me where you want to go."

"Right, um, sorry. That way, please, straight up the main street." Cécilie and Handmaiden were already charging that direction, and Squire bolted after them.

Nachton's gallop through Capital City was exhilarating. Squire was going so fast that the wind whipped through Nachton's hair, and the occasional arrow zipped by close enough to keep the Loremaster's heart thumping rapidly too. On their right, they passed countless gleaming white buildings that might have come straight out of Shanagrailia—some as much as five stories tall—with plants flowering out of windows, doors, and balconies. The buildings on their left, meanwhile, couldn't be more different. Even if it weren't for Nachton's catapult attack, it looked like most of the imps' rickety shacks were one strong wind away from falling over. The sturdiest-looking homes in the Slums were actually the stands of pencil-like trees where the spooks roosted.

As Nachton and Cécilie and the others approached the center of Capital City, little people in chains began appearing out of homes on the right, or at intersections. They were cheering excitedly, and Nachton looked back to confirm that members of Amélie's army were stopping to free the slaves from their shackles and hand out weapons. Every time that happened, Amélie's army got even bigger.

The Little Quarter, with its gleaming white buildings, went on and on out of sight—ironically the biggest section of the city. But on Nachton's left, the Slums eventually gave way to the great glittering lake of the Aquatic Quarter. Then they were galloping along a raised roadway beside a sandy beach, and the Citadel came into sight atop a ridge ahead.

Suddenly, Nachton realized how dark it had gotten. He looked up, expecting storm clouds, but it was just the dome itself blocking all direct illumination from the Sky Light. He hadn't even thought of that; if the Vizier were allowed to finish this dome over Capital City, the citizens here would be trapped forever in complete darkness. The Shadowlander creatures would probably love that, but Nachton couldn't imagine how miserable that would be for everyone else.

And the Citadel loomed over everything. Some of the buildings within the compound were beautiful, with exquisite stained glass windows. But surrounded by those tall brown walls, presided over by the Vizier's tower with its great black flag, the old capitol complex had become a sinister place.

Nachton asked Squire to halt at the foot of the ridge where the Citadel stood, in a wide paved area labeled on his maps as the parade grounds. Looking back south, toward the entrance to the city, Nachton saw the roadway packed with an unbroken stream of Amélie's followers. Fighting had broken out between them and the impmen at a dozen places along the way, but Nachton paid no attention to that. He could see Amélie and her centmen now, not far behind. And Cécilie was still at his side, perched atop Handmaiden.

But where was *Ewan?* Turning every which way, Nachton searched desperately for his little brother, but he saw no sign of the little boy. Capital City had become a madhouse, imps and spooks swooping all around in the gloom, good guys firing arrows or throwing spears, and everyone yelling even louder than before.

Something big landed right next to Nachton, shattering the cobblestones with a *crack* and causing Squire to stumble. For a moment, Nachton thought someone had fired a catapult at him, but then the dust settled, and he recognized the nightmarish shape of the drachman Warlord.

"Ah, little Conjurer," the villain growled.

"It's Loremaster now," Nachton corrected him.

"This grows confusing," the Warlord snarled. "I care not *what* you call yourself, so long as we finish what we started on Eqland." Then, in the blink of an eye, he was whirling. His long, barbed tail swept the legs from beneath

three nearby eqmen, even
as he swung his staff in
a powerful blow at the
middle of Nachton's
chest. Nachton wove a
blue shield to catch the
staff, but it still struck with
bone-jarring force, knocking
him out of Squire's saddle.

Furious and aching,
Nachton scrambled to his
feet and reached for his
magic again, instinctively
weaving flows of green and forming fireballs in
each hand. The Warlord was pushing through the ranks of
Amélie's army, half-flying and half-slithering, knocking
people aside—clearing a space in the middle of the parade
grounds where he and Nachton could fight without
distractions. Raising both hands, Nachton prepared to
bombard the drachman with destruction...

But then he saw Cécilie, staring at him with wide eyes.
Realizing what he was about to do, Nachton clenched his
fists, extinguishing the fireballs. He would *not* use the green
magic again. But how would he fight the Warlord? Blue
magic was defensive only, wasn't it? Nachton also carried a
small side sword, but it was little good against a drachman's
thick skin—especially when so few of the creatures remained
in Overtwixt. If it came down to a choice between death or
using the green magic, could Nachton really hold himself
back?

By now, everyone else had fled the center of the parade
grounds, and the Warlord turned to face Nachton again. In
the gloom beneath the dome, the drachman's midnight-
black fur made his shape indistinct; he truly was a creature

of shadow. All Nachton could see clearly were the beast's sharp red eyes and glistening white fangs. The Warlord ran his tongue over those fangs now, smiling evilly. "Are you ready to die, little human?"

Nachton hesitated another long moment, itching to conjure a green fireball. "If that is my fate," he replied at last, weaving several blue shields instead.

The Warlord attacked. Alternating between the ends of his staff, the drachman struck Nachton's shields with blinding speed. Nachton took a step back, then another, and another. The Warlord whirled, sweeping his tail to take out Nachton's legs, and Nachton jumped over it—but that's what the drachman intended, for in that moment, he struck with his staff *again*. And because Nachton was no longer grounded, the blow sent him flying.

"There's something different about you," the Warlord said conversationally. "You hesitate to reach for the green."

"I serve only the greater good, now."

The Warlord roared with laughter. "Perhaps I will let you serve *my* greater good. When the dome is finished and you are trapped in here for eternity, I will ask the Vizier to give you to me as my own personal manservant. How does that sound?"

Furious and aching more than ever, Nachton offered the monster a wordless scream and moved to attack—but what could he do, without the green magic?

Then a blinding streak of blue shot between them, and the Warlord gasped. Nachton had to blink rapidly to clear the afterimage; when he was able to see clearly again, the Warlord was grasping his upper arm in a taloned paw... and yellow smoke was seeping through his fingers.

"*Captain!*" the drachman bellowed.

"I am here, fiend," the centman responded, appearing out of the crowd, flanked by the Operative and the Volunteer. He finished reloading his crossbow and fired again, another streak of blue.

The Warlord leapt into the air, spinning through a tight corkscrew and narrowly avoiding the blue Bolt, which he knocked out of the sky—touching only the shaft—with a swat of his paw. He collided with the Captain, bearing him to the ground, and the Operative and Volunteer immediately moved to their commander's defense. They jabbed the Warlord repeatedly with their spears, eliciting cries of pain but no further puffs of yellow.

"Nachton!" Amélie cried, and Nachton finally spotted her on the other side of the fighting, still mounted on Ranger's back. "Where's Ewan?!"

Nachton could only shrug helplessly.

"Find him! We'll deal with the Warlord."

That actually made a lot of sense, considering the Captain bore one of Sovereign's Relics that was *meant* to be used as a weapon. Such a weapon was likely the only thing capable of taking out the Warlord.

But where to start looking for Ewan? In the Citadel itself? Sure, that's where the little boy was probably headed, but there's no way he could have gotten inside without help. The Captain had explained the use of the secret entrance to Nachton, but no one had told Ewan. They didn't *want* him to know, for fear he would do something exactly like this, running off on his own. In his desperation, Nachton whirled one direction and then the other, searching everywhere for his wayward brother, without luck.

Again, something struck the ground right next to Nachton, shattering the cobblestones. *Again*, Nachton immediately thought someone had fired a catapult at him... and this time, he was closer to the truth. When this newest cloud of dust settled, he saw a ragged chunk of bricks and masonry in a new crater beside him. What in the world?

Another chunk of masonry struck nearby, and then another, this one smoking an unfortunate raiman. Eyes widening in realization, Nachton looked up at the Citadel.

There, standing way-way-way up top on the highest balcony of his tower, the Vizier was staring down at Nachton with obvious hatred. The villain seemed shorter than before, but there was no mistaking those black clothes. Even as Nachton watched, the Vizier tore another chunk out of his own tower wall—with his bare hands!—and hurled it across the distance between them with amazing strength.

Nachton dove out of the way, his blood immediately beginning to boil. The very sight of the Vizier brought back all of the fury and fear he'd felt after that disastrous night in the Archives. Nachton had managed to repress his thirst for vengeance until now because he *knew* it was wrong— completely contrary to the wisdom the Diamond Lens was trying to impart, a wisdom Nachton had finally learned to appreciate. But to face that monster again, to see how desperately the villain wanted to harm Nachton and his family...

The glow of his spectacles began to flicker irregularly.

Coming out of his roll, Nachton staggered back to his feet and looked toward the Citadel again; but this time, it was a flash of blond hair that grabbed his attention, not the Vizier. A little boy was running along the top of the Citadel's outer wall, toward the Vizier's tower, and that little boy was accompanied by a *spook*.

Ewan was already inside the Citadel! And worse, he had clearly fallen for more of the Charlatan's lies.

Rage finally overwhelmed Nachton, and the glow of his spectacles winked out entirely. His anger at the Vizier was nothing compared to his hatred for the Charlatan. Nachton had always known who and what the Vizier was, but "Shark" had gone out of his way to prey upon Nachton's little brother—convincing him he was a friend, then flying off to tell the Vizier all their secrets. *That* little monster's crimes were much more personal than the Vizier's. He had betrayed the most innocent person Nachton knew.

And now the filthy creature was betraying Ewan all over again.

No, not again, Nachton swore. *You won't hurt my brother again.* The only emotion Nachton felt stronger than anger, right then, was a terrible sick worry for his brother's wellbeing. *I won't let them hurt you this time, Ewan. And I will make them pay for the harm they already caused you.*

Fortunately, the secret entrance to the Citadel was just a hundred feet away at the base of the ridge. Unfortunately, Nachton had lost track of his sisters again in all the confusion. Supposedly his family needed to confront the Vizier *together*, all four of them, or else capturing him would be impossible.

But in that moment, Nachton's worry, fear, and hate overwhelmed his ability to think clearly. He didn't have time to search for his sisters. He would save his brother alone, and he would put down the Vizier and the Charlatan. For good.

Nachton pushed through the crowd and made his way toward the ridge. Within minutes, he was ducking into the secret passage's cleverly disguised entrance, then beginning his climb into the Citadel itself.

· twenty-six ·
(Amélie)

The parade grounds had become the center of the battle. Most of Amélie's armies were inside the dome by now, and all the remaining forces of darkness were converging on them here.

Amélie didn't know how to fight, not with her own two hands; that had been made painfully clear to everyone during the assault on Gaoland. But she *was* learning how to lead, and her followers seemed eager for orders, so that's what she gave them. "Find me a place where I can see the whole battle!"

"At once, your majesty," the Ranger said. Even so, he hesitated, looking at the Captain and the other guardsmen. Ranger obviously didn't like the idea of leaving them to face the Warlord alone, but his primary duty was to protect the Empress, and he knew it. Besides, that fight was going to last a while. So he clenched his jaw and pushed through the crowd toward a nearby hill, just east of the parade grounds.

Cécilie and her retinue followed after them, and they picked up a lot of other stragglers as they went along—a handful of raimen and even a dagman—who formed a sort of honor guard around their Empress. When they reached the hill, Ranger climbed to the very top and turned around, putting the sheer cliff face of the ridge at their backs, so no one could attack them from that direction.

Amélie was finally able to see the entire battle. No one had formed battle lines this time; it was just one big free-for-all, spilling onto side streets. On the sandy shore of the Aquatic Quarter, the dagman army she'd seen earlier had broken apart to fight spooks one on one, using those nets to pull them out of the sky. With alarm, Amélie noticed a big group of impmen headed that direction, enough to overwhelm the dagmen.

"Engineer!" she cried, noticing that he had followed Cécilie onto the hill. "Go warn those dagmen! Tell them to retreat into the lake!"

"They won't do it, Empr'ss," her own new dagman guard said. "Our kind, we don' run from a fight!"

"But they'll be slaughtered! They don't have their tridents anymore!" The dagman just shrugged sadly, so Amélie began thinking furiously. "Engineer... tell them it's not running away. Make them take you underwater, to that passage going outside the city—the one the Vizier blocked off. Figure out how to get it open again, so all the other aquatics can get inside. Tell them I have ordered you into their care, that they're to guard you with their lives!"

Her dagman guard's bug eyes bugged out farther, shining brightly. "Can I go too?"

The Engineer looked horrified. "You want *me* to go... underwater? But I can't swim."

Amélie gave him an encouraging smile. "You don't have to swim. Just hold your breath and let *them* do the swimming. Now go! Both of you, go!"

Amazingly, the little gnoman obeyed, and the dagman tagged along gleefully.

Next, Amélie's attention was captured by the sight of imps landing on the top balcony of a tower at the edge of the Little Quarter. Their arms were filled with bundles of arrows, enough to keep them shooting for the next hour. "Princess Cécilie?" she asked politely. "Would you lead some of your eqmen to take care of those archers?"

"Yes! Handmaiden, Wrangler, let's go!"

"Wait!" one of Amélie's new raimen said. "The eqmen, they'll have a hard time fitting through that door, much less up the stairs."

"But *you* could fit!" Cécilie said excitedly, looking around at all the raiman stragglers. "Can you guys ride?"

The potbellied little creatures looked at one another in horror. "Us? Um, no."

And they probably wouldn't be worth much in a fight, either, Amélie suspected. She searched the battlefield for inspiration. "There!" she cried, pointing. There was a group of gnomen trapped in an alley near the building in question. They weren't being attacked, but they were so small, they couldn't get through the crowd either. "Cécilie, take your friends and pick them up. Give 'em a ride to that tower, so *they* can take out those archers."

Wrangler and Handmaiden were already on their way, Cécilie looking very grown-up on the unicorn's back. Matron and Scholar and three others went with them, the Squire staying behind as the only remaining eqman in Amélie's guard. And *he* was still desperately craning his neck in all directions, trying to catch a glimpse of Ewan somewhere.

Amazingly, Amélie didn't seem to need any guards at the moment anyway. They had left the banner behind on the plain, and here in the shadow of the ridge—which itself stood in the shadow of the dome—they seemed to escape the notice of all the bad guys. Amélie felt a little guilty about that.

"Ranger," she said softly, "I'm safe here. Return to your comrades. They need your help against the Warlord."

The centman didn't answer immediately, and Amélie joined him in watching the other centmen fight the drachman. In truth, it was less a fight than a hunt, Amélie realized, because the Warlord really was afraid of the Captain's Diamond Bolts. He kept darting away from the centman, keeping gnomen and eqmen and even impmen between them, sometimes grabbing a random person to throw in the Captain's direction. He had lost his staff somewhere, but even so, the Warlord was an absolute terror on the battlefield, attacking good guys and bad guys indiscriminately. Yet his fear of those Bolts always kept him on the ground—because flying into the air would give the Captain a clear shot. And so the drachman was never able to get *too* far away from his pursuers.

"Go," Amélie told the Ranger again, dismounting.

Nodding finally, he addressed the Squire. "You protect her, you understand? With your life."

"Of course, of course," the Squire said distractedly.

Ranger galloped off.

"Your majesty," the Squire said suddenly, still sounding distracted. "Those gnomen over there. They're being slaughtered!"

Amélie saw where the horse was looking, and her heart climbed into her throat. Then she remembered who she was talking to. "Squire? *You're* concerned for the gnomen?"

"Yes!" he cried. "They..." He seemed embarrassed suddenly. "They're my allies. Some are friends now."

Overcoming prejudice had been one of the things the Guide tasked Amélie with doing, that first day in Overtwixt, because building trust among the races had been an important part of uniting them. Of course, she'd had nothing to do with healing the rift between the eqmen and gnomen; that was all Cécilie's doing. Even so, seeing this very personal evidence of that healing brought tears to her eyes.

"Go," she told Squire, as she had told Ranger. The big black horse should have been with Ewan anyway, helping protect the little boy through this battle—but Ewan was nowhere to be found, and those gnomen needed help now. "Rescue them," Amélie told the eqman. "Be the hero they need." And so Squire galloped off too, leaving Amélie alone with the raimen.

Now that Amélie had started crying, she couldn't stop. Everywhere she looked, people were hurting one another. Maybe it was impossible to be killed here in Overtwixt, but these people locked in battle were still suffering terrible pain. And watching them suffer, she was overwhelmed with compassion—for allies and enemies alike.

In the shadow of a nearby building, she noticed something she had ignored before: a different group of gnomen was torturing some defeated imps instead of the other way around. These bad guys were flat on their backs, the little people standing on their wings and poking them with swords—just hard enough to hurt without fully smoking them.

"You!" she said, touching one of her raimen and pointing. "Tell them to stop that."

The pot-bellied little creature waddled off quickly, and soon enough, that injustice was ended. But looking around, Amélie realized it was not an isolated occurrence. More and more, the battle was turning in Amélie's favor—and more and more, her own followers were turning into the aggressors, hurting the impmen just like the impmen had hurt them in the first place.

"Raimen!" she called to the ones still standing with her. "Go throughout the city. Tell my armies to exercise mercy.

Offer our enemies a chance to join our side, swearing themselves to serve me and fight *against* evil. But even if they refuse, we shouldn't disgrace ourselves by becoming like them. Tie them up or smoke them if we have no choice, but don't torture them. That's beneath us."

Amélie's raimen clearly didn't like these orders. "But Empress—" one of them began.

"Do you trust me?" she asked. One by one, they nodded. "Then go. Please. Tell my people to be merciful and loving."

They obeyed. And as they descended the hill, she abruptly realized just how ridiculous she was being. Had she really just ordered her followers to show mercy and love to those disgusting impmen? The very same creatures who had shown nothing but spite toward the good people of this realm since Amélie arrived? What was she thinking?

It was the Crown, she realized—the Diamond Crown of Compassion. While she wore it, it was influencing her thoughts and feelings. Realizing this, she very nearly called the raimen back... but no. She desired mercy and love when *she* was wrong, didn't she? And she *had* been wrong, many times since coming here.

She did not call the raimen back.

So now Amélie was all alone, here on this hilltop. Staring out at a battle that no longer inspired feelings of adventure or victory within her.

She searched until she found the centmen and the Warlord again. By now, the Captain, Operative, and Volunteer had been joined by the Ranger, and they were steadily herding the Warlord toward the ridge. Soon he'd be trapped against the cliff face, with nowhere else to run, and no choice but to face the Captain's crossbow.

As Amélie watched, the Warlord darted between two eqmen fighting an imp, only to encounter the Operative. The centman jabbed him with his spear, and the drachman howled; whether or not it caused serious damage, he clearly didn't like the feel of that spearhead. Backing away, he grabbed one of the eqmen to throw at Operative, then hurled the second eqman in a different direction—turning several other combatants to yellow smoke and opening up a route of escape. He darted that way as the smoke began to clear...

And found himself face to face with the Captain.

It happened so suddenly, even the Captain was surprised. He raised his crossbow quickly, for he would never get a better shot than this—point blank, with no chance of hitting a friend on accident. But the drachman ripped the weapon out of his hands. Tossing it to the ground, he stomped on it, then howled in rage and pain when it refused to break. Snarling furiously, he picked it up and hurled it far away instead, to splash into the lake.

The Captain didn't waste any time getting upset. Instead, he shoved his sword tip straight into the wound he'd made earlier in the Warlord's arm.

The drachman *screamed*.

Leaping into the sky with powerful strokes of his leathery wings, the Warlord opened up distance between himself and the centmen. With that crossbow gone, he didn't need to fear giving the Captain a good shot anymore. Instead, he gripped his arm in one hand, groaning at the steady stream of yellow smoke. Turning toward the ridge, he began flying toward the Citadel—

—and noticed Amélie hiding in its shadow.

Their eyes met, and the drachman threw back his head, howling victoriously. Then he changed direction, swooping straight towards her.

· twenty-seven ·

(Nachton)

The secret passage into the Citadel—the old capitol complex—opened directly into the Baron's original throne room. Nachton closed the stone door behind him, wincing at the scraping sound it made, and turned to survey the room.

The audience chamber was completely empty, dust thick on the marble floor. The throne chair itself had been completely demolished, but aside from that one act of juvenile vandalism, it didn't look like anyone had been here since the Vizier seized control. In the distance, Nachton heard the clash of weapons and screams of battle; but here in this throne room, all was quiet, all was still.

Hurrying across the vast chamber, Nachton peeked out the door and down the hall, then hurried on. A minute later, he stepped out beneath the city-wide dome again.

And there, on the far side of the courtyard, was Ewan. The little boy was barely fifty yards away, hurrying through the ground-floor entrance to the Vizier's tower.

Nachton felt a surge of relief. "Ewan!" he called.

Ewan whirled, a look of surprise and delight on his face. "Nock!"

The traitor Charlatan was still with Ewan too, and the expression *he* gave the Loremaster was much less encouraging. The little bat whispered something in Ewan's ear, then grabbed the boy's shirt in his claws and started pulling him toward the tower entrance.

"C'mon, Nock!" Ewan called. "I know where to go! He showing me where to go!"

"Ewan, no! He's a bad guy!" Nachton's voice cracked as he began running their direction. "Don't listen to him! Shark's a bad guy!!"

But Ewan *was* listening to the spook, and not to Nachton. The vile creature had literally sunk its claws into the little boy, and Ewan willfully followed it into the enemy's lair.

So Nachton chased after them. Sprinting across the courtyard, he crashed through the entrance to the Vizier's tower, almost knocking the door off its hinges. There were rooms here on the ground floor, but he didn't bother searching them; he heard shoes slapping on stone steps above. Nachton had yet to see anyone *else* in the Citadel—the imps and spooks were surely all out in the city, locked in battle—so that must be Ewan he heard upstairs.

Ewan... or the Vizier.

Nachton spied a staircase off to the right and started climbing it at a run. It turned gently to the left, seeming to follow the inner curve of the tower's outside wall. "Ewan!" he hissed. "Ewan, wait!" But there was no reply.

The top of the staircase opened onto a short hallway, just one story up from the ground. Nachton charged down that hall, looking into open doorways as he passed. No sign of Ewan, of course. The little boy was almost certainly climbing to the top, where they had both seen the Vizier hurling bricks from that balcony. Nachton found another sweeping staircase at the other end of the hall, curving up to the left once more. He charged ahead.

This went on for the next six floors, and never once did Nachton even hear his brother again. He got a terrible cramp in his side, but he pushed himself onward, fueled by anger and worry. He *would* protect Ewan this time, no matter what. He kept climbing at a run, doing his best to prepare himself for the fight to come—summoning his strength, firming his resolve, and thinking through his spells... both the blue *and* the green.

The ninth story was different from the ones below. Instead of a hallway with rooms on both sides, most of this floor was open, laid out like the Baron's throne room. The Vizier had an ornate chair of his own at one end, and beautiful stained glass windows set in the walls. Open doorways lined just one side of the chamber, and Nachton was getting ready to search them for Ewan when he finally heard something—*voices* this time, coming from above.

Dashing to the next staircase, Nachton threw himself up the steps and into another large room at the top. This floor was even more open than the last, and it was immediately obvious Nachton had reached the top floor of the tower. There were no more staircases. Just a large four-poster bed, exquisite rugs and furniture, and a balcony overlooking Capital City. The Vizier's opulent bedchamber.

The voices Nachton heard were coming from the balcony. "I assure you, dear girl, I have no intention of risking myself amidst that rabble." The speaker had a very deep—and very recognizable—voice.

The Vizier.

"Of course not, master," a mewling female voice replied. "But your majesty, you are still at risk. A single well-aimed arrow, or even a rogue catapult shot—"

"And that is why you must tread on my very feet?" the Vizier interrupted, sounding amused and dangerously annoyed, all at once. "Tell me, have your reflexes softened so much that you cannot protect me just as well *from one yard away?* Give me some space. You stifle me."

Nachton frowned. The Vizier clearly wasn't talking to Ewan... and if Ewan wasn't on the balcony, he obviously wasn't on this floor at all. The little boy must've been in one of the side rooms Nachton passed one floor down.

The Loremaster considered sneak-attacking the Vizier right then and there. He *desperately* wanted to give the villain a taste of his own medicine. But saving Ewan from Shark was more important. Cursing his haste, he turned to slip back out again—and stepped right on a squeaky floorboard.

"Master!" the unknown voice cried, "get down!" There was a thump and a cry of pain from the balcony, then something slithered rapidly into the room with Nachton.

It was a drachman, that much was immediately clear, but smaller and more slender than the Warlord. Faster too, if such a thing was possible. A drach*woman?* She saw Nachton and thrust a finger in his direction. "You there! Halt in the name of the Emperor."

Nachton was taken aback by the terrifying creature. "Oh, um, hi. You must be the Blackguard," he babbled, his heart racing. "Don't mind me—I got turned around down below. Sorry if I disturbed you... I'll, um, be going now."

The Blackguard narrowed violet eyes at him. "I said *halt*, human."

The Vizier stumbled in from the balcony and backhanded the drachwoman across her muzzle. "Throw me to the ground again," he told her under his breath, "and I will skin you alive. Do you understand me, cur?"

The Blackguard ducked her head subserviently, acting just like a dog whose master kicked it often. "Of course, your majesty, of course!" Nachton's apprehension immediately faded again.

"I have nothing to fear from this one," the Vizier continued, turning to face the Loremaster for the first time.

Nachton ground his teeth painfully. It took him a moment to realize the Vizier *was* shorter than before—much shorter than Nachton, and probably no taller than Amélie.

The Vizier sensed Nachton's surprise, and he scowled. "There are... trade-offs... where magic is concerned," he said. "Even an amateur like you must know this by now." He smirked suddenly, then walked onto his balcony once more—and ripped a chunk of stone right out of the railing with his bare hand! He hefted the masonry, then crushed it in his fist. As he did so, the ruby necklace hanging around his neck throbbed with green light. "I think this amulet is worth the indignity from time to time, wouldn't you agree?"

"Hey!" a childish voice cried. "That *mine!*" Ewan came running into the room, his attention all on the Vizier, but Nachton grabbed him by the shoulders. "Let me *go*, Nock!" He focused on the Vizier again. "Give dat back!"

There was no sign of Ewan's spook 'friend', but both the Vizier and Blackguard were grinning now, eyes alight with evil. "You fools," the Vizier spat. "Didn't you learn anything from our last fight? You come at me even weaker than before, while I am stronger than ever." He stroked the ruby. "You, little Knight... you're not even wearing your precious Armor." He chuckled. "Not that it did you much good last time."

The Vizier was right, as much as Nachton didn't want to admit it. His desire to hurt the villain warred with a small inner voice that reminded him this was *not* how their rematch was supposed to occur. The plan had been to face the Vizier together—all four siblings, preferably with Squire and Berserker and all four guardsmen too.

Still, with rage clouding his judgment, Nachton *felt* more than capable of taking out the Vizier all by himself. He shoved Ewan back toward the door, then turned, immense green fireballs suddenly filling both hands.

But then Ewan dashed around him and charged the Vizier! The little boy had gotten a sword from somewhere, and it was way too big for him, its sheath dragging along the floor as he tried to draw the blade out.

"Ewan," Nachton cried, "no!" In an instant, his hate for the Vizier was replaced by concern for Ewan; and just that quickly, Nachton's fireballs winked out as he started weaving flows of blue magic.

The Vizier gestured. "Blackguard, deal with him."

The beast moved almost faster than Nachton could see. Before Ewan even got his sword out, she lashed out with one big paw. Nachton barely finished his spell in time—segments of bubble armor leaping into place over each part of Ewan's body, formed entirely of bright blue light—just as the Blackguard struck him. The little boy tumbled aside, rolling halfway across the room with a yell. But when he doggedly returned to his feet, he was obviously unharmed.

The Vizier stared for a long moment, then turned to Nachton in confusion. "You're using *Sovereign's* magic?"

"I guess I've learned a *few* things since last time," Nachton said grudgingly.

From behind, the Loremaster heard the sound of the door slamming shut—Ewan's only way out of this room, closing behind them. Spinning around, Nachton was just in time to see the Charlatan turning a key in the lock. He lunged for the bat, fully intending to wring its neck, but Ewan's filthy little 'friend' was too fast. It dodged out of the way and darted out a window. Nachton watched in mingled fury and horror as the vile creature released the key, allowing it to drop ten stories to the courtyard below.

"Ah, Charlatan," the Vizier said warmly. "My most trusted servant."

The bat circled the tower and reentered via the balcony, coming to rest on the Vizier's outstretched arm—perching on top like a parrot, rather than hanging below like a bat would normally do. The Blackguard hissed jealously at the little bat, and Charlatan bared his fangs in return at the drachwoman.

"Now, now, ladies," the Vizier chided them.

"I *told* you not to trust the spook," Nachton complained at Ewan. "Now he's betrayed us again, and we're trapped here. Wait—" He spun to face the Vizier and the spook perched on his shoulder. "*Ladies?*"

"You assume too much, human," the spookman—no, spook*woman*—said in that raspy voice. "Even now, you don't know half as much as you think you do."

Ewan never said a word. But he did finally get his big new sword out of its scabbard.

The Vizier barely glanced at the little boy, merely flicked a finger in his direction. "Blackguard, *please?*"

The drachwoman spun about, dropping low onto her forearms, and roared directly into Ewan's face. The little boy staggered back from her ferocity—but as soon as it was over, he wiped the slobber from his cheeks and raised his sword again. Then he stepped toward her.

The Blackguard erupted in harsh laughter and spread her arms wide, trusting her impervious skin to protect her. "Go ahead, little human. Take your best shot."

Ewan stabbed her right in the middle of the chest, burying his new sword to its hilt. The drachwoman whimpered and was gone a moment later, leaving behind a great cloud of yellow.

The Vizier whirled to face Ewan, jaw dropping open in shock. "What!? How did you do that?" Then he noticed, at the same time as Nachton, that Ewan's bubble armor wasn't the only source of bright blue light in the room.

Ewan was holding the old Baron's magnificent *Diamond* Sword, one of Sovereign's Relics. And *it* was glowing too.

"*No*," the Vizier said hoarsely. "I locked that up, in my laboratory. No one could have gotten in. No one except..." His eyes widened, and in that instant, the little spookwoman sprang from his shoulder. The Vizier lunged for her but missed. "*You?*" he demanded. "*You* let him into my most sacred place?" He kept trying to grab the little bat, but she always stayed just out of reach. "Why?" he asked, on the verge of tears. "Why would *you* betray me?"

Nachton gaped, wondering the exact same thing.

"I never betrayed anyone," the Charlatan rasped. "Least of all *you*. I never served you in the first place."

"But—"

"I was the Baron's friend all along." The little bat sucked in a huge breath, then yelled at the top of her lungs, as if speaking to all of Overtwixt. "Do you hear me!? I was *always* loyal to the Baron!"

The Vizier's face contorted with rage.

"Who do you think stole your amulets the night you fought him?" the spook rasped. "Who do you think destroyed your research?"

The Vizier's face began turning purple.

In contrast, Nachton felt some of his own fury leach away, replaced by confusion. He turned to see Ewan's reaction, but the little boy was standing right where he'd slain the Blackguard, casually propping that beautiful

Diamond Sword against his shoulder. When Ewan saw Nachton looking, he gave his big brother a *very* self-satisfied I-told-you-so smile.

"TRAITOR!" the Vizier screamed, spraying spittle. Bending over, he seized hold of a chunk of masonry from the balcony railing he had destroyed earlier. Clearly, he meant to fling it through the Charlatan's smiling face, smoking the little spook in midair.

But the chunk didn't even twitch. All the villain managed to do was wrench his own arm out of its socket.

"*What?*" he gasped. Automatically, his hand went to his neck, feeling for the amulet ribbon. It was still there... but the ruby itself was gone.

Grinning bigger than ever, the spook opened one clawed foot to reveal what she'd been hiding—the ruby, which she'd quietly stolen while perched in that position of trust on the villain's shoulder. Very deliberately, she now let the amulet tumble free, dropping it into the courtyard below, just as she'd done with the key earlier.

"NO!" the Vizier bellowed. Ewan stepped toward him, brandishing that amazing Sword, but the Vizier dodged him. Running all out, the villain circled the room and threw himself at the door in an attempt to escape.

But the door was locked—and suddenly, Nachton understood. The Charlatan had *not* trapped Nachton and Ewan... she had trapped *the Vizier.*

"Surrenner!" Ewan yelled.

"Never!" the madman yelled in response. Giving up on escape, he turned to face them and began weaving.

This was Nachton's moment. The Vizier was weakened, off-balance, distracted. In an instant, Nachton could wrap the villain in ropes of green, then pummel him into submission with fireballs, then... then...

Then what? Take his revenge?

Nachton's spectacles flickered weakly, and he finally recognized an important truth: he couldn't trust himself to fight the Vizier. He couldn't trust his own judgment *at all* in this situation. The Charlatan had just proved that beyond a shadow of a doubt! If Nachton allowed himself to keep fixating on his hatred for the Vizier, he would only keep repeating the mistakes that had gotten Ewan smoked in the first place.

With a monumental effort of willpower, Nachton released the anger he continued to harbor against the Vizier. And he focused on the love he held for his brother Ewan.

Once again, blue magic leapt to Nachton's fingertips, replacing the sparks of green that had briefly appeared. "Ewan," Nachton yelled. "We need to work together. Not like last time! If we *cooperate*, we can defeat him." Nachton took a deep breath. "But *you*'ll have to take the lead." He could only hope that would be enough. After all, the Guide made it sound like Amélie and Cécilie were needed to defeat the Vizier also, even though neither one could fight.

"You think this little boy could take me?" the Vizier cackled. "Just because I lost that stupid necklace? Ha!" He was clearly teetering on the edge of insanity. "Nothing has changed from last time. Remember *this?*" And he finished his spell, flinging a tempest of green magic at the two brothers.

Their last encounter with the Vizier was all Nachton could think about right then: how Ewan had gotten stuck in a freezing mist of Nachton's own making, then was cut down. Except *that* was a mere cloud of mist, like a fog. *This* was so much more powerful—a maelstrom, a *hurricane*, lit from within by bolts of crackling green lightning.

Desperately, Nachton wove another spell to enhance his brother's armor, filling every gap and joint, even crafting a transparent facemask—encasing the little boy entirely, so not even a wisp of that evil could squeeze past his defenses.

And sure enough, the evil storm passed Ewan by, with no effect whatsoever.

Urgently, Nachton began crafting a shield of his own, but it was far too late to protect himself. He had barely managed to shield his face before the maelstrom reached him, a dozen forked lightning bolts lancing out at his body. The overwhelming power of that magic froze Nachton from the neck down, locking his hands in place and rooting his feet to the floor.

He couldn't move an inch, couldn't even feel the rest of his body now—and somehow he knew that this freezing spell would not wear off quickly. The Vizier really did wield the green magic better than Nachton ever had.

And now the villain was advancing on Ewan, drawing his elegant saber and raising it in a flourished salute.

Nachton almost told his brother to run, even though there was nowhere to go. Then he remembered the Guide's words, that last time they saw the centman on the plain at Pholand: *Trust one another, and rely upon no magic except the Sovereign's... and the Vizier cannot stand against you.*

Nachton took a steadying breath, then spoke calmly. "Um, Ewan? I'm not gonna be able to help after all. But you've got this. I believe in you. You can defeat the Vizier!"

· twenty-eight ·
(Cécilie)

Cécilie and her eqmen had finally fought their way through the battle to rescue the gnomen in the alley, and now the little men were all mounted up. "Let's go take care of those archers!" she yelled.

A terrible scream filled the air, coming from the parade grounds. Everyone turned to look as the Warlord flew into the sky gripping his arm, which was leaking yellow smoke.

"Yay!" Cécilie's followers cheered.

"Get him!" a gnoman screamed. "Make him suffer!"

The Warlord whirled in midair and paused. Suddenly, he threw back his head and howled again, different from before. This time, he sounded *happy*.

And then he tucked his wings against his back and dove, straight toward Amélie's hiding place near the ridge.

Before she knew it, Cécilie was riding Handmaiden at a gallop in the same direction. "Hurry!" she cried.

"I'm hurrying," the unicorn said. Her voice was anguished, and Cécilie knew she was scared for Amélie's safety too. Handmaiden dodged among the combatants, spearing one imp that got too close, but mostly avoiding everyone to get through the crowd faster.

By the time they reached the ridge, the centmen had already caught up to the Warlord, but he was ignoring them. His back turned to everyone else, the drachman was hunched over someone. "Amélie!" Cécilie screamed. "I'm coming!"

With no thought for her own safety—or what she would even do to help—Cécilie threw herself off Handmaiden's back. She tripped, falling and rolling painfully, but climbing to hands and knees and pushing onward. She was small enough to squeeze between the centmen's legs and keep going, even though she should have been trampled. The Diamond Armor protected her.

And then she was between the Warlord and the centmen with their spears—and she saw Amélie. The Warlord had backed the older girl against the ridge, into a cleft in the cliff face. The Empress was clearly terrified, but she also stood as straight and proud as possible. She still wore her new Crown, and she raised her chin defiantly.

"Coward!" the Captain was screaming, more emotional than Cécilie had ever seen him. "Face me, fight *me!*" Striding forward, he dodged the drachman's barbed tail and hacked with his curved sword, but it was no use. He couldn't squeeze between Amélie and the Warlord. "You *coward*," he sobbed. "Turn and fight me like a man!"

Well, just because the Captain was too big to squeeze past the Warlord, that didn't mean Cécilie was.

Continuing forward on hands and knees, Cécilie squeezed underneath the Warlord's belly, then stood up in front of Amélie. Drawing her short sword, she jabbed the drachman right in the nose.

He yelped, swatting the blade out of her hand.

Cécilie was crying by now, terrified for herself and Amélie both. "Leave her alone, you monster!"

One paw clasped over his muzzle, the Warlord stared at her, stunned. And he wasn't the only one—all the centmen gaped in horror too. Somewhere behind them, the Handmaiden screeched, "Princess, no!"

Cécilie glanced over her shoulder at Amélie, her big sister who made her so angry sometimes, always bossing her around and treating her like a little kid. Sometimes she felt like she hated the older girl... but she also loved her no matter what. And in that moment, Cécilie knew she would do *anything* for her sister.

"You wanna hurt someone?" Cécilie said, turning back to the Warlord. "Hurt me instead. Not her—me!"

The Warlord began to laugh, each low chuckle puffing across Cécilie's face. His breath smelled of decay, but Cécilie faced him with chin held high, following her big sister's example.

"Cécilie, no," Amélie whispered behind her.

"Oh, there's no need to fight over the honor," the drachman said. "I will hurt you *both*." He grinned, and a glob of saliva slid down one exposed fang to splash across Cécilie's Diamond breastplate. "But since you volunteered, little one, I'll start with you."

The centmen renewed their attack, all of them crying out angrily, the Captain's anguished wails louder than any of the others. The Warlord ignored them all. Quick as lightning, he grabbed Cécilie by the ankle and jerked her feet out from under her. The next instant, she was lying flat on her back, seeing stars. Before she could even think about getting up again, the Warlord pressed his fanged muzzle right against her ear. "Nighty night, stupid human." Then he straightened and brought one massive paw crashing down on her chest.

The force of the blow drove Cécilie down into the hillside with a sound like thunder. The weight of the beast, *standing on her chest*, was enough to crush her. It *should* have crushed her, should have sent her off in a puff of yellow smoke—and clearly, that's what the drachman expected. For in the next moment, he released her, reaching forward to fasten his paw around Amélie's throat instead.

But Cécilie wasn't crushed... because she was wearing the Diamond Armor. A Relic of Protection, crafted by the Sovereign himself.

Coughing in the dirt kicked up by the Warlord's violence, Cécilie tried to pull herself out of the newly created crater, but she was caught. The Armor had protected her, but now it trapped her. And even if she *could* get out, the Warlord's leathery chest still pinned her to the ground. Meanwhile, Amélie gagged weakly, and Cécilie knew the drachman was choking the life out of her.

Groping desperately for a weapon, anything, Cécilie cried. "Help! Anybody, help me, help Amélie, please!" She could barely get the words past the dust in her throat. "*Guide*, help us!"

Her left hand found something. It wasn't long at all, and the sides weren't sharp, so it wasn't a sword or dagger. A stick? It didn't matter; Cécilie was desperate. Without hesitation, she plunged the thing into the Warlord's belly.

She plunged it *into* the Warlord's belly. Past his impenetrable skin, and deep inside.

The Warlord straightened instantly. "What?" he gasped, then roared, "No! Impossible!"

And the very next instant, he disappeared in the biggest cloud of yellow smoke yet.

Amélie collapsed on her knees next to Cécilie. "You're alive!" the Empress sobbed. "Oh, Cécilie," she cried, "you're alive, you're alive!" Unable to pull Cécilie out of the crater, she threw herself across Cécilie's chest instead, the closest she could get to hugging her.

Still staring up from the ground, Cécilie saw the Captain appear above her, waving a hand to dispel yellow smoke. The Ranger and Operative came into view also, all of them looking amazed. The Operative pulled Amélie gently to her feet, then the Captain knelt, got a good grip, and heaved Cécilie out of the stony ground.

"He's gone," the Ranger said softly, voice awed. "The Warlord—you smoked him." He shook his head. "*You* did that, Princess, when none of the rest of us could. *How?*"

Everyone was staring at Cécilie. Slowly, she raised her left hand, curious to see what exactly she was holding.

It was one of the Captain's Diamond Bolts, its crystalline arrowhead still glowing blue. She was holding one of Sovereign's Relics. *That* was how.

The sight of that crossbow Bolt, still glowing brightly in Cécilie's human hand, seemed to shock the Captain more than anything that had come before. "That *is* impossible," he gasped. "You are human, and that Relic is for centmen. Besides, you already wear a Relic of your own. You cannot bear *two*. It breaks all the rules. It's... it's impossible!"

Cécilie nodded, dazed. She *knew* it was impossible.

"Maybe," Amélie said slowly, "there's no such thing as impossible where the Sovereign is concerned."

· twenty-nine ·

(Ewan)

The Vizier smiled and started walking toward Ewan. He was dressed all in black, just like always, with a cool cape blowing behind him, just like *all* bad guys wore. He waved his sword in the air again, even more fancy this time, like he was trying to be extra special scary.

But Ewan wasn't scared of him. Not anymore. Thanks to Shark, *he* had a *better* Sword. And thanks to Nock, he had new awesome armor. Viziguy couldn't do anything to hurt him this time, so Ewan gave the bad guy his biggest smile.

"I. AM. IM-VIZIBLE!" he bellowed.

Still frozen in place, Nock cleared his throat. "Invincible, buddy. Not invisible. Invisible means no one can see you. In*vinc*ible means no one can hurt you—"

"I. LOVE. DIS. PLACE!" Ewan interrupted joyfully, then pointed his new Sword at the Vizier. "Time for bad guy gonna go bye-bye! For Overchix! For Empress Ommie and OVERCHIX!" And he attacked.

The Vizier stepped sideways and stuck out his foot. Ewan was going *way* too fast to stop, and he tripped, falling flat on his face. With a smirk, Viziguy raised his sword and brought it down on Ewan's back.

But it bounced right off, all shaky and wobbly.

Smiling even bigger now, Ewan rolled onto his back and swung the Diamond Sword at the bad guy's legs. The Vizier yelped and fell backwards trying to get away.

Giggling loudly, Ewan got to his feet and attacked again. He forced himself to slow down and fight the way Fight Guy taught him, but he had *fun* doing it. The Vizier was a pretty good sword fighter too, but that didn't bother Ewan. He *wanted* this to last a long time!

Ewan swung the Sword again and again, in lots of different ways, a sequence of sword strikes he had learned from Fight Guy. Each time, the Vizier blocked the Diamond Sword, making lots of little green sparks. Then the bad guy launched another attack of his own, and Ewan had to take a step back, blocking rapidly.

"You think you can defeat me?" Viziguy snarled. "I'm a master swordsman! I defeated the old Baron, even though he wielded that very Sword. I can certainly defeat a *child*."

Ewan smiled big. He *liked* telling insults. "Oh yeah? You bweff stink."

"Huh?"

"You nose too big."

"*What?*"

"You face *uggy*."

"Ewan!" Nock said in his best Dad-voice. "You *know* Mom doesn't like you talking that way."

Ewan faked like he was gonna swing the Sword at Viziguy's face, then stepped back and swung at the bad guy's feet again instead. And again, the Vizier yelped. He wasn't used to fighting someone so short. Ewan was actually *scaring* him every time he attacked his legs.

They fought back and forth across the room. When they got near the bed, Ewan jumped on top and fought Viziguy face to face. When the bad guy stepped back to catch his breath, Ewan shrugged and destroyed the bed, cutting off all four posts and slicing up the sheets and blankets.

"How *dare* you!" the Vizier snarled, and Ewan giggled, taking a running jump off the mattress and attacking him midair.

Ewan never managed to touch Viziguy with the Sword, but Viziguy had a hard time touching Ewan too—and every time he did, his sword bounced right off. It made Ewan bolder and bolder, while Viziguy just got *mad*.

"You're better than I expected," the Vizier finally muttered. "Then again..." He smiled suddenly. "You essentially learned everything you know from me."

"No I didn't!" Ewan yelled. "I learn from Fight Guy!"

In answer, the bad dude reached into his robes and pulled out a new necklace—a pearl on a gold ribbon. "This look familiar? I *am* Fight Guy now! The greatest Weap—"

With a screech, Shark dove out of nowhere. He slashed Viziguy's hand and flew away with the pearl.

No, wait-wait-wait. Ewan kept forgetting: Shark was a *girl*. SHE dove outta nowhere, slashed Viziguy's hand, and flew off with the pearl—which she dropped over the side of the balcony, so Viziguy couldn't use Fight Guy's skill.

The bad guy screamed. "Stop. DOING. That!"

Remembering what the Vizier did to Fight Guy in the jail made *Ewan* mad now, and he attacked again. He *would* defeat this bad guy so the Vizier could never hurt anyone ever again.

Viziguy barely got his sword up in time. He blocked Ewan's attacks, again and again—but each time, he took a step backwards. Ewan was swinging the Sword *hard* now. He backed the Vizier all the way out onto his balcony.

Then the bad guy surprised him. With a yell, he *threw* his sword at Ewan, then started shooting green fireballs at him. Ewan whacked the saber out of the air, but the fireballs hit him in the chest. The armor protected him, but the fireballs still knocked him over, onto his back.

The Vizier stepped close, weaving his hands like he was gonna try something new, destroying Ewan's armor or something. Even though he was dizzy, Ewan reacted immediately, swinging the Sword at Viziguy's legs again.

The bad guy yelped and jumped backwards, like he did last time, right to the edge of the balcony. He lost his balance and groped for the railing to catch himself—

But the railing wasn't there. Viziguy himself had destroyed it earlier.

"NO!" the Vizier screamed, falling over the side. Waving his arms, he barely managed to catch the edge of the balcony with one hand.

Ewan didn't even think about what he was doing. He dropped the Sword and dove forward on hands and knees. Reaching over the edge, he grabbed the bad guy's hand in both of his, trying to keep him from falling.

"Surrenner!" he said.

"Never!" the Vizier yelled.

"Don't let him fall!" Nock called from inside. "We have to capture him!"

"You too big!" Ewan said. "Let Nock go. *He* can pull you up. We don't gotta be emenies!"

Viziguy looked into Ewan's eyes with wonder. "You really mean that, don't you?"

Ewan nodded emphatically.

That made Viziguy mad again. "No. We will *always* be enemies."

"If you fall down—"

"If I fall," the Vizier snarled, "I will wake again on Gaoland, surrounded by the allies your armies slew today." Staring up at Ewan over the edge of the balcony, holding on by only one hand, Viziguy started to laugh like a crazy guy. "This is not the end. There will *never* be an end! *I* rule here, and none other. You cannot defeat me!"

And with that, he ripped his hand free of Ewan's.

He fell... and fell... and then made a little puff of yellow smoke in the courtyard far below.

For some reason, that made Ewan really sad. He *wanted* to rescue him. It didn't matter that the Vizier was a bad guy.

Shark landed on Ewan's shoulder and sighed. "He's right, you know. Don't misunderstand me, you've won a great victory here today—"

"No, WE won today," Ewan said, grabbing his friend and hugging him—her!—really tight. "You part of dat, Shark! I make sure evveybodies knows. People gonna start tusting you again. They *gotta* now."

Shark blinked rapidly. "I... thank you."

Nock stepped out onto the balcony with them, free from that freezing cloud now that Viziguy was gone. Looking embarrassed, he got on his knees before Ewan and Shark. "I was wrong about you, Charlatan. You *were* the Baron's friend all along, and Ewan's too—the best kind of friend Ewan could have. Can you ever forgive me?"

Shark squirmed out of Ewan's arms, then hopped up on Ewan's shoulder. "Yeah, whatever. You promise to treat me like a lady from now on, the way I deserve?"

Nock blushed. "Uh, yeah. Sorry about that too."

Shark bared her teeth in a smile. "You're forgiven." She sighed again. "But what will we do now? I was starting to say, the Vizier was right—this isn't the end. When next we see him, he'll be at the front of another army, this time attacking with *all three* drachmen, *both* phomen, and probably a few new amulets while he's at it. Meanwhile, we're all out of surprises. I've played my hand, and so have you. He won't be caught unprepared again, and... What in the world is so funny, little human?"

Ewan had started giggling. "Nuffing."

"Tell me!"

"Tell us!" Nock agreed. "What is it?"

Ewan just shrugged. "I dink Viziguy is all 'feated now. No more battles."

Nock narrowed his eyes. "How can that be?"

Ewan just shrugged and tried to look innocent. "Tust me." He stood up. "C'mon, let's go find Ommie and Sessy and have a party. We won. We WON!"

The End of

Part III

Part IV
Return

Sovereign's Relics
for the Human Race

Command Relics

for Wisdom:

 The Lens of Discernment

for Humility:

The Crown of Compassion!!

Combat Relics

for Protection:
The Plate Armor of Assurance

for Correction:*
The Great-Sword of Justice

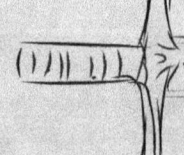

** for use as a last resort only!

· thirty ·

(Ewan)

"I had a feeling I'd be seeing you again soon," Jail Guy said. He was sitting on top of the wall on Jail-land as Ewan and his brother and sisters and all their friends walked up from Fo-land. "Gimme a sec," the dwagon added. "I'll let you in."

A little bit later, the repaired drawbridge lowered and the Jailer pulled himself through on muscular forearms. A whole bunch of Ommie's troops got ready to shoot him with bows and arrows. "Hole you fire!" Ewan yelled. "He a good guy."

"That remains to be seen," the Captain said. "Tie him up." Now a bunch of no-mans ran forward with chains.

"No," Ommie said loudly.

Ewan and everyone else turned to look at her. She was looking at Ewan. "I think my little brother has proven himself a good judge of character. Better than the rest of us, certainly."

Captain looked like he was gonna argue, then he hung his head. "I suppose he has." He gestured, and the no-dudes backed away from Jail Guy. The dwagon bared his fangs and smiled really big at Ewan.

Ewan ran up to his friend and threw his arms around him. The big guy was so big, Ewan was mostly just hugging his belly. "What happen?" he demanded. "Tell us what happen!"

"Well," the Jailer began, "it was a funny thing. A week after you left me here, locked in a cell, a couple Soldiers showed up with the Vizier's spare keys. They let me out of my cell, and I realized I had a choice to make."

"What choice was that?" Nock asked.

"Whether to follow the Vizier's orders—letting all of his other minions out of their cells, to return to Twixt—or whether to follow my heart."

"So... what did you decide?"

The dwagon gave everyone another toothy smile. "Come inside and I'll show you."

Ewan followed his friend immediately, reaching up to scratch Shark's head when the spookwoman landed on his shoulder. She seemed to really like that. No one *else* was in a hurry to go inside the jail, until Ommie took a deep breath and chased after Ewan. Then everyone came in.

It was dark inside, just like Ewan remembered. But when his eyes got used to it, the first thing he saw was two cent-guys. "Your majesty!" both of them cried, bowing low before Ommie. "Please forgive us."

Ommie looked confused. "For what?"

"For falling in battle," one said.

"And for not returning as soon as we were able," the other added.

"Why didn't you?" Ommie asked slowly. "I notice you aren't locked up."

"That's correct, your majesty. The Jailer released us immediately and nursed us back to health. But he needed help. There are still many prisoners here, all the Vizier's forces who were smoked. We've been guarding, patrolling, making sure they stay locked up."

"Just the two of you?" Nock asked.

"Oh, no, Master of Lore. We were joined by all the others who fell while fighting for you in the Battle of Capital City. There are more than two hundred of us here, which is good... since there are almost a *thousand* of the Vizier's minions to look after."

"And the Jailer let all of my allies out of their cells?" Ommie said, making sure she understood.

"Yes, majesty. And kept all our enemies locked up."

Everyone seemed to relax, and a couple people even smiled at Jail Guy. That made Jail Guy smile and wink at Ewan, so Ewan smiled and winked at Ommie, then Nock, then Sessy, then anyone else who would look at him.

"Jailer," Skire Horsey asked. "On the morning of the prison break, was it you who threw us the keys?"

"Yes."

"Why you no say so?" Bazooka asked loudly. "You could have come with us!"

"My place was here, caring for the prisoners. I knew the Vizier would send someone with keys eventually."

"So the Knight was right," Skire said. "You were a good guy after all."

Jail Guy swallowed, looking ashamed. "A good guy never would have followed the Vizier in the first place."

"But you free us!" Ewan protested.

"One good act does not cancel out past crimes," the dwagon replied. "And it certainly does not undo the consequences." He gestured at the cells around him. "I helped build this place. Even if my intentions were good, to soften the Vizier's rule, I still helped put him on the throne *and* keep him there. I could not simply walk away from my responsibility to these prisoners, even after you convinced me of the Vizier's evil. There is too much I must atone for."

"Well," the Captain said, "I for one am glad you stayed. I'm not afraid to admit it now!" he told Ommie when she raised an eyebrow at him. "If not for the Jailer taking responsibility, we'd be facing a very different sort of welcome right now."

"Yes, you've already atoned for a lot," Nock said.

Jail Guy only grunted, like he wasn't sure he agreed. "I suppose you'd like to see him?"

"The Vizier?" Ommie asked. "Yes, please."

"Follow me."

Jail Guy led them down the same hallways that Ewan remembered from before. Every cell was filled to bursting with wimpmen, and there were smaller cells with mesh walls for holding spooks. Lots of the bad guys yelled and spat when they saw Shark, but others turned away, ashamed. Some begged for mercy from Ommie.

Ewan's group passed through an area that had bigger cells for the dwagons and fo-dudes. All four of *these* bad guys moved away from the bars when they saw Ewan and his brother and sisters. Bwackguard Yady hugged herself and whimpered, and War-Dwagon Dude wouldn't look Sessy in the eyes. Both the fo-guys pretended to be cleaning under their wings, but they got *really* tense when Nock and Ommie and Captain walked by.

The very last room of the jail was the same one where Ewan and his friends stayed while they were here. That was where Viziguy was locked up now, arms around his knees, rocking back and forth and muttering to himself. He didn't seem to notice he had visitors.

"Ha!" Nock said, shaking his head and laughing softly. "I was right. The magic he poured into these cells *was* strong enough to hold anything—even himself."

The Jailer nodded. "When I wouldn't let him out, he yelled and screamed and cursed me for days. Tried all sorts of magical spells, but nothing he threw at me could pass between the bars. It was his own magic fighting against him, canceling itself out. Eventually he gave up, and he's been muttering about the Adversary ever since."

"Da Addersarry?" Ewan asked. "Who dat?"

Jail Guy shrugged. "No idea."

But Nock frowned. "The Guide has mentioned him. The Adversary of the Sovereign, his greatest enemy."

"Shh, listen," Jail Guy said quietly.

Everyone leaned in to hear what Viziguy was saying.

"*I trusted you... You promised I could have* everything, *rule* everything... *Everyone betrayed me... Don't betray me too, not you... Please... I trusted you... You* promised..."

"It just keeps repeating from there," the Jailer said.

Ommie shivered. "That's disturbing. What does it mean?"

"I don't want to know," Sessy said, shivering too.

"So what now?" Nock asked.

"Now we deliver on the rest of our promises," Ommie said. "We rebuild the bridges, so we can return all these criminals to their real worlds. And so we can go home too, finally."

Everyone smiled big at this. "I'll get the Engineer started right away," Nock said. "Nothing would make him happier than a project like this."

· thirty-one ·

(Nachton)

The bridge back to the Inquisitor and Enforcer's real world was the first to be rebuilt. The Engineer chose to start there because it was the simplest of all the bridges, not even really a "bridge" except in the most abstract sense. It was more like a cool rock formation in the shape of an arch, which acted as a magical *portal* to the phoman real world.

Almost as soon as the last rock was put in place at the top of the arch, the enclosed space began shimmering and glowing; then a veritable army of phomen came streaming out into Overtwixt. The centmen and eqmen in charge of guarding the Engineer's team very nearly attacked the newcomers, until everyone remembered it was the Vizier who banished the other phomen in the first place. Strange and scary as the skeletal horses were, they were no allies to the Vizier.

The leader of the newcomers—a phoman called the Zealot—demanded the immediate return of the Inquisitor and Enforcer, who were promptly escorted home to face prosecution. The Zealot promised that, as the very least of their punishment, the two criminals would never set foot in Overtwixt again. After that, the Zealot and his followers proceeded to rebuild their villages on Pholand, which had fallen into disrepair. Within a week, there was even talk of reestablishing trade with Shanagrailia.

Now, another week after that, the bridge back to the drachman real world was nearing completion too. And following the scare with the phomen, no one was taking any chances. A combined army of centmen, gnomen, and dagmen flanked Nachton, Ewan, and the Jailer—and *all* of them kept a close watch over Warlord and Blackguard, whose wings were chained tight against their bodies. On top of all that, the Zealot's phomen had agreed to provide air support.

As the Engineer supervised placement of the final bridge supports, Nachton looked out over the nightmarish landscape of Drachölm: hardened black lava flows, punctuated in places by bubbling pools of red and yellow magma. Jailer said this was what the most habitable regions of his real world looked like, and honestly, that kinda scared Nachton. Pretty much no one thought the drachman real world was a place they'd want to visit, even if such a thing were possible.

"You sure 'bout dis?" Ewan asked, and Nachton turned around. The little boy was talking to the Jailer, sniffly and teary-eyed.

The Jailer sighed. "I'm sure, little one. I don't deserve to stay here any more than they do." He nodded at his cousins, the Warlord and the Blackguard.

"But you never wanted to hurt people," Ewan insisted. "You heart was *pure*."

"Perhaps. But it's not only our intentions that matter. We must take responsibility for our actions too." He had tried explaining this several times already, but the little boy still struggled to understand. "It is time for me to go," the kind-hearted drachman said firmly, "and past time to take these two back home as well. Besides, they need me."

"You don't owe those two anything," Nachton said bluntly. "Even if they *are* family."

"I don't think even you believe that, Loremaster. We always bear a responsibility to family. Our love for them requires it." The drachman shifted, and the chains he held—connected to collars around his cousins' necks—jingled in his hands. "I hope and believe they can still be redeemed, as I was. The first step is removing them from Overtwixt and all its strange magics and powers, which are too much temptation for them to resist. But at every other step along the way, they will require a good friend by their side. Just as I had." He gazed down at Ewan with obvious affection.

"But I gonna miss you!" Ewan said, sniffling.

"As I will miss you, little one."

Nachton kept his mouth shut. Ewan was still willfully ignoring the fact that he would be leaving Overtwixt soon too. He would end up missing the Jailer even if the big drachman chose to stay.

"*All done here!*" the Engineer yelled in the distance. "*Bridge is active!*"

Jailer straightened and threw back his shoulders, as if settling a great burden. "This is it, then. My last act as Jailer. When I step through to the other side, I'll be freed of these chains, a jailer no more. I can go back to being the man I'm supposed to be, the man I was when I first arrived."

Ewan twisted his lips and tried really hard to pronounce the word. "Puh— Puh-ruh— ugh!... I *still* can't say dat!"

The Jailer roared with laughter, wiping tears from his eyes. "I needed that, thank you. The Proprietor. That's what I used to be called."

"What do it mean?" Ewan asked.

"It means I own and run a hotel, where I see to the needs of my guests. I keep them warm and well fed and, above all, happy."

"That *perfick* for you!" Ewan blurted. "It what you did for da pwiz-o-ners!"

"All except the part about happiness. I'm looking forward to making people happy again also."

"I hope you get happy too," Ewan said.

The Jailer gave him a big hug, then marched away, head held high. The other two drachmen slithered after him, muttering under their breath.

Nachton and Ewan watched until the threesome faded into whiteness across the bridge. A minute later, the Jailer reappeared alone, gave them all one last smile and thumbs-up, then disappeared for good.

The armies turned to leave.

"Now all that's left is the Vizier," Nachton said. "He grows weaker with the departure of each major ally, but there's still more to do. His power must be broken before we can finally drag him out of Overtwixt too."

"Like what?" Ewan asked, swiping at his eyes.

Nachton pretended not to notice. "Well, Amélie and Cécilie are working on part of that right now..."

· thirty-two ·
(Amélie)

"**A**nd I promise t' serve the greater good for as long as I stay here in Overtwixt," the imp named Flunky said, repeating after Amélie. "I promise t' help in the rebuildin' of Shanagrailia and Eqland, and to preform any other reputations—"

"Reparations," she corrected.

"—reparations," he agreed, "or renovations—"

"Restitutions," she corrected again.

"—right, restitutions, that um... um..." The Flunky's scrunched-up prune-like face got even more wrinkly with confusion.

Amélie sighed. "You promise to help pay for anything your people broke while you served the Vizier."

His face cleared. "Yeah, that! I promise that."

"And above all, you renounce the Vizier."

"You bet!" the imp gushed. "That fool was the worst thing ever happened to—"

"Say it."

"I pronounce the Vizier!"

Good enough. Amélie offered the former bad guy a smile. It was getting easier to smile now that the line of war criminals was nearing its end, here on the outdoor lawn at the center of Gaoland. "Then by the power vested in me as Empress, I pardon you for past crimes and grant you your freedom. So long as you and all the other imps and spooks follow through with your commitment to rebuild and repay, you may continue here in Overtwixt for as long as you wish."

"Thank you!" he gushed. "Oh, thank you, Empress!"

"Report to the Charlatan for your first assignment."

"At once!" And the imp leapt into the air as soon as the centman guards untied his arms, freeing his wings.

"Next?" Amélie called, and a little spookwoman hopped forward. Like the Flunky, she accepted pardon in exchange for speaking the same oaths and promises, as did the spook after that, and the pair of impmen that followed. Then came two more of the gargoyle creatures—a wife and husband—who flatly refused to renounce the Vizier or pay for any of the harm they'd caused. The two of them were returned to their cells; they would be transported to Impstead and escorted back to their real world as soon as reconstruction of their bridge finished.

Soon, all the imps and spooks were processed, and only a single prisoner remained: a sullen centman named Scout. The two centman guards pushed him forward roughly, their faces angry.

"I am prepared to pardon and forgive you," Amélie told her former friend. "You only need to confess your wrongdoing and promise never to repeat it."

"I freely admit that I conspired against you," the Scout said loudly. "But I do not apologize for it. I would do it again, for the good of my people."

"Traitor," one of the guards muttered.

"You acted in your own self-interest!" the other guard said. "You wanted to rule over us, as the new Baron!"

"Better that than some filthy human!" Scout cried. "It would have been better for *all* centmen!"

"Enough," Amélie spoke calmly. She stood up from her makeshift throne, approached the Scout, and held out her hand to him. "I offer you one more chance. You don't have to swear to serve me or any other human. I'm leaving Overtwixt soon, and the centmen will return to self-rule. You can be part of their community again. Only confess your wrongdoing and promise never to repeat it."

"I will not admit I was wrong," the Scout snarled.

Amélie tried not to show how much this hurt her. "Then I remand you into the custody of your people, to be returned to your real world at the earliest opportunity." She gestured, and the guards took him away.

She sat back down on her throne and massaged her head beneath the Crown of Compassion. Wearing the thing was tiring, sometimes. Loving people, especially people who had hurt her, was *hard*. But as long as she served as ruler of this realm, she could not take it off. She needed its help too much.

Cécilie approached, carrying a small chest. "Ready?"

Amélie nodded. "Are they all here?"

Her little sister set the chest down and opened it. Inside were dozens of amulets—gemstones of all sorts, mostly hanging from ribbons, though a few were loose. "They're all here," Cécilie assured her. "Including the ruby and pearl, which Shark threw into the Citadel courtyard."

"Okay. Let's get this over with."

Cécilie handed her the pearl first, and Amélie studied it for a moment. The bright white jewel was beautiful, but it glowed a sickly green. She and Nachton had talked a long time, trying to figure out how to destroy these things, until Nachton realized the answer was simple. The amulets were fueled by green magic and hate, right? How better to reverse that evil than using blue magic and love?

Cupping the pearl in her hand, Amélie focused her thoughts on the person whose talent had been harvested to create it. She had never met the Weaponsmaster, but she found it easy to love him anyway, because he'd been such a good friend to Ewan. Her heart filled with compassion for the shaman, horror at the injustice he had endured, and her Diamond Crown throbbed with blue light.

The pearl shattered in her hand—and with a *pop*, a shaman appeared out of thin air.

Amélie almost fell off her throne, and Cécilie screamed. The centman guards rushed forward to defend the girls, but Cécilie recovered quickly. "No, it's okay!" she squealed joyfully. "It's him! It's the Weaponsmaster! He's okay—are you okay?"

"'Course I'm okay, doll, 'course I am," the shaman told the younger girl with a needle-toothed smile. "But how did *you* get here?" He blinked and looked around. "Wait a sec... How did *I* get here? Where *is* here? Oh boy, I don't think I feel so great." And he sat down quickly on the ground, cradling his head in his hands.

Amélie gestured to the guards. "Please take care of him. Nurse him back to health, the way you did for all the prisoners that appeared in cells after the battle."

"But remember," Cécilie said, "he's a hero!"

The centmen agreed to take good care of the shaman. As they led him away, Amélie heard the little guy say, "Do I know you? Well, I'm the Weaponsmaster! Expert in various and sundry forms of combat..."

Cécilie looked at all the amulets still in the wooden chest, then started rhyming: "All you do is lie... you only made me cry... you're not my friend at all... so time to say goodbye!" Her finger landed on the ruby amulet, which had granted Ewan superhuman strength for so long. Amélie had no idea whose talent the Vizier had harvested to collect so much brawn; but wearing the Crown, she was able to love that unknown person anyway.

With another *crack* and *pop*, the ruby shattered. This time multiple people appeared out of thin air: five huge lugmen like Berserker.

Each amulet Amélie destroyed released one or more imprisoned people: a phoman from the obsidian, *eleven* eqmen from the topaz, and an incredibly tall centman from the emerald, which had been the Vizier's favorite. The amethyst—Cécilie's own favorite, at one time—produced the oldest raiman they'd ever seen, even more wrinkly than the Mystic. And there were dozens more. Every person Amélie freed was extremely disoriented, with no memory of recent events.

When it was done, Cécilie's wooden chest was full of broken gemstones, and the Gaoland lawn had turned into a triage area for yet another group of the Vizier's victims.

By then, the Sky Light was setting for the day. Nachton and Ewan had returned from Drachölm, and preparations were beginning for the next day's departure from Gaoland.

It was the start of their last adventure in Overtwixt.

· thirty-three ·

(Cécilie)

The victory parade began at first light. Exiting Gaoland via the prison's north drawbridge, the children and all their allies made slow but steady progress up the slender niland of Impstead. They stopped at every village they passed, making sure every impman got a chance to see the Vizier.

The former "Emperor" was shackled hand and foot, each iron bracelet and anklet linked to a chain held by Cécilie and her siblings. Even the Vizier's *fingers* were tied tight against each other, to prevent him from weaving the smallest spells. The good guys were taking no chances.

By the end of that first day, the impmen had begun booing their former master.

Just before dark, the one-eyed Dockmaster and his crew of impmen started ferrying parade participants across the gap from Impstead to Dagmoor, using their flying barges. The Captain didn't like the idea, but Amélie wanted to set a good example. As far as she was concerned, the war was over, and people needed to start trusting each other again. She had united all of the oppressed races in order to defeat the Vizier, but the impmen hadn't been part of that coalition; so now Amélie gave them a way to prove themselves worthy of trust.

And everything worked out just fine.

The children and their allies camped for the night on an island in the middle of the Dagmoor swamps. They enjoyed a luau and freshwater seafood feast hosted by the dagmen, and Amélie made a formal show of returning the ancient King's scepter to the dagman leadership; after all, the King had been a dagman himself. To Amélie's obvious surprise, the bug-eyed creatures immediately fiddled with the scepter until they found the catch—and with a *snick*, the golden tube of the scepter's shaft slid smoothly off the end, revealing a long Diamond staff beneath. All this time, the part of the scepter Amélie had been gripping was nothing more than a kind of scabbard. The scepter itself was almost entirely Diamond.

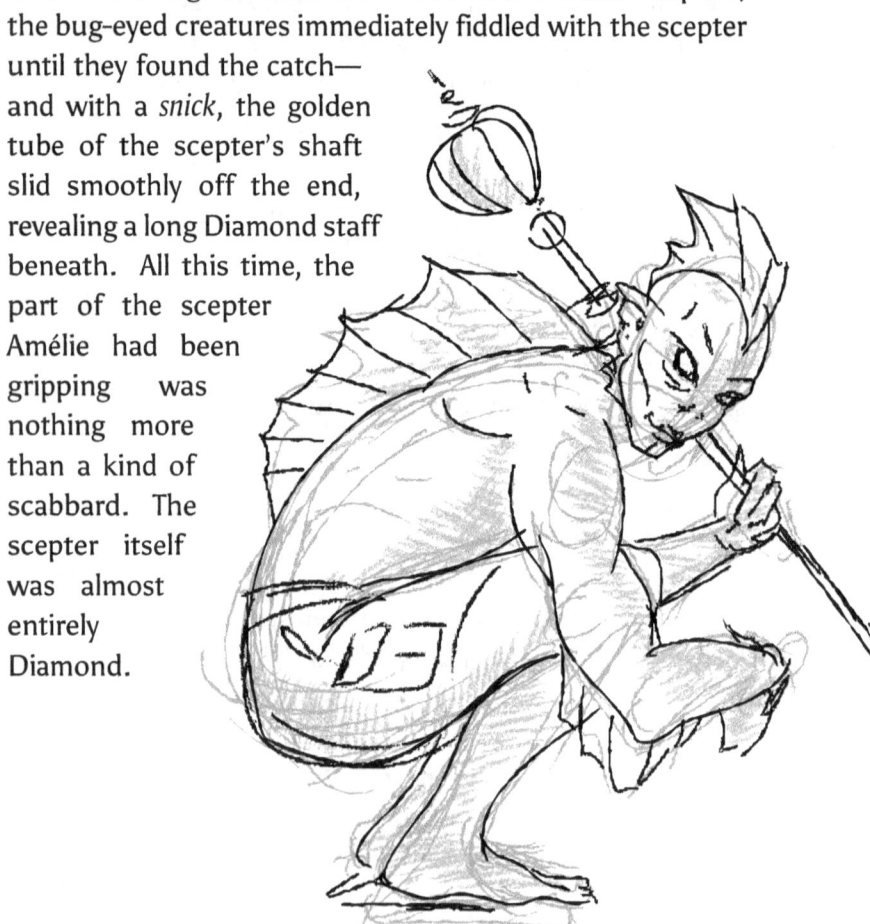

"What?" one of the dagmen asked innocently. "It's one o' them Sovereign's Relics, of course. You just couldn't use it, on account of it bein' a *dagman* Relic, see?"

Amélie only shook her head and began to laugh. Clearly she knew something that Cécilie didn't.

After that, everyone settled in around a crackling fire to talk. Their hosts had even built a cage to hold the Vizier for the night, so that Cécilie and her family could just relax.

Cécilie waited until the hour was late, and people were getting quiet and drowsy around the fire. Then she asked, "Why are we doing this?"

Everyone turned to look at her. "Which part, doll?" the Weaponsmaster asked. "The luau? The fire?"

"The parade. I mean, the impmen are our friends now, right?"

All eyes turned to the Dockmaster, who sat picking his fangs with a small stick. The imp was still super-ugly, with a patch over one eye and a scar running down that side of his face, but he seemed less scary since becoming a good guy. "Yeah," he growled. "We's friends now. What's it to ya?"

Cécilie folded her arms and huffed at the man's rudeness. "What's it to *you*, prune-face?"

Suddenly, the mood turned tense, and several people rested hands on their weapons. But the ugly Dockmaster just eyed her for a moment, then slowly flicked his toothpick into the fire. "You's alright, kid."

Everyone relaxed again.

"So...?" the imp prompted her. "Us bein' friends matters because...?"

Cécilie shrugged, trying to act casual even though her heart was now thumping a little; maybe the Dockmaster was still a *little* scary. "If we're friends now," she said, "I'm just wondering why we don't fly your barges all the way to

Huland, so we can get home faster. Instead of doing this whole parade thing."

The Captain nodded understanding. "Because it's important for all the people of the realm to see the Vizier in chains." Everyone turned to look at the villain in his cage, some distance away where he couldn't hear them talking.

"But why?" Cécilie pushed.

No one answered for a moment, then Nachton spoke up. "The Guide once asked me what gave the Vizier his power. He said I would need to figure that out if we ever hoped to remove him from Overtwixt." He looked around. "Well? Anyone want to guess what it was that gave the Vizier his power?"

"Was amulets!" Berserker said firmly.

"That's right," Weaponsmaster agreed with a shiver. "His relics, his spells, *all* that terrible magic."

Squire tossed his head. "That and the support of powerful allies. The Vizier never would have grown so powerful himself if not for the Warlord and the phomen."

"Maybe," the Crafter spoke up. "But even with a handful of drachmen and phomen, all the magic in Overtwixt wouldn't be enough to subdue the realm." He shook his little gnoman head. "Much as I hate to say it, the Vizier built an impressive bureaucracy. Otherwise, he never could've managed so many slaves or quarried all the stone he needed in order to build that dome."

"Plus he had us imps doin' stuff for him," the Dockmaster growled, picking his nose now.

Crafter sighed. "That's *literally* what I just said."

"Loremaster," Ranger added thoughtfully, "didn't you say it was being the only human—or one of just a few—that gave the Vizier his greatest power?"

"No," Shark said, shaking her head. "It was fear. *Fear* gave him his greatest power. That and deception—convincing the masses that he was even more powerful than he actually was."

Nachton was smiling. "At different times over the last several months, I was convinced that each of those was the right answer. But in the last week, I've come to realize they're *all* right answers. It was no single thing that gave the Vizier his power, but all of those things together."

"That's why we've been removing those sources of power," Amélie said, "one by one. So that, when we finally arrive in Huland, we'll be able to drag the Vizier back across the bridge and out of Overtwixt forever." She looked at Squire. "We started by banishing his most powerful allies." She turned to Crafter and Dockmaster, who were now glaring at each other. "Then we gave the imps and spooks a chance to renounce him as their master." She nodded to Weaponsmaster. "After that, we destroyed his amulets, and every other one of his relics we could find."

"And now," Shark concluded, speaking to Cécilie, "we are undertaking this parade so that all peoples of the realm can see the truth: that there is no longer anything to fear from the Vizier."

"Which leaves the power he wields by being one of just a few humen," Nachton said. "And we'll address *that* when the four of us drag him back to reality with us. Something only the four of us humen, working together, can accomplish—since we're the only ones capable of returning to our real world." He shook his head in wonder. "All this time, that's what the Guide meant about us cooperating to defeat the Vizier for good."

"But why can't we stay here after that?" Ewan sniffled. "Why we gotta go too?"

Nachton and Amélie traded looks. "Aside from the fact that Mom and Dad are probably worried sick?" Amélie asked. "Well, it's not fair to the people of this realm if *anyone* holds that kind of power. So we need to go too, or else make sure more humen cross the bridge to join us. Personally, I'm ready to go home."

Cécilie thought maybe she was too, but it was gonna be hard saying goodbye. Ewan sniffled some more, but Cécilie knew he was ready to snuggle with Mommy again.

The next morning, the parade continued, climbing the treacherous, moss-covered steps from Dagmoor to Caymerdelphia. Cécilie woulda liked to use the slide bridge instead—her new dagman friends insisted it was the most elaborate water slide ever created—but of course, it only went the other direction, from Caymerdelphia to Dagmoor.

In Caymerdelphia, they visited the Amphitheater in the middle of Crystal City for a public reading of the Vizier's crimes. Cécilie barely paid attention, because there were way too many things to distract her: dolphins and mermaids everywhere she looked, and glittering glass towers disappearing into the empty white sky above.

From Crystal City, they traveled across the aqueducts to Delphyrd and from there to Shanagrailia. They stopped short of riding the waterfall the rest of the way to Alabaster City; only dagmen were *that* crazy. Instead, they took a more meandering route around the mountain to enter the secluded valley of the little peoples. Here, the Mystic set up a platform for the Vizier to stand upon; and for three days straight, a long line of gnomen, shamen, nagmen, and raimen passed by, one at a time, in silent accusation. And at the end of it, *they* celebrated too.

The day after that, there was some talk of crossing the skyway from Shanagrailia to Twixt, and traveling on to Eqland from there. But the Engineer put an end to it, insisting Twixt was no longer stable. So they took the more mundane bridge back to Shaland, and started up the great white arch to Eqland on the day that followed.

Midway across the white arch, Cécilie looked over the side and saw for herself why the Engineer insisted on this route. The hubland of Twixt, grandest niland in all the realm, was crumbling. The Engineer explained this was the way of hublands. They came into being at the junction of one or more bridges, symbolizing the alliance of peoples; then they grew in proportion to their own population. With the Baron long gone, the Vizier in chains, and Capital City now deserted, Twixt had become an uninhabited wasteland. It wouldn't last another week.

On reaching Eqland, Cécilie hosted her friends and family at the Palace, then said a tearful goodbye to the Mayor, Steward, Matron, and other friends before the parade continued towards Centwick the following morning. They stayed that night at the Grove, where the centmen had prepared yet another feast. Cécilie only picked at her food. It was all green plants—*yuck*.

And finally, they began the last leg of their journey. By now, their parade procession was much shorter than when it started, since they'd left people behind at every stop along the way. Their last night in Overtwixt, they camped in the outer court of the old Baron's abandoned Castle—just Cécilie, Amélie, Ewan, Nachton, and their ten closest friends.

And the Vizier, of course.

And when the Sky Light dawned on the morrow, they crossed the bridge to Huland, where this whole adventure had started so many months before.

· thirty-four ·
(EVVAN)

When they crossed the very last bridge to Hyoo-land, they turned left and followed the dusty road along the edge of the floaty island. Evveybodies started getting sad. Skire Horsey kept trying to talk to Ewan, but Ewan didn't feel like talking.

"Remember that time you grabbed my mane and wouldn't let go?" the horsey said hopefully. "And I thought you were a filthy gnoman?"

"Hey!" Crafter called.

"No offense."

Ewan shrugged and looked away. He didn't want them to see him crying.

"What about the time we went to Lugard and attacked Berserker?"

"I remember!" Bazooka boomed, laughing. "You call me Rhino Guy. You swing me by ankles 'til I give up!"

Ewan swiped at his cheeks.

Nock was walking next to him. "Talk to your friends, squirt. They're gonna miss you too, y'know."

"Why we gotta leave?" Ewan whined.

"We have to get back to Mom and Dad."

"Why can't *they* come *here?*" he demanded yet again.

"I don't really think that's an option, buddy. Not immediately, at least. We've been gone months. They'll be back home at the house by now, worried sick about us. We'll have to find a police officer to call them."

"How will we ever explain?" Ommie asked.

"They'll never believe us," Sessy said.

"We'll think of some way to tell them," Nock insisted. "And maybe someday we *can* bring them back here with us. But for now, we need to say our goodbyes."

"I don't wanna say goodbye!" Ewan yelled. "Why stuff gotta change?"

"Oh, little human," Shark said, landing on his shoulder and nuzzling up against his cheek. "Change is part of life. Things never stay the same for long... and if you try to *stop* change, you might miss out on a lot of joy."

"And if you never change, puny human," Bazooka boomed, "you never gonna grow big like me!"

Ewan scowled at the lugman, but his lip started twitching, and finally he had to smile.

"Besides," Skire Horsey said, "you're not gone *yet*. Maybe we can still have a little more fun before you go."

Ewan's smile got a little bigger. "Wanna race?"

"I would be delighted, sir Knight."

The horsey knelt down, and Ewan scrambled into his saddle. "First one to da rope bridge a rotten egg!" Ewan squealed, then kicked Skire in the side. "Charge, horsey!"

Skire sighed. "Some things will never change."

"*Go*, Skire! 'Zooka gonna beat us!"

They galloped like the wind along that dirt road, Bazooka loping easily beside them. To Ewan's surprise, Sessy caught up to them a minute later, riding her unee-corn.

There was no way Skire and Ewan were gonna let two *girls* win, so they really started racing then.

When they got to the rope bridge, Ewan jumped out of the saddle and tackled Bazooka to the ground. He knew the big guy was just pretenning, since Ewan wasn't wearing his magic ruby necklace anymore, but that was okay; Ewan decided after his fight with Viziguy that pretend fighting was better anyway. Nobody got hurt.

By the time Nock and Ommie and the others got to the bridge, Ewan was feeling much better. But saying goodbye was still hard. He threw his arms around Skire Horsey's neck. "I love you, Skire."

"I love you too, sir Knight." And when Ewan let go, he saw big tears sliding down the horsey's cheeks.

The little boy turned to face his other friends. "And I love *you*, Fight Guy."

"I'm fond of you too, kid. Hey listen, don't forget to keep practicing your skills. Just 'cause you're going back to the real world is no excuse for getting soft, y'hear?"

Ewan laughed. "Hey 'Zooka? I lo—"

"In my world, we no say such things," the lugman boomed quickly. "We just feel them inside."

"But—"

"Please," the big dude begged. "I have reputation!"

All Ewan's friends laughed at this. Shark was still sitting on his shoulder, and Ewan started scratching her head the way she liked. "I dink I gonna miss you most of all," he whispered.

"Oh, my dear boy," she rasped in his ear. "I will miss you terribly. A truer friend I never had. You trusted me when no one else would, and—" She cleared her throat and started blinking rapidly. "I will never forget you."

"I never forget you neither, Shark."

Nearby, Sessy was hugging her unee-corn's neck tightly, sobbing into her long pink hair. And Nock was giving awkward high-fives to the no-mans.

Ommie's guards were giving her a much more formal goodbye. Ranger Guy, Opera Dude, and the Captain had crossed their arms over their chests to make an X. "It has been a great honor, your majesty the Empress."

"I can never thank you enough for all you've done," Ommie told them. "I will miss you all terribly." And then she was hugging them too.

There were more goodbyes after that. Sessy hugged Ranger Guy, and Nock laughed with all Ewan's friends, even Shark. But eventually, everyone got serious and quiet.

"I had hoped to see the Guide one last time too," Ommie said finally, looking around. "Um, Guide, can you hear me?"

The Guide did not appear.

The Vizier, still chained up so tight he could barely move, laughed under his breath. This surprised everyone, because the bad guy barely made a noise the whole time since they left the prison.

Ommie looked discouraged, but Nock hugged her. "Remember what he said. He's always near, even if we can't see him."

"It's true!" Sessy said. "I asked him for help when I was fighting the Warlord, and he guided my hand to the magic crossbow Bolt!"

"I know," Ommie said with a small smile. "I just wanted to say goodbye."

"I was hoping to talk with him again too," Nock admitted, looking sad. "To... apologize. After promising I would never use the green magic again, I almost used it against the Vizier in that final fight. I jeopardized everything because of my hatred and need for revenge."

The Captain clasped Nock on the shoulder. "Being tempted to commit evil is not the same as *doing* evil. If the Guide were here, I think he'd say he was proud of you for not succumbing. Even if you could have made better choices to avoid that temptation."

Nock slowly nodded, though he was still sad.

"We'll see the Guide again someday," Ommie said. "Somehow, I'm sure of it." She stood up straighter. "In any case, it's time."

Everyone gathered in a circle around the Vizier, and the kids took a firm grip on the four chains.

"In my last act as Empress," Ommie said solemnly, "I hereby banish the Vizier from Overtwixt forever."

Viziguy's eyes blazed. "This doesn't have to be your last act," he told her earnestly. "*You* could stay here forever."

"We have no interest in that—" Nock began.

"You could have power, the likes of which you've never dreamed. I could show you. We could rule together, the three of us—the *five* of us humen."

"No," Ommie said firmly.

The bad guy looked to Sessy.

"No thanks."

He looked at Ewan hopefully.

"You face still uggy."

The Vizier started to get desperate. "You don't understand! All of my progress, the power I've amassed... I lose that the moment I cross back over to the real world. Even if I return tomorrow, I would start from scratch—"

"That's the idea," Nock said. Then he made a blue magic glob to cover Viziguy's mouth. "Empress Amélie? You were saying?"

She nodded regally. "I hereby banish the Vizier from Overtwixt. And once we return to the real world, I will do whatever I can to ensure he never returns. However..." She turned to look at the bad guy, and her Diamond Crown started glowing really bright blue. "As an act of mercy, I will *not* have you executed as you deserve, even though you executed so many in your rise to power. I do not wish that agony on anyone, even you... and you already suffered much when you fell from your tower in the Citadel."

The Vizier glared at her with fierce hatred.

"But please know," Ommie concluded, "if you ever *do* manage to find some way back to Overtwixt, that will be the fate that awaits you. This is my decree. Let it be read aloud in all the cities of the realm, and entered into all historical records."

"It will be as you command, your majesty the Empress," the Captain said. He was writing down everything she said in one of Nock's notebooks, which Nock had to leave behind.

Ommie turned toward the rope bridge, then suddenly looked unsure. "Do we need to leave Sovereign's Relics here before we go?"

"No, doll—erm, majesty," Fight Guy said. "When you cross the threshold to your real world, they too will return home automatically. It's part of their magic, built into them by the Sovereign. 'Sides, you best keep them on you 'til the very end, just in case this one tries something." And he jabbed the Vizier in the side with two of his flippery fingers.

Ommie nodded and took one last big breath of Overchix air. Then she and Sessy stepped onto the bridge, leading the Vizier after them with their chains. Ewan waved a final goodbye, then he and Nock followed.

· thirty-five ·

(Amélie)

The rope bridge back to the Atlanta airport stretched into the distance before Amélie, fading into nothingness like it was being swallowed up by a cloud. It looked just the same as it had that first day, before the Warlord tore it down. The Engineer's team had done its job well.

"C'mon," Amélie whispered, pulling the Vizier's chain and clasping Cécilie's free hand in her own.

The bridge creaked and swayed as they walked, and they were soon enveloped in whiteness. Amélie tried to look back toward Huland, but it was out of sight by now too. When she faced forward again, she noticed the wooden planks of the bridge had been replaced by carpet.

The whiteness cleared, and Amélie saw a wall where the rope railing had been moments before. Amazed, she raised a hand to touch it—then jerked in surprise when she realized she was now holding a cell phone. *Her* cell phone, which she'd lost all those months ago. Its screen was still cracked, too, but that didn't matter. What happened to the chain she'd been gripping in that hand? Heart thumping, afraid the Vizier had gotten away somehow, she whirled to face him—

But he was gone too. In his place was a short, greasy-haired teenage boy.

This was the *Vizier?*

All of the kids looked different now, wearing their original real world clothes again, carrying backpacks. Nachton was staring in wonder at his paperback novel, and Ewan looked really unimpressed with the plastic action figure he now held. Everyone seemed disoriented, especially the short teen Vizier, who was stumbling along in terrible confusion.

Ewan tossed the action figure over his shoulder and came up next to the kid. Taking his hand, he said, "It okay, buddy. Follow me." And the 5-year-old took the lead, dragging the teenager—the Vizier!—after him. He marched right up to the top of the jet bridge, shoved the big metal door open, and re-entered the brightly lit airport concourse.

"Kids!" Mom yelled, rushing up with Dad at her side.

Amélie stared in wonder. They were still here? All these months later, and her parents had stayed *here*, waiting for them to return?

In that instant, Amélie forgot all about the Vizier and Overtwixt and all their adventures, and she ran to her parents. All four Ollivaros kids collided with them at the same time, making a giant six-person hug. "Oh Mom, Dad, I love you so much!" Amélie blubbered. *All* of the kids were blubbering.

"What are you doing?" Dad asked, sounding annoyed. "Let go! We're gonna be—"

"I thought I'd never see you again!" Cécilie sobbed, burying her face in his shirt.

"Oh, Cécilie, stop being so dramatic all the time. You were barely out of our sight a couple minutes!"

"What?" Nachton blurted.

"Still," Mom said, "someone should do something about that door. It shouldn't be left unlocked like that." She, at least, seemed relieved at seeing them again, but not hysterical the way Amélie had expected.

Dad was forced to pry himself free of all four kids, even Nachton. But when he realized how emotional they were, his face softened. "Hey, I'm glad you're all okay. Believe me." His face twitched in a small smile. "I guess I *was* worried... just a little. But if we don't hurry—"

"Honey, look!" Mom was pointing at the greasy-haired teen. "Do you think that's the other missing boy?"

Dad blinked. "I bet you it is. Officer? Officer!" He began waving to a policeman who was standing nearby, talking to a woman who had her arms wrapped around a second teenager, a red-headed boy.

"It's crazy," Mom said. "They've been making announcements about those two missing children all day. And all that time, they were both hiding in the same place!"

"Up to no good, I'll bet," Dad said darkly. He had finally gotten the policeman's attention.

"Wait," Nachton said. "They found the other missing kid too?" He glanced at Amélie, but she only vaguely remembered hearing those announcements over the airport loudspeakers, so long ago.

"Sure," Dad said, and he pointed to the red-headed boy. "Didn't you see him back there? You must've walked right past each other, just a couple minutes ago."

Nachton stared. "Yeah... Yeah, we mighta bumped into each other."

The red-head was staring vaguely in their direction, but he seemed almost as disoriented as the Vizier. Still, when his eyes met Amélie's, he smiled—and Amélie liked him instantly.

Somehow, she knew this was the old Baron. "How long was he missing?" she asked Dad.

"All day, according to the announcement," Dad said.

Just one day? "The Captain was right," Amélie whispered, thinking back to what he'd said back when they first arrived. "Time really *does* pass strangely in Overtwixt."

"In keeping with the Third Fundamental Law," Nachton said in an answering whisper. "Just think, the Baron was there longer than all of us. He lived an entire lifetime! And he still got home in time for dinner."

Amélie elbowed her brother hard for that one. It wasn't funny. Well, maybe a little.

The police officer was trying to talk to the teenage Vizier now, but the former villain still seemed dazed. Suddenly, Amélie remembered that she had one last duty to perform for the good of Overtwixt. "Officer? Sir, there's something you should know."

"What's that, young lady?"

"This boy, he wanted to destroy the bridges."

The policeman stared at her. "What bridges?"

"You know..." she said, gesturing vaguely in the direction of the rope bridge to Overtwixt. Too late, she realized that the full truth of the Vizier's crimes would be meaningless to the police officer.

And yet the policeman's eyes suddenly widened. "You mean the jet bridges? The bridges to all the airplanes?"

"Um... yes?"

"But young lady, that door doesn't go to a jet bridge. Just a hallway and some supply closets."

"Oh." Amélie tried to play it cool. "Well, that's what he *said* he wanted to do—destroy all the bridges."

"That way he could stay here forever and never have to leave," Nachton added.

"That is a very serious accusation," the officer said sternly. He turned to face the teenage Vizier. "Is this true?"

Amazingly, the boy blushed and nodded.

It *was* true, or as much of the truth as anyone in the human real world would ever understand. Hopefully it would be enough to get the Vizier banned from the airport for life.

"What about the other one?" the officer asked, turning to point at the red-head.

"Oh, he tried to stop him," Nachton said hurriedly.

"But he went missing first!" the officer said in disbelief. "What's he been doing all day?"

"That I can't tell you," Nachton said apologetically.

"We were barely in there a couple minutes ourselves," Amélie explained. "We took a wrong turn."

"Of course, of course," the officer said, his attention back on the Vizier again. "Thank you for your help, kids."

"Look at that," Mom said, pulling Nachton and Amélie into another hug. "My kids doing their civic duty. You're a pair of heroes in my book."

"Me too!" Ewan blurted. "I fought dat guy with a *Sword*—"

"Time for stories later," Nachton interrupted quickly.

"That's exactly right," Dad said, smiling at Nachton in surprise. "For now, we've got a flight to catch—and if we don't hurry, we really are going to miss it."

The red-headed boy was still watching Amélie. He mouthed two words at her: *Good job.*

"Fortunately," Dad went on, "we don't have far to go. That's our gate right th—"

"Wait!" Mom shrieked, sounding panicked.

"What?" Amélie asked. "What is it now, Mom?"

"It's *Cécilie!* She's disappeared—again!"

· epilogue ·
(Cécilie)

For the second time ever, Cécilie stepped off the last wooden plank of the rope bridge and onto the niland of Huland. She sat down in the grass, dismayed. She had just been here minutes before, saying goodbye to her friends... but now there was no one else in sight.

"What are you doing back already?" a kind voice asked.

Cécilie's heart soared. "Guide!" She leapt to her feet and rushed toward the bearded centman, who was suddenly standing a short distance away on the blanket of soft grass. He knelt on his forelegs, and she collided with him in a big hug. "I changed my mind," she blurted. "I'm not ready to leave."

"But your family..."

"They'll never even know I'm gone. I can have more adventures, stay here for *years*, then still go back and I won't miss anything." Without releasing their hug, she leaned away and looked hopefully into his eyes.

"You're saying that further adventure is what you desire?" the Guide asked, raising an eyebrow. "Another villain to fight? More scary escapes through the woods, wondering if you'll be captured and thrown in jail?"

"Well... no."

"Then why aren't you ready to leave?"

Cécilie thought about it honestly for a moment. "Because I'm special here."

"No more or less than any other person from any other world."

"But I'm not special *at all* at home."

The Guide snorted. "Of course you are."

"I'm not a princess!" she argued, her lips beginning to tremble.

"Aren't you? As far as your Daddy is concerned, you are the only princess in all the real world."

Cécilie sniffled and tried not to roll her eyes. "So what if *he* thinks that? That's not the same thing as—Wait." She looked at the Guide suspiciously. "How do you know my Daddy calls me that?"

The centman just gazed at her innocently.

"Did you see my Daddy at the airport? Did you hear him call me princess?" Suddenly she realized something, and her eyes opened wide. "*Wait* a sec. Wait, wait, wait. That first day in Overtwixt, you told Nachton that no one can travel to any real world except their own. You said that's why Overtwixt exists, so everyone can meet in the middle!"

"Yes," the Guide nodded calmly. "That is still absolutely true."

"But you *were* in my real world, in the airport! You looked like a human, and you were waving at us to hurry!"

Now the Guide was smiling slyly.

"But you just said that's impossible, unless—" Cécilie sucked in a sharp breath. "You're *him*. You're the Sovereign!"

"Whoa, that's a big leap. What makes you say that?"

"He's the supreme ruler of all the infinite dimensions of the cosmos—you said so! So *he* can visit any real world! And since *you* can visit any real world too, that means..."

The Guide smiled, confirming her suspicions.

"I knew it!"

"I and the Sovereign are one," the Guide said. "He is I, and I am he... though we are each also ourselves." He chuckled. "I don't expect you to fully understand it, young one. It is enough for you to realize that his power and authority are mine as well, and we can never be in opposition to one another."

Cécilie was kinda awestruck, but she nodded. Still, this changed everything she thought she understood about the Guide. "I don't get it, though. You knew all along what the Vizier was doing. If you and the Sovereign are the same guy, that means you coulda sent help to defeat the Vizier and his followers!"

This time, the Guide laughed out loud. "I *did* send help. I sent you and your brothers and sister."

"But *you* coulda defeated the Vizier, all by yourself!"

He shrugged. "True. But I preferred to work through your family."

"Why?" she asked, completely amazed.

"My reasons are many, and mostly beyond your understanding," the Guide said with that small smile again. "But giving you this opportunity to learn and grow would have been reason enough, all by itself."

That made Cécilie feel even more special—and humble too—when she stopped to think about it. She supposed she *had* learned a lot while she was here, lessons she could take back with her to the real world. Maybe going back to her normal life wouldn't be as boring as she feared. Maybe it would be an adventure now too.

"So I really have to go home?" she asked anyway, just to be absolutely sure. "Today? Now?"

"That would be best," the Guide assured her.

"Will I ever visit Overtwixt again?"

The Guide only smiled.

"I'm gonna miss it... and you."

"How quickly you forget. I'm never far, whether you can see me or not. All you need to do is speak to me—even quietly, in your own head—and I will hear you."

Cécilie smiled at this, then rushed forward and gave the Guide another big hug. "Can I maybe get one last ride before I go?"

The Guide laughed delightedly. "Absolutely." And he lifted her smoothly onto his back, just like he'd done that first day so long ago.

The Princess and the Guide rode the entire perimeter of Huland, galloping at breakneck speed, never stopping to rest. And though Cécilie's heart soared with exhilaration, she never felt any fear, because she trusted the Guide.

By the time they came back where they started, the Sky Light was setting for the night. Cécilie gave the Guide one last hug, then hurried across the rope bridge without any further argument. She had to keep wiping tears from her eyes, but she didn't slow down or turn around.

"There she is!" Amélie announced, as soon as Cécilie walked back into the airport. "I told you she wouldn't just disappear again, Mom."

Daddy took a firm grip on Cécilie's hand. "C'mon, pumpkin, no more dawdling. We've got a flight to catch."

"Please don't call me that, Daddy."

He looked at her with surprise, and then he smiled. "Very well, princess. If her royal highness would kindly come with me, her coach is waiting."

Cécilie lifted her head high and smiled regally, just like the Matron had taught her. "That's better."

Daddy laughed, and the Ollivaros family moved together towards the next gate. The very human gate agent—who looked nothing like the Guide—took their tickets and let them onto the plane that would finally, *finally* return them home.

Behind them, a pair of airport workers closed and locked the big metal door that led to Overtwixt, never knowing it was a gateway to a magical world. They only pulled the door tight and jiggled the knob a few times... all the while wondering how a bunch of kids ever got past that door in the first place.

Nachton, Amélie, Cécilie, and Ewan will return to Overtwixt someday, this time with more of their family! But much will change in the world of bridges between now and then...

Be on the lookout for:

OVERTWIXT3
THE KAISERLANDS

In the meantime, begin an all-new adventure set in Overtwixt's ancient past, in the time of Caymerlot and its unlikely King...

THE CIRCUS OF
DAGMOR™
Book 1 • The Golden Age of Overtwixt

Or continue the adventures of Nachton, Amélie, Cécilie, and Ewan with these tie-in stories, one for each of the children:

The Knight and His Friends • picture book

The Princess and Her Throne • chapter book

Perilous Flight • novella
(bridges the gap between Overtwixt *and* Escape from Overtwixt*)*

Scavenger Hunt • novella

glossary
of persons, places & things
(with pronunciation clues in bold gray)

Note: *[Ew.]* indicates a "Ewanism," unique pronunciation or slang used by Ewan Ollivaros for words he cannot pronounce.

Adversary, *unknown race* – mysterious enemy of the Sovereign

Alabaster (AL-uh-bass-tur) **City** – major metropolitan area on Shanagrailia

"All you do..." – one of many counting rhymes created by Cécilie; full rhyme goes: "All you do is lie; you only made me cry; you're not my friend at all, so time to say goodbye!"; see also "Batter you lick..." and "Cows go moo..."

Amélie (AWM-uh-lee), *huwoman* – 12-year-old human girl, second of the Ollivaros children; see Empress

Amphitheater (AM-fuh-thee-uh-tur) – main meeting hall of the Assembly of Caymerdelphia, a circular open-air pool of water capable of "seating" more than a thousand people

Aquatic Quarter – the section of Capital City originally populated by aquatics

aquatics – general term referring to the cayman, dagman, delphman, and merman races

Archives (AR-kyvz) – the main eqman repository of knowledge on Eqland

Archivist, *eqman* – administrator of the Archives

Arts-and-Crafts Dude *[Ew.]* – see Crafter

Assembly – the voting population of Caymerdelphia, comprised of any aquatic with an interest in making his or her voice heard in current affairs

Baron, *human* – former ruler of the humen and centmen, who reigned from the Castle; later ruled all the United Lands from Capital City, until overthrown by the Vizier

bat-dudes/guys *[Ew.]* – see spookmen

"Batter you lick…" – one of many counting rhymes created by Cécilie; full rhyme goes: "Batter you lick could make you sick; you look fine so you're my pick!"; see also "All you do…" and "Cows go moo…"

Bazooka *[Ew.]* – see Berserker

Berserker (bur-ZUR-kur), *lugman* – huge companion of Ewan who loves to fight

Blackguard, *drachwoman* – sworn bodyguard and secret admirer of the Vizier

Bwackguard Yady *[Ew.]* – see Blackguard

bweff *[Ew.]* – breath

bwudder *[Ew.]* – brother

caparison (kuh-PAR-uh-sun) – an elegant ornamental covering for a horse, like clothing

Capital City – major metropolitan area on Twixt, and foremost city of the United Lands

capitol complex – see Citadel

Captain, *centman* – companion and leader of the guardsmen sworn to protect Amélie; formerly served the Baron in the same capacity

Cartographer, *shaman* – expert mapmaker who surveyed and plotted the nilands of the United Lands

Castle – former seat of the Baron's rule on Hucentia

caymen, *race* – see Nachton's Reference Book

Caymerdelphia (cay-mur-DELF-ee-uh), *niland* – hubland joining Caypool, Merpool, and Delphyrd originally; bridges were later built to join Dagmoor as well

Caymerlot (CAY-mur-laht) – ancient name for Caymerdelphia

Caypool, *niland* – portland of the caymen

Cécilie (SESS-ill-lee), *huwoman* – 8-year-old human girl, third of the Ollivaros children; see Princess

cent-dudes/guys *[Ew.]* – see centmen

centmen (SINT-min), *race* – see Nachton's Reference Book

Centwick (SINT-wik), *niland* – portland of the centmen

Citadel (SIT-uh-dell) – seat of the Vizier's rule in Capital City; formerly the capitol complex, under the Baron's rule

Committee – ruling body of Caymerdelphia; historically responsible for voting on motions put forth from the Assembly and acting as intermediary between the Assembly and the Underlord; comprised of eleven members elected from all four of the aquatic races

Conjurer (KON-jur-ur) – title assumed by Nachton Ollivaros for a time

Council – ruling body of Centwick; comprised of two centmen and two centwomen

Councilmember – member of the Council of Centwick

"Cows go moo..." – one of many counting rhymes created by Cécilie; full rhyme goes: "Cows go moo while they chew; you look nice so I pick you!"; see also "All you do..." and "Batter you lick..."

Crafter, *gnoman* – companion of Nachton who is talented at fabricating needed items

creatures of darkness – general term referring to the drachman, impman, phoman, and spookman races; see Shadowlands, or forces of darkness

Criers (KRY-urz), *spooks* – any of several spooks renamed by the Vizier to pronounce his decrees throughout the United Lands

Crystal City – major metropolitan area on Caymerdelphia

dagmen, *race* – see Nachton's Reference Book

Dagmoor, *niland* – portland of the dagmen

Debby – nickname for the Debutante

Debutante (DEB-yoo-tawnt), *eqwoman* – friend of the Handmaiden who was smoked during the Vizier's conquest of Eqland

Decrepit Damsel (dee-KREP-it DAM-zuhl) – alternate name for the game Old Maid, as used in parallel dimensions (other real worlds)

delphmen (DELF-min), *race* – see Nachton's Reference Book

Delphyrd (DELF-urd), *niland* – portland of the delphmen

dink *[Ew.]* – think

Dockmaster, *imp* – one-eyed leader of the flying barge crews; wears a patch over his missing eye

drachmen (DRAWK-min), *race* – see Nachton's Reference Book

Drachölm (DRAWK-holm), *niland* – portland of the drachmen

dwagons *[Ew.]* – see drachmen

eck-dudes/guys/mans *[Ew.]* – see eqmen

Eckwind *[Ew.]* – see Eqland

emenies *[Ew.]* – enemies

Emperor – title assumed by the Vizier after overthrowing the Baron and taking control of the United Lands

Empess *[Ew.]* – see Empress

Empress – future ruler over all sixteen races of the United Lands, and rival to the Vizier; role chosen by Amélie Ollivaros upon entrance to Overtwixt

Enforcer, *phoman* – the Vizier's minion primarily responsible for imposing punishments throughout the United Lands

Engineer, *gnoman* – former slave freed by Cécilie; later companion of Nachton who is skilled in mechanics, construction, and woodworking

epoch (EP-uhk *or* EE-pok) – any period of time during which a race inhabited Overtwixt, marked before and after by periods of non-habitation; for example, the 782nd Human Epoch refers to the 782nd period during which humen visited Overtwixt; also known as eras by some races

Eqland (EK-luhnd), *niland* – portland of the eqmen

eqmen (EK-min), *race* – see Nachton's Reference Book

era (AIR-uh *or* EER-uh) – see epoch

Ewan (YOO-wun), *human* – 5-year-old human boy, youngest of the Ollivaros children; see Knight

Fight Guy *[Ew.]* – see Weaponsmaster

Five Fundamental Laws – basic rules governing the innerworkings of Overtwixt, as established by the Sovereign when Overtwixt came into being; listed at the start of this book

Flunky, *imp* – one of the Vizier's minions responsible for guarding niland bridges; also see Stooge

fo-dudes/guys *[Ew.]* – see phomen

forces of darkness – general term referring to the Vizier's minions; see creatures of darkness

fwend *[Ew.]* – friend

Gaoland (JAIL-luhnd), *niland* – mysterious hubland joining Impstead, Pholand, and Spookwood

glowstone – stone mined on Gnobury that gives off a natural amber (yellow-orange) light; used by the gnomen to provide illumination and act as signposts

Gnobury (NO-bur-ree), *niland* – portland of the gnomen

Gnocentia (no-SINCH-yuh), *niland* – hubland joining Gnobury and Centwick

gnomen (NO-min), *race* – see Nachton's Reference Book

Go Trawl/Go Troll – alternate names for the game Go Fish, as used in parallel dimensions (other real worlds)

goss *[Ew.]* – gross

Grand Library – the main human repository of knowledge on Huland

Grove – primary settlement of centmen on Centwick

Guide, *centman* – the first person to greet every new visitor to Overtwixt; responsible for presenting newcomers with three paths to choose from; otherwise provides assistance and guidance as requested by the visitor

Handmaiden, *eqwoman* – adolescent companion of Cécilie who serves as her primary lady-in-waiting

Heights – the section of Capital City originally populated by centmen and eqmen; home to the Citadel

horseys *[Ew.]* – see eqmen

Hostess, *delphwoman* – friend of Amélie who first welcomes her to Caymerdelphia

hubland – a hub niland, any new niland created by the inhabitants of Overtwixt when two or more peoples desire to come together for mutual benefit

Hucentia (hyoo-SINCH-yuh), *niland* – hubland joining Huland and Centwick

Huland (HYOO-luhnd), *niland* – portland of the humen

humen, *race* – see Nachton's Reference Book

hungy *[Ew.]* – hungry

imp – slang for any impman or impwoman

impmen, *race* – see Nachton's Reference Book

Impstead (IMP-sted), *niland* – portland of the impmen

Innkeeper, *dagman* – owner/operator of a glass tower hotel in Crystal City near the Amphitheater

Inquisitor (in-QUIZ-it-ur), *phoman* – the Vizier's minion primarily responsible for interrogating the Vizier's enemies

Ivan (EYE-vuhn), *human* – cousin of the Ollivaros children

Ivory (EYE-vur-ee), *huwoman* – cousin of the Ollivaros children

Jail Guy *[Ew.]* – see Jailer

Jailer, *drachman* – kind-hearted minion of the Vizier responsible for imprisoning the Vizier's enemies

Kaiser (KY-zur), *drachman* – former ruler of the Shadowlands who reigned from the Fastness, until the Vizier fabricated evidence to have him banished from Overtwixt

King, *dagman* – ancient ruler of Caymerlot

Knight, *human* – primary defender of a ruler's honor; role chosen by Ewan Ollivaros upon entrance to Overtwixt, after which he served his sisters the Empress and Princess; also a historical figure who served the ancient King of Caymerlot

little peoples – general term referring to the gnoman, nagman, raiman, and shaman races

Little Quarter – the section of Capital City originally populated by little peoples

Loremaster, *human* – chief advisor to the Empress, responsible for researching issues and uncovering lost knowledge in libraries, then rendering judgment or providing counsel; role chosen by Nachton Ollivaros upon entrance to Overtwixt

Lugard (LOO-gard), *niland* – portland of the lugmen

lugmen, *race* – see Nachton's Reference Book

man-bat-dudes/guys *[Ew.]* – see impmen

Matron (MAY-truhn), *eqwoman* – friend and advisor of Cécilie who trains her in the proper "comportment" of a lady

Mayor (MAY-ur), *eqman* – leader of Pastoral City

mermays *[Ew.]* – mermaids; see mermen

mermen, *race* – see Nachton's Reference Book

Merpool, *niland* – portland of the mermen

Messengers, *spooks* – any of several spooks renamed by the Vizier to carry messages to and from his allies throughout the United Lands

Mystic (MISS-tik), *raiman* – former leader of the little peoples who ruled from Alabaster City before abdicating in favor of the Baron

Nachton (NAWK-tuhn), *human* – 15-year-old human boy, oldest of the Ollivaros children; see Loremaster and Conjurer

Nagland, *niland* – portland of the nagmen

nagmen, *race* – see Nachton's Reference Book

niland (NY-luhnd) – an island landmass floating in nothingness

no-dudes/guys/mans *[Ew.]* – see gnomen

Nock *[Ew.]* – see Nachton

Ollivaros (awl-iv-VAIR-os) – last name of Nachton, Amélie, Cécilie, and Ewan

Ommie *[Ew.]* – see Amélie

Opera Dude *[Ew.]* – see Operative

Operative, *centman* – one of the Captain's guardsmen, sworn to protect Amélie; formerly served the Baron in the same capacity

Overchix *[Ew.]* – see Overtwixt

Overtwixt – the world of bridges, where all parallel universes (or alternate dimensions) intersect

Palace – seat of the Prince/Princess's rule in Pastoral City

Pastoral (pass-TOR-uhl) **City** – rustic major population center on Eqland

pease *[Ew.]* – please

perfick *[Ew.]* – perfect

Pholand (FO-luhnd), *niland* – portland of the phomen

phomen (FO-min), *race* – see Nachton's Reference Book

Pincess *[Ew.]* – see Princess

portland – a port niland, any landmass that exists where a real world intersects with (bridges into) Overtwixt

Prince, *eqman* – former ruler of the eqmen who reigned from the Palace, until the Vizier fabricated evidence to have him banished from Overtwixt

Princess, *huwoman* – future ruler of the eqmen; role chosen by Cécilie Ollivaros upon entrance to Overtwixt

prolly *[Ew.]* – probably

Proprietor (pro-PRY-it-ur), *drachman* – role chosen by the Jailer upon entrance to Overtwixt, before the Vizier renamed him

pwiz-o-ner *[Ew.]* – prisoner

Raibourne (RAY-burn), *niland* – portland of the raimen

Raibournian (ray-BURN-ee-un) **Rummy** – raiman game originating on their portland of Raibourne

raimen (RAY-min), *race* – see Nachton's Reference Book

Ranger, *centman* – one of Captain's guardsmen, sworn to protect Amélie; formerly served the Baron in the same capacity; also a companion of Cécilie for a time

ray-dudes/guys *[Ew.]* – see raimen

relic – any magical artifact

rhino dudes/guys *[Ew.]* – see lugmen

Scholar (SKAWL-ur), *eqman* – intellectual and academic, often a companion of the Archivist

Scout, *centman* – one of the Captain's guardsmen, sworn to protect Amélie; formerly served the Baron in the same capacity

Seamstress, *gnowoman* – former slave freed by Cécilie; an expert dressmaker who sewed new gowns for both Cécilie and Amélie

Sessy *[Ew.]* – see Cécilie

Shadowlands – general term referring to any of the nilands of the drachman, impman, phoman, or spookman (and occasionally dagman) races, which are generally overshadowed by the nilands above; see creatures of darkness

shaggy pony guys *[Ew.]* – see nagmen

Shaland (SHAW-luhnd), *niland* – portland of the shamen

shamen (SHAW-min), *race* – see Nachton's Reference Book

Shanagrailia (shaw-nuh-GRAIL-yuh), *niland* – hubland joining Shaland, Nagland, and Raibourne originally; tunnel bridges were later engineered to join Gnobury as well

Shark *[Ew.]*, *spook* – controversial friend of Ewan

Skire *[Ew.]* – see Squire

Sky Light – one of countless celestial artifacts put in place by the Sovereign to provide illumination to the nilands of Overtwixt; bright like a sun one side and dim like a moon on the other, it rotates on its axis to simulate daytime and nighttime

Slums – the section of Capital City originally populated by creatures of darkness

smoke, *verb* – to hurt a person badly enough to eject him or her from Overtwixt; example: "The Kaiser got smoked," meaning the Vizier executed him; see yellow smoke, and the Five Fundamental Laws

Soldiers, *imps* – any of several impmen renamed by the Vizier to serve in his armies throughout the United Lands

Sovereign (SAWV-rin), *unknown race* – distant supreme ruler of all the infinite dimensions of the cosmos

Sovereign's Relics – special magical artifacts of enormous power that can only be used by the pure of heart for the greater good, of which four were gifted by the Sovereign to each and every race when Overtwixt came into being

Spies, *spooks* – any of several spooks renamed by the Vizier to move quietly throughout the United Lands, spying on the populace and gathering information

spook – slang for any spookman or spookwoman

spookmen, *race* – see Nachton's Reference Book

Spookwood, *niland* – portland of the spookmen

spooky-bats *[Ew.]* – see spookmen

Squire, *eqman* – primary companion of Ewan who carries him into battle

Steward, *eqman* – individual responsible for the day-to-day operation of the Palace

stick-and-chain thing *[Ew.]* – nunchucks

Stooge – one of the Vizier's minions responsible for guarding niland bridges; also see Flunky

Thieves, *spooks* – any of several spooks renamed by the Vizier to steal items of interest to him throughout the United Lands

Twixt, *niland* – hubland joining Caymerdelphia, Shanagrailia, Hucentia, Eqland, and Drachölm

uggy *[Ew.]* – ugly

Underlord, *merman* – former ruler of the aquatics who reigned from Crystal City before abdicating in favor of the Baron; left Overtwixt immediately thereafter

unee-corns *[Ew.]* – see eqwomen

United Lands – the realm of Overtwixt united and ruled by the Baron, later isolated and ruled by the Vizier

uvver *[Ew.]* – other

Vizier (viz-ZEER), *human* – the villain who schemed and plotted to unite the realm beneath the Baron, then overthrew the Baron to assume control himself, destroying bridges and building walls to secure his reign

Vizier's tower – the tallest tower of the Citadel, which houses the Vizier's residential chambers and preferred audience chamber

Viziguy *[Ew.]* – see Vizier

Volunteer, *centman* – newly recruited member of the Captain's guardsmen, sworn to protect Amélie

War-Dwagon Dude *[Ew.]* – see Warlord

Warlord, *drachman* – supreme commander of the Vizier's forces of darkness; formerly served the Kaiser in the same capacity

Weaponsmaster, *shaman* – companion of Ewan who trains him to be a swordfighter

wimpmen *[Ew.]* – see impmen

wimpy-bats/dudes/guys *[Ew.]* – see impmen

Wrangler (RANG-glur), *eqman* – former slave and shy companion of Cécilie who is quick to help anyone

yellow smoke – the emission that appears when a person is hurt badly enough to be ejected from Overtwixt

yug-dudes/guys *[Ew.]* – see lugmen

Zealot (ZEL-uht), *phoman* – leader of the group of phomen newly returned to Overtwixt

'Zooka *[Ew.]* – see Berserker (abbreviated form of Bazooka)

introduction to the
ancient languages of Overtwixt

(condensed from a primer
by the Ancient Wizard of Merlyn)

Observant visitors to Overtwixt (in any age or epoch) will soon notice that they can easily understand the speech of other races, even though each people speaks one or more languages unique to its own dimension. This is one of the passive magical functions of Overtwixt, to facilitate communication and understanding.

The written word is translated automatically in much the same way. Any book a person reads (in one of the many libraries or elsewhere) will appear to be inscribed in the reader's own language.

With just two exceptions.

The oldest treatises are written in one of the two ancient languages that originated within Overtwixt itself. The first is **High Epitopian**, a graceful script that was used during the First Age in Epitopia, the earliest society in the world of bridges. The Epitopian language relies on simple, easy to remember rules of grammar and spelling, and the words for many concepts are spelled symmetrically. However, these many rules are rigid and unyielding, such as the requirement that Epitopian always be inscribed from right to left. It also has a limited lexicon, and many concepts simply cannot be expressed in Epitopian.

Example *(right-to-left):*

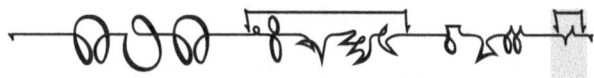

!rule (of (Human race, *lit. The Stubborn Ones*)) Doom [is] *[FUT]* ←

The other ancient language is **Unterstygian**, which was developed in the ages after the Schism as a proposed improvement on Epitopian. It employs a boxier, utilitarian script, and is much more flexible in its use. Unlike Epitopian, Unterstygian can be inscribed in any direction: right-to-left or left-to-right, top-to-bottom or bottom-to-top, or even some combination of the above, with lines of text changing direction as needed. Unterstygian's only unbreakable rule is that words are *never* spelled symmetrically.

Example *(left-to-right):*

→ *[FUT]* [is] Destiny (of (Human race, *lit. The Proud Ones*)) rulership!

Interestingly, vocabulary and pronunciation are both highly similar between these two languages, since again, Unterstygian evolved from Epitopian. However, varying connotations and subtle gradations of meaning between the two can result in significantly different interpretations.

As one might expect, many of the oldest tomes written on the subject of Sovereign or the blue magic are inscribed in High Epitopian, while the morally flexible green magic is typically documented only using Unterstygian.

OVERTWIXT
Reference Book

Your Guide to Overtwixt

See, it's the **Guide** (get it?)

Prepared by Nachton Ollivaros,
782nd Human Epoch

INDEX

The Peoples of Overtwixt

Warning ~ This document deals with topics that are perhaps less interesting to younger readers.

Introduction ~ Having been in this place called Overtwixt for a few weeks now, I will now endeavor to document my observations. Overtwixt is not a "world" or "planet" as we would normally define such things. It is a conceptual realm where all real worlds intersect, and where the people of those worlds can interact. Even though it's NOT a physical place, our minds still visualize it that way, because the physical world is most familiar to us. That's why we find ourselves walking on land (or swimming through water, in the case of the aquatics). I also think that our non-physical link to this place accounts for the irregular and relative passage of time, much as we experience when dreaming.

About Nilands ~ Overtwixt has no core structure, and it only obeys the laws of physics when it feels like it. It appears to consist of unending white nothingness, with an infinite number of "nilands" floating inside. (Just as an "island" is land floating in water, a "niland" is land floating in nil, or nothing.)

Portlands - For each real world that intersects Overtwixt, a single port niland—or "portland"—occurs naturally. (Huland, for example, is the portland linking Overtwixt to the human real world.) Portlands are then linked to each other by bridges of all sorts.

Hublands - New nilands can be created by the inhabitants of Overtwixt if two or more peoples want to come together for mutual benefit. These hublands must be "planted," at the intersection of two or more bridges, by bringing together soil from

2

each of the linked portlands. The new niland is then "cultivated" through inhabitation. The more people come to live on the burgeoning niland, the greater the landmass (or body of water) will become as it grows to accommodate its population.

About Flora and Fauna ~ As a conceptual realm, Overtwixt has no naturally occurring species of animal life. Each niland DOES feature plant life reminiscent of its linked real world(s), but these plants are not truly alive. They are simply mental constructs created by the niland's inhabitants—the mind's way of surrounding itself with the familiar.

About the Peoples of Overtwixt ~ Since no true flora or fauna exist, the only real life in Overtwixt is INTELLIGENT life. That's why Overtwixt exists, after all—to bring together every people from every dimension of reality, for a "meeting of the minds."

Each race represented in Overtwixt (as far as I know) has both males and females, and they are referred to as men and women (or boys and girls), just like in OUR real world. It isn't two arms and two legs which makes someone a man or woman. Instead, it is the state of personhood—the existence of a personality and a soul. It's taken some getting used to, but I've come to recognize (for example) that a merman is just as much a "man" as I am.

The rest of this notebook represents my initial attempts to study and document just sixteen of the infinite races present in Overtwixt—the peoples of this realm who have been trapped by the Vizier.

3

(or lads & lasses / maids, as some peoples prefer)

About the Ollivarian system of classification ~
The longer you study the peoples of Overtwixt, the more clearly a pattern emerges: every race is essentially a hybrid of two other races (and each of THOSE races is a hybrid of the first and yet another, and so on and so forth).

Examples ~ Humen and eqmen (physically identical to horses from our real world) are distinct races sharing no physical attributes. However, centmen and lugmen might both be described as a cross between humen and eqmen. To be extremely simplistic, a centman (like a centaur from our mythology) is essentially the top half of a human and the bottom half of an eqman (horse). The lugman (like a minotaur) is the same mix in reverse: the top half of an eqman (horse) and the bottom half of a human.

As I've noted, this methodology of describing all races as hybrids of each other is simplistic. But it's not far from the truth. For my system of classification, I think of the contributing "halves" in terms of dominant and secondary, as follows:

- DOMINANT ~ upper body features, including circulatory, respiratory, and (usually) integumentary systems (body covering like skin, fur, hair, scales, feathers, etc.)

- SECONDARY ~ lower body appendages and overall stature

Notation – All peoples, therefore, can be classified as having one dominant half and one secondary half. For example, using the races discussed above:

- Humen – Hu>hu
- Centmen – Hu>eq
- Lugmen – Eq>hu
- Eqmen – Eq>eq

Base races – The "halves" used in this notation (whether dominant or secondary) always reference what I call "base races." Base races are those races I've identified as being physically identical to organisms from Earth. (I acknowledge this is a very hu-centric way of thinking. No offense toward non-humen is intended by this.) Base races include:

- Hu – humen
- Eq – eqmen – horses
- Del – delphmen – dolphins
- Spu – spookmen – bats
- ... and many others, undoubtedly

~~This system of classification is not without its flaws and exceptions. For example, not all hybrids with dominant delphman attributes are aquatic, therefore their respiratory system must come from their secondary half.~~

Correction: I'm an idiot. Delphmen (like dolphins) are mammals; even though they are aquatic, they must surface to breathe air, which they process through lungs. The pattern holds—and the Ollivarian system of classification works.

Same for Dagmen, despite their fishy appearance

5

Humen

Ollivarian classification: **Hu>hu**

Traditional liege lord: Baron of Hucentia
                               (historically a human)

Nilands occupied: **Huland**, Hucentia

Anatomy: Your garden variety human being, as
    originating from Planet Earth; two arms, two legs, so
    forth and so on

top: Vizier, Baron
bottom: Empress, Knight, Princess

Culture: As best I can tell, there has seldom existed any great population of human in Overtwixt; at many times in history, Overtwixt has gone a long time without any human at all, hence our method of recording human history within Overtwixt as occurring during human epochs. (My own visit to Overtwixt marks the 782nd Human Epoch—the 782nd time humans have come here.) From what I have read, ~~the only epoch~~ that lasted long enough to establish a true human society was Epoch 394, when travel between Overtwixt and Ancient Greece was almost commonplace. Not surprisingly, much of Classical Greek mythology was influenced by events taking place here during that time... Perhaps MORE surprisingly, that era of Overtwixt's history bled back into our real world AGAIN much later, in the form of legends regarding King Arthur and Camelot. I fully intend to study/document more about the ancient human Knight and ~~his~~ involvement with the utopian niland kingdom of Caymerlot as soon as I get the chance.

one of *several* epochs

right: ~~Anglos Allustrous Lonister~~

7

humble
Loremaster

Centmen

Ollivarian classification:	Hu>eq
Mythological cognate:	Centaurs
Traditional liege lord:	Baron of Hucentia (historically a human)
Nilands occupied:	Centwick, Hucentia, Gnocentia

Culture: Centmen prize loyalty and wisdom above all other character qualities, and are famous for demonstrating those same qualities themselves. A person cannot ask for a better bodyguard or advisor than a centman, or so most people believe. In the absence of a ruling Baron, the centmen in Overtwixt are led by a Council of four elders (two men and two women) identified as the wisest among their people.

Anatomy: The upper body of a human attached at the waist to the four-legged lower body of a horse, covered in its entirety by a pattern of skin and hair; the hair grows especially long down the back of the human upper body (much like a horse's mane) and in thick tufts along the equine back haunches, forming patterns similar to zebra stripes; the females of the species, which are generally more slender, grow an even shaggier pelt below the shoulders to protect their modesty, while the males are known to braid the hair down their backs.

9

Eqmen

Ollivarian classification: **Eq > eq**

Base Race cognate: **Horses** (male)

Mythological cognate: **Unicorns** (female)

Traditional liege lord: Prince of Eqland
(historically an eqman)

Nilands occupied: **Eqland**

Anatomy: Identical to the Arabian stallions of Earth;
the males of the species exhibit the same variety of
coat colors normal on Earth (browns, blacks); females
tend to be markedly smaller and display more
whimsical colors (including white, pink, and red coats,
with even more vibrant and varied manes and tails);
the eqwoman's forehead horn is undoubtedly what
gave rise to the human legends of unicorns.

Culture: Eqmen are sometimes considered primitive by the other races, partly because they lack fingers or opposable thumbs (even though they've developed their own forms of technology which seem magical by comparison with our own), but also because of their overwhelming interest in simple pursuits: running, eating, and talking. Nevertheless, eqmen are renowned deep thinkers, and their Archives (essentially a library of philosophical audio recordings) rivals that of many other races.

Eqmen are also very adventurous. At times in the past, they established trade with other races, both for the construction of their settlements and for the acquisition of the seashells they use at the Archives.

An eqwoman's horn is like a work of art.

Lugmen

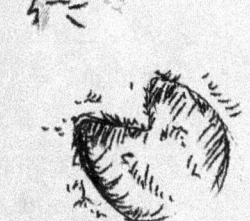

Olivarian classification: Eq >hu

Mythological cognate: the Minotaur

Traditional liege lord: none

Nilands occupied: Lugard

Culture: Lugmen have little culture to speak of, at least not in the traditional sense. They are isolationist with respect to other races and warlike amongst themselves, constantly fighting with little need for provocation. They fight most viciously with close friends and family members, though they always stop short of doing serious harm. Family reunions and other gatherings typically consist of a feast followed by a free-for-all with blunted weapons.

Anatomy: Bipedal thanks to secondary human traits, but immense, with a horsey head and face; males and females both feature a single thick horn sprouting from the end of the muzzle; despite this similarity in appearance to a rhinoceros (or the fact that lugman facial features are equine, not bovine), I am convinced the lugman is the inspiration for our human myth of the Minotaur. Lugmen of both genders grow great shaggy pelts over the upper chest, similar to a buffalo; their upper arms end in hooves like a horse, but articulated into three fingers and an opposable thumb. Most lugmen wear trousers or kilts but otherwise hate clothing.

I'm glad
this one's on
our side!

13

Gnomen

Ollivarian classification: Hu>spu

Mythological cognate: Gnomes

Traditional liege lord: Mystic of Shanagrailia

Nilands occupied: Gnobury, Gnocentia, Shanagrailia

Culture: The gnomen are a people most comfortable underground. As such, their portland looks like nothing more than an un-navigable chunk of stone from the outside. On the INSIDE, Gnobury is riddled with warrens and tunnels, hence its name (equivalent to Gno-burrow). Gnomen are incredibly crafty, very creative, and quick with their hands, and this area of Overtwixt knows no better stone masons or sculptors.

14

Anatomy: Short of stature, like all races with secondary spookman attributes (those races generally called "little peoples"); at a glance, gnomen are easily confused for small humen, or young humen not yet fully grown, primarily because of their dominant human traits and their propensity for wearing clothes; on closer inspection, gnomen prove to be extremely bowlegged, with the same padded and clawed feet as bats; young gnomen of both genders typically grow thick, peach-fuzzy beards, but the hair falls out by the time the gnoman reaches middle age.

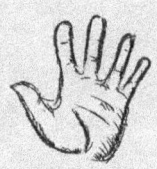

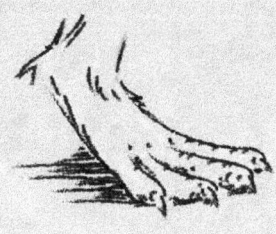

Nagmen

Ollivarian classification:	$Eq > s\, pu$
Mythological cognate:	none
Traditional liege lord:	Mystic of Shanagrailia
Nilands occupied:	**Nagland**, Shanagrailia

Culture: Nagmen are cliff dwellers, but there is nothing primitive about their habitats, which they carve meticulously from sheer cliffs in geometrically-precise shapes. Known as peacemakers and lovers of harmony, nagmen have been compared favorably to the hippies of Earth's 1960s. Nagmen play a wide variety of musical instruments unique to their real world (many of which they have recreated in Overtwixt) and are famous for producing more talented musicians per capita than almost any other race.

Anatomy: One of the so-called "little peoples" (short-statured, thanks to secondary spookman attributes), nagmen are capable of walking naturally on all fours or on back legs only, as humen do; reminiscent of nothing so much as Earth's Shetland ponies, though much smaller; like lugmen, their front hooves have articulated "fingers" (three, plus an opposable thumb); nagman hair grows uniformly across the entire body, thick and shaggy, though a recent fad among younger nagmen involves shaving that coat in places in order to wear gnoman clothing.

Raimen

Ollivarian classification:	**Delzea**
Mythological cognate:	none
Traditional liege lord:	Mystic of Shanagrailia
Nilands occupied:	**Raibourne**, Shanagrailia

Culture: Raimen enjoy a strange reputation among the other peoples. Known as wise and insightful, they are also mocked for their tendency to speak in riddles (and for their physical appearance too, of course!).

Many a pilgrim has sought answers to some great question in the Alabaster City of Shanagrailia, only to turn away confused at the end. This has given rise to the saying, "A raiman would set you straight, if only you could get a straight answer." The raimen lost significant political clout when the current Mystic (a raiman) was forced to abdicate as a result of the Baron's campaign of unification (which led to the Vizier's eventual seizure of power). The raiman portland of Raibourne is one of the most isolated nilands in this part of Overtwixt.

(Having now met the Mystic, I can confirm: he's clearly a smart dude, but I've got NO CLUE what he's saying 2/3 of the time!)

18

Anatomy: The same hybrid mix as a cayman, but in reverse—the head of a dolphin affixed to the body of a miniature horse—the entire body covered with smooth gray skin; raimen tend to be rotund, with stubby little legs barely long enough to keep their bellies from scraping the ground; raiman heads feature a unique growth of cartilage running like a fringe from just above the eyes to the back of the head, and this ridge contains olfactory and secondary breathing apparatus (operating much like a human nose or dolphin blowhole).

Shamen

Ollivarian classification: **Del>spu**

Mythological cognate: none

Traditional liege lord: Mystic of Shanagrailia

Nilands occupied: **Shaland**, Shanagrailia

Culture: Shamen are the most outgoing and widely traveled of the "little peoples" who come together in Shanagrailia. By some quirk of their real world culture, adult shamen devote their lives to a single field of study, within which they seek to become an unparalleled expert. That is why shamen often attach themselves to prominent individuals of other races, to serve as coaches, trainers, or advisors.

Anatomy: The upper body of a dolphin attached at the waist to the lower body of a bat, including upper appendages that seem a cross between the dolphin's fins and the bat's winged arms; the shaman's arms are broad and flat, ending in extremely dexterous articulated fingers; vestigial webbing grows from the armpit to the elbow, but does not grant the ability to fly; shamen have sharp, carnivorous teeth; they often wear pants and shoes, and sometimes bowler-style hats with ponchos (especially for the shawomen), but their underarm webbing makes it impossible for them to wear actual shirts or tunics.

21

Caymen

Ollivarian classification: Eq>del

Mythological cognate: Hippocamps

Traditional liege lord: Underlord of Caymerdelphia

Nilands occupied: Caypool, Caymerdelphia

Culture: Caymen are essentially the eqmen of the sea,
  though more sedate and individualistic. They have
  the same propensity for lengthy philosophical
  discourse, and are favored speakers at the
  Amphitheater in Caymerdelphia. More so than any of
  the other aquatic peoples, caymen prefer to remain in
  their underwater environs, ignoring groundwalkers and
  surfacing only for air—or to debate their aquatic
  brethren about some topic or another.

Anatomy: A cross between a
  horse and a dolphin, they
  look more like a mix of
  sea horse and manatee;
  they are physically
  ponderous, even if they
  ARE known to be
  quick-witted.

23

Dagmen

Ollivarian classification: **Del>hu**

Mythological cognate: various

Traditional liege lord: none

Nilands occupied: **Dagmoor**, Caymerdelphia

Culture: Dagmen are renowned pranksters and thrill-
seekers. One of Overtwixt's most versatile species,
dagmen are comfortable on land or in water (though
they must rehydrate their skin at regular intervals
while out of the water). Dagmen are nomadic,
sometimes banding together with like-minded associates
rather than members of their birth families. Outside
of Dagmoor and Caymerdelphia,
roving bands of dagmen
have historically
provided entertainment
for the other races,
by putting on
carnivals or building
amusement parks.

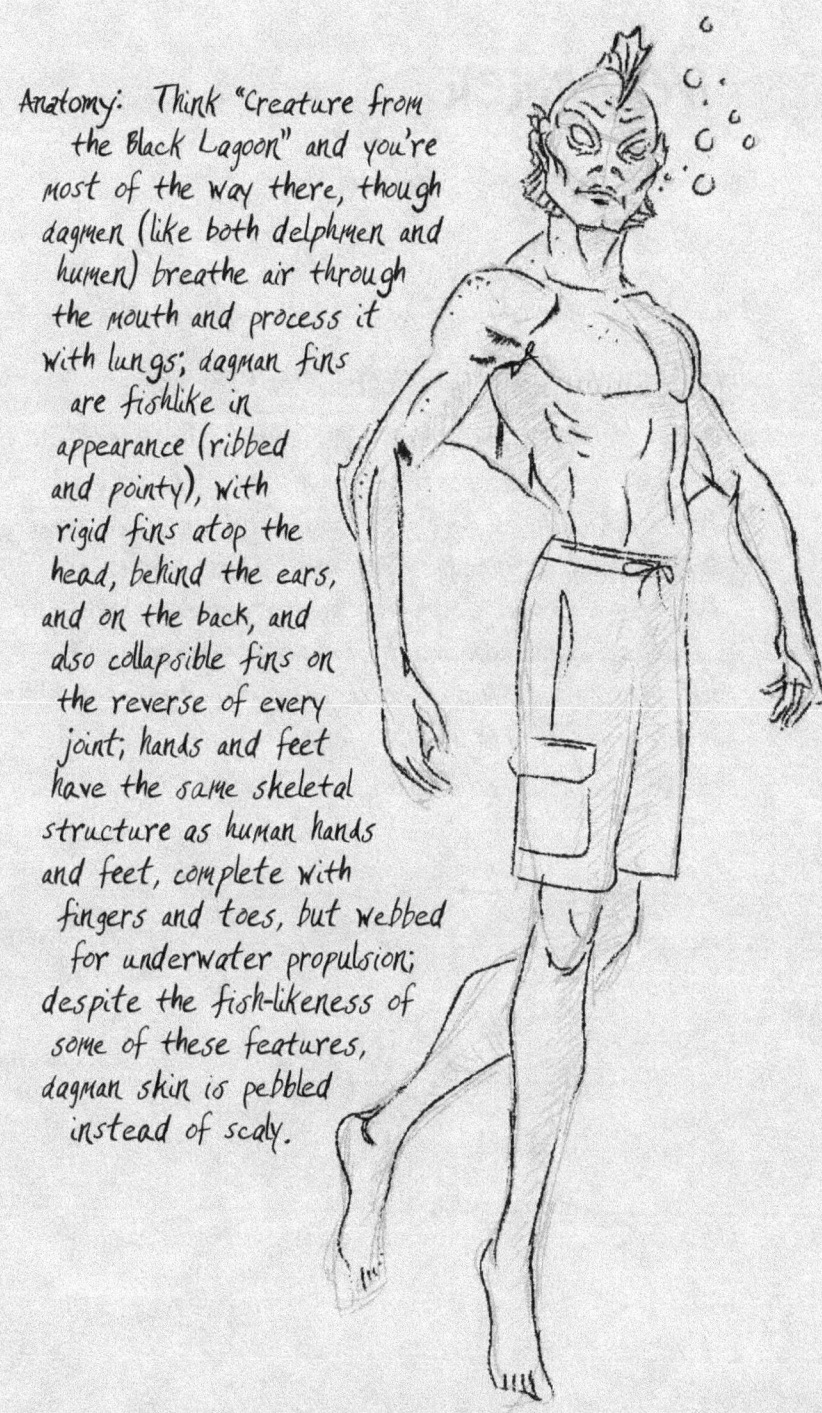

Anatomy: Think "Creature from
the Black Lagoon" and you're
most of the way there, though
dagmen (like both delphmen and
humen) breathe air through
the mouth and process it
with lungs; dagman fins
are fishlike in
appearance (ribbed
and pointy), with
rigid fins atop the
head, behind the ears,
and on the back, and
also collapsible fins on
the reverse of every
joint; hands and feet
have the same skeletal
structure as human hands
and feet, complete with
fingers and toes, but webbed
for underwater propulsion;
despite the fish-likeness of
some of these features,
dagman skin is pebbled
instead of scaly.

25

Delphmen

Ollivarian classification: **Del>del**

Base Race cognate: **Dolphins**

Traditional liege lord: Underlord of Caymerdelphia

Nilands occupied: **Delphyrd**, Caymerdelphia

Culture: Delphmen are widely considered the friendliest and most welcoming people in this area of Overtwixt. They are known as care-free and fun-loving, but their play has less of an edge than the dagman pranksters. By their lifestyle, delphmen illustrate their belief that responsibility must be taken seriously, and that life contains many serious moments—but that life should never be taken TOO seriously.

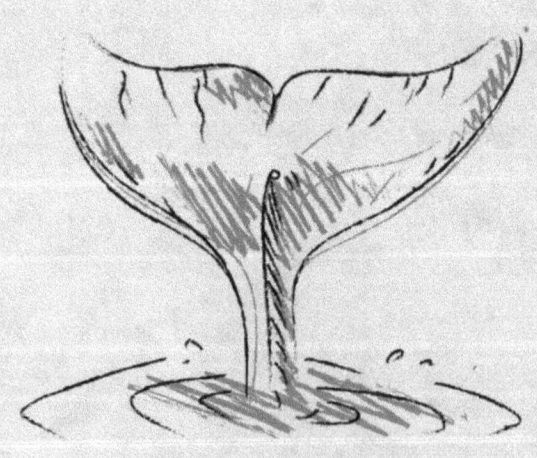

Anatomy: Identical to the bottlenose dolphins of Earth, with smooth gray skin covering a thin layer of blubber; the males of the species exhibit a broad, dark gray band from nose to tail along the back, while the females are distinguished by thinner, lighter gray stripes running in wavy lines along their sides; similar to eqwomen, delphwomen also have a small horn just above the eyes, but very short and stumpy, barely breaking the surface of the skin.

Mermen

Ollivarian classification:	Hu>del
Mythological cognates:	Mermen/mermaids
Traditional liege lord:	Underlord of Caymerdelphia
Nilands occupied:	Merpool, Caymerdelphia

Culture: The merpeople hold beauty in high esteem, and are sometimes considered vain and self-important as a result. But they care as much for inner beauty as outer, and much of their culture revolves around the creation of artistic masterpieces. They are famed for the masterful glassblowing they perform on their hot sandy beaches, which results in small works of art as well as delicate underwater towers.

Anatomy: The upper body of a human attached to the lower body of a dolphin; for the females of the species, the transition occurs just below the shoulders, while the males transition at the waist, exposing a muscular human torso; in both cases, the lower body is covered in the blubbery gray skin of a dolphin; only the females have a dorsal fin. Both the men and the women wear their hair long, either loose or in dreadlocks.

29

Drachmen

Ollivarian classification:	Spu>del
Mythological cognate:	Dragons
Traditional liege lord:	Kaiser of the Shadowlands (historically a drachman)
Nilands occupied:	Drachölm

Culture: Bombastic and always the largest person in a room, drachmen are used to being the center of attention. In a social setting, that makes them the life of the party; in a political or military setting, they have a thirst for command. The Kaiser of the Shadowlands was always a drachman, ever since the days when the first Kaiser conquered Impstead and Spookwood, making its inhabitants his minions. It is no coincidence that all three races now serve the Vizier, led by a drachman Warlord.

Anatomy: The largest of the races I've observed in Overtwixt, drachmen are best described as huge bats, their muscular bodies long, slender, and sinuous from shoulders to tail, covered entirely in thick black hair; drachmen have two sets of shoulders, the lower equipped with meaty forearms and (prehensile) hands, the upper with immense wings that fold along the back; the drachman's ears are huge and side-facing, and its long body ends in two pairs of crossed, dolphin-like fins that give it the appearance of having a barbed tail.

"prehensile" means being able to grab or hold things, like tools... or throats

30

31

Impmen

Ollivarian classification:	Spu>hu
Mythological cognate:	Gargoyles
Traditional liege lord:	Kaiser of the Shadowlands (historically a drachman)
Nilands occupied:	**Impstead**

Culture: Impmen have strong clan ties and typically flock in large groups. Much like the ducks and geese of Earth, they are fond of <u>long flights during which they sing in five-part harmony</u> while flying in rotating formations. Impmen do not have strong leadership tendencies, and historically have been quick to accept outside authority. Some few impmen break the mold, forming small companies and hiring themselves out as mercenaries that fight or offer airlift services.

Think ↳
sea shanties,
sung loud and
dissonant, but
Kinda fun ⌐

What they lack in musical talent, they make up for with pure raspy enthusiasm...

Anatomy: Closely resembling the body of a human, with a
well-muscled torso, but the head of a bat; the bat-
like wings attach directly from the creature's back
to its strong human arms (as opposed to being
mounted on the back, as with the gargoyles from
human stories); impmen have very human hands, but
with sharply taloned fingers; most impmen wear
nothing more than patterned trousers in bright
colors, with ripped cuffs, while impwomen add colorful
strips of cloth to protect their modesty; most
prefer to go without footwear,
except when flying into battle.

Phomen

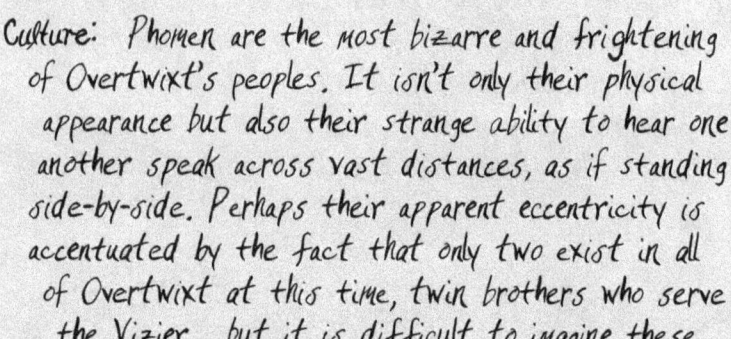

Ollivarian classification:	**Spuzea**
Mythological cognate:	various
Traditional liege lord:	none
Nilands occupied:	**Pholand**

Culture: Phomen are the most bizarre and frightening of Overtwixt's peoples. It isn't only their physical appearance but also their strange ability to hear one another speak across vast distances, as if standing side-by-side. Perhaps their apparent eccentricity is accentuated by the fact that only two exist in all of Overtwixt at this time, twin brothers who serve the Vizier... but it is difficult to imagine these creatures as anything other than villains.

Anatomy: The body of a horse, so gaunt that every bone shows beneath the hairy black skin; while equine in shape, phoman heads retain bat-like features (oversized ears, upturned nose, exposed fangs); phomen have two sets of wings: vestigial webbing beneath the forelegs and a larger set folding behind the back when not used for flying; phoman tails are hairless like a rat's; size-wise, phomen are comparable to horses and theoretically could be ridden; as such, I imagine they are the inspiration for Pegasus from myth... though how these monsters ever inspired such a beautiful creature, I'll never know.

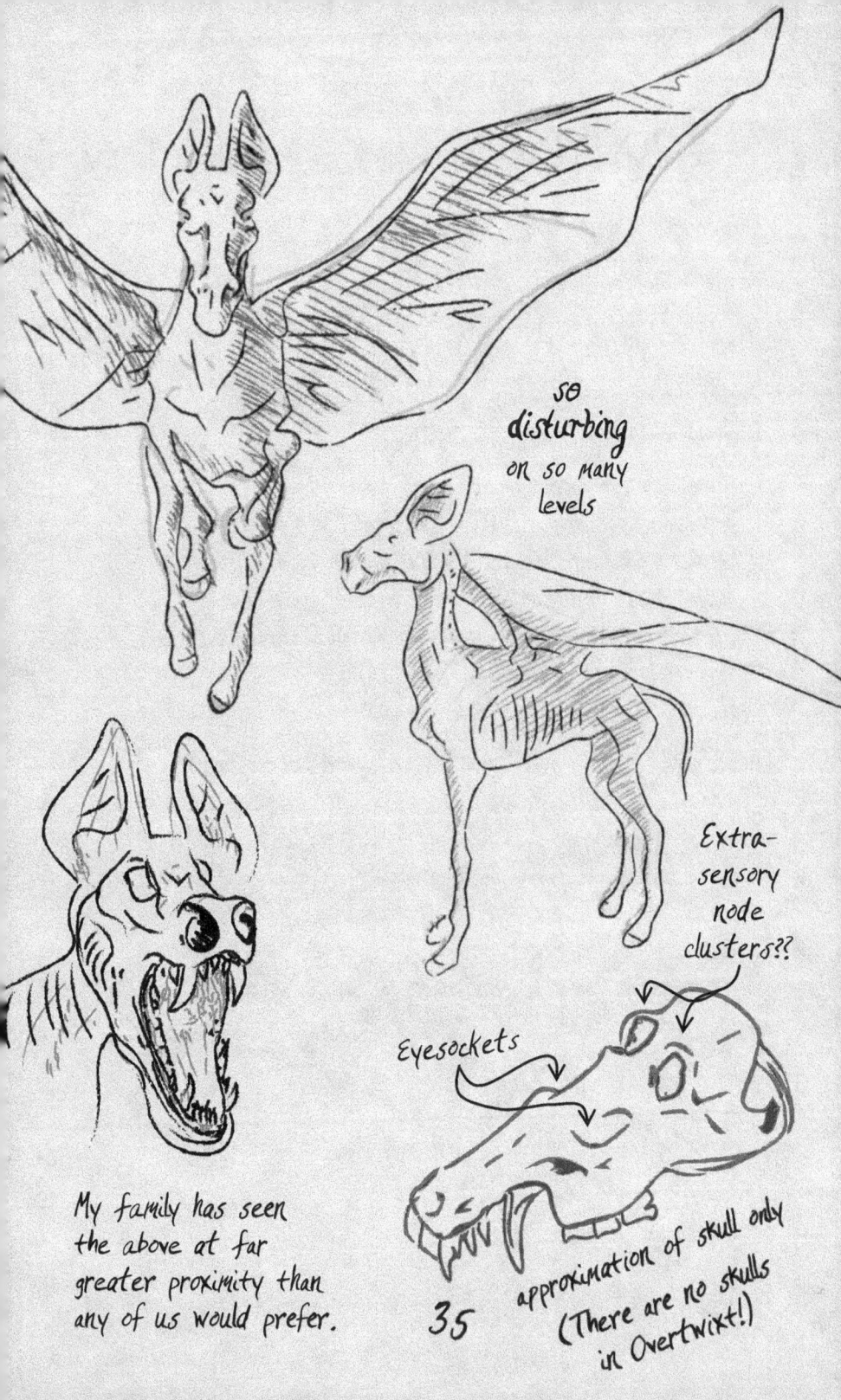

so
disturbing
on so many
levels

Extra-
sensory
node
clusters??

Eyesockets

My family has seen
the above at far
greater proximity than
any of us would prefer.

35   approximation of skull only
(There are no skulls
in Overtwixt!)

Spookmen

Ollivarian classification:	Spu>spu
Base Race cognate:	Bats
Traditional liege lord:	Kaiser of the Shadowlands (historically a drachman)
Nilands occupied:	Spookwood

Culture: Much like humen, great variety exists in spookman social patterns; some prefer to live in large groups (called "legions") while a significant minority have loner tendencies. Incredibly crafty and dexterous, with prehensile hands and feet both, spookmen have a well-deserved reputation for being thieves and con-artists. They are not to be trusted.

Anatomy: Most similar to the vampire bat of Earth, roosting upside down (in caves, but more preferably from the upper reaches of forest trees), spookmen are also capable of walking/running on all fours and of course flying; spookmen or "spooks" are the smallest of all the races I've observed in Overtwixt, ranging in size from that of a rat to that of a small lapdog.

acknowledgments

Overtwixt and *Escape from Overtwixt* began as a single volume. I suppose, therefore, that the people I most need to thank for the existence of this separate second volume are the literary agents who said, "It's how long? No thanks!" Beyond that, many of my acknowledgments from the first *Overtwixt* apply to this installment as well, since those folks proofed the original combined version of the story.

My wife still tops the list—many different lists, in fact, but in this case the list of people deserving gratitude. Sarah (role: Countess), thank you for continuing to cheer me on, and for offering constructive criticism as I sought to capture the essence of our children in the characters of Nachton, Amélie, Cécilie, and Ewan. Thank you also for not getting (too) angry when I left your beloved Ewan in such a terrible state at the end of book one.

Next up are Nate, Emme, Sadie, and Ian (my real children). Thank you again for being you. I know it was hard seeing your alter-egos making mistakes in the first book (even though that was *them*, not *you*), but now we've reached the payoff. I hope you're as happy as I am with the lessons they learned and the heroism they've demonstrated in this second book. P.S. Sorry for all the times I've accidentally called you Nachton, Amélie, Cécilie, or Ewan by mistake.

Jesse Lewis, you brought Overtwixt to life once again with your wonderful illustrations. Thank you as always for all your patience and hard work.

Thank you to my parents, Ruth and Les Akers (Lounge Pianist and Salesman), as well as my Aunt Beth Paul (Minstrel)—for continuing to give me good (if sometimes difficult) feedback on every new story I craft, and for encouraging me that I have found my sweet spot, writing young adult fiction.

Monica Robinson (Defender), thank you for your consistent encouragement on *all* my Overtwixt books, and for championing these stories to others.

Heidi Burch (Sorceress), thank you for reining me in on my overuse of italics... though I fear your "encouragement" has left a mark. I can no longer type command+i without *feeling* your disapproval.

Faith Reeves (Chronicler), thank you again for recognizing the most important messages I was trying to communicate, and for resonating so enthusiastically with them. Thank you also for your last minute proofing of Overtwixt's four modern day tie-in stories. I hereby bequeath you a glass house on Caymerdelphia, per your request.

In addition, I remain grateful to the Marrs, Matthews, Cobbs, and Amblers for investing in this story—not just as readers, but also as contributors. Overtwixt is a better place because of you. And yes, I still have the proof copies scribbled in by Kylie, Ryan, Kaeden, and Ben, and I still treasure all of those handwritten opinions and suggestions. They are a true encouragement to this author when he needs a pick-me-up!

Last and foremost, I again acknowledge my Lord and Savior Jesus Christ, who is my guide and teacher and sovereign king all at once. I guess it's now safe to admit (without spoiling the story) that he inspired the most admirable character to be found in Overtwixt! May the investments I make in the world of bridges always please and honor you.

about the fonts

The text of this novel was set in 11-point Asul Regular, a baroque humanist typeface designed by Mariela Monsalve. With its subtle semi-serifs, Asul is perfectly suited (in the author's opinion) for younger readers.

Since Asul lacks an italic variant, italicized text was set in Amerigo BT Std Italic, a typeface designed by Gerard Unger in 1987, which complements Asul nicely.

"Nachton Hand" and "Nachton Hand Title" were designed by the author using real quill and ink, scanned and digitized and packaged into a font with multiple variants per character to make it feel more natural. Nachton's handwriting is based on the author's own, which has not improved much in the three decades since HE was fifteen.

Section headers, illustration text, and many place names on the maps were set in Mercator Regular, designed by Arthur Baker in 1995. Mercator's calligraphic strokes give it a hand-scribed feel that's ideal for this application.

Finally, all hublands on the maps were beautifully identified using ITC Locarno Italic (in all caps), designed by Alan Meeks in 1922.

about the author

R.L. Akers loves stories. He loves hearing them, loves telling them, loves embellishing them, and loves forging them from raw materials. He is convinced that every person who ever lived has an interesting story, and he's only met one person in his life who came close to proving otherwise.

Holder of an undergraduate degree in computer science and a master's degree in business administration, Akers has worked in software development as well as non-profit fundraising and publicity. His love for children has led him in the past to be a foster parent and a coordinator of the K-5 ministry at his church. His interests include graphic design, orchestral movie soundtracks, and anything remotely creative.

Akers lives in West Virginia with his wife Sarah and the four children he loves most in this world. Visit him online at RLAkers.com.

about the illustrator

Jesse Lewis is an award-winning published illustrator and graphic artist, who specializes in breathing life into worlds beyond our own and the characters that reside within them. After studying for and attaining his bachelor's degree in fine arts at Savannah College of Art & Design, Jesse went on to expand his skills through numerous book-, video game-, and animation projects both within the U.S. and around the world.

While always pursuing continued development of his own skillset, Jesse has also kindled a passion for sharing his knowledge and experiences by educating new generations of aspiring artists.

Instagram: jnoah.art
Facebook: jesselewisdesign